A JACK STERN ADVENTURE

a Priest, *a* Brothel *and the* Fox

M J JURAND

ISBN: 978-1-925952-39-1
Published by Vivid Publishing
A division of Fontaine Publishing Group
P.O. Box 948, Fremantle
Western Australia 6959
www.vividpublishing.com.au

 A catalogue record for this
book is available from the
National Library of Australia

CONTENTS

1
ADVANTAGE TAKER

Jack Stern was awake. It was 5:30am. The sun had just started to appear on the horizon. Warm golden light filtered through the lace curtains and painted the naked body of his latest conquest. She was French. Exceptionally beautiful, a vibrant blonde, one whom any man would worship and have as his wife, but to Jack, she was just another toy, something to occupy his time for a brief moment or two and discard once he had lost interest. It was not that Jack mistreated or abused women, on the contrary, he had always handled them in the most chivalrous manner, attending to their every need in minute detail. The problem was that he could not warm to them. Everything that he did was mechanical, almost programmed, all as a result of his attitude to business and the ridiculous fashion in which he could make money. Floating on such immense wealth, all that he had to do was cast that line with nothing more than a look, a word and women were his. As Jack lay there contemplating, he was unaware that his recent catch, Michelle, was awake and beginning to play with his manly bait. As the waves of sexual pleasure spread through his body he began to think about the different forms of ecstasy and wondered if they possessed a common thread. Was spiritual and sexual ecstasy one and the same? He closed his eyes and focused his attention upon Michelle's desire to start the day on a beautiful note.

The Classical Music of Gabriel Faure's 'Pavane' filled the sumptuous interior of Jack Stern's red Ferrari. Everything in his life had to be just right, well balanced, a sense of style, beauty and of course, performance. He glanced at his gold Chopard wristwatch; it was later than he had anticipated. He gunned the engine, the car leapt forward in total contrast to the music. He changed lanes and sped past numerous cars, a motorcycle policeman and several heavy duty lorries. In a matter of seconds Jack sensed that the chase was on. With siren on and lights flashing, the policeman was in hot pursuit. Jack loved a challenge, especially if it had anything to do with any aspect of the law. He was late for the office and did not have the time to deal with the petty minded antics of a traffic cop. Jack put himself into automatic mode; his senses surveyed the traffic in front, behind and to the sides of his Ferrari. Decision made, he changed the radio to CD, the song 'I am always one step ahead of you' blared out. It was a catchy tune, a good rock and roll number that he and a friend had collaborated on. Jack put up the volume, clutched out and changed down a cog, the Ferrari leapt again, Jack turned the steering wheel sharply to the left and then to the right so the car instantly slid sideways in the same direction as it was previously travelling. The tyres screamed with agony as they dragged across the bitumen and then they gripped once again, propelling the car forward across the stream of heavy traffic. Before anyone could respond by braking or blowing their horns he was away diagonally and down the off ramp to the city. The policeman had no chance, as maneuverable as a bike might be, his reactions were too slow. 'Oh well,' he foolishly thought, 'there will be a next time.' Jack changed the CD back to radio, Tchaikovsky's 1812 Overture now played. Perhaps the cannons are an omen of today's events he thought, as he motored his way to his "Global Balancing Act" business offices .Once he entered the private parking lot, he stored his car in his reserved bay and made his way towards his plush offices. As he confidently made his way in, he was greeted by the voices of women hysterically screaming, shouting and crying. His secretary, Miss Julia Sutton was trembling. She was white with fear as she tried to deal with two very large opponents. The Ricci twins were threatening to destroy the entire office and kill everyone in it, especially Mr. Jack Stern once they laid their hands on him. Papers and magazines were already strewn about. The reception desk's vase of fresh flowers decorated the wall behind it in a hundred pieces. Several of the glass framed paintings had met with similar fates. As soon as Jack appeared, all eyes were upon him. The Ricci women lunged at him, attempted to tear out his eyes and hair. With cat-like ability he sprung away and was able, in a gentlemanly fashion to dispatch each one of his assailants simply by side-stepping, bobbing and weaving. Each woman encountered the same end, unconsciousness.

Without a hair out of place, Jack Stern looked at his secretary, smiled and asked, "Now Miss Sutton, would you please tell me what this is all about?"

"Yes sir, but can you please give me a moment to regain my composure," she shakily replied.

"Of course in my office in ten minutes…?"

"Yes sir, thank you sir," she hastily replied and took her leave.

Building security and maintenance were called in to repair the damage and usher out the bewildered assailants. Jack waited patiently in his office for his secretary's arrival. "Now, who were those women and what did they want?"

"They claimed that they are the twin daughters of the late Mr. Giovanni Ricci who recently committed suicide. He had lost a company and a huge sum of money during a recent share deal. They claim you were involved. They say you are responsible for everything. His death, their financial loss, their diminished fortune and future income, they came seeking revenge. I fear that they are very serious about this and unless they receive some sort of compensation, they are going to do just that."

"Now Miss Sutton do not overly concern yourself what I did was perfectly legal, I just happened to take advantage of some opportunities one might say that presented themselves in law."

"Even so sir, I think you should take precautions. There is no telling what they might do next. They might even… " She put her hand up to her mouth and held her breath.

"Hire an assassin." Miss Sutton's eyes widened with fear. "Yes sir." Jack stood up, approached her, took her hand and firmly squeezed it. With a smile on his face, he continued. "Julia, you have had a very traumatic experience this morning. Why don't you take yourself home, have a nice warm relaxing bath, listen to some classical music, take a few days off. This was nothing more than a storm in a teacup. I tell you what, I shall make arrangements straight away so that you can go and enjoy a week or two at the corporate holiday home. Everything will be supplied; you need not worry about anything at all."

"But, but sir, the office will not run efficiently without me."

"That is very nice of you to say that Miss Sutton, very well, take as much time as you need, come back whenever you wish, I admire your loyalty. Now, what I also need to tell you is that I shall be away for at least two weeks. When I return, I want to see you totally refreshed, okay." Julia accepted his proposal and took her leave, but remained quite uncertain of the future and her employer's safety.

The reception area was now restored to normality. The cleaners had done away with the mess and one of the other secretaries had taken charge of the reception desk. Jack Stern called a meeting of his staff that numbered six in total for that afternoon. This morning's activity, plus his glorious start to the day had given him quite a healthy appetite. Food now, was the foremost thought in his head. He could smell the freshly brewed coffee, oven baked croissants and lightly scrambled eggs. With those thoughts in mind he went in search of his favourite café.

"Gentlemen, as you are aware, I have decided to take a break of about two weeks from the office to oversee my new acquisition, the community service centre out in the mid west. This has nothing to do with this morning's incident and it is not an attempt by me to go into hiding. I simply want to be there to fine tune the operation and other matters as you well know. I have left a file for each one of you and I expect that the contents of each will be completed by the time I return. Do not telephone me, except for the utmost urgency and only on my ultra secure private line. I expect that each one of you will be as efficient as always, to the maximum degree of course. After all, each one of you is handpicked and expert, any questions?" The room remained silent, just as Jack had anticipated. Each one of his employees was a quiet achiever, more than capable at his or her respective tasks. As they left his office, he fiddled with his attaché case and once satisfied that he had everything that he required, he locked it, closed the door behind him confident that unless a disaster happened, his office would run with Swiss German precision.

The journey to the newly acquired community service centre would be quite long between 10 to 12 hours in total driving time. Jack decided to motor, rather than take a bus, or train or plane because he enjoyed the pleasure of spending time with, as he affectionately called her, 'my timeless lady'. She was his red Ferrari, complete with V12 engine. It had to be so, for symbolically and in the numerological sense the number 12 reduced to 3 and to Jack this represented immense strength. It stood in his mind, as an equilateral triangle, the strongest structure known to man. In his mind his timeless lady responded in a similar fashion. Although she enjoyed the short trips to and from work and the episodes of stunt driving, she often yearned to stretch her legs and run a marathon at speed. Her engine simply purred as she drove out of the city onto a route that would guide him to his destination. The cabin was filled with the angelic music of Mozart's Ave Verum Corpus. As the music played, Jack reflected on days gone by. The scene was one of… The convent's chapel was silent. The congregation awaited the procession of altar boys and priest, the signal, for the start of mass. The altar had been made ready. It was richly decorated with flowers left over from the previous day's wedding ceremonies and bathed in a myriad of colours that shone from the upper left stained glass windows. People swore that when the lights came from a particular direction during a particular time of the day, you could make out the image of the Virgin Mary, with the baby Jesus in her arms on the right hand wall of the sanctuary, but you had to be quick, for it only lasted a brief moment or two. Jack's mother sat with her husband in the centre aisle pews, seven rows back from the front. She was overjoyed that her son had become and remained a devoted altar boy. Now nearing eighteen years of age, she hoped that he would consider becoming a priest, just like his Uncle Tom. She prayed for that at every mass and said numerous rosaries in between with the same intention.

It seemed that her prayers had been answered, for Jack accompanied his Uncle Tom every time he went on a mission of pastoral care, bringing communion to the sick and saying mass in remote areas. Jack had become so good at observing and remembering, that Father Tom quite frankly said, "You might as well let Jack say the mass." On many occasions when it was obvious that the distribution of communion was going to be a laboured affair, he would allow Jack after saying the necessary blessing, to assist in giving out the consecrated hosts. People often thought that Jack was a trainee priest, or even a deacon. Such was his angelic disposition, but something went wrong. That something wrong if you wish to call it that came in the form of a woman.

2

THE HANDSOME SAINT

As he descended the stairs from the altar he sensed that today something was about to change in his life. Holding ciborium in his left hand, he gently withdrew a consecrated host with the fingers of his right hand and proceeded to hold it up before the first adoring worshipper and said in a soft voice "body of Christ". He gently placed it on the man's tongue and continued to administer host after host with the same passion until she stood before him. "Amen," she said, whilst flicking her tongue from side to side and then deliciously licking her lips before finally extending her moist tongue in the most provocative, seductive manner. She was not exactly suitably dressed for church. The skirt was too short, too tight, and the blouse was very tight and obscenely low, showing more than an ample bosom that heaved rhythmically with her deep breathing. He froze, not knowing what to do. The host remained almost suspended in mid air. He gathered his senses and placed the host on her eagerly awaiting tongue. Before he could retract them, she had wrapped her lips around his fingers, drawn them into her mouth and started to perform fellatio in the most delectable manner. There was no argument about it. His trapped fingers and penis were one, both enjoying the forbidden, even though it was by mental association. He could not bring himself to cry "stop woman," aware of what the congregation might be thinking. He extracted his fingers as best as he could. The woman simply smiled, bent forward and in a low whisper said, "see you again, confession perhaps?" Father Brendan O'Reilly visibly shaken did a quick about face, dashed up to the safety 'of the altar' washed his hands in the finger bowl provided and hurriedly sat in his chair. The acolyte was left to complete distribution of the holy sacrament whilst Brendan mentally attempted to reduce his swellings and regain his composure. He thanked God that his vestments were loose, allowing room for any expansions. He kept his head low and prayed for strength. When it came time to say the final prayer and blessing Father Brendan avoided eye contact with any member of the congregation. Once safe in the sacristy, he buried his face in his hands and tried to come to grips with the blatant assault upon his sexuality and the quite receptive manner in which his body had responded. This had not happened before; perhaps the years had finally taken their toll. He realised that just because he was an ordained priest it did not confer immunity against attack of any sort. He was flesh and blood and although the spirit was willing, his flesh for the first time was weak. Surely this was just a chance event. "I will make sure this won't happen again" With that thought, Brendan O'Reilly returned to the nearby presbytery to enjoy breakfast. The rest of the day was to be spent attending to the list of items left behind by the parish priest, Monsignor Monahan. This included banking of the Sunday mass offerings, visitation of the sick at the nearby hospital and later in the afternoon, marriage guidance lessons for couples wishing to marry within the Catholic Church. The day remained relatively uneventful in contrast to the morning however, Father O'Reilly began to wonder why all the duty nurses at the hospital seemed to be so friendly. Whenever he would pass anyone of them, they would invariably smile, giggle and even wink. They would even walk up to him and ask not once, but many times, "Is there anything I can get you? Can I do anything for you? Anything at all" Father Brendan O' Reilly thought that being new they were simply trying to make him feel at home. They were being as hospitable as possible. The woman patients that he visited also appeared to be very friendly. In his presence, they all seemed to be revived, re-energised, not at all sick, as they were meant to be. In fact, some even left their beds and sat next to him. Many kissed him when he had finished saying the prayers and blessings.

Many held his hand for as long as they could, whilst they said, "Stay a little longer, I feel so good now that you are here." This made Father Brendan feel appreciated. As he left the hospital, he thought to himself, 'sacraments, the priesthood, the power of prayer, they all work.'

The late afternoon marriage guidance lessons also went well, especially for the women. They eagerly involved themselves in the discussion section, describing in intimate detail how they were prepared to look after a man. How devoted and attentive they would be, whilst all the time they continually smiled and stared at Father Brendan who listened intently and admired their verbal commitments. Their prospective husbands however sat and thought, 'who is this person sitting next to me.' When Father Brendan O'Reilly returned home to the presbytery a message from the Monsignor awaited him. He was instructed to run the parish by himself for the next few weeks as the Archbishop of the region had a range of important duties that needed urgent attention and required additional help. Father O'Reilly had only been in the parish for part of a week and as yet, had not become fully conversant with the weekly timetable of priestly events. Previous to that, he had been posted to a dozen different locations for no longer than six month durations. He searched for the parish diary in the Monsignor's room, but to no avail. He then asked the housekeeper if she knew of its whereabouts. Mrs. Greenwood obliged and quickly produced it, explaining how the Monsignor kept it in the most unusual places. Father O'Reilly studied the contents of the book over dinner to which he had invited Mrs. Greenwood. She was not used to such generosity. Between the two of them, he was able to obtain an idea of what was expected of him in the forthcoming weeks. After he helped Mrs. Greenwood with the dinner dishes, he retired to bed with a copy of the Marion magazine.

The week proceeded without incident. Each day was busy with answering telephone calls that dealt with a variety of matters, births, deaths, baptisms, questions of theology, interpretation of the same, help in domestic matters, the odd crank call as was to be expected and Monsignor, who rang daily to see how Brendan my boy was coping. Besides all of this, Brendan visited the schools to conduct religious instruction for various grades and even found time to help Mrs. Greenwood with household chores. It was as if the proverbial calm before the storm was about to happen. The gods had decided that Saturday was the day that Father Brendan O'Reilly would start his tempering in earnest. Any incident before that was merely an introduction to what lay ahead. Saturday's schedule appeared uncomplicated. It started with early morning mass at 6:30am. A baptism at 10:30am, a parish council meeting at 1:00pm, confession or reconciliation as some preferred to call it, between 3:00pm and 5:30pm, finishing the day with the evening mass at 7:30pm. One would normally expect for the early morning mass about 15 to 20 elderly people to turn up. However, this morning, around 150 people were present, most of them young school girls between the ages of fifteen to eighteen years of age, all still wearing their night attire, namely pyjamas, nighties etc., by all sorts of designers, the most popular being Play Boy. When Father Brendan O'Reilly stepped out onto the altar and saw what awaited him, all sorts of scenes raced through his mind. He had no acolyte to assist him. Would the distribution of communion become finger licking good? Father O'Reilly tried to take as much time as possible to reach the climax of the mass, namely consecration and the partaking of communion. It was not a tactic that worked well. The girls remained patient and said the prayers with him in the softest seductive voices. It was as if he was glued to a couch with a dozen naked women next to him, constantly tantalising him with 'dirty sweet talk'. In the cool of the early morning he was sweating profusely. His throat felt parched and the sweet wine, when it came time to consume it, did not alleviate his thirst, it worsened it and his self control. Father Brendan O'Reilly felt like a demon possessed with only one wish to consummate! Consummate! Consummate! The words raged in his head becoming louder and louder as it came closer to distribute Holy Communion. Then they stopped, silence, he sighed with relief, his eyes fixed on the elevated host as he said to the young girl who stood before him, "Body of Christ."

"Amen Father," she replied, ever so sweetly gazing deeply into his eyes. One by one it was the same, an almost endless parade of firm young bodies cheekily showing glimpses of erect bosoms, nipples, smooth long thighs and perfect belly buttons that cried out, "Just press to turn me on." The sexual excitement in Father Brendan O'Reilly reached fever pitch. He hoped that he was not going to experience 'a day time wet dream'. Certainly the fluids were there, the pump primed, ready to deliver with the hand firmly on the trigger ready to squeeze off a round or two. The line of communicants seemed almost endless, he even thought that the girls were coming back a second time with further revealing intentions. He felt suspended between agony and ecstasy and no matter which way he wished to go, that choice became the other. The sheer mental anguish of it all prevented Father Brendan O'Reilly from disgracing himself. He was thoroughly drained. Once mass was over, he slowly tidied everything away and returned home. There he lay on his bed forsaking breakfast. Instead, he focused on his sexual apparatus.

"Father… Father… are you alright?" asked Mrs. Greenwood as she gently tried to stir him. Brendan lazily opened his eyes and nodded. "Father, it is almost 10:15, you have a baptism in fifteen minutes, the church is locked and the parents, their baby, family and friends are waiting."

"What baptism? Good lord!" Brendan shouted as he sprang to

his feet and then he raced to the bathroom, spent a frenzied thirty seconds brushing his teeth, combing his hair and throwing about the wrong body cologne. It was the Monsignor's love musk that he had mistakenly used. He ran out of the house and slowed down as he approached the party of people who were patiently waiting at the church. Brendan apologised profusely and then after he introduced himself to everyone, he opened the church, turned on the lights and ushered the party to the area about the baptismal font. The handsome priest then excused himself, went into the sacristy, donned the correct vestments, collected the correct prayer book, blessed sacramental oils and emerged looking rather composed, ready to perform the ceremony which progressed rather nicely. The parents beamed, the baby was angelically radiant, both sets of in-laws approved, as did the invited guests. The baby did not even cry when the cold water was poured over her head, but as the ceremony came to a close, she started to become unsettled to the point that the only way left to pacify her was to make the breast available. The mother of the baby being modestly shy asked if she could use the privacy of the sacristy, once the ceremony had concluded. Brendan obliged. He let her in made her comfortable and left to mingle with the guests. When he returned the baby was contently sucking away. "I see she is happy now," he said. "Is there anything that you need?"

"No, I'm fine," and then without warning, and in complete contrast to her normal behaviour, she asked, "Would you like some?"

"Pardon...?"

"You know, do you want a bit?" she asked, pointing to her other breast. It was at that moment that her husband walked in. Luckily he had not overhead what had just been said; otherwise he would have planted Father O'Reilly then and there. He was a jealous man, devoid of all humour. "Rather strong aftershave you are wearing." He roughly said.

"Yes something that I picked up." Brendan sheepishly answered.

"Careful Father, the girls will be after you, they like a man who smells good. Isn't that right wifey?" The uncouth husband coarsely said as he looked at his wife who blushed, nodded and looked quickly away. "That's what attracted my wife to me all that sweat from a day's hard work. Hard to get rid of even after a good long hot shower, gives one's aftershave a certain bite, lets a woman knows who's a real man. Isn't that right wifey?" She nodded once again, and said nothing. "Has bub finished?" Her husband asked.

"I think so," she replied as she nervously adjusted her clothing.

"Good, let's go down to the pub and celebrate. Care to join us Father? I know it was meant to be the Monsignor, but you will do. What do you say?" The rugged husband asked in a friendly tone of voice.

Brendan thought over the proposition very carefully and declined the offer, using the parish council meeting and his inability to handle alcohol as convenient excuses.

3

CONFRONTATIONS

Father Brendan O'Reilly spent his time in solitary confinement after the baptism. He avoided all female contact, even the housekeepers. His only companion was the book of Psalms, which he read over and over again, looking for guidance, an answer to a prayer, no, not a prayer, an overwhelming erectile problem. Could it be that he had made a mistake. Perhaps he was not suited for the priesthood at all. Did Christ suffer similar temptations? Had he succumbed? The Bible did not say. How much was missing? How much do we really know? The more Brendan read the deeper became his despair. Perspiration started to bead on his forehead, he felt uncomfortably hot. His heart began to race, his breathing became laboured. He felt powerless and then with supreme effort he recited in a whisper the Lord's Prayer and all became still once more. His mind became quiet. His animal nature subsided. Lust, lust, lust, that's all it is, he reflected. I must learn to control it. No more weakness, I am strong, I am in control of my body, no one else. He sat motionless in an almost hypnotic state and then his internal clock summoned him. Brendan stood up to his full 182 cms, stretched upwards as though he was reaching for heaven and maintained a strong erect posture, a picture of confidence and strength. He marched into the Monsignor's office and collected the parish hall's keys and proceeded to the old gothic styled multipurpose building called the parish hall. Several elderly people were eagerly awaiting his arrival. Upon seeing him, they stood up and gingerly greeted him. "Father Brendan O'Reilly?" They said in unison.

"Yes." Brendan answered and waited for them to formally introduce themselves one by one.

"I am Mario Perucci the head of the parish council. This is my wife Rita and over here we have Mr. and Mrs. Abraham Isaacs, newly converted Christians from the Jewish faith Mr. and Mrs. Donald Fullham and finally Ms Rosita Lindenmyer." Brendan smiled, but avoided shaking anyone's hand. "Shall we go in," he gestured. Perucci led the way. Brendan opened the door, turned on the lights and kept the door open whilst everyone entered and took their favourite places. Brendan was the last to be seated. "Father," Perucci began, "Monsignor has instructed us to continue these meetings and ensure that the parish fund-raising program progresses in a successful fashion while he is away. He suggested that you may have some good ideas as the past parishes to which you have been assigned did re-markably well under your guidance." Brendan swallowed hard. "We have not run a fete for a number of years and were considering this avenue again. We would like to have something completely different, whilst remaining inside church guidelines. However, we feel that we may have to step outside of these as the big world has much more to offer and we should therefore endeavour to compete with it, offering a somewhat liberal fresh approach to entertainment. Mr. and Mrs. Isaacs have much experience in these fields, having run various amusement centres and parks. We need to act quickly as church funds are low and therefore we were considering running the fete next weekend in the church grounds. Here is a list of amusements and activities that we feel would make the public embrace the church and not only fill its coffers, but attract people back to Sunday mass. All it needs is your approval." Brendan was forced to swallow hard again. He was literally in the hot seat; he scanned the list of activities. They were mild, however, some leapt out of the page.

No 1 – seal your fate with a kiss from the Adonis himself, our own handsome parish priest.

No 2 – sensational sizzling satin burgers.

No 2 – huge Mormon Bible bonfire complete with Jehovah scarecrow and fireworks.

No 4 – Baptist doll-throwing competition.

No 5 – sample the latest hair care products – Gabriel's dazzling shampoo enriched with Lourdes' water.

Brendan tried desperately to smile, was this the Jew's way of making a mockery of his holy church? Was it right to deride other religions just because they did not dance to the Catholic Church's tune? Did they not realise that just because they were Protestants they still had their origins in the church and still belonged to it, just like a prodigal son? Was this the way to go for the sake of raising a few dollars? "I will have to give this some thought," he said.

"The matter is urgent, we can't wait. Monsignor has approved it so we don't need your approval to proceed."

"All that we really need are your kissable lips," Rosita Lindenmyer lustfully said as she ran her tongue across her lips and looked Brendan in the eye.

4

HELP ME, FOR I HAVE SINNED

The confessional box was cool somewhat musky in odour, a welcome relief, a sanctuary in which to hide away. Here at last, he could be in control of his situation. It was still the old fashioned way, priest in his cubical, separated by a non see-through purple curtain for the confessee. Time dragged on slowly. No one had called since the innocent child at 3:30pm. It was now 5:00pm and Father Brendan O'Reilly began to feel rather tired. The day's assault on his sexuality had left him feeling quite exhausted. Strange, how an outpouring of adrenalin does that to you. His whole body felt heavy and although he sat upright upon a hard wooden chair, he imagined that he was horizontalal in a bed of soft cushions with his head on the lap of an angel. She spoke soft comforting words as she stroked his forehead and cheeks. The vision took him back to his childhood of days when it would be just him and his mother sharing a bed, sharing intimate moments that only a mother and a young child knew, a bonding that lasted a lifetime and beyond. Was this vision just a memory or was it an access to his spiritual mother and a future that lay ahead.

"Excuse me Father." Silence, the words fell upon deaf ears. "Hello is someone in there, hello."

"Oh yes, I am sorry," replied Brendan in an apologetic startled fashion. "I was miles away, how can I help you child?"

"I am not a child."

"I am sorry your voice sounded so sweet and innocent, I thought that you were."

"Are you still conducting confessions?" she asked.

"Yes." Brendan softly answered.

"Well, can you hear mine and help me in the process?"

"As best I can."

"You are the closest person to God that I am able to talk to, aren't you? That is what happens to priests isn't it?" Brendan nodded. "I did not hear you Father, did you say yes?"

"Of course my child…. now what is your problem?" Brendan answered stumbling on his poor choice of words.

"I have sinned."

"Okay, let's hear your confession."

"I am married to a good man, I think, he has never beaten me and does provide for me and the children, but after ten years of marriage I am thinking about other men and even dreaming about having a relationship with someone else."

"Why do you think that is so?" Brendan asked

"I don't know, but it might have something to do with what a bunch of women were talking about some time ago."

"And that was?"

"Orgasm…..what is it Father? I have asked my husband but he does not want to discuss it. He becomes very embarrassed and a little angry."

"Why not read about it in books?" asked Brendan.

"I can't read very well or understand big words."

"Did you ask the bunch of ladies?"

"No."

"Why not….?"

"Because I don't belong to their group, I am an outsider."

"What about the doctor?"

"I never get sick, besides being a priest, being so close to God, I thought you could find out and tell me all about it. I was brought up to believe in the church and that it always looks after its flock, so can you help me Father?"

Brendan felt pity for the woman. He wanted to help her desperately beyond explaining orgasm and so he started by delicately saying "Orgasm usually occurs when two people, that is a man and a woman make love."

"You mean sex?"

"I would prefer to call it lovemaking."

"So when does it happen then, say in a woman?"

All of a sudden, the sanctuary was no longer. The confessional became hot, confined, cellular. Brendan struggled to reply. He had to rely on his memory of high school human biology. He searched for words, pictures and then with an air of shaky confidence, he said, "When she has been sufficiently stimulated."

"You mean banged?"

"No…. made love to"

"I have never experienced that, all my old man does when he comes to bed is takes his knickers off, sticks it in, jiggles for a while and falls asleep. Does he have an orgasm then?"

"I can't answer that question."

"Why not…?"

"Because it happens in the mind of the person"

"What happens?"

"Orgasm."

"So wwwhat is it?"

"I believe it is like an explosion in the head."

"Like a big bang, a firework, is that it?"

"No, it is usually associated with a feeling of warmth, your whole body tingles, you feel no pain, your body floats."

"You mean like people who get spaced out on drugs, that sort of thing?"

"Perhaps not."

"Why not?"

"Because orgasms are natural, not drug induced, they are gifts from God."

"So why do some people say that sex is dirty then?"

"I don't know. It does not make any sense does it?"

"Father, have you had an orgasm?"

"Not sexually."

"When then?"

"In deep prayer…. concentrating on the beauty of the Virgin Mary."

"Did she give you an orgasm then?"

"Only in my mind and soul."

"So the Virgin keeps you happy."

"Yes."

"Now I understand why priests don't marry. The Virgin looks after all of you, she must be very busy. I wonder if God gets jealous."

"Why?"

"'Cause She is married to Him."

Brendan was becoming increasingly frustrated.

"Did I manage to answer your questions my child?"

"No, not really."

"Why not?"

"Because the only way that I will ever know what an orgasm is, will be if I experience one. Reading about it, listening to others won't let me experience it. Even if I imagine it, it still won't be the real thing will it? So Father, tell me how to achieve orgasm please."

"Your husband needs to help you."

"I told you what he is like. Can I do it myself, like you do in prayer?"

"Sexual orgasm is different."

"Why?"

"Because it is a physical act."

"What do you mean?"

"You have to touch yourself."

"Where?"

"On your private parts, the vagina and clitoris."

"My what?"

"Vagina and clitoris."

"How?"

"There are toys I believe."

"Action figures?"

"No, not quite"

"What then?"

"I believe they are called vibrators."

"What do they do?"

"They shake a lot."

"What… like my husband?"

"Deeper and longer until the batteries run out…!!!"

Brendan could feel himself losing control. He hoped he had not shouted the last phrase out loud

"I am upsetting you aren't I? I am sorry, I will go now," she very timidly said.

"No, wait, I apologise. I will explain as best I can."

"You don't have to. I don't have any spare cash for those toys. They sound expensive anyhow. Thank you Father."

"Please wait."

"Why?"

"Because if I can't help you then no one else can I am supposed to be closest to God, remember."

"Alright, what do I have to do?" Brendan paused, hoping to be filled with the Holy Spirit and then he began.

"When you are alone at home, lay down on the bed, very carefully and gently after removing all of your clothes, discover the little button that lies above the entrance to your vagina."

"You mean my love cave?"

"Please think about calling it vagina. That is the proper anatomical description."

"Okay, then what?"

"Then very gently stroke it in a way that gives you the greatest pleasure."

"Why?"

"Because this button will trigger an explosion in your head. Don't be afraid, continue to stroke until it finally happens."

"How will I know?"

"Believe me, you will. It is like I explained before. Continue to practice, you will then become healthier and a happier person."

"Will I still think about other men?"

"I don't know, but I think you may not."

"Thank you Father. Can I come back and ask you for more help?"

"Yes, my child, but only during confession time, never outside of that. I don't want people forming wrong ideas and starting gossip. For your penance, say five Hail Mary's and try not to think about other men again, okay. Stay faithful to your husband, no matter what and when you feel confident, discuss orgasm and lovemaking with him in a kind and gentle way. Many people feel embarrassed about it, so you will have to be caring and in this way, lovemaking will become a joyous experience. After all, that is the way God intended it to be."

"How do you mean?"

"Man learns from woman and vice versa so that they can become one in all aspects of their relationship."

"Thank you Father." She quietly said and left.

Brendan collapsed into a heap of exhaustion. When he came to, it was 7:15. Oh my god, he thought, I am late for mass. As he left the confessional box he saw that the church was rapidly filling with worshippers, which was unusual for the 7:30 mass. Monsignor said it would be quiet, only a handful of souls would attend. As he entered the sacristy he was relieved to see that the altar boys were present and had correctly prepared the altar and laid out all of the vestments necessary for the mass of the day.

"Good evening Father," they both said.

"Good evening boys, and who might you be?" he politely asked.

"I am Stuart," replied the older and taller of the two.

"And I am Leslie," said the other

"Thank you for preparing everything." Brendan genuinely replied.

"That's okay Father. Monsignor thought you might need a hand until you settled in and knew your way about. The church looks really full tonight, did you advertise something special?"

"No, I didn't."

"We have never had such a full church, not even at Christmas or Easter time."

"Is that so" Brendan replied starting to look a little worried.

"Yes," the younger boy replied.

"You're not a movie star are you Father?" The other boy asked

"No, why do you ask?"

"Because you look like one, you know, handsome and all that."

Brendan dismissed the remark and finished donning his attire, he looked at the two altar boys and said, "Okay boys, let us say a prayer before mass."

And they did so with complete reverence.

As they walked onto the sanctuary, Brendan was awe-struck by the sheer volume of the congregation. It dawned on him that the girls who had attended 6:30am mass had invited one and all to view the new boy on the block. What was it that had made him so popular? Was it as the altar boys had suggested, that he looked like a film star? And if so, which one? Brendan did not follow the popular press and therefore he did not know who the current megastar was. His self determined mission in life was to discover what Christ really came to teach. Some of the great saints of the church had discovered and demonstrated it by the extraordinary feats that they had performed. It was his belief that he could do the same and in his mind, it could only be attained by the pathway of purity, celibacy and self-sacrifice to the point of locking oneself away from the world entirely. Today he could not do that. He was out in the open. The best he could do was to inspire the congregation into embracing his philosophy of Christ's teachings. He was determined to do that during the homily. Mass proceeded very nicely the congregation as a whole behaved itself quite obediently. But as the time drew closer to the homily, Brendan sensed an air of restlessness. Once the second reading had been over and done with, he approached the pulpit and stepped onto it and as he did so a thunderous wave of applause greeted him. A super star had certainly stepped into the spotlight. The congregation was now a frenzied crowd wanting to cheer, touch and applaud. Brendan tried to settle them down. It was of no use. The crowd drew nearer, eager to embrace and smother. It was soon upon the steps of the sanctuary drawing closer and closer. Afraid for his spiritual and personal safety Brendan ran out towards the adjoining sacristy door, found the church's rear entrance and dashed across the grounds and made a beeline for his car, which was parked behind the presbytery. Luckily he had remembered to keep the keys on him that day and with the utmost urgency he withdrew them from his trouser pocket, fumbled for a moment before, unlocking the door. He then jumped in and without even looking around him raced away to safety.

5

FATHERLY ADVICE

It was 11:00pm when Father Brendan O'Reilly finally arrived at the 'Palace' as it was affectionately known amongst the priests of the State. The imposing building was where the Archbishop resided. A magnificent two storey Georgian style mansion surrounded by extensive parklands and surprisingly no fences. The Archbishop believed in divine providence and that it would provide all of the necessary protection. Brendan pounded on the front door and shouted, "Let me in, let me in."

His antics were enough to startle the neighbourhood dogs into barking. The porch light went on and the housekeeper, cautious as always, peered out from behind the partially opened door and asked in an agitated voice.

"Who is there, what do you want?"

"Father Brendan O'Reilly, I want to see the Arch now," The handsome priest demanded.

The housekeeper opened the door a bit more, but kept the safety chain on until she was convinced that it was indeed, Father Brendan O'Reilly who had spoken. She peered at the man before her and slowly the image of Brendan coincided with her memory.

"Father Brendan, come in, please," she said as she unlatched the door.

"I go fetch the Archbishop, but I make no promises, he very tired, busy day."

Brendan thanked her and sat down in one of the chairs made available for visitors. It seemed like hours before she returned.

"I am sorry Father, the Archbishop says it does not matter how urgent it is, it can wait until the morning."

'Damn his arrogance!' thought Brendan.

But he realised no matter what he would do or say the Arch was immovable. The housekeeper could sense Brendan's despair. She looked lovingly at him and asked, "Father, are you not a very long way from your parish?"

"Yes."

"Then you must stay the night and see the Archbishop in the morning. Come; let me take you to the guest room. I think you also need a good night sleep."

Brendan agreed. She looked at him again.

"When you last eat?"

"Some time ago."

"I think you have not eaten since lunch time, si, you look terrible, very white. Come to the kitchen, I make you something good and quick."

Brendan obediently followed. The housekeeper was right, after some food his mind would become less cloudy, he would regain some sense of rationality once again. Angela De Jesus was a simple middle-aged Italian woman who had devoted her entire life to the church. She wanted to become a nun; however, circumstances precluded that from happening. She was a very efficient housekeeper. There was a rumour that she and the Archbishop were romantically involved, but in reality, it was more like an intense brother/sister relationship that evolved over the years. Angela was a very imaginative cook. Within minutes she had prepared for Father Brendan a plate of scrambled eggs with mushrooms, bacon and chives expertly folded in. He devoured this within seconds and sat like a contented puppy licking his lips.

"Would you like freshly brewed coffee?"

"Yes please," he said quietly.

The aroma of the brew was overpowering. It infused itself into his anatomy giving a welcome relief from anxiety and tension.

'Funny how I have never tasted the aroma in the coffee itself, too volatile I suppose,' he thought to himself as he held the cup.

Brendan's mind went blank. Without a thought in his head, he suddenly felt an aura of cold shame descend upon him.

"Father, are you alright?" asked Angela.

"I don't know, I think I may have made a fool of myself by coming here."

Angela remained briefly silent. She walked up to Father Brendan O'Reilly, looked him straight in the eye and said, "Don't doubt yourself, you are a very fine priest, a very capable man. I think you have been a little rattled, that is all. Come to bed."

'What, not you as well... Angela,' thought Brendan. 'Doesn't it ever stop?'

The next morning Father O'Reilly woke quite refreshed, but still felt guilty. He had not fulfilled his obligations to the parish that he had been looking after. The early morning churchgoers would have found the church locked; no mass today. No priest, no knowledge of his whereabouts, a flock without its shepherd and he decided that perhaps he should just slip away unnoticed back to where he came from but a knock at the door changed all of that.

"Father Brendan, are you awake? Father......."

Brendan stirred out of his pessimistic daydreaming.

"Yes, I am, just a moment please."

He opened the door and was dressed only in boxer shorts; the Archbishop's secretary stared at him wide eyed. He was not accustomed to seeing members of the cloth almost naked. He cleared his throat and gestured to Father Brendan to follow him.

"But I am not fully clothed."

"It does not matter, the Archbishop is very busy, he can spare a few moments only, come on."

Brendan reluctantly followed. It was 6:00am. Luckily it was still summer, the air temperature was comfortable, the Palace was warm. Brendan could smell breakfast being prepared. Angela was at it again, creating more culinary delights. Apart from that, everything else was still. The Archbishop's office was at the end of a long hall at the rear of the Palace. It overlooked the gardens. The door was open and he was standing looking somewhat worried, as a father should be. As Brendan entered the room, the Arch flew to him and embraced him warmly. My Golden Boy, "I understand you are somewhat distressed."

"I am," Brendan replied visibly embarrassed.

"O'Reilly, come sit down and tell me all about it, then we can decide how to solve what troubles you."

"I don't know how to phrase this, it is very delicate."

"There is nothing that delicate Brendan."

"Well Your Grace, it is about my sexuality."

"How do you mean?"

"There have been so many assaults on it lately that it is driving me crazy."

"You mean, physically?"

"Almost…..."

"Almost…..! Does that mean you have lost your virginity?"

"No."

"You masturbated?"

"No."

"What then?"

"My head is full of sexual desires. I feel as though I have reached the point where I can no longer want to be a priest. I want to taste the pleasures of the world, the flesh of a woman, yet I know that if I do, I will never reach my goal in life."

"And that is?" asked the Bishop.

"I would rather not say. All that I can tell you is that I feel that the church has let me down."

"This is something that I did not wish to hear," said the Archbishop as he frowned. "Especially from you, we have been grooming you for a long, long time."

"Grooming me!"

"Yes."

"For heaven's sake; what for; the asylum? I have been tormented everywhere I stayed. How could you do this to me? This is entirely your fault."

Brendan was starting to lose control. He held his breath and tried to relax his tensing muscles. The Archbishop lowered his voice and looked at him steadily.

"Brendan, nothing of what has happened to you has been intentionally done. It has happened by chance. You are indeed a very handsome man. Women will be easily attracted to you. Be aware however, that there is a breed of women that we call Black-trackers that will do anything in their power to seduce a priest."

"Then I must have met every one of them in the last six months," interrupted Brendan.

"We can only suggest sending you to an older community where there is very little likelihood of this happening again. Give the church another chance, she needs you, she cannot survive without you, please."

Brendan accepted the Archbishop's sorrowful plea, but with some reservation.

"Okay but if this does not work out what then?"

"We will have to consider other options."

"And they are?"

"We will look at these later. For now, let me outline in detail the place where you are going."

Brendan listened attentively, but could not come to grips with anything that the Archbishop had just said. There was going to be a change, but not as the Archbishop described, or as Brendan imagined it.

6

DOES HE KNOW?

"Good morning Monsignor."
"Good morning Your Grace" replied the Monsignor
"Looking very relaxed" he continued, "I believe you and Father O'Reilly met earlier this morning

"We did."

"Did he suspect anything?"

"I don't think so. However, he is very sexually frustrated."

"That is understandable"

"Where did you send him?"

"To the R and R Centre"

"The R and R Centre…?"

"Yes. He should be safe there."

"How long will you leave him there?"

"Until I need him to resurrect another ailing parish"

"Well then, that could be next week," laughed Monsignor.

"Oh no, that would be rather improper. I think he needs as least two months to cool down."

"You know, you are quite the devil Your Grace in the way that you easily manipulate people."

"I can only do it with your help, after all, Monsignor, you are the States spiritual master, they all flock to you when they have problems, they confide in you with absolute trust, but little do they know," His Grace replied with a sly smile

"Quite so Your Grace quite so."

7

DRIVE TIME

The journey to the R and R Centre would take Father O'Reilly at least twelve hours. The Archbishop suggested that Brendan go by coach, but he refused. He thought that a drive would do him the world of good, a chance to unwind, to reflect and in any case, he would be alone. No female company to offer temptation. The R and R Centre was in fact Saint Pious Parish located 950 kms north of the Palace. It would be easy to reach as a major highway almost connected the two. It would require at least three pit-stops along the way. Brendan was going there as an assistant priest, the workload would be very light, mostly visiting an abundance of nursing homes that proliferated in the area. In fact, Saint Pious Parish had the dubious distinction of being known as the narcotic capital of the nation. All of the nursing homes specialised in the care of cancer patients and those needing chronic pain relief. To ease the torment of the previous weeks Brendan played Mozart's Ave Verum Corpus, followed by a selection of Bach, Beethoven and Brahms compositions. Whilst these played on his car stereo, he quietly recited the rosary and stayed alert with respect to driving conditions. He had decided to dress in civilian clothes. These would camouflage him against the Black-trackers. The first garage stop was uneventful; no one looked at him, just another lonely traveller, nothing special about him 'Perhaps the Arch was right; women are attracted to the uniform, nothing to do with me after all'. Brendan continued to motor on. One hour later when the tape had stopped he switched to radio. As he flicked through the available stations he managed to find one that played light classical music. Berlioz, The Planets, Mars, the bringer of war was being played and then the radio announcer interrupted the program.

"Ladies and gentlemen, sorry for this break in transmission, we have been advised to broadcast an urgent weather warning. The Bureau says that a storm is rampant along highway N86, motorists are advised to proceed with the utmost caution. High winds, gusts to 120kms and heavy hail have been encountered. Just repeating that; normal broadcasts will now resume."

'It must be a long way from here,' thought Brendan as he surveyed the sky, but twenty-five minutes along the highway things were very, very different. The first hailstone hit the roof of Brendan's car with an almighty bang. Brendan thought that it was a meteorite descended from the heavens he slowed the car down as the incident had really shocked him. Then a succession of large hailstones hit in machine-gun fashion. A wind gust ripped across his car, throwing it off balance. The tyres struggled to keep hold of the road. The window wipers groaned as they swept the splattered hailstones off the windscreen. Brendan had never experienced anything like this before. He struggled to keep control

"This is no place for me." He anxiously concluded and he decided to drive very carefully as he looked for an off ramp. "I certainly do not want to be involved in any pileup."

Brendan prayed as he nudged his car along. Two kilometres further on an exit presented itself, with a large sign advertising N86 Road House Café 200 metres. Brendan would not have seen the exit had it not been for the red flashing sign, as the rain was torrential. He manoeuvred the car through the deep torrents of water hoping that it would not give out. There were very few automobiles in the parking area. He positioned his Ford as close as possible to the café, shut down the engine, made certain that all the doors were locked and then he made a dash for the café's main entrance.

The N86 Road House was largely empty. Brendan looked for the cleanest available table and sat down. With one eye he looked at the menu that was stuck to the surface of the table and with the other, he looked outside. Water dropped onto the table from his wet hair. He picked up a napkin and wiped it away. Brendan became mesmerized by the falling rain. It seemed to him that it fell in a repetitive pattern and as he stared, he could even make out nebulous forms conducting the rain. Music filled his ears and he understood how the great musical composers came to write their scores, they simply listened to nature. He became one with the events outside and was unaware of the waitress standing by his side trying to attract his attention.

"Excuse me sir, excuse me."

Brendan looked up into the face of an angel; she was exceptionally pretty, light blue eyes, flaxen blonde hair, a peaches and cream complexion, no more than sixteen years of age.

"Can I get you something?" she politely asked.

"Oh, oh yes I would like some hot coffee and let me see, um, what time is it?"

"4:00 o'clock in the afternoon sir."

"Oh, very well, perhaps I will have an early dinner. The mixed grill with salad looks fine, thank you."

"Thank you sir"

'Such sweet innocence,' thought Brendan as he watched her disappear into the kitchen.

He returned his attention to the water symphony that was being conducted outside. As the wind and hail crashed and thrashed about, the image of a man dressed in black attire with baton in hand formed in the midst of it all. The elements obeyed every movement of his wrist, it was a delight to behold, and then as his arms descended into rest, so did the hail and wind lessen. He turned his back on his orchestra and walked towards the building. Brendan rubbed his eyes to make certain that he was not imagining what he had just seen. The tall dark stranger entered with an air of authority, paused, looked about and then approached Brendan.

"Good afternoon, my name is Jack Stern, would you mind if I joined you on this miserable afternoon? It looks as though you could do with a little company."

"Not at all, please sit down." Brendan cordially answered and was struck by the fact that this man was not wet at all, yet for the past fifteen minutes Brendan thought that he had had watched him conducting the storm outside. What had Brendan really seen?

"Your name would be?" asked Jack.

"Brendan O'Reilly."

"That's a nice Irish name. Mum and dad Irish are they?"

"Yes."

"Born here?"

"Yes."

"Enjoying the storm?"

"Yes I was, in a rather romantic way."

"Bit of a dreamer are you?"

"I suppose."

"This weather stimulates my appetite, how about you?"

"Same."

"Have you ordered?"

"Yes."

"May I ask?"

"The mixed grill with salad."

"Sounds good." Jack Stern agreed and signalled the waitress to take his order. "Same as this gentleman here for me please." She nodded in reply. "Going far?" asked Jack.

"Yes, to Saint Pious Parish."

"That's about four hours drive from here down the highway."

"I suppose, I haven't been there before."

Before Jack Stern could ask another next question, the waitress arrived with Brendan's meal.

"Mmmmmm that looks great," Jack said, and then he continued by saying "I can hardly wait for mine."

"That shouldn't be very long sir," the young waitress sweetly replied. Jack flashed a smile and then watched Brendan as he ate with obvious enjoyment.

8

PROPOSITION

Brendan O'Reilly was right the storm had created an air of romance within the café. There was nothing comparable to enjoying a warm delicious meal whilst watching nature's fury outside. Nothing except perhaps, sharing that moment with a beautiful woman. The young waitress interrupted Jack Stern's daydreaming by saying, "Excuse me sir, your meal."

"Oh, yes of course, thank you."

"Is there anything else I can get you?" She asked

Her question sent shivers down Brendan's spine.

"Cappuccino coffee later would be nice." Looking at Brendan he added, "For two please and a dessert menu."

"Yes sir, thank you."

"Mmmm this really is quite delicious."

"Yes, mine was," replied Brendan. "Thank you for ordering coffee for me."

"Oh, it is the least I could do after all I did impose myself on you. You did say you were going to Saint Pious Parish."

"Yes."

"Does that mean you are a priest?"

"Yes I am."

"Well then, I suppose I shall have to behave myself in your holy company."

"No, just be natural."

"It is quite strange."

"How do you mean?" enquired Brendan.

"Well, I haven't been to church in almost ten years and on the stormiest of nights when one could expect to find one's life in danger, one finds a priest, quite coincidentally, almost as if the gods are trying to tell me something."

"God; not god."

"Thank you for correcting me," countered Jack. "You know, I have often wanted to become a priest, but somehow I could not bring myself to do it. Almost as if I needed to know the world before I could know God. In that respect I suspect we are opposites."

"How do you mean?"

"Well, I know the world better than you and you know God better than I. This means that each one of us is lacking in our make-up. Each one of us is incomplete. Heaven wouldn't want us then, they only want complete beings."

"How can you say that?"

"It is easy, the world has taught me."

"The world?"

"Yes, the world."

"That can't be possible. It is a conglomeration of billions of people; you can't possibly expect me to believe that the world is a teacher."

"But it is, the earth is a living entity, it is one of our teachers, one of our gods."

"I am afraid you are wrong."

"Am I? Prove it!"

"I can't." Brendan paused. "Yes I can. The Bible has all of the answers."

"Perhaps in terms of a period of relationship between man and some of the gods, but it does not describe the mechanism by which the gods act."

Brendan was stumped. He could not argue like a religious fanatic. He was above all intelligent and this aspect of him that made him seriously think.

Jack Stern continued. "I, like you, believed in the Bible and that is not bad, for it gives people a good code to live by, especially the New Testament, however, when you begin to think about events contained within it, many questions spring into your mind."

"For example?" asked Brendan.

"Well, one day when my father and I were discussing religion, he asked me a curious question. The Jews in the old testament had a covenant with God."

"What is a covenant he asked me?"

"I answered I do not know."

"Well, he suggested, surely it must be a contract, that would seem reasonable."

"If it is so, what does God's signature look like?"

Brendan laughed. "You're kidding me; most of those things were symbolic."

"Why, how can you possibly say that? Do you realise how difficult it would be for you to convince those people who take the Bible literally. You haven't come across these have you? You have simply led an over sheltered life dealing only with obedient Catholics. Well Father, perhaps for the first time in your life, let me introduce you to a real live disobedient one, me."

Jack Stern extended his hand. Brendan gingerly accepted it and shook it. Silence descended. Jack continued to enjoy his meal. Brendan sat there quite solemnly shifting his gaze between Jack and the storm outside. Was this man right, was his education as a priest lacking? Could it be true that the entry into heaven demanded more than being a priest? Was the priesthood nothing more than a job? What did Brendan have to learn in order to qualify? A fear suddenly gripped him, perhaps it was not coincidental perhaps this storm was an act of God. The past months had indeed been a stormy troubled time and it had now well and truly broken. Was this physical reality of God's actions telling Brendan to listen to this man? Was this man or divine, a messenger of God; an angel perhaps? After all, he did walk through the rain without getting a drop of water on him. Jack Stern stopped eating. He wiped his hands and mouth with the table napkin provided.

"You're very quiet. Have I said anything to upset you?" He asked the handsome priest

"No, quite the opposite, I find our conversation rather stimulating." Brendan awkwardly replied.

"Well then, where do we go from here?"

"How do you mean?" questioned Brendan.

"As I see it, we both need to enlarge our education, especially yours."

"How about yours…?" Brendan asked in defense.

"Not really, I have had plenty of practice as an altar boy. My uncle was a priest I saw what he got up to in the name of God and the church." Jack replied with a frown.

"What do you propose that I leave the priesthood?"

"No, just take a short holiday."

"I can't do that."

"Yes, you can, you can do anything you want, remember what Christ said, faith moves mountains."

"What does this have to do with faith?"

"Everything, faith is that energy, that activity that creates reality. Your reality is acceptance into heaven, but it is dependent upon education. So become educated, for the Catholic Church does not provide it."

"Why not?"

"Because it is too dogmatic, it is run by humans, not the gods. For Christ's sake, they haven't even got the Bible correct. You do realise it has been subject to manipulation, political and otherwise and to incorrect translations etc, etc, etc."

Brendan's face whitened. This man spoke with such persuasive authority.

"What am I to do?" Brendan asked almost panic stricken.

"Take a step forward and be embraced by the greatest teacher in life, the world. I can provide you with that step."

"How?"

"I have a community service business on the outskirts of the town where Saint Pious is located. I suggest that you run it for a while, say a month."

"And the parish?"

"I can look after that for you."

"You're suggesting we exchange places."

"Yes, for a while. Look, when I was with my uncle, I ran the parish while he was away doing his pastoral duties."

"Things have changed since then."

"So have I. Remember, I am of the world, not outside of it."

The prospect was inviting, but Brendan was still reluctant and Jack sensed this.

"I tell you what, let's have a good stiff drink and mull it over while the storm blows itself out… waitress!" Jack politely said as he summonsed the young girl with a wave of his hand.

The angelic girl responded quickly.

"What do you have to drink in the alcoholic way?"

"We have a large selection of beers, wines and spirits sir."

"What do you fancy?" Jack erotiucally asked the handsome priest

"I don't really drink."

"Oh yes you do, altar wine is a very good sherry. I remember that the priests that used very little altar wine at consecration usually saved it for later come on try something harder how about brandy?"

"Okay, brandy it is. French if you have it please Miss"

Jack was surprised.

"I am only guessing, I don't drink, I have overheard people saying how good the French are"

"Okay then, what brand would you like?"

"What do you have?" asked Brendan.

The waitress ran through the variations from memory. "Courvoisier, Remy Martin and Martelle"

"Brendan?"

"Remy Martin please."

"Why that one?"

"I think we have a well known church in that district of France"

"For two please and could you also bring us the dessert menu."

"Yes sir," she very politely answered.

Brendan and Jack eyed each other, neither saying a word, yet each knew that their souls were interacting, deciding on the most appropriate course of action which Jack would use to his advantage.

9

DECISION TIME

The first sip of Cognac took Brendan's breath away; it burnt his tongue and throat but once they settled, the beauty of sun-drenched grapes intermingled with majestic oak hit him.

"You approve?"

"I do," said Brendan in a vow-making fashion.

"A lifelong association?"

"It has its possibility," he replied.

"Like the priesthood? How many sips will it take to convince you?"

"Another 2 or 3 and then I shall probably agree to anything."

"Anything?"

"Yes, anything."

"The French are rather good at what they do, that is why they are so arrogant." Jack suggested

"Really?"

"Haven't you seen that amongst some of your fellow priests?" Jack asked

"Come to think of it, I have, especially the bishops."

"Do you want to become like them?"

"No! I would rather be like Christ and mix with the ordinary people. You know, say the tax collectors and prostitutes."

"Noble thoughts, he wasn't a priest you know, just an ordinary man."

"The son of God," added Brendan

"A master soul, one of many that has guided mankind through its evolution," Jack added without any further confrontation. "The question is, are you ready to confront your fears and to fulfill your noble ambitions?"

"I would like to," Brendan replied sincerely.

"Well, what is your delay?"

"I have never had the opportunity."

"Until now I represent that opportunity. Grasp it Brendan, it may never appear again. You cannot appreciate how well the world will teach you. Take her hand and let her guide you upon the most exciting educational tour of your life."

Stern's argument was certainly bedazzling especially in the way that he seductively delivered it and it was hard if not impossible for Brendan to resist.

Brendan quietly replied, after much thought. "Okay, I'll do it."

He drained his glass and sat in submissive silence.

A smile spread upon Jack's face as he glanced at the storm, it had started to subside. Brendan noticed it as well. He ordered another drink.

"Rather ambitious of you Father."

"Yes, my son, it's not a case of Dutch courage, more in the way of educating one's taste buds. I think they need another lesson. Tell me, do you think we will get away with it?"

"And why not? What is there to prevent us?"

"Nothing I suppose. We do look very similar."

"All it needs is for us to never let our tongues slip. You are an actor now, you will become me. As Shakespeare said, we are many actors on many stages in life, so act; it is not difficult, nothing is impossible in life." Jack said with conviction

"Brave words."

"No, true words, it is only impossible for those who allow fear in all of its forms to dominate and frustrate them. Having said that, it makes you wonder why the religions are so pre-occupied with instilling fear into people."

"We have to, otherwise we would not know how else to control the flock. It is the case of reward for good deeds done."

"Do you really mean it?"

"Yes I do. I have known it for a long time, which is why I felt so uneasy hearing confessions and giving out penances."

"Boy, has the alcohol loosened your tongue. Are you sure it is you that is talking?"

Brendan giggled like a tipsy young lady.

"I think we had better sober you up," Jack signalled to the waitress.

"More coffee please this time, double short blacks."

It was a while before Brendan regained his composure. As he did, so did the weather. The wildness had slowly dissipated. The light of day began to filter through, bathing the outside scenery in golden ponds of shimmering light.

Jack Stern paid for the meal much to Brendan's disgust.

"I'm not poor you know."

"Maybe not financially, but in other respects you are. Consider it another blessing, divine providence looking after you."

Brendan frowned.

The angelic waitress bade them farewell. The air outside of the café was crisp and refreshingly clean.

"Where is your car?" Jack asked.

"Just over there, the white Ford."

"Looks like you're in for quite a change then," Jack laughed. "Do you think you can handle it?"

"What do you mean?"

"Two cars to the left of yours, as you can see, is a red Ferrari, it's mine. I mean yours for a while. It is a mechanical version of a hot woman with one exception."

Brendan blushed. Jack pretended not to notice.

"And that is?" Brendan asked as he cleared his throat.

"You are in control," Jack replied as he and Brendan walked towards it.

"Now, take a seat, let me run through her operational assets." Jack erotically said as he carefully pointed out all of the right buttons to press in order to turn her on and keep her purring.

"These are the stop/go pedals and here is the most important part, the gear stick. Some women think it is a phallic symbol."

"Really, I would never have guessed." Brendan naively replied

"Comfortable."

"Yes thank you."

"Think you can handle her?" Jack asked in a serious tone of voice

"Yessss, it I mean she reminds me of an old tractor my uncle once had." Jack remained unmoved; obviously the priest was beginning to show some sense of humour, something to be expected from a non-materialistic soul.

"Okay, let's exchange clothes," Jack said, as he looked Brendan up and down.

"What here?"

"Why not plenty of bushes to hide behind....."

Their previous estimations were quite correct, they both wore similar-sized clothes. Jack had no trouble in stepping back into basic wear whereas Brendan felt uneasy in his upper market designer labels.

"We are not however going to completely change identities and identification."

"How do you mean?" Brendan asked feeling a little uneasy about the swap.

"I am keeping the mobile phone and credit cards. I still need to keep in touch with the office. It's not that I don't trust you."

"Okay, that's fair, I understand." Brendan replied a little relieved.

"Good. As for everything else, I am you and you are me. Wallets less some money and car keys now, here is the address of where you have to go, remember it is a community service organisation. You will have no trouble in running it. It is a very religious concern. People are very devoted to it. They just keep coming back for more."

"I have never done anything in the private sector before. Are you sure I will be able to cope?"

"Of course you will. You have the performers, just like in the church, you have a paying congregation, a daily ritual, you have plenty of giving, even pseudo confessions."

"Really?"

"Really" confirmed Jack, "it will be perfect for you."

Jack ushered Brendan into the Ferrari and closed the door.

"Start her up. Before you go, here's my card. Any problems, call the mobile number."

Brendan nodded. He adjusted the driver's seat to his requirements. Inserted the starter key and coaxed the lady into life. He looked somewhat hesitant at Jack, forced a smile and gently eased the Ferrari towards the main highway. Jack watched as his lovely lady disappeared out of sight 'God is with you, he thought.' He walked towards the white Ford and as he did so, he congratulated himself on his negotiating skills, and upon the realisation of one of his many wicked dreams, namely, to run a Catholic church with a difference. The Ford was a dramatic contrast to what he was presently used to, but it did have a wonderful air about it the kind that you perceive in any Catholic church. A certain stillness; a certain peace, a sense of belonging, a feeling of being embraced by many unseen heavenly creatures. I wonder what mum would think. Blasphemy, outrageous behaviour I suppose. Does it matter? What really makes a priest a holy man? Is it the passing of man-made exams or is it the passing of that test of completeness that heaven demands? Heaven can wait, time to have some fun. Saint Pious, here we come.

10

THE INFIRMARY

Brendan O'Reilly awoke the next morning in the most comfortable bed he had ever slept in. The Hotel Large had provided the best room it had to offer for one Jack Stern. It was not the usual 5 star rated, as Jack would have demanded, but it was opulent by Brendan's standards. It was already 7:00am, late for Brendan who was used to getting up early in preparation for 6:30am mass. The room was surprisingly quiet and still, almost like a church. The silence was broken by a knock at the door, followed by, "Good morning Mr Stern breakfast sir."

Father Brendan rolled out of bed, donned a hotel dressing gown and proceeded to open the door. A middle-aged waiter wheeled in a trolley bearing a smorgasbord of breakfast delights.

Brendan's eyes widened in sheer disbelief 'So, this is how the rich live,' he thought.

"Can I get you anything else?" the waiter enquired.

Brendan did not answer immediately. He stared at the array of food and replied after a moment, "Ah, no thank you."

The waiter nodded, excused himself and took his leave.

Brendan was used to breakfasts of toast and jam with a cup of tea, certainly nothing like this. If the parish could afford it, he would have bacon, eggs and sausages once a month. The memory of that caused him to struggle with the idea of partaking in such an extravagant fashion.

'I hope this is not the last breakfast,' he thought.

'Too early in the morning for such morbid thoughts, it is a sin to waste such good-looking food, better dig in, as mum would say.' And with that, he proceeded to enjoy the most heavenly breakfast that he had in a long, long while. Meanwhile, across town, Jack Stern had to contend with the opposite. Sub standard bedding, a very cold room and the most appalling breakfast he had ever confronted in his life. Yet he relished the atmosphere of it all. It represented a new challenge, a new era of achievement. Once Brendan had finished his breakfast, he fell on his knees and recited the rosary. It represented both thanks and the asking of forgiveness in case his actions had disappointed the Lord. Intuitively he realised he had not. This temporary leave of duty was for him to explore and learn from. His meditative mood was disrupted by the waiter and the housemaid.

"Can you give me ten minutes?" he said. "I need to shower and shave. I am rather slow this morning."

"Of course sir, we will be back in half an hour."

"Thank you that will give me plenty of time."

Within fifteen minutes Brendan had prepared himself for his next adventure. He made certain that he had everything. He double-checked the hotel room and made certain that he had not left anything behind. He started to make his way out of the hotel to the private car park, almost forgetting that it was a red Ferrari and not his own car that he had to make for. But before he left, he did ask the desk clerk for directions to The Infirmary upon which the clerk blushed deeply. An elderly bell boy overheard the request and was more than pleased to advise him.

"Marvellous laddie simply marvellous, spent the best hours of my life in there, you know. Came away totally drained and renewed at the same time," he said with a cheeky gleam in his eye.

"I believe there is a great devotion there," Brendan remarked.

"And more…The stories, I can tell you. Must go, lots of work to do, enjoy, enjoy," the bell boy shouted as he scurried away.

Although the morning was cold the Ferrari sprung easily into life. Brendan drove it slowly down the hotel's private road as he admired its beautifully manicured gardens. He later realised how picturesque the town of Newburn was as he made his way about the streets. The Infirmary, an ornate three-storey building complete with verandas surrounding each level and international flags adorning the roof's perimeter, was located at the end of a cul-de-sac. On the front, written in bold gold coloured letters was The Infirmary – We know how to take care of your alements. It certainly gave the impression of a welcoming and caring establishment. An unusual way of spelling ailments, thought Brendan to himself. He drove the Ferrari into an available staff only parking bay, shut the engine down, secured the precious lady and walked away very slowly towards the front entrance. The aroma of freshly brewed coffee coupled with that of newly baked croissants reached his nostrils and lured him through the door.

"It's a bar, they sell liquor. They have waitresses with big breasts and long legs, what am I doing here?" he screamed in his mind.

"Looking for something to eat sir," asked a buxom blonde who just happened to be at the main door.

"Welllll, actually no," replied Brendan as he stared at her cleavage and then when his composure returned he added, "My name is Jack Stern, I am the new owner." This time he shifted his gaze and directed it into her bright blue eyes.

"Welcome Mr Stern, a pleasure to meet you sir. Where would you like to begin, out here or in the Manager's office?"

"The Manager's office" Brendan nervously replied with a lump in his throat.

"Okay, follow me."

The buxom blonde led the way upstairs with a wiggle of her hips.

"Here we are sir, after you."

Brendan nervously entered the lavish suite. The Infirmary's Manager immediately stood up wiped the hair from his brow and in an almost sinful voice said, "Ah, Mr. Stern, we have been expecting you. We thought you might have arrived yesterday. The storm probably delayed you, is that right?"

The manager said as he held out his hand awaiting some form of acceptance and recognition. Brendan looked at him as a priest would when a sinner enters an open confessional. 'The Manager, a Mr. Louis Badcock, certainly had something to hide,' thought Brendan and refused to shake Badcock's hand.

"Yes it did."

"You drove through the storm." Badcock asked a little disappointed with Brendan's cold reaction.

"No, I took shelter in an off road café, quite pleasant it was."

"Gave you the time to think about what you would do once you arrived here. I suppose now that you are the new owner, changes will be made. The staff members are very nervous about their jobs."

"You couldn't meet a more charitable man than me Mr Badcock."

"We were led to believe that you were quite the efficiency expert, the type who values the bottom line of any operation, rather than the welfare of its people."

"You shouldn't listen to rumours."

"It was first hand information."

"Really! Care to tell me from whom it was?"

"I can't."

"I respect that. Well, let's change the subject. Could you bring me the turnover books, say for the last six months? I would like to study them in my own office."

"Office?" asked the buxom blonde

"Yes," replied Brendan as he turned to look at her.

"You don't have one sir."

"I don't!"Brendan replied appearing a little annoyed

"Since your last visit we had to make alterations under the wishes of the previous owner. It's now been incorporated into the red room so your quarters are now located in a quieter part of the complex, on the top floor overlooking the rear car park and gardens. The suite has a secret staircase to the red room so that discreet encounters can be made."

Brendan wondered what she meant and was about to ask when he was interrupted by Louis Badcock.

"If memory serves me correctly, it has been at least twelve months since your last visit so it would be appropriate if we showed you around. Consider yourself a guest today at our expense. Familiarise yourself with the operation, examine the books at your leisure before you decide to implement your ideas."

Brendan nodded

"Good, the girls will look after you very well. By the way, are you married?"

"No."

"Then it is even better. Girlfriend?"

"No."

"Better still, no guilt then."

Brendan frowned, clearly showing his confusion.

"You can enjoy the benefits of the king size bed, it's just new, never been slept in and it will be your pleasure to christen it in any way you please."

With that, he answered the phone that had just started to ring. The buxom blonde took Brendan's hand and said, "This way sir."

Brendan had never been in the company of such a warm inviting girl before. He could feel his entire anatomy reacting to the touch of her hand in his. She guided him with such confidence that he imagined her to be more divine than human and for a brief moment saw her as a being of white light. By now they had reached the ground floor of The Infirmary.

"Excuse me Miss, I've just realised I don't know your name."

"Mr Stern, I am sorry, I should have mentioned it before; it's Christina."

"Well Christina, how long have you been here?"

"Fifteen months sir."

"And, what sort of work do you do?"

"General sir waitressing in the kitchen, cleaning up, that sort of thing. But never anything else, my parents wouldn't approve. It is bad enough that I work here. The money is good and will come in useful when I return to do my studies."

"What are you thinking of studying?"

"Social work, especially psychology where I can help people with their marital problems, we see so many here, that's why we do so well in the restaurant and bar."

"The place sells lots of liquor, yes?"

"You're very funny Mr Stern, very funny indeed"

Funny, since when is an obvious conclusion funny, pondered Brendan.

They stopped walking and stood in the middle of the restaurant/bar area.

"As you can see, the restaurant seats around 150 people; the menu is extensive, children are not allowed as it is not a family restaurant. Our clientele is mainly male, with a few women now and then, especially those with different tastes."

"Your Chef experiments…?"

Christina tried not to laugh. "Males either come alone or in groups, especially as business luncheons and treats. We have live music, discreetly played of course."

'There is that word again,' thought Brendan as he asked himself. "What is all this pre-occupation with discretion?"

"The walls and ceilings have been sound-proofed; it is for the comfort of the clientele and adds certain warmth to the place. When the gentlemen are ready, they signal the waitress, make their selection, pay their account in advance of course and they are escorted via entrances 1, 2 or 3, depending upon their chose of menu."

"You mean to say, I come in, look at the menu, make my choice and pay in advance."

"Yes sir. It is the only way we can guarantee payment otherwise they will want a freebie."

"What about the poor and destitute. Do you ever consider them?"

"No sir, they are not allowed in here."

"Really?"

"Yes, really."

"Does the menu change?"

"Yes sir, every day. It depends who is on."

"Can I have a look?"

"Of course you may."

Brendan sat himself down while Christina fetched the day's menu. On her return she politely asked, "Would you like a cappuccino coffee sir?"

"Just a glass of water thank you"

Brendan could see that the menu was exhaustive to say the least. The opening pages pre-occupied themselves with all sorts of different ales that were available from different parts of the world, including an impressive selection of local and imported beers. This was the same for the wines and liquors. The food section was almost an encyclopedia in itself, with a heavy leaning towards ingredients that made your manly juices flow. Oysters, caviar, asparagus were heavily scattered throughout. Only main meals were offered. The dessert section was divided into two parts, exotic and erotic delights. Under exotic were all sorts of heavenly laden chocolates sweets, complete with tropical fruits. The erotic section was seemingly sealed.

"Have you reached the erotic sweet section?" asked Christina, startling Brendan in the process.

"I haven't."

"Well, please have a look and a gander."

"I was just about to spread the pages apart."

"You should, there is nothing like the picture of a naked woman with her legs apart displaying her personal heaven to get a man going, unless you prefer to meet the woman in person, that is." Brendan glanced down avoiding eye contact with Christina and tried to look a man of the world as he gingerly opened the erotic sweet section. Listed under three separate headings were a host of highly suggestive sexual experiences

Section 1 – Sweet and Gentle

1 Smooth Mousse Licked Off Your Body –The Way You Like It

2 Jelly Cup Alaska – Your Choice of D or E Cup, Decorated with Lashings of Meringue, Lick to Your Heart's Content

3 Pop-U-Go – Can't Hold Back With All of That Chocolate Sauce on It.

Second Section – Temperatures Are Rising

1 Banana Cherry Surprise – She Won't Keep Her Hands Off This One

2 Whip Me Nuts – What One Can Do With Liquorice Straps

3 Horny Angel's Delight – Black Mischievous and Laced with Sambuca

Third Section – Hit The Showers

1 Iscream Fantasy – How Quick Will The Iscream Melt?

2 Position Impossible – You Will Need All Of Your Strength For This One

3 Missionary Mania – Let Your Imagination Go Wild and Design Your Own After Dinner Fantasy

"Well, what do you think?"

"Very imaginative…." Brendan answered almost stuttering.

"Yes, but what effect does it have on you, does it just make you water at the mouth?" Christina cheekily asked.

"Water, yes, of course water, may I have another glass of water please?" Brendan asked as by now his mouth and throat were extremely parched, a result of excessive sexual excitation.

11

SAINT PIOUS

Jack Stern relished his newfound adventure in life. His appalling breakfast was uplifted by the warm attention showered upon him by the parish housekeeper, Miss Yvette Bell. 'Such a lovely attractive girl, pity she has devoted her life to the church, she would have made such an excellent lover and wife. But then, one never knows, supposing her true vocation in life is to keep the priests from leaving the church,' Jack thought, as he surveyed her wonderfully fine features and started to become physically drawn to her.

"Yvette."

"Yes Father."

"Are you French?"

"No, I was born here, but my parents are."

"So you were raised in the French tradition?"

"Yes, I was, quite strictly."

"Ever been back to France?"

"Twice with my parents when I was much younger. It is a wonderful place, full of culture, but somehow I did not fit in. I am sort of lost between two worlds, living here in this great country with its particular way of life and realising that I also don't fit in entirely because

France is the home of my soul but my body wants to be elsewhere. It is very difficult. That is why I have chosen to be here in this parish, it offers a sanctuary until I sort myself out."

"You are very beautiful."

"Thank you Father."

"Not at all, I suppose you have plenty of male suitors." Jack asked testing the waters.

"Not really, I spend most of my time praying and am patiently waiting for the Virgin Mary to answer my prayers."

"What are you asking for?"

"That is personal Father."

"I am sorry I asked." Jack pretended to apologise.

Jack watched as Yvette's countenance changed from that of shy efficient housekeeper to that of a blushing virgin. Their eyes met briefly and in that moment, Jack contacted with something that he had never experienced before, the essence of innocence in all of its glory. A smile spread across the face of the lovely Yvette a smile that made her radiantly beautiful, invitingly so. Jack raised and assumed a somewhat defensive priestly aloofness that would tell him whether or not she was another cleverly disguised Black-tracker. He then briefly returned the smile and without saying a word, took his leave and made for Father Kelly's office. There he found a list of instructions to be followed while the priest was away on retreat. The parish did not need the services of two priests; there was only enough work for one. He sat down at the desk and looked around the room. The walls were decorated with the customary crucifix, a picture of the sacred heart, last supper and the Immaculate Conception. Even the carpet wore symbols of Christianity with rose and cross motifs. In front of the desk were two hard timber chairs for client's use, all in all, the room omitted a vibration that was a mixture of oldness, truth and deceit. Father Kelly had laid out a daily schedule and what was to be expected of the locum. It seemed quite straight forward, nothing out of the ordinary. On Monday, Wednesdays and Fridays weekday mass was celebrated at the parish church at 7:00am, at 7:00pm on Saturday evenings and 9:00am and 11:00am on Sunday mornings. On Tuesdays and Thursdays mass was held at Longevity Plus Nursing Home at its own private Grotto. This was a replica of that found at Lourdes, France. On these two days, the locum was expected to visit the sick at the complex and perform the necessary rites as required. Banking of the monies was to take place on Monday, Wednesday and Fridays, apart from that, there were no other instructions. Today was Tuesday, no need to say mass. However, like a true boy scout, he decided it was best to be prepared, off to the sacristy to familiarise himself.

He found Yvette cleaning the bathroom, she was on her knees, scrubbing the floors, God knows why, it really was clean enough. Jack's heart was filled with sympathy as he stood and watched briefly, he cleared his throat. Yvette looked up smilingly. "Yes Father?"

"May I have the keys to the church?"

"Yes, of course, but wait, I will go with you if you give me five minutes to finish here."

"Can I help?" Jack pretended to care.

"Oh no Father, this is not your work."

"And why not?"

"Because Father Kelly or the others don't do this sort of thing, they are too busy praying to God and performing all sorts of miracles."

"Miracles!" Jack asked cynically as he knew better

"Yes miracles."

Jack looked puzzled.

"Haven't you done the same?" she asked as she continued to vigorously clean.

"No, not recently." Jack truthfully replied.

"I thought you had. They only send priests with those special powers here, unless…" she paused thoughtfully.

"Unless what?"

"You are to be trained in their ways."

"I have simply come to do a locum, nothing more."

"Okay Father, I won't say anymore. Come, I am ready."

She put away the cleaning cloths and bucket. Together they left the presbytery and walked across the road to the parish church. As with all Catholic establishments, the primary and secondary schools were on the same block of land. When they reached the other side, they were greeted with wolf whistles.

"Someone finds you attractive Yvette."

She blushed and replied, "It happens quite a lot."

"You must be very flattered."

"I am, but I am not interested. Those sorts of men treat girls like sexual objects for brief moments of sexual pleasure and then dump them. I have seen too many beautiful girls with broken hearts and unwanted babies."

"It doesn't mean that it will happen to you."

"I am certain of that. The Virgin is looking after me, which is why I am here at Saint Pious."

"I see." Jack replied whilst he began to think that she was a religious freak

They passed through the gates leading to the church. The pathway was flanked by tall poplar trees, the leaves chattered merrily in the cool morning breeze. Rose beds were everywhere in arrays of magnificent colours and fragrance. The church was built in the traditional cross shape fashion. It was made of limestone blocks and every stained glass window depicted a different biblical story. Yvette unlocked the main entrance. As she opened the door, a whoosh of air escaped followed by the aroma of freshly burnt incense.

"Has anyone been here this morning?"

"No not that I know of."

"Why does the air smell like this?"

"It often happens Father, it is rumoured that ever since a priest died at the altar while saying mass, strange noises and happenings have occurred, but never to me. If we have a ghost, he must be very friendly."

'What a lot of nonsense,' thought Jack.

"Ghosts indeed, superstitious hocus pocus. There is always a proper explanation for everything. What was the name of the priest and how long ago did he die?"

"I believe his name was Father Patrick McCran and he died some twelve years ago."

"How long have you been here?"

"Just two years."

"You must have been very young when he passed away."

"Yes, I was. We didn't even live here then. You ask a lot of questions Father."

"Just familiarising myself with my new surroundings and the people"

Jack assumed an air of priestly confidence as he walked through the door. He paused to bless himself at the holy water font, Yvette followed and then he proceeded to slowly walk up the central aisle, taking careful note of all of the church's internal beauty. The stained glass windows created a visual feast of colour and patterns as the morning sun cast its life-giving rays of light through them. The coloured light literally danced with laughter as it brought the entire church to life. Even the dust in the air sparkled like multi-coloured gems. Jack reached the altar and as memory would have it, genuflected and made the sign of the cross. He relived his childhood memories of being an altar boy and could see himself walking beside the priest, helping with distribution of Holy Communion. The scene seemed so real to him, that momentarily he was transported into another world. Regaining his focus, he then ascended the stairs and walked towards the open sacristy. There he allowed Yvette to show him where everything was kept, namely the different items of ceremonial clothing, mass and prayer books, candles, incense, thurible, holy water and oils. Jack took down the holy missal and mass of the day book with its suggested procedures from the shelves above the dressing table and decided to study them then and there in preparation for saying mass later in the day at the Grotto. As he read, past images of him and his Uncle Tom travelling together and performing pastoral care projected themselves onto his mind reinforcing all that he read. When he had finished, he went looking for Yvette. He found her attending to the flowers at Our Lady's Altar. She was lovingly arranging the display, making sure that the Virgin would approve. She was obviously deep in thought, preoccupied with her particular cares and life.

"I am ready to go Yvette I will see you later for lunch."

"Anything special I can make for you?" She sweetly asked.

"Yes, smoked salmon, camembert cheese, avocado and lettuce sounds good."

"You joke Father, this is Saint Pious, the best I can do for you is tomato and cheese sandwiches."

"With a little mustard and pepper please."

"Only if the mouse hasn't stolen it, I will see you at about 12:00 noon?"

"12 o'clock it will be, God bless."

"God bless you, Father."

Jack left the church and went back to the presbytery. It was 10:00am. There in true businesslike fashion he proceeded to become intimate with the monetary situation of the parish and dig up any dirt that he could after all it was a good read.

12

BUSINESS IS BUSINESS

As hard as he could try Jack Stern could not find anything relating to Saint Pious financial records. The bank deposit book that Father Kelly had left behind was new. No old books to peruse, no hidden compartments in the bookshelves, no secret drawers, the barest safe with the simplest lock. Perhaps the church was as poor as the impression that Yvette gave. Jack Stern stood in the middle of the room looking around and pondering when the phone rang.

"Hello, Saint Pious, Father O'Reilly speaking."

"Oh, hello, this is Matron at Longevity, may I speak to Father Kelly?"

"Father Kelly is away on retreat, may I help you?" Jack smoothly replied

"Are you the replacement priest?" Matron abruptly asked.

"Not exactly, I am helping out until Father Kelly returns, how can I be of assistance?" Jack replied in a highly polished priestly voice.

"Well Father, it is already 10:30 in the morning, Father Kelly is usually here by 8:00am attending to the needy patients, didn't anyone tell you," shouted Matron in a somewhat agitated voice.

'Typically aggressive,' thought Jack as he replied, "No, but if it is that urgent, I shall come over immediately. Can you give me directions how to get there please?"

"With pleasure," she replied sarcastically.

As Matron detailed the quickest route, Jack reflected as to why Yvette had not informed him. Slipped her mind, deliberate action or was she not privileged to Father Kelly's movements? He continued to listen to Matron barking away while he looked over Father Kelly's schedule of notes. The only mention made, was look at the sick as required. Jack thanked matron, cradled the phone and ran back to Saint Pious church. He found Yvette in the sacristy putting away some freshly laundered garments.

"Yvette."

"Yes, Father."

"I have just spoken to Matron at Longevity hospital, it seems I am supposed to be there visiting the sick."

"I didn't know that. Father Kelly comes and goes as he wishes. He tells me very little."

"I see. Well, does he have some sort of case that he uses when he visits the sick at their homes?"

"Yes, it is over here," said Yvette pointing to a black case with the initials RIK embossed in silver.

"What do these stand for?" Jack asked as he opened the case.

"Reginald Indigo Kelly, Father."

"Indigo? Blue man of the Nile."

"No Father, he is white. I believe Indigo was included when his own father saw how blue he was at birth."

"Blue blooded then."

"Only in the Catholic sense," replied Yvette quite defensively as she continued to work away.

'Obviously she has a soft spot for him,' thought Jack as he prepared to leave.

"Well this case seems to be well stocked. I will be at Longevity if you need to reach me, otherwise I will see you at 6:00pm for dinner, nothing too lavish, okay. Sorry we can't lunch together," Jack said light heartedly as he turned to depart.

Yvette did not reply and kept working. Complex woman, Jack muttered to himself as he made for the car.

Longevity Hospital and Nursing Home was a pleasant 20-minute drive away. It was situated in thirty hectares of parkland, very serene, so close to nature that one of its features was to have tame deer, goats, ducks and geese and the like wandering about. It even had its own lake fed by a natural stream. The entire complex was completely surrounded by high stonewalls. The entry and exit points were manned by security guards at all times. Security was also present on the grounds, with several guards disguised as patients. Jack approached the gates to the entrance. He was stopped by a big beefy security guard who looked more like a delinquent biker, he imagined that underneath his uniform he was complete with hideous tattoos and body jewellery all designed to frighten. 'All brawn and no brains,' thought Jack, as the oaf signalled for him to lower his driver's window.

"Get out of the car," the oaf bellowed. Jack obliged.

"Identification."

Jack silently produced O'Reilly's driver's license and showed it to the obnoxious oaf.

"Priest huh."

"Yes I am." Jack unemotionally answered

"Don't know you," he said in a loud drawl.

"I have taken over from Father Kelly while he is away."

"Oh ya, I'll check." The guard grabbed his two-way radio in a vice-like grip and shouted

"Jim, you dar? Got new priest here, O'Reilly, claims to have taken Kelly's place, that okay? What, say again, thanks"

The big oaf clicked off. "Okay, you go through O'Reilly."

"God bless you my son," replied Jack mockingly 'I suppose these are the types Yvette refers to,' Jack thought, as he drove along the private road to the designated parking lot.

He parked the car, and as he walked towards the main entrance, he noticed more oafs dressed as patients sitting and wandering about. They stood out quite stupidly to the observant eye.

"Good morning Father," sung a group of young nurses.

"Good morning girls," replied Jack, admiring the seductive way in which they walked in their ever so tight white uniforms.

Once through the revolving doors Jack was immediately seized upon by a female version of the oafish security guard.

"Finally," she shouted. "You're here."

Jack turned slowly around to face the human hippo, 'his girlfriend,' he thought, 'what a match.' Everything about this woman was round, round face, body, legs, arms and fingers. There was nothing angular at all. It would take at least two entire cowhides to clothe this beast in leather. Still, she must keep oaf at the gate happy, God knows how

"Good morning Matron."

"Well O'Flattery, you're here at last, go to it."

"O'Reilly."

"Oh really, no need to be sarcastic, off you go," she said pointing the way with her rude finger.

'Deaf as well,' thought Jack, as he stood there glancing at the piece of paper that was violently thrust into his hand. He looked around, hippo had disappeared. Somewhat lost, he asked the receptionist for a map of the complex and then set off to find his first sinner.

Room 121, first floor, east wing. He knocked on the door.

"Come in Father," said the elderly voice.

"How did you know I was a priest?" he asked as he entered the room.

"Because the Lord told me, He visits me you know and tells me everything," said Rosa Mazzoli, a woman in her late 50s who was sitting upright in bed.

Jack dismissed this as the ramblings of a religious fanatic or of a person in some sort of drug-induced dementia.

"I watch all of the evangelist programs every morning at 6:00

o'clock, they're very inspirational. If God can talk to them, then he can talk to me as well and he does," she said most emphatically.

"There is nothing wrong with that," replied Jack as he studied her drug chart.

Mrs Rosa Mazzoli's drug resume was a cocktail of high potency drugs, especially morphine and some of the newer opioid analgesics mixed with antipsychotics.

"You must be in a lot of pain to be receiving these medications Mrs Mazzoli."

"Oh, yes, spinal cancer you know. I was lucky that my doctor spotted it so soon. I thought it was a slipped disc, but noooo, cancer. So here I am, receiving the best cancer treatment and a cure. Doctor said that this was the best place for such a miracle. Either the doctors cure you or the priests do."

"The priests cure the sick," queried Jack

"Do not play dumb with me Father, you know they do. You are one of the healers, otherwise you wouldn't be here. In any case where is Father Kelly?"

"He is on retreat."

"No he's not he is probably learning more ways of curing people."

"And how does he do it?" Jack asked disbelievingly

"Surely you know Father. Oh, I understand, you want to know his techniques, is that right?"

"But of course."

"Well, after we all assemble as a group in the common room, Father first starts with the anointing of the sick. He uses his own special blend of oils. These have a wonderful heavenly scent and then we all have to say the rosary out loud by ourselves. We have to say fifteen decats and when we are all exhausted and dry in the mouth, we are given a drink of Lourdes' water. Many of us feel the holy spirit fill us."

"What happens then?"

"Some faint, some cry, others stand with arms wide apart looking upwards and praise the Lord, just like the evangelists do. Would you believe that some even talk in strange tongues?

"All after drinking the Lourdes' water?"

"That's right!!!!"

Jack tried to hide his laughter and disbelief.

"Why is your name on the list?"

"Well, I didn't want to see you; I had an appointment with Father Kelly. Not very happy that he did not tell me he was leaving."

"So I can't help you?"

"Not in the least, good bye Father." Mrs Mazzol bluntly said as she waved him away

'What an utter waste of time,' thought Jack. He forced a smile and left closing the door behind him. A nurse stood opposite him in the passageway attending to notes on her drug trolley.

Jack approached her and politely asked, "Excuse me nurse, can you tell me how long patients stay here for?"

"Depends Father"

"Depends on what?"

"On their condition, most of them stay about two weeks and then they leave, usually completely healed or cured."

"Really"

"Yes Father. We have the country's best reputation for curing the sick."

"And why is that?"

"Because the Director, Doctor Joseph Reed has developed a brilliant resume of drugs to treat serious diseases."

Jack raised an eyebrow.

"It's true"

"Okay, what about Mrs Mazzoli?"

"Oh, I don't think she is really sick at all, she comes and goes on a regular basis. Usually stays a week and then disappears for three and then returns. Every time she comes in she claims to have a different condition. I think she is a hypochondriac or neurotic, one of the two. At least she pays the bills."

"Thank you sister"

"A pleasure Father will you be here for long?"

"Oh about two weeks"

"I look forward to seeing you next time."

"Thank you," replied Jack as he looked at his list of names, which was quite extensive; more than he had previously realised. There would be no time left for a common room assembly before mass. The best he could do would be to visit each person briefly introduce himself and say a little prayer. It was in this manner that Jack worked as he made mental notes of the patients he had seen and of the condition that they suffered from. He reflected on these as he sat at a quiet table in the hospital's café after he enjoyed a well made cappuccino and a salmon Caesar open sandwich. Two very attractive nurses decided to join him.

"Hello Father, do you mind if we sit next to you?"

"Not at all, please make yourselves comfortable." Jack replied as he mentally undressed them.

"New here?"

"First day"

"We thought so, Father Kelly on holidays then?"

"Yes he is."

"First day on?"

"Yes."

"We saw you looking quite lost as you walked around." Jack initially took this as a slight insult. He thought he was in control. But then if that was his outward appearance, then he was in control and his priestly portrayal was working just fine.

"Was it that obvious?" asked Jack.

"Just like a little boy."

"I suppose you've come to rescue me." Jack ambiguously responded

"That's what we're here for."

"Well, rescue away," Jack jokingly replied with a sexual inflection in his voice.

"You're very cheeky for a priest."

"Do you really think so? I am actually not a priest at all."

"Oh Father, do pull the other leg."

"Really! I'm not. You know, what is really funny, is when you tell the truth and no one believes you."

"That's what confession is for Father?" reminded the nurse.

"To tell lies."

"Exactly."

Jack nodded his head in agreement.

"So Father, what are your first impressions about Longevity?" asked the cute nurse.

"Everyone seems to be so seriously sick and everyone expects miracles."

"Quite right, except we don't cure everyone, only about 80 – 85%. Some die I suppose, they do that to make us look good."

"What do you mean look good?"

"Well, if we had 100% success rate, no one would believe it would they? Even 85% is hard to accept."

"And it's all due to the Director I gather?" asked Jack.

"Yes, he is quite a brilliant man."

"I have studied the charts of some of the patients I have visited, they appear to be on different cocktails of drugs, but everyone appears to receive a narcotic and an antipsychotic. Does that mean they're all in pain and crazy?" he asked.

"Oh, the Director Doctor Reid believes that each one of these is essential to the treatment. Take away the pain and anxiety and the body will heal faster. Most people believe that the cool dude always wins a sporting match. In this case, the goal is simply winning back your life, so why not stay cool in a different way."

"Seems plausible"

"Gets great results"

"And if it fails?"

"Well, then it is up to the likes of Father Kelly and you."

"I don't know if I am qualified. Everyone keeps telling me that it is a case of mind over matter."

"Perhaps, but it still needs a mediator. Not many people can go it alone."

"You're very intelligent and perceptive." Jack said complimenting the nurse in more ways than one

"Of course I am. After all, I am a woman," she said with a gleam in her eye.

Jack smiled whilst admiring her cheekiness.

"Well, I better be off, I have to conduct mass at the Grotto soon."

"Bye Father."

"Until next time."

"Buy us a cup of coffee then," they both said in unison.

Jack nodded, "Surely."

13

LIFE AT THE GROTTO

Jack was mentally unprepared when he rounded the corner of the garden hedge and saw the huge grotto that lay before him. It was an exact replica of that at Lourdes, with one exception, instead of crutches decorating the walls there were miniature empty coffins and wheelchairs, macabre and amusing to say the least. In front of the altar were rows of collapsible chairs, enough to seat 600 or 700 people. The entire area was enclosed by masses of trees which provided a canopy of shade and peace. All varieties of birds were abundant in the branches. They were happily singing, chattering, jumping to and fro, flying hither and thither and bringing good news to their many listeners. The Lord certainly does work in strange ways, thought Jack, as he found the rear entrance to the sacristy. He tried the door handle, it was unlocked. He gently opened the door and peered inside. All was quiet, except for the flicker of the electric tabernacle light. If it goes out, does it mean that God is out? He found a light switch to the right of the doorframe and turned it on. In front of him on the opposite wall stood a wardrobe full of vestments two of its doors were complete with full-length mirrors. A collapsible table was attached on the left-hand side. The day's colours were already laid out, as were the books, ciborium and two crucibles one filled with water and the other with sacramental wine. Jack took seven deep breaths of air; slowly intoned a variant of "OMMM" to himself, the energy of this mystical manoeuvre filled him with enhanced confidence and courage. He took off his jacket and donned the alb and then wrapped the cincture around his waist. As he did so, he noticed a television monitor above him. The control lay on the collapsible table. Jack picked it up and pressed the 'on' button. The congregation in front of the Grotto appeared on the screen, the view taken from above the altar. Already about 150 people were seated. 'Fine, what about some real television,' thought Jack. He repeatedly switched channels however; every channel was connected to another view of Longevity's complex. Twenty channels of nonsense he surmised, but then again, perhaps not. He carefully looked at each scene to see what significance it had. At this stage nothing, unless the sacristy was used by security after hours as a surveillance station. That made sense. Jack looked at his reflection in the wardrobe mirrors. A smile blessed his handsome features. Definitely saintly and very good looking he mumbled to himself. No altar boys or helpers must do mass by myself he concluded. Jack placed all of the liturgical equipment on a long plate and very solemnly walked out onto the altar.

The entire congregation stood up. Jack placed the plate on the credence table at the side of the altar, took the necessary books and walked behind the altar facing the worshippers. He noticed the red button with a microphone symbol on it and pressed it.

"Good afternoon ladies and gentlemen," he jovially said.

"Good afternoon Father," they replied all together.

"As you may see, I am not the parish priest he is presently away on retreat. My name is Father Brendan O'Reilly. I shall be attending to your needs in the interim period. Let us begin this holy mass with the opening prayer written for the blessing of the sick."

The crowd stood in silence and Jack recited the words with the utmost divine authority. Having finished these, he went on to say.

"Today, I will do away with the gospel reading by simply saying the word came to dwell among us. This is the Word of the Lord, please be seated."

At this point, silence reigned supreme. It was as if Jack had command over his surroundings. The trees, birds and wind were still, daring not to move or speak.

"I notice on the Grotto there are many empty miniature coffins and wheelchairs. I don't suppose these belong to the little people?"

A ripple of laughter spread through the congregation.

"Correct me if I am wrong, but these were put there by those who had been cured, and I suppose many here today are hoping for such a personal outcome and are looking to the Virgin or me to obtain this. The truth of the matter is that the cure lies inside of you, it has always been there, but because this world as you know it is controlled by humans, it is unfortunately based upon deceit and it is your goal in life to both realise that and discover the truth that has always existed inside of you."

Jack could sense that some of the weaker members seated were uneasy with this radical concept, whilst others were glad that they had finally come across someone who confirmed their reasoning's.

"Judging by the mixed reaction I am receiving from you, I intend to teach you the glory of your own power. After all, that is what Christ came to teach, the power within. These series of homilies will be held here and also at Sunday mass. Tell everyone you know to attend, for now is time that the power is returned to you. God bless you all."

To call the silence stunned was an understatement. It was more like unconscious, if that is at all possible. When the impact of his statements had subsided, he continued with the mass, conducting it with such an air of confidence and belonging that some members taken by his countenance later swore to seeing lights about his persona. Everyone that afternoon whether they accepted his philosophy or not, went to Holy Communion. Everyone afterwards agreed that it was not the novelty of a new priest that caused this to happen, but rather the magnetism that he exuded. Everyone agreed that this was no ordinary man. When mass had finished, although it sounds quite corny, the congregation broke out into spontaneous song, not of the liturgical nature, but a popular version of the song 'Drink, Drink, Drink' from the Student Prince. It symbolised perfectly the cup of knowledge that Jack had intended to share with his fellow man. All however, were not amused.

In the security surveillance room a small dark figure was heard to say, "He could spoil all of this for us, we better investigate this evangelist and deal with him appropriately. I want him watched 24 hours a day. Report everything to me and do it NOW."

14

SANCTUARY IN DISGUISE

Brendan O'Reilly survived the sexually exhausting tour of The Infirmary and could finally rest in his own private quarters located on the top floor, which overlooked the erotic gardens. Tall phallic cacti grew amongst blooming rose bushes. Hedges were carefully manicured into all sorts of suggestive body positions, whilst fountains depicting astrological preferred sexual positions poured forth their liquid assets. Brendan surveyed his new abode; it was enormous, even more sumptuous than the hotel suite he had previously occupied as Mr. Jack Stern. The décor was classically Roman, complete with 3D murals on some of the walls. The window dressings and carpet were thick, ideally so, to ensure that the state of the art audio visual equipment delivered its best. The furniture was extremely comfortable, covered in velvets and leather. A cocktail bar complete with the finest spirits, liquors and French champagne sat discreetly in one corner. The colour scheme was in soft tones of blue and red, with a dash of gold here and there.

Brendan laid on the king size bed. It was covered in the finest cotton percale bearing a heraldic motive. Large eiderdown pillows provided additional comfort. He could not quite come to grips with his role in this establishment. What was he meant to do, play the part of an overseer, examine the books periodically or make important executive decisions? Brendan felt totally bewildered, abandoned, what a fool he had been. How could he have been so stupid as to be seduced by Jack Stern? Hell, he didn't even know the man, a stranger bearing a gift of escape; nothing more. Panic started to take hold of Brendan. He leapt out of bed and searched franticly for his rosary beads, a symbol of hope an instrument of belief. Damn it, Mr. Jack Stern has them, Brendan cursed to himself. He sat on the edge of the bed and only then did he realise that he was the rosary, for there were ten digits on his hands combined, a decat. I am a living rosary, I am my own sanctuary, I am a trained priest and yet so blind. Jack was right, heaven only takes complete people. He fell to his knees, closed his eyes and prayed the Hail Mary on each finger of his hands until he felt as though the wings of an angel embraced him and the room was full of the fragrance of freshly crushed rose petals, a certain sign in his mind that the Virgin was perhaps present.

"Mr. Stern, Mr. Stern, we want to talk to you."

Brendan opened his eyes. A group of young scantily clad women stood before him.

'God, now what?' he thought as he breathed in their rose perfumed scent.

"So you are the new owner; Jack Stern, I believe Mr. Badcock called you," shouted a well endowed and determined brunette appearing to be the leader of the group. "Well Mr. Stern, we are not happy, not happy at all and we demand changes to our working conditions, you hear?"

Brendan stood up and faced his adversary

"I'm sorry I didn't catch your name."

"I'm F F"

"And that stands for?"

"Fabulous Felicity."

"Your stage name?"

"No, my working name"

"Your real name?"

"The same," she angrily retorted "Stop the interrogation it's us that want answers. You're the new owner, we are sick and tired of being screwed for peanuts and want a decent wage otherwise you can forget about your erotic delights, Capisce!"

"Screwed for peanuts!" These ladies are prostitutes, bloody hell, Mother of Mary, help me. 'What am I doing here?' thought Brendan.

"Looks like I will have to examine the position," he awkwardly replied.

"Doggy style, woman on top, knee trembler, which pays most?"

"Would you like a drink?" Brendan blankly asked after a long pause.

"Pardon?"

"Would you like to sit down while I pour you a drink and work out the situation?"

"You're nuts, just trying to soften us up, get us drunk, just like the previous owner. All you want is to sample each one of us, I know what you are up to, you devious bastard."

"Actually no"

"But eventually you will. All you men, you are all the same. Expect us women to work, bring in heaps of money then screw us. Do this, do that and we are supposed to like it because you give us a job, shelter and support our habit. Have you any idea what you are doing to us?"

Brendan remained silent while Felicity continued to rant with the support of her sisters.

"It's no wonder that we hate you. It's no wonder that we prefer our own kind and it doesn't matter whether we are working girls or girls that work, it is all the same. Men; you are all dickless wonders!"

"But surely..."

"No buts, you have no idea of the mental pain we go through, having to deal with all these dicks, revolting they are. We are nervous wrecks, we spend hours in the shower trying to wash off the filth, but it doesn't go away, it stays. The smell; the sliminess; the images the deceit"

Felicity's pent up anger prevented her from breaking down into a sobbing mess. Her sisters stood by her side expressing sorrow in all of its forms. She took a deep breath and bravely continued.

"Okay, you look a little better than the last slimy bastard we had, god was he terrible. He had a fat podgy belly, shiny skin-head, fat round face and red swollen protruding eyes. He walked slowly, dragging himself around, with his jackal smile, dinosaur teeth and sewer breath. We had to service him on demand."

Now Felicity was close to crying. The scene was so reminiscent of past confessions that it allowed Brendan to take charge in a caring fashion.

"I really do think that we need a drink, come on Felicity make yourself comfortable sit down ladies."

He beckoned with hands showing the way. The girls looked at each other and then wearily sat down, all eight of them.

Brendan then asked each one in turn what they preferred in the way of alcohol. Each cautiously replied with her own personal choice. He dutifully poured these out and chose a fine Oloroso sherry for himself. It was as close to altar wine as he could find and with the utmost reverence he handed the drinks out. The girls remained silent, focusing on Felicity who sat motionless reflecting on her torrid past. Anger was still visibly present on her face, her generous lips remained tight. Brendan hoped that the relaxing effect of the alcohol would allow him to explain the situation. However before he was able to begin, Felicity interrupted.

"I'm sorry; I got a bit carried away."

Brendan approached her and put his finger to her lips, and softly said, "Shoosh child it's okay I quite understand."

Felicity resisted. "You can't possibly you just bought this place to make money, that's what it is all about. How can you expect us to believe anything else, it's just lip service to get us on side, so you can work us even harder." Felicity retorted and quickly drained her glass.

Brendan could feel what the girls had gone through and felt powerless to help them. He pensively swirled his drink and in a moment of inspiration asked, "If it is not too traumatic can each one of you, if you are willing, tell me why you are doing this line of work."

"Circumstances, no opportunities, easy money, no self esteem, lots of reasons," answered Felicity.

"And more," a voice said quietly.

Brendan looked at the shy redhead.

"Tell me more," he asked, as he gestured seeking her name.

"Naomi."

"Well Naomi, how did you end up here?"

"My friend introduced me to it, I was very insecure, couldn't get a boyfriend. I believe it was because I was too good looking. Boys were afraid of me, so my friends suggested, they meaning the boys paid for it."

"Do you like it?"

"It's okay, I don't like working when I am not in the mood for it, or during my period, it is pretty messy, having to put up sponges all the time."

"It can't be very healthy."

"But it makes me feel good that men want me."

"Do you have any regrets?" he asked.

"Not really." She answered truthfully

"Why not?"

"Because these days sex is so rampant in open cultures, girls do it for fun, have heaps of encounters, so there is no difference between them and us. In any case, I might well be helping to save a marriage."

"Explain."

"Most of our clients are married men, and others are just boys who have had no experience with girls, so somehow we help them out."

Unlike other women, this group did not threaten Brendan's sexuality. Inwardly, he breathed a sigh of relief. For once he felt comfortable with sexually attractive women. Brendan listened very attentively. It soon became apparent that he was genuinely interested in the welfare of 'his workers'. For the next hour or so, the girls opened up to him until the intimacy of the gathering was disrupted by the arrival of Mr Badcock's hammering at the door.

"Mr. Stern, may I come in?" he bellowed as he marched into the penthouse.

"Please do," replied Brendan.

"We have a problem, it's the girls," he stopped and stared menacingly.

"Are here with me," Brendan said.

"So I can see, we have paying customers downstairs becoming quite restless. They need seeing to if you know what I mean," he said in a commanding and irritating tone of voice.

Brendan looked Badcock in the eye, unaware of the effect that Badcock's words had had on the girls. They reacted with a conditioned response and quickly fled to their 'offices' to do business.

Badcock arrogantly smiled, completely satisfied, he smugly turned around and left to keep a further eye on the girls activities. Brendan watched him leave and turned to face an empty room. He wondered how Badcock had managed to have such power over the girls and then he thought about the scriptural life of Christ. Jesus went after the prostitutes, was he executed because he had interfered with an organised Roman crime syndicates activities, he wondered? Was Jack Stern a Mafia boss? Brendan suddenly feared for his life.

15

RE-EDUCATION

In the following days Brendan looked rather worried as he walked about The Infirmary. Badcock on the other hand, assumed a somewhat arrogant, if not, domineering persona. His body language loudly stated, 'you're not the boss here, I am!' It was a complete about face to the original man that Brendan had first met. It made him wonder if Badcock already knew that he was not the real Jack Stern. It also made Brendan increasingly suspicious of Mr Stern's motives. How much involvement had he with the Mafia? Was he using the disguise of a priest as a convenient escape? If Badcock knew that Brendan was not the real Stern, who had informed him? Brendan was torn between his own survival and that of the prostitutes. He wished he could change everything and be back in the sanctity of his beloved church.

Sunday morning would provide him with that opportunity, even though it was to be as a congregational member. Half an hour before the start of Mass, Brendan was seated in one of the pews halfway down the church at 8:30am. He felt at home, safe, in a state of temporary ecstasy as he passionately interacted with the statues and the Holy Sacrament in the tabernacle of the altar. To him, every one of these was alive. You could see and feel this only if you were a true believer. Everything about this church felt just about perfect. Brendan shifted his gaze and watched as Yvette applied the finishing touches to the altar decorations. The choir had assembled and began to sing a selection of hymns written by Handel. The congregation stood up as the altar boys carrying the processional crucifix and altar candles made their way into the sanctuary. Jack Stern, alias Father Brendan O'Reilly, followed closely behind. Brendan breathed an inner sigh of relief as he saw another priest behind him. The mass went very smoothly. Brendan concluded that Jack had either studied to become a priest or had been an acolyte at least.

Everything in Brendan's mind was now at ease, until it came time for the homily. Brendan expected the proper priest to deliver the sermon. Instead, Jack approached the pulpit without any indication of prior priestly approval.

"Good morning fellow Christians," greeted Jack.

'That is a good start,' thought Brendan.

"As some of you already know I am a stand in whilst your parish priest is away on retreat. My name is Father Brendan O'Reilly and I am here to educate you in the proper ways of Christ."

'Oh really,' thought Brendan.

"I have already indicated this at the first mass that I said earlier this week, at the magnificent Grotto which I believe is an exact replica of the one at Lourdes. The Grotto as all of you know is located in the grounds of Longevity Plus Hospital. Today is Lesson One; I suggest that from next week onwards, you bring pencil and paper if you wish to make notes. Otherwise, the information I will impart should be very easily remembered. I understand that this parish and the Grotto enjoy a widespread reputation for miracles, these being cures for terminal disease and other life threatening illnesses. It is suggested that these have come about because of the administered medical treatments, prayers offered up, or Father's anointing and blessings of the sick, and as a consequence."

"All do very well," Brendan said sarcastically in a low voice. Jack paused and then added, "Supposing there is another explanation." Again, Jack paused for the congregations' reactions and then continued.

"Suppose not one of these things actually happened. Suppose the real reason was that the people willed themselves to become better. Well, you might argue that the medicines and the sacraments, the priest, must have done something, and of course you would be right to a degree, with those who are not sufficiently informed or enlightened. However, I have met people in my life who were given only weeks to live and are still alive today. Why..... because they used the power within. That's right, the power within. So easily accessed and yet you are deprived of it because you are all led to believe that you are sinners and it is only God that can help you. Well he did, and he did it in the form of giving each one of us the talents, the gifts, the mechanisms of thought and belief. Jesus Christ demonstrated and taught those abilities, but then so have many others that followed him.

What made him special was the timing and the place. Within the Catholic Church's history there have been dozens of saints who also demonstrated the same and went one step further, they left a part of themselves behind, their bodies did not corrupt. Instead, they are still here today doing quite extra-ordinary things such as, their heart beats, their blood liquefies, or their body emits a heavenly scent now and then. All of these discovered the principle, which was given to you at birth. And that is?"

Jack searched the congregation for an answer, but only blank expressions sat before him. Again he asked, "Well, do any of you know?" Again no reaction, finally, he asked once again. "Would any one like to have a guess?"

Silence reigned supreme.

"The answer is imagination. Think about it. Remember it was reported that Christ said the Kingdom of God belongs to children who naturally and freely use their imagination. When they believe what they have imagined, it comes true. It is that simple, nothing more, nothing less. The world in fact, the entire universe is one enormous system with a limitless amount of intelligent energy just waiting for your thought commands. Tell it what you want, feed it belief, faith, exercise patience, divorce yourselves of time and before you know it, the reality of it all stands before you and becomes a part of you. This then means that life has the ability to express itself in infinite ways; the universe has been so designed. This phenomenon applies to everything, whatever its nature might be, there are no limits."

Again, the congregation remained silent, afraid to challenge. After all, it had been like that since the origins of the mass, remain silent, never question the artificial authority of the priest and his church. Today, something different, an invitation to ask, but the fear is still present, until an old man bravely stands up and asks, "Are you sure it is so simple, where is your proof?"

"I have none," replied Jack.

"So how can you expect us to believe?"

"I can't, but all that I ask of you is to experiment, start small and then proceed to larger projects."

"You expect us to believe that we can cure ourselves."

"You can, you determine how healthy you want to be you don't have to become sick."

"Surely you jest," said an enraged medical student.

"No I don't. Remember the cliche – What a tangled web we weave when we first start to deceive."

"Sooooo."

"The entire civilized world as we know it is based on two fundamental aberrant principals, fear and deceit. There was a book written in the 1920s or 30s, it doesn't really matter when; it was called 'The Science of Getting Rich'. In this, the author writes about the certain way which dictates the road to seek richness. I quote: 'If you want to become rich, you must not make a study of poverty'. Things are not brought into being by thinking about the opposites. Health is never attained by studying disease and thinking about disease. Righteousness is not promoted by studying and thinking about sin and no one ever gets rich by studying poverty and thinking about poverty. Medicine as a science of disease has increased disease. Religion as a science of sins has promoted sin and economics as a study of poverty will fill the world with wretchedness and want."

These statements shook the real Brendan O'Reilly to the core of his body as it did the medical student. The old man who remained standing throughout Jack's answer continued his questioning.

"You expect us to believe that doctors deliberately made some of these people here today sick, that the Catholic Church makes us into sinners and that we could all be rich."

"Exactly, and in doing so, I am asking you to disbelieve the world and listen to your hearts which will never lie to you. If your heart tells you that you are healthy, believe it. Not what others may teach; which is that you are surrounded by disease. It is belief in health that keeps you healthy, not the contrary. It is not opposites that attract, but likes that attract each other. Remember what Christ taught, 'more is given to the rich man and even more is taken away from the poor man'. So remain rich in positive thoughts and more is attracted to you. Remain negative and watch and experience all of the bad things that can happen. Each one of your existences is nothing more than the outcome of the summation of all of your positive and negative thoughts on a daily, yearly and lifelong basis."

Another man stood up, "Father, I agree with what you are saying, my experiences in life confirm it."

"Then why are you standing here?" asked the old man.

"You mean why do I go to church?"

"Yes."

"Because I have been waiting for someone within the Catholic Church to confirm my thoughts….."

Murmurings spread throughout the entire congregation. It gained momentum and became louder and louder until it erupted into numerous verbal battles.

Jack shouted into the pulpit's microphone, "Quiet please, quiet, you are after all in God's house."

"What sort of house do you call this," shouted the medical student loudly. "I am devoting my life to treating the sick and you are telling us that there is no such thing as disease. Next you will be telling us that doctors make people sick and that the medical cures seen here in this town are hoaxes."

Jack looked directly at the medical student and with authority said,

"Firstly, this house of God is pre-occupied with the truth and secondly, wouldn't it be strange that what you have just said is true. Namely that all of the cures that have happened here are indeed hoaxes."

A solitary small dark figure with displeasure written all over it stood up, looked threateningly at Jack and left abruptly.

16

REFLECTIONS

Brendan O'Reilly sat ever so quietly in the church after mass had concluded. He had to admit that Jack Stern had done a good thing. He dared to think and speak differently, but at what cost. How long before someone would ring the Archbishop and complain. Days, weeks, months, what effect would it have on his personal reputation and how would he explain it all? His deep train of thought was abruptly halted by the swift rising of the congregation. Everyone it seemed wanted to be outside. Brendan wondered why, as he sheepishly stood up and followed. Outside, the assembled crowed had surrounded Jack Stern, all wanted to touch him, to experience his power, his profound insight. All wanted, including the disbelievers, to share his wealth of true knowledge. It's like the Christ time again Brendan thought Jack, it could be observed, was not overcome by the attention lavished upon him. Instead, he remained calm and had complete control, smiling all the time, allowing himself to be touched, exchanging handshakes and constantly blessing the children. No one took any notice of the priest by Jack's side. The joyous scene was not shared by everyone. Across the way on the road bordering the church grounds, a man was watching through binoculars and reported everything he saw into a mobile phone. Brendan glanced at the priest who gestured with a nod of his head that they should return inside the church and meditate. Brendan agreed and waited for the priest to join him. Together they walked, not saying a word, side by side. And so it continued until they sat in complete silence before the Immaculate Conceptions Altar, forever it seemed, until the light of the candles signalled that night had come and it was time to leave. Ladies of the night; prostitutes, why did Christ love them so? Was it because some of them had the Christ principle? Is Jack right, in that like attracts like? With these thoughts in mind, Brendan walked back to The Infirmary reflecting along the way, imagining how it could have been in Christ's time and land.

He hadn't eaten or drunk anything since early morning, yet he was neither hungry nor thirsty, he felt satisfied. He remembered the story, about the girl in Alexandria Greece who lived for fifteen years on nothing but the mystical host given to her on a daily basis by the Archangel Michael. Curious things these hosts, so much debate about them, we Catholics believe that once consecrated, they remained the body of Christ indefinitely. The Anglicans say once mass is over they revert back to the host form, nothing holy about them at all. An acolyte used to take them home and give them to his underage children, contrary to canon law. Too many laws, Christ was right, there is only one law and that is the law of love, love for all living things.

A man once said, "We should look at words, turn them inside out, back to front and see what hidden messages they contain." God became dog, flog was golf, I suppose that is what they do; flog themselves with a stick, but love reverses to be evol. The first four letters of evolve, the first four steps to becoming perfect. So does this mean that people who never truly love never evolve? What can I do with the ladies at The Infirmary to help them evolve, to discover love? Supposing they already know how to love the only problem is they have misdirected it. How can I change their lives and still preserve

The Infirmary, or make it better? What is it that they are good at besides the obvious? Mary Mother of God, it is written that you have given so much help to the human race with all of your apparitions, your blessings, and folk lore has it that you gave women a herb to cure them of all of their health problems, lady's mantle I think it is called. Why is it that you don't protect your kind from becoming prostitutes, what is it that I don't understand? Is it merely a matter of exercising one's free will and damning the consequences?

"That's part of the answer, but certainly not the damning my son."

Brendan stopped and looked around. The priest that he meditated with stood by his side.

"Where did you come from?"

"I have been by your side all the time."

"No you haven't."

"Yes I have. You only see me when you want to. It is like that with most things you know."

"Meaning?"

"All answers, all things necessary are out in the open, right before people's eyes, but most people are blind."

Brendan looked at the priest more closely and then realized his lips were not moving.

"Mother of Mercy, how can I hear you?" he exclaimed.

"Because I am in your head, you have always been looking for that perfect priest, well, here I am. What's the matter, not exactly what you expected? Well, look closer, deeper and you will begin to see yourself."

Brendan thought he was going mad, hallucinating, lack of food, that's it.

"No its not, this is really happening, yes it is, it's not divine intervention, but it is in a complete sort of way."

"What are you saying?"

"I am here to help you."

"Why me?"

"Because I also need your help."

"What sort?"

"I am grounded here on earth; I broke a few karmic rules and am obliged to repay the debt."

"By using me?"

"Not exactly, but sort of."

"How?" Brendan asked in a worried fashion.

"By hearing my confession"

"Right here and now I suppose."

"It is neither the time nor the place; I will tell you when you are sufficiently attuned."

"And how long will that take?"

"That depends on you." With that the priest's image faded from view.

A clap of thunder shook the air, and it began to pour with rain. Brendan listened to its whisperings as it fell about him, but not on him.

17

ATTUNEMENT

Brendan walked bone dry into The Infirmary quite oblivious of that fact. He made his way to an empty table, sat down and glanced at the menu. It was hard for him to focus considering his situation and the past events of the day.

Christina approached his table, cleared her throat and gently asked, "Mr. Stern, will you be eating in the restaurant tonight?"

"Mmmmmm," he replied in a dazed fashion. "Yes I will."

"Are you sure sir, wouldn't you be more comfortable in your apartment?" She thoughtfully asked

"No, the answers are out in the open, so I will stay here."

"Are you alright?" Christina asked rather concerned about Brendan's state of mind

Um, yes, quite." he replied in a daze

Christina sat down opposite Brendan and surveyed his transfixed features. She had admired his handsomeness before, but this time, she saw him in a different light. He did not have that hard edge she previously imagined, but rather, he possessed an innocence she remembered in her brother when he was a young playful boy. In that moment, she thought that perhaps Brendan did not belong here.

"Something troubling you sir?"

"You could say that," replied Brendan as he stirred out of his trance.

"Terrible weather outside"

"I hadn't noticed." Brendan freely admitted.

"Decided what you would like for dinner?"

"No, I am rather lost I am afraid. Could you order for me?"

"Okay, I shall," replied Christina in a thoughtful fashion.

"Thank you very much."

Christina took the menu stood up and walked away, looking back every now and then, wondering what was troubling her new boss.

Brendan sat pensively, his senses straining to find those 'out in the open solutions'. The restaurant was full of men, all driven by their genital fires, irrespective what stage of dinner they were at, they blazingly pre-occupied themselves with the agonizing decision of which erotic sweet they wanted to indulge in and hopefully it would not be limited to one serve per customer. Out of the corner of his eye, Brendan caught Christina emerging from the kitchen carrying he sensed, his evening meal. He relaxed his concentration, sighed deeply and stretched out his legs.

"There you are sir, a perfect marriage of food," said Christina as she placed his meal before him.

"What did you say? Perfect marriage, that's it. Thank you Christina, thank you very, very much." With that he jumped from his chair, embraced her warmly and kissed her on both cheeks. Realizing what he had done, he withdrew apologetically.

"I am sorry, I did not mean to."

"It's okay."

"Please join me for dinner," he said as he sat down.

"I can't, I am still on duty, Mr Badcock wouldn't approve."

"I am supposed to be the boss."

"Yes I know that sir, but in our contract it is not you who fires or hires, it's Badcock."

"Does that extend to all staff?"

"Yes, I believe it does."

"So what is my role?" asked Brendan

"To collect the money and count the huge profits, that's what the previous owner did."

"You seem to know a lot about the goings on."

"I keep my ears and eyes open sir. Please don't mention this to Badcock, he can be very nasty."

"How do you mean?" Brendan asked becoming increasingly curious.

"Some of the girls have received terrible beatings at the hands of strangers."

"For doing?"

"Anything that Badcock saw or heard or took an instant dislike to."

"If as you say, huge profits are made here, why did the previous……" Brendan paused to correct himself, "Owner, I wonder, sell to me?"

"I heard he lost a fortune in a bad share deal or something like that."

"Funny, nothing was mentioned to me," said Brendan, pretending to be vacant about the matter.

"Why should he? If he had, people would have forced down the selling price of this place wouldn't they? You know very well when someone is in trouble, the vultures swoop in."

"Quite so," answered Brendan. "Well it seems as though I have paid too much then."

"I am sure you will get it back very soon, just look how packed this place is with hungry men. It is like this every day of the week, it never lets up. Those poor girls upstairs, honestly, they must be rubbed raw by now; I don't know what keeps them going."

"Neither do I," replied Brendan looking genuinely concerned.

"Do you care for them Mr Stern?" Christina asked as she looked at him directly.

"Yes I do."Brendan truthfully answered.

"You are not lying are you?"

"No I'm not." Brendan sincerely replied.

"I guessed you weren't, you're different from the others perhaps you are the saviour the girls were looking for. Better watch out for Badcock though, in case he bushwhacks you."

"Why?"

"Well, I have heard he gets a percentage of the profits. I believe it is his responsibility to promote this place to the max."

"Really, well that explains it."

"Mr. Stern, surely you knew all of this?"

"Umm, not really, the sale went through a broker and was quite rushed; I hadn't had time to examine all of the finer details."

"You just looked at the bottom line."

"Precisely" Brendan said attempting to lie.

"Well then you are a very poor businessman, aren't you, or should I say, just greedy?"

"Poor, yes, very poor. Actually, I don't have a cent to my name, it is all tied up elsewhere, I just manage to receive food, lodging and travelling expenses, greedy not at all."

"You poor man," Christina replied sarcastically. "Next thing you will be telling me you're celibate and can't indulge."

"Well, as a matter of fact…"

"I have to go" Christina interrupted "Badcock's secretary is here, she is just as bad as he is if not worse."

Brendan quickly caught on and thanked Christina for bringing his meal and waved her away.

Badcock's secretary walked about the restaurant checking on the staff's efficiency ensuring that the customers were well attended to. Brendan quietly observed her as he slowly ate his food. He finished his meal with coffee and after dinner mints. When it was safe to do so that is when Badcock's secretary had left Brendan in an authoritative fashion went from table to table and suitably questioned his patrons until the 'out in the open solution' was clearly defined in his mind.

Brendan then took the elevator to his apartment and prepared for bed. As he did so, he could not prevent himself from sensing that something was not quite right. He felt that an uninvited stranger had been there on some sort of devious mission. Again, he feared for his life and took this and other fears to bed. After the 5th decat of the rosary, he managed to fall asleep.

Brendan dreamed a muddle of visions in total disharmony with each other from which emerged a canvass of ideas that clearly painted his next day's actions. The artist with a pallet of letters held in his left hand was initially two headed, one was belonging to himself, the other to the priest with whom he meditated at Saint Pious. As the dream proceeded, the artist's heads fused symbolically together, with the pallet of numbers changing to that of brilliant primary colours, the process of attunement had begun.

18

CONFIRMATION

"**G**ood morning Brendan, I see you slept well and that the process has begun." A familiar voice whispered into his ear

Brendan sleepily opened his eyes to find the priest standing at the edge of his bed.

"You were there?" he asked in a laboured tone of voice.

"'Course I was."

"Is nothing sacred?" he angrily said.

"It's the opposite of what you think. I saw you on the astral plain where dreams are made of."

"Astral plain? What a lot of metaphysical nonsense."

"So you have heard of it? Well, come now Brendan, leave your doubts and ignorance behind, you are on the road to attunement, don't stop the process now, I understand it comes as a shock to you, but deep down you knew it was like this all along. You know very well that the soul goes astral travelling during sleep. People often ex-perience that sensation of falling and suddenly waking up abruptly feeling quite shaken. This is when the soul re-enters the body, sometimes with a bang."

"So what are you saying?"

"On the astral plain of dreams your subconscious, the problem solver goes there to find solutions, I was present, merely as an observer to see how it went about it."

"And?" queried Brendan.

"I was suitably impressed."

"Tell me more."

"The process is quite complex, it acquires the body to fully accept what the subconscious has found and it often does not happen."

"Why not?"

"Because one needs to understand the dream process one dreams under various physiological conditions, it depends on the local and internal environment. Dreams can be caused by the room being too hot or too cold, or if the person has a belly full of food or other substances, or when the person goes to bed with the day's problems and the mind tries to resolve them, by constantly thinking it over. In all of these situations, the person wakes up exhausted because the subconscious has not been engaged, but if it is allowed to, then a truly magnificent event occurs, a mystical experience, one which allows the person to be properly taught in the ways of the cosmos; that is attunement." The priest stopped and looked at Brendan quite seriously.

"You're suggesting I had one of these," asked Brendan.

"The events of the day will tell you."

Brendan bent down to pick up his clothes and said, "Tell me more."

No answer was forthcoming. When Brendan looked up the priest was gone. Brendan reflected on the conversation, only to be startled by Badcock pounding away at the door. Brendan hurriedly dressed himself and answered the commotion.

"Well, it's about time you were up Mr Stern," shouted Badcock.

"Oh what's the matter Badcock?" Brendan calmly answered

"You should know, you caused it all!"

"Caused what, might I ask?"

"The strike, the girls are all on strike," Badcock shouted hysterically

"I was here all night sleeping; I came up straight from the restaurant."

"No you didn't, you were caught on videotape going to the girls' quarters, at 3:00am I might add. What were you there for, something on the house or was it something else? Well?" Badcock demanded to know.

"Look, I am telling you, I was nowhere there, I was asleep," Brendan snapped back defensively.

"Oh, really, well take a look at this," screamed Badcock, as he produced a surveillance videotape.

"I can't believe you Badcock I repeat, I was in my quarters asleep all night long!"

Badcock's eyes bulged; his face reddened as he shoved the videotape into the video recorder and forcibly pressed play. On the screen in perfect picture clarity was the face and body of Brendan O'Reilly walking down the corridor to the ladies' quarters at the recorded time of 3:00am. A blaze of victory shone on Badcock's face. Brendan stared in total disbelief.

"Well Mr Stern, I think that if you want this business to continue doing well and if you don't want to incur my wrath, you'd better settle this strike ASAP," Badcock screamed as he pointed his finger in a threatening fashion.

Brendan lost for words reluctantly nodded his head, Badcock having got his point across turned and goose-stepped out of the apartment and slammed the door behind him.

Brendan continued to stare at the image on the television screen.

"I told you it was happening."

"What's that?" Brendan mentally asked.

"The process of attunement."

"That really isn't me, is it?"

"Of course it is."

"But I was asleep." Brendan answered

"Only your body not your soul; you haven't transferred that information to your body yet," said the priest with authority.

Brendan turned away from the television and looked at the priest.

"Where did you go?"

"Away, Badcock was coming, I couldn't chance it that he saw me, could I?"

"I suppose not. What is this, was that an impostor?"

"Not at all, it is the talent of bi location"

"But Father, it is only restricted to the great saints." Brendan humbly replied

"So what makes one great, it is only relative you know, no big deal."

"You're saying I have the talent?"

"We all have."

"When will I remember what happened last night?"

"When you want to, that's the next stage namely, when your soul and body are one, intimately and irreversibly connected something for you to meditate on."

"How?"

"Just think about it and intone the word 'OMRA' eight times, it works really well."

"OMRA?"

"Yes."

"What did Jack say about turning words around?" Brendan mentally asked himself

"From this I get roam, to move about, Roma, the city of Rome Italy, the site of the Vatican, the centre of Catholic religion. The centre, amour, love" He then said out aloud

"And more," interrupted the priest, as he continued, "Do not restrict to the English language, always look afar, beyond in everything you do. Only then will you understand the depth of creation, but for now, you must remember last night." And with that the priest faded from view.

Brendan returned his gaze back to the television and played the same scene backwards and forwards, backwards and forwards as he sat there intoning in a low voice the mystical word "Omraaaaaaaaaa."

19

REMEMBERING

In an almost surreal atmosphere Brendan found himself walking down the corridor at 3:00am of the present morning, a process of re-living an event in an automatic, but distant fashion. He knocked on the door of the girls' room and gently opened it. All of the girls were awake, not one noticed him. All were looking very tired, haggard from having to endlessly perform. Many had tears in their eyes and sorrow in their hearts with a sense of abandonment. The Adagio from Dvorak's New World Symphony played softly on the stereo in the far corner of the room. The scene touched Brendan's heart, compassion filled his soul and tears flooded his eyes.

"I suppose you're here to sample," said Felicity as she stood up holding a wooden hair brush in one hand. After all, it's been five days; curiosity is probably getting the better of you, 3:00am, girls off duty, what better time, that's what the last boss did."

Brendan took a white handkerchief embossed with the cross out of his pocket and dabbed his eyes. He looked at Felicity with love and softly said, "I've come to change things."

"Really, Well I suppose it will be 4:00am or 5:00am screw time instead," she viciously replied in a sword-like fashion that cut deeply into his soul.

"Neither of those actually, more like never."

"You're lying." She hit back with vengeance.

Brendan remained silent and stood still while he let his body language interact with Felicity's intuition and searching eyes. She mellowed.

"You're telling the truth?"

"I am." Brendan softly answered

"But why?"

"Because I took an oath and I am always supposed to." Brendan replied without letting on that he was a priest.

"To what?"

"Help."

"And how will you do that, apart from shooting Badcock? You know he is the boss here, you only count the money, that's how it's always been it's in the contract."

"Contracts are nothing more but words on paper, paper burns words disappear," Brendan confidently answered.

"He has too many copies, too many hiding places you will never defeat him that way."

Brendan nodded in acknowledgment and walked towards the other girls and seated himself on one of their beds and listened attentively to their miserable murmurings.

"There is always a solution to every problem. In fact, there are many solutions," he interrupted.

"I admire your courage, but not your stupidity," Naomi caustically replied

"What do you know of the previous owner?" asked Brendan.

"Everything, in fact, we know just about everything that goes on in this town," answered Naomi.

"And that is why some of us have been beaten and one of us has even been killed, we believe," Felicity sadly answered choking on her last words.

"So you live in fear of your lives?"

"All the time we only discuss amongst ourselves what our clients tell us," Naomi disgustedly replied.

"So what about the previous boss?" Brendan asked again.

"As we told you days ago, revolting he was, as were his two fat sisters or daughters, or whatever they were."

"Daughters?"

"Yes, they used to come down here and instruct us on new sexual techniques, especially devised for their business cronies, bloody awful it was. That's when one of us, Cherrie over there, almost had a nervous breakdown doing it," Felicity painfully explained.

"All of you have been to hell and back."

"Still are," they replied. "You have no idea of the deviates that Badcock throws on us and what he expects and commands us to do."

"So are you still seeing the old boss' friends and associates?"

"Yes we do."

"But why? I thought with him gone, they would have gone elsewhere."

"They either like the service or Badcock gives them special deals."

"I don't know how I am going to do it, but Badcock has to go."

Every girl instantly shouted "Yes! Please! As soon as possible!"

"And now for all of you, I have a suggestion."

The girls looked at Brendan with a mixture of apprehension and excitement.

"It is my thought that you all should become sexual therapists, to what degree you want; that is up to you. So, effectively from now, no more hanky-panky, you are all officially on strike and the menu changes." Brendan then outlined the girls' new roles over the next two hours. His suggestions were met with cheering, laughter and celebration even though the girls found it hard to accept their new found luck.

The television image flickered before Brendan's eyes he was back in present time. Effective word 'OMRA', don't you agree?" asked the priest, as he appeared by Brendan's side.

"I wonder what else I am supposed to remember."

"Lots more, but until then, I have a puzzle for you to solve."

"A puzzle?"

"Yes, I want you to find an intensely coloured red rose, bearing white petals, and marry it to a man who bears a five-pointed symbol."

"Don't you think I have enough to deal with?" Brendan angrily replied.

"It is only the beginning."

"Of what may I ask?"

"The events that associate themselves with the letters 'V' and 'E'"

"For God's sake, what are you talking about now?"

"Nothing out of the ordinary."

"Maybe not to you, but for me it has been quite a day."

"The dawning of a new era for mankind."

"Pardon?" Brendan asked, becoming increasingly frustrated.

"Nothing."

"You are toying with me."

"Teaching you would be a better description."

"Well teacher, what is the next lesson?"

How well can you duck and weave?" the priest asked with a radiant smile on his face as he disappeared from view.

Badcock was back at the door attempting to kick it down with the heel of his shoe before he managed to forcibly open it and once he stepped into the apartment he did not allow Brendan to say anything by hysterically screaming "What the bloody hell do you think you are doing?"

Brendan spun around to see Badcock thrusting a menu into his face.

"You changed the bloody menu, what is this shit?"

"Sexual therapy" Brendan innocently answered as he pushed

Badcock's hands away

"We don't sell that here. That's for the academic loonies, we sell sex you idiot, sex, do you understand? That is what makes money, you are in breach of contract Mr. so either fix this or pay up," Badcock screamed.

"I will do neither," Brendan replied calmly as he stood up to face Badcock.

"Change your mind now Mr. Stern," Badcock demanded as he narrowed his eyes in a threatening manner.

"I won't."

"Its war then" Badcock roughly declared as he shook his fist at the handsome priest.

"If you wish," Brendan calmly answered.

"You bloody started it, you stupid fool, and I will end it," Badcock retorted, slamming the door behind him as he stormed out.

'What can he do to me,' thought Brendan un-phased by the violent encounter?

"You obviously didn't read the contract," said the priest

"You're back again."

"Yes."

"What do you know about the contract?"

"Not much, it is probably very complicated as are all legal documents and more so if gangsters are involved."

"Gangsters?" Brendan almost shrieked

"Who do you think run the brothels? There is always a criminal element involved. Either that or a crooked cop."

"How do you know so much?" Brendan asked now starting to show his built up fear.

"By hearing confessions," he answered.

"I am scared," Brendan admitted.

"You shouldn't be," encouraged the priest.

"Discover the power within, the attunement, it won't fail you and if you are in real danger, then I will leave you with a word of protection – Mathrem."

Brendan remained motionless feeling somewhat assured as the priest's face and body shone brilliantly and enveloped Brendan's.

20

SEXUAL WINNERS

With the abrupt departure of Badcock from The Infirmary, Brendan and the girls nervously proceeded with the education of their clientele, over the following days. All of them however, could not escape the shadow of Badcock's threatening words and constantly watched over each other's safety and whereabouts.

During the process, Brendan found himself researching the art of lovemaking. Only then did he realize how beautiful it really was, and to what heights it was written that orgasm could take any individual, and furthermore how important it was for the proper functioning of man and woman. He realized what a task it was for a man to exercise extreme patience and fully satisfy a woman even before he had his own pleasure, but then, that was a wrong word, for it was not pleasure, but rather an indispensable part of life, as important as eating, drinking and breathing. Lovemaking was a spiritual experience, a precursor to ecstasy. At the seat of all of it was the pineal gland and its stimulation by light; god-given light. How important it really was and how unfortunately it was misunderstood by the masses. Brendan was no longer afraid of the subject or of his own sexuality. However, he was somewhat unhappy in that his vow of chastity prevented him from reaping the benefits of glorious sacred lovemaking. And so it was that through his reading and his love of his fellow man Brendan was able to interpret correctly and teach the girls how to influence their clientele for their benefit.

The revolution in man's thinking started with a few who decided to bring along their wives or girlfriends. They realized that the sexual fault lay with themselves, rather than with their women, and so the two received instructions from the girls never to look back or consider anyone else. The men became winners, not only in the sexual sense, but more importantly, in the phenomenon of true unconditional love. Marriages and other relationships whether new or old, even if rocky, became stable again. The men realized that previously when they were having sex with the prostitute, they were wishing and thinking all the time of their own wives or girlfriends, and that the reason that they sought out these girls was that they were welcoming, even though they were being paid to be so. The women on the other hand learnt that lovemaking was not dirty in any aspect, and the introduction to it was nothing more than being playful with childlike simplicity. Over the week the environment of The Infirmary changed from being a highly sexually-charged restaurant to one of a fine eating and higher education. Its motto of 'We look after your ailments' was truly satisfied. The girls changed character, gone was their need to perform. Tension was replaced by happiness. The end of day was joyous, not sad. Sleep was restful and not troubled. They revelled in their new roles of hands-on teachers. Each one of them in time became specialized in certain fields of lovemaking so that the course of instruction became as varied and as long as the clientele wished. Brendan was very pleased with the outcome, especially for the girls, it gave them a new lease of life, but all the time the spectre of Badcock remained at the back of his mind. This fear had to be dismissed otherwise attunement would be staid.

Brendan sat quietly opposite Felicity and Nicole the trio was enjoying a well deserved mid morning cappuccino break.

"I don't know what you did," remarked Nicole, "but Badcock seems to have disappeared into thin air."

"As have all of his gangster friends," Felicity said thankfully.

"But," Brendan paused, "do you really think he has gone?"

"Perhaps the contract wasn't that tight in the first place."

"I don't know," replied Brendan, "I have never seen anything like it, most convoluted it was."

"Probably written by Badcock for his advantage and flawed in the process," suggested Felicity. "He's a coward, one that will use other people to do his dirty work like that poor pharmacist."

Brendan's ears pricked up. "Pharmacist?" he asked.

"Yes, he was one of our regulars before he committed suicide." Felicity grimly replied

"Why would he want to do that?" asked Brendan

"Well, he told one of the girls that he was laundering drugs."

"How do you launder drugs?"Brendan asked becoming increasingly puzzled.

"I don't exactly know, but he said that he had the machinery for it and it had something to do with Longevity Plus. We suspected Badcock was involved in it as well."

"So do you think he has forgotten about us and involved himself with other ventures?" Brendan asked and hoped that his suggestion was true

"No, he loves money and wants it all. He would sell his mother for body parts if he could, that's how we believe one of our girls met her fate," Nicole suggested.

"What do you mean?" asked Brendan.

"Seems through no fault of her own, she found out a little too much about the pharmacist and Longevity Plus and she just disappeared."

"And then Badcock bought himself that fancy car," said Felicity with a disturbed look on her face. She paused briefly and then continued, "After all, I believe you can get good sums of money for things like livers, kidneys, pancreas', corneas, especially on the black market."

"Is the world really like that...?" Brendan asked not realizing that such atrocities were wildly rampant.

"Where have you been Mr. Stern," Nicole and Felicity asked simultaneously, "a monastery?"

"A different sort of shelter, rather self-imposed," Brendan innocently replied. The two girls stared at him unconvinced.

"An academic institution is that right, considering your knowledge?" enquired Felicity.

"You could say that."

"Changing the subject, do you think Badcock will return?" Nicole asked

Brendan was about to answer her question but abruptly stopped talking for a brief moment when he saw the real Jack Stern dressed in civilian clothes walk into the main restaurant. Brendan pretended to ignore him but continued to observe his movements out of the corner of his eye, as he listened and conversed with the two girls. The real Jack Stern talked in a most refreshing manner with the staff as he stolled about and then sat down to order coffee and study the various available menus. He pretended to ignore Brendan. Once the girls had finished their coffees they excused themselves to attend to their next pupils. Brendan stayed to enjoy another cappuccino, he stretched to make himself more comfortable, and as he turned, he made eye contact with Jack Stern who gave a nod of approval. Brendan hoped that it was genuine and breathed a sigh of relief.

21

CONFESSION NEW VOGUE

Brendan needed to know from Jack Stern's own lips whether or not he approved entirely of what he was doing. A gut reaction on his part was not enough. He imagined the safest place for this to happen was in his beloved church and the safest time was probably confession.

Confession was scheduled for late Saturday afternoon, as was the norm with most Catholic churches. This allowed the sinners to repent, cleanse themselves and become worthy to receive Holy Communion as canon law dictated. Yet, even if people did not go, priests still administered communion to them, what was it then, the love of his fellow man that allowed it, or simply thanks in return for their offerings? Brendan often wondered for there was no way of determining how good a person was when they were about to receive the Blessed Sacrament. Brendan was so absorbed by these thoughts that he stopped listening to the music that played. When he finally emerged, the CD track entitled 'Golden Hearts' caught his ear. There in that moment he understood that for all of their failings, humans needed religion and it did not matter what it was, provided it did not harm anyone, but what if it did? How did his heavenly father deal with it? What was the right religion?

"Love my friend."

"You're back again," said Brendan.

"I never left you," replied the priest. "Forget all of the canon and other laws. Our master Jesus, after examining all that mankind had invented, with respect to religions and governments, taught that one word alone was enough. 'Love' in all its glory, its manifestations and applications."

"It is still difficult."

"Quite so because you have to deal with men's ego and their excessive greed for power and possessions….."

"So teach me how to deal with these people."

"That time is coming, just remember the words I have taught you." Again, the priest faded from view.

'I wish he wouldn't do that,' thought Brendan.

The apartment was still, the music had finished playing only the sunshine's creatures danced and played on the window sill as photons do when they stream in through open windows.

Brendan stood up, checked his attire in the full length mirror and made his way to the street below. He thought twice about taking the Ferrari, walking was a better option he concluded. The afternoon was warm, the sun and clouds played with each other, casting abstract shadows across the landscape and the town's buildings. One could see, hear and smell so much more when walking.

More than using any form of transport as one is immersed in life's activities instead of being cut off from it. Brendan wished more people would walk, rather than isolating and pre-occupying them-selves with mechanical art forms and electronic gadgets that isolated them from the real world.

It wasn't long before Brendan found himself at Saint Pious and saw that cars were everywhere. Probably a big wedding he thought.

He made his way to the church doors and found the entire church packed. There was standing room only, but not one to despair Brendan found a neat tight corner under an oscillating fan to retreat into. This couldn't possibly be the queue for confession he thought, as he looked around and spotted Yvette who was attending with intense devotion to the Blessed Virgin's Altar. There was no doubt that she was stunningly beautiful, perhaps one of the most perfect women Brendan had ever seen. The parish priest was certainly blessed to have such a wonderful housekeeper. The longer Brendan observed her, the more he realized that she possessed extra-ordinary qualities. A hush spread throughout the congregation as Jack Stern, alias the parish priest, walked boldly onto the altar. He genuflected in front of the Blessed Sacrament which was on display in its monstrance, and as he ascended the pulpit, he made the sign of the cross.

He began, "In the name of the Father, Son and Holy Ghost, good afternoon fellow Christians. It is a pleasure to see all of you here this afternoon. As there are so many of you present, we will have an open confession."

"An open..." Brendan almost splattered out aloud in sheer disbelief as it was contrary to church law

"I understand that many of you may think that this is unusual, but it is not if you know what I mean. Each one of us confesses during Sunday mass when we say the credo and so today, we will be extending that prayer and I shall do nothing more than confirm that each one of you is absolving yourself of sin. Yes, you yourselves will do the absolution, for in each one of us, is a fragment of the creator and therefore, why wouldn't the creator forgive itself of sin. Sin is not a terrible thing, in fact, it is man-made as you know and as you now realize. What is sin one day, is not sin the next, depending upon the lawmakers' whims and fancies. If you want to be driven crazy then listen to them, but if you want to be happy, then listen only to your hearts, which will never lie to you, and above all, learn to love yourself. There is however but one sin, and that is the failure to develop your talents. I understand that circumstances may make it difficult for you to realize this at times, however, it is only an excuse, there is nothing impossible in life everything necessary is available for you to realize your destiny."

Brendan searched his heart to find what he had failed to do, which he sensed each member of the congregation present was also doing. Yvette was still at our Lady's altar, looking lovingly at Jack. Her heart was filled with admiration, perhaps a little more besides that, Brendan thought. Yvette's eyes sparkled as she listened. Jack looked at her and smiled. For that brief moment, it was as if they knew each other from a life long ago.

"Tell us more," a middle aged businessman shouted.

"Yes, tell us more," the congregation erupted.

"There is nothing more to tell, life and love is simple, it is to be experienced, to be enjoyed, but then again, there is something else that I need to tell you."

"And that is?" a young woman asked impatiently.

"How to achieve true happiness"

"What is happiness?" the same woman asked.

'This is going to be interesting,' thought Brendan.

"We have all come to believe in one way or another of the existence of God, of a creator. I believe that it or he or she is a playful child with limitless imagination and power. What greater happiness is there in life than to be with a child, playing with it, teaching it, feeding it, lavishing love on it? Why not then whenever you can, because the creator is not of this physical world, spend as much time dreaming with our creator in the realm of its imagination and giving thanks for that gift. Whenever you do this, you will push the limits of our physical existence, in fact, all physical things to their utmost and in the process, you will create a so called miracle."

"Is that how Jesus walked on the water?" one of altar boys asked with childlike simplicity.

"Quite so," Jack replied.

"And all the other miracles as well....?" The same altar boy then asked

"In the same fashion," Jack replied. Now let us divorce ourselves from that ugly word 'Confess'. Instead, let us rejoice by saying from today onwards, "We will never again think of sin, but instead, we will listen to our hearts and develop our talents" and in doing so, we shall fill our life with happiness, because we will become creators in our own right. Let us now say the 'Our Father' as thanks, and as we do so, the choir will sing the famous Ave Maria by Gounod.

The atmosphere of intense prayer and song brought tears to the eyes of those who understood, others less fortunate sat somewhat bewildered. Brendan was awestruck, absolution was complete.

An hour later the church was deserted, Brendan was kneeling at the Blessed Virgin's Altar. Jack quietly approached him from behind and tapped him on the shoulder.

"Well, how goes it my friend?"

"Alright I suppose," Brendan replied nervously.

"What's the matter, you look rather..."

"Yes I am; can you hear my confession please Father?" Brendan answered a little flustered.

"Come into the confessional box and tell me what troubles you my child," Jack said in a priestly fashion, as he showed Brendan the way.

Once there, Brendan knelt down and confronted Jack with his fears. He bravely told him what he had done with The Infirmary, to which Jack replied, "Well done, it is exactly what I had hoped you would do."

Brendan looked at Jack's smiling face and saw the priest standing behind him

"Are you looking at me or the ghost behind me?" Jack asked without any warning

"You know he exists?"

"That's what I have been told and I have felt his presence, but you I sense, can see him is that right?"

"Yes, he even talks to me in my head."

"About?"

"Attunement."

Jack smiled again but said nothing. Brendan changed the subject back to The Infirmary.

"You really don't mind what I did to The Infirmary?"

"Look Father, it is exactly what I would have done. Women are not there to be abused, taken advantage of, they are there to be appreciated and cherished. In fact, if you hadn't done it, I would have once we reverted back to our normal selves. You need to realize that I don't do that sort of business, I don't like making money in those ways," Jack stated emphatically.

"I on the other hand don't know if the church would approve of your running of this parish, in fact, I will probably need to do a lot of explaining as to why you were here."

"It may not come to that."

"What do you mean?"

"Well, how many people know that you are here?" asked Jack, looking directly at Brendan

"Two that I know of, the Monsignor and the Archbishop, I have told no one else."

"Well, what is the problem? Surely there can be two Brendan O'Reilly's as priests in this great nation of ours, quite common names I would think you will find."

"I wish it was that simple."

"It is, trust me, all will be fine. In any case, look how I have managed to fill the church, that's what it is all about. In any marketing game, it is all about numbers. After all, you are doing nothing more than selling God, but me, quite the opposite. I came to teach and that is much more worthwhile and important. People want to discover themselves to be free, cut the strings and let them be so, that is what the church should be doing, she would gain far more in the long run."

"Now you are lecturing me," Brendan said defensively.

"Not really, more like sharing. I see a little of me in you and for that reason, I would like you to share my level of enlightened consciousness. It is called attunement."

Brendan remained silent, somewhat aghast.

"Did I say something to shock you?"

Brendan swallowed. "No, not at all, I was merely day-dreaming." Jack smiled and knew otherwise.

"Are you sure you haven't spoken to the priest?" Brendan asked

"Not at all…."

"Well I suppose it won't be long before we can go back to our former selves."

"I didn't remember there being a time limit about it, do you? In any case, I haven't quite finished here; there are some other matters that need tidying up." Jack replied as he was thoroughly enjoying his adventure

"Such as…?" Brendan asked a little distraught.

"That is my personal business, sorry, can't tell you anymore. Well my son, if you have nothing else to confess, perhaps we should leave it at that. Now for your penance, go home to The Infirmary and continue your good pastoral work. I am sure Christ will be pleased, after all, he did the same." Jack replied tongue in cheek

Brendan looked at Jack curiously and wondered what he really meant.

22

24 HOURS FROM HELL

The middle aged harsh looking man, dressed mostly in black, rang the front doorbell at the Palace. It was 8:00pm. The porch light cast shadows on his face and accentuated his hard features. He was not one to be tampered with. Within a few minutes the housekeeper Angela opened the door and ushered him in.

"Come, wait in here, I get Monsignor for you."

He remained silent as he followed.

It wasn't long before Monsignor Monahan rushed into the waiting room and closed the door behind him. The room was dark, except for a small glowing table lamp. Tension filled the air.

"Why have you come?" the Monsignor asked nervously.

"To correct problems," he coldly answered.

"What problems?"

"You should know," he replied as he paced about the large room.

"Not at all," the Monsignor answered him. "As far as I am concerned, everything is running smoothly, I can assure you of that."

"Really? Well, let me tell you otherwise. Our auditors have found that there has been a disappearance of substantial amounts of money, something our brothers are not happy about. What makes it worse is that it is ongoing and getting worse."

"And you're suspecting us?" Monahan asked.

The Harsh Man evaded the question.

"There is more, our joint venture has been sabotaged by your man, Father O'Reilly and some friend of his. It appears to us that your conscience has got the better of you and that perhaps you wish to cleanse yourselves of our interests. If that is true, the only people who will be doing the cleansing are us."

The Harsh Man looked at the Monsignor who by now was rather worried and confused. His breathing became laboured and perspiration formed on his forehead. The Monsignor produced a white handkerchief, a sign of truce, and fumbled nervously with it in his hands. The Harsh Man continued to walk around the dimly lit room awaiting some sort of reply until he stopped with his back to the door. The Monsignor beset with fear looked at the Harsh Man and the priest standing next to him.

"Who are you?" were the last words he uttered as the bullets smashed into his forehead and chest. He fell to the floor and lay there motionless. The Harsh Man smiled meanly; partially satisfied he opened the door behind him, and turned to look outside. All was still. Very quietly he crept across the foyer and up the stairs to find the Archbishop's sleeping quarters.

His Grace was comfortably seated in a well upholstered high backed recliner. He was making notes as he simultaneously watched the discovery channel on his wide-screen television and talked to an unidentified person on his cordless telephone. In a world of his own, he was oblivious to the assassin's entrance. The Harsh Man raised his gun, took aim and squeezed the trigger. In that moment, a woman's screams filled and echoed throughout the entire building. The Archbishop jumped from his chair in response, dropping the phone as two bullets slammed into him, propelling him forward. He crashed with an almighty force into the fireplace and passed out. The Harsh

Man with no time to spare fired two more bullets and hurriedly departed with ease escaping detection. Commotion reigned supreme as Angela continued to scream; lights switched on everywhere as the Archbishop's secretary and other staff came alive.

Brendan O'Reilly, after blessing himself with holy water from the font at the main entrance of the church, made his way back to the road outside of Saint Pious. By now, all of the church gates had been locked and the place and its surroundings looked quite deserted. A lone car was parked some 50 metres from where he stood, and taking no notice of it Brendan continued to walk in its direction. As he passed it, a voice from within said, "Excuse me Mr. Can you help me?" Brendan stopped and saw an elderly lady looking somewhat out of sorts seated in the passenger seat.

"Pardon madam, would you mind repeating that?"

"I am feeling very unwell, I don't think I can drive, I don't want to have an accident and I don't want to stay out on the streets, not at my age, it's not safe you know."

"I don't have a car madam. I am on foot as you can plainly see."

"Yes, you can drive though can't you?"

"Yes."

"Well, can you drive me home? It's not far. Please?" she convincingly pleaded.

"How far is it?"

"Oh… about five kilometres." She faintly answered

"In what direction?" he asked, seemingly concerned for the elderly woman's well being

"East of here."

"Very well."

"Thank you, I will make it worth your while, I promise." The old lady weakly said

"No, it's okay, I am pleased to help" he said as he walked around to the driver's side.

Once seated Brendan found that the keys were already in the ignition and in the 'on' position.

"How long since you turned the ignition on?" he asked.

"Oh, about forty five minutes I think."

"I hope you haven't drained the battery." Brendan said as he turned the key, the starter motor strained to turn over, and then with a groan the motor managed to jump into life.

"Thank God for that," He said as he shifted the gear stick into drive

"I'll say that again," the elderly lady thankfully replied. "I don't know what I would have done if you hadn't come around."

"Someone else would have helped you."

"Oh no, it had to be you." The elderly woman firmly said

Her remark made Brendan feel good and he carefully pulled the car out onto the road and drove according to her directions.

About two kilometres on he was waved down by an on duty policeman. Brendan stopped the car and wound down the driver's window.

"How can I help you officer?" he politely asked

"Routine sir, I need to see your driver's license, registration of the car and perform a breathalyser test."

Brendan produced Jack Stern's license, asked the elderly lady for the car's papers, as he explained why he was driving her car. The policeman listened attentively and agreed that all was in order. He then asked Brendan to step out and undertake the random breathalyser test.

"This is a relatively new unit sir, it requires you to inhale first and then exhale vigorously with your lips firmly on the mouth-piece."

Brendan nodded that he understood he wrapped his lips around the plastic disposable mouthpiece and breathed in. As soon as he inhaled, consciousness left him and he fell heavily to the ground.

When he came around, he found himself reclining on a dentist's chair covered in plastic. His wrists were securely strapped down, as were his ankles. The room that he was in was brightly lit; everything in it was painted or decorated in brilliant white. It had an eerie clinical feel about it.

A video surveillance camera was present in each corner of the room. Next to the chair, was a stainless steel trolley with all manner of strange looking surgical devices designed to cut, probe and remove. A selection of jars clearly labelled to accept specific body parts lay next to them hungrily waiting delivery. The priest appeared.

"Well, looks like someone doesn't like you."

Brendan was in no mood for such humour; now more than ever before he genuinely feared for his life.

"No need to do that my son, you are well equipped to deal with this situation," the priest said.

Brendan remained silent hoping that the priest was right. He remembered what the girls had told him about losing some of their kind, and how it was suspected they were sold off as body parts, and it certainly looked as though this fate awaited him.

A door opened and in walked Badcock, two extremely fat women and a sinister looking middle aged man with harsh features who was dressed in a laboratory coat and full-length plastic Wellington boots.

"Well Mr. Stern, I see that you are awake. You didn't think for one moment I was going to let you ruin my operation and simply walk away, there are too many players involved, too much money at stake for a simpleton like you to get in the way."

Badcock pulled out a cigarette case. He was about to extract one when the Harsh Man said, "Not now, I don't want the organs being contaminated."

"So the girls were right, you do deal in body parts," Brendan grimly said

"Only when we wish to dispose of the evidence, nothing must be wasted, most things can be recycled. We have a waiting list for livers, kidneys, corneas etc, etc, why not satisfy the market," Badcock answered in a sinister tone of voice. "But that is not the reason why we are here Mr. Stern. You see, you have a choice, either you sign back The Infirmary to the Ricci girls, or we will kill you. You can do it peacefully, or we will encourage you with the use of various surgical techniques. Well, which will it be?"

"Neither," Brendan answered in sheer disbelief at his own words.

"Surely you jest, have you seen yourself lately? You miserable cretin, you are immobilised, incapacitated," Badcock angrily said as he scoffed at the handsome priest

Brendan did not answer; instead he just lay there and mentally intoned 'OMRA' seven times.

"Not the most brilliant word my son, try the other," the priest whispered into Brendan's ear.

With that Brendan quietly intoned, "Mathrem."

"Get on with it" Badcock ordered the Harsh Man.

The Ricci twins looked on squeamishly, as the Harsh Man took a long barbed probe and attempted to insert it into Brendan's left ear. The point of the probe stopped at the entrance to Brendan's ear canal.

"What are you doing man, get on with it," Badcock shouted as he looked on.

"I am, but if refuses to go in."

"What complete nonsense, push it in like a man." Badcock angrily commanded.

The Harsh Man attempted with all of his concentrated might, but nothing happened. The probe refused to budge. Badcock, incensed at his failure, grabbed the probe from the Harsh Man hands and boasted, "Let me show you how it is done." He took aim and pushed with all of his might. The probe shuddered to a halt, as if repelled by an overwhelming force field. Badcock's sweaty palms lost their grip, slid down the barbs and ripped open his hands in a serrated fashion. He screamed with pain, blood poured profusely from the wounds and he fainted at the sight of it.

The Harsh Man quickly summoned the Ricci girls to help him, as he attempted to stem the flow of blood.

Meanwhile, the priest re-appeared.

"Convinced?" he asked.

Brendan nodded.

"Excellent….now free yourself,"

"How?"

"It is all a matter of perception. If you realise how little material exists in those restraints holding you down; when you realise how much space there really is in comparison then you easily conclude its weakness which increases your strength and makes your body denser, giving you the advantage and you simply break free."

Brendan focused he altered his breathing, intoned OMRA, and closed his eyes. He saw the true reality of his restraints and arose easily from the chair breaking the bonds that held him captive. The Ricci girls gasped in horror; screamed with fear and then both of them fainted. The Harsh Man, threatened by Brendan's sudden freedom, grabbed a scalpel and threw it at the handsome priest's chest. The blade hit its target without penetrating it and unexpectedly turned around and flew back at his assailant. The Harsh Man winced as the blade penetrated deeply to its full length into his left shoulder. Racked with excruciating pain, he grabbed another surgical device and threw it at Brendan. The same thing happened, except this time, it lodged in the Harsh Man's right arm. The Harsh Man struggled to come to grips with the reality of his situation. He could not accept that he had been defeated by an opponent who hadn't even raised a hand. He stared wide-eyed at Brendan with a mixture of fear and hatred. He shouted, "What sort of frigging freak are you?"

Brendan simply smiled and concentrated even more, he pointed at the surveillance cameras, and as he did so, each one of them exploded into tiny fragments. He then pointed his finger at the Harsh Man who was terrified at the prospect of the same thing happening to him. Brendan's pointed finger gestured, 'Come here.' The scalpel and the other devices removed themselves from the Harsh Man's body and fell to the ground. Blood gushed from the open wounds. Brendan walked towards the disbelieving Harsh Man who lay in a pool of his own blood and was about to go into shock. Brendan touched the Harsh Man's wounds, the bleeding stopped and the wounds healed over immediately.

'This is all an illusion, this is not happening; I am a cold-blooded killer who enjoys killing. I am being hypnotised by this freak,' thought the Harsh Man as he sort ways of defeating Brendan.

He sprung to his feet and briefly stared at Brendan in the eye, before he threw a series of wild punches at Brendan's head and stomach as hard and fast as he could.

Brendan shook his head to say, "No, don't do that." And with a flick of his finger, he threw the Harsh Man's body across the room and crashed it into the wall behind him. The Harsh Man remained suspended on the wall for a brief moment before he slid down it onto the floor into a crumbled heap.

"Quite impressive my son first you protect yourself, then you minister to his wounds and then you discover the power of telekinesis. You're a fast learner," the priest proudly said.

"Just discovering the Christ principle or should I say attunement" replied Brendan.

"Well said my son, I wonder what else you will in time discover about yourself."

Across town a similar reign of terror was about to occur. The real Jack Stern alias Father Brendan O'Reilly sat in relative comfort at the desk of Father Kelly in St Pious Priory. He was studying what seemed to be an old copy of the official King's version of the Bible. But in fact, it was a disguised financial ledger dealing with the parish finances, the priest's personal finances and the joint venture between Monsignor Monahan, the Archbishop and a group called 'The Brothers in Black'. Jack would not have discovered this book had he not gone looking for a specific prayer book. This 'Bible' somehow did not belong amongst the collection of old holy books. Its vibrations were all wrong, its cover was old, and its pages it could be gleaned, were far too young in comparison. The analytical mind of Jack Stern slowly and surely began to unravel the convoluted relationship between all of those recorded. The night was still, the only sound that reached Jack's ears was the sweet classical music that Yvette had chosen to play on the household's ancient stereo that was situated in the main dining area. From the corner of his eye, Jack saw a large dark shadow sweep past the window, followed by another. Sensing that something was not quite right he dimmed the room lights and went in pursuit of Yvette, turning off house lights as he searched for her. Yvette was in the kitchen preparing to leave for home. Jack signalled to remain quiet by putting a finger to his lips. He turned off the kitchen lights and joined her side.

"What's wrong Father?" she whispered nervously.

"We could have a problem, intruders I suspect, come with me," he said as he took her hand. A surge of emotion immediately flowed between the two of them, only to be broken by the shattering of the front and rear doors.

The darkness of the presbytery was pierced by the intense light of torches seeking out their prey. Yvette started to shake. Jack sensing her panic drew her close and used his muscular strength to calm and comfort her. Loud coarse voices accompanied by heavy footsteps came closer and closer towards them.

"Come on, find them, quick, come on."

"Okay, okay," another muffled voice answered.

These sounded familiar to Jack. He did not waste time trying to identify them, as his mind was more pre-occupied with Yvette's safety and calculating an escape route. The kitchen was located to the right of the central passage; behind them were the laundry and a spare toilet. There was no direct door leading to the outside, one had to go through the passage. Damn it, thought Jack, can't escape unnoticed. He strained his ears in an attempt to count the number of intruders, one, two, three at the most probably very heavily built and armed.

"Quick Yvette, take off your shoes and hide in the toilet behind the door and lock it, don't come out until I come for you."

"Father don't go, they sound very big and mean you'll get hurt!" Yvette begged as she held on tightly to him

"I'll be okay, I will surprise them with my innocence, go quickly now." Jack urged as he pushed her away

Yvette meekly obeyed and tip toed to her hiding spot as quietly as she could. She locked herself in, and strained her ears to hear above the noise of her beating heart, what was about to happen. The murderous voices came from all directions and echoed throughout the house as the thugs violently searched and finally converged on the kitchen.

Jack managed to fit his slim muscular physique neatly behind the kitchen door. As the thugs entered, his senses were proven correct there were three of them, each armed with a semi-automatic pistol complete with silencer. Jack on the other hand, only had his intelligence and a large open container of finely ground extra hot cayenne pepper. One thug stood legs apart with his back to the entrance, the other two walked about shining their torches into everything. As they made their way towards the laundry and spare toilet, the window of opportunity briefly presented itself. Jack slipped from behind the door stepped forward on the ball of his foot and kicked the large oaf between his legs from behind with all of his might. The man screamed with pain, dropping his gun and torch as he was propelled forwards. As he did so, Jack hit him hard to the back of his neck knocking him unconscious and then he leapt forwards across the kitchen table, throwing the pepper into the masked faces of the other two who had turned around. Bull's-eye the pepper hit its targets, stinging and burning their eyes and throats, both thugs shot their guns wildly as they struggled to regain their sight.

Jack was crouched on the floor in front of them. He grabbed the right arm of the bigger one of the two and smashed it into the face of the other.

"What the hell did you do that for, you stupid bitch?"

"Don't call me a bitch," she yelled as she slapped him in the face.

With egos bruised and tempers flaring, the two began to pummel each other, quite oblivious to Jack's presence .He calmly collected and holstered all of their weapons and stood in the corner witnessing the comical battle of the sexes.

'Domestic violence at its best,' he thought, as the warring couple resorted to throwing kitchenware and food at each other.

"That's quite enough," he shouted, as he flicked the light switch on. "Don't either of you have any respect for church property?" he asked as he pointed a gun at them. "Well, well, who do we have here? If it isn't Matron from Longevity Plus and the guard at the main entrance I gather from your performance that you appear to be romantically linked. I wonder what possesses the likes of you to invade this holy place and cause so much damage. Are you looking for somewhere different to make love?" Jack flippantly asked as he kept the semi automatic trained on both of them.

"Nah, just following orders," the oaf said, as he nursed his sore head.

"Whose orders?"

"Mine of course," Matron snapped.

"Have I done something to upset you, too much penance or not enough altar wine?"

"We don't like your kind here," she spitefully answered with a hiss

"Oh, so you think I am black and you decided to tar and feather me, is that it?"

"Sort of"

"Perhaps the truth is that I rocked the establishment. What do you say?"

The hideous Matron remained silent

"Well," Jack said demanding an answer

"I am not saying."

"Supposing I told you otherwise, supposing I told you that I have seen a book of records that tells me exactly how you run your establishment."

"You're bluffing," she said, tight lipped as she cast a vicious look at him.

"Am I?" he questioned, as he looked directly at her.

"Oh well, it was worth a try," Jack said after a pause. "In any case, it looks to me as though you two lovebirds are dying to hold hands and continue your foreplay" He then said as the oaf looked sheepishly at the human hippo, who cast a menacing look full of daggers at Jack.

"How about a little bondage to your foreplay, hand-cuffs anyone?"

The oaf giggled and pulled a pair from his back pocket.

"Now that's what I like, an obliging fellow, now put Matron's hands behind her back and cuff them together, good. Kiss her tenderly on the neck, nice, turn around, hands behind, good."

Jack then handcuffed the oaf's hands with the pair that he had retrieved from the unconscious thug.

"Yvette, come out," he gently called out.

Yvette appeared looking quite pale and shaky. "Come over here child, take this, point it at them, put your finger on the trigger and shoot them if you have to."

Jack positioned the human hippos back to back and tied their hands together using electric cord. He then untied their shoelaces and interconnected them.

"Well then, I wonder who will fall on whom," he jokingly said. "What shall we do with the drunken sailor Yvette?"

She forced a smile without knowing what Jack was hinting at and shook her head.

"Think he has had enough punishment?"

"Yes, but how did you do all of this, you are supposed to be a man of peace?" She asked a little confused by outcome of the situation.

"And that I am, I have brought peace back to this place, but most importantly I have restored you're peace of mind and am happy that you are safe," he said, as he took hold of her arm.

Yvette mellowed as she felt her heart flutter. Finally, a real gentleman, pity he is a priest she thought.

"Come now, let's leave this place fancy a cappuccino?" he asked in a most chivalrous fashion.

She smiled, quite besotted. "I'd like that."

"Good, let's go then."

The enraged human hippos tried desperately to break free. A large crash sounded as Jack and Yvette left through the front door.

As they approached Father O'Reilly's white Ford a police car with lights flashing came down the driveway. Jack and Yvette waited and looked at each other as the sole police officer emerged from the vehicle's driver's seat.

"Good evening Father, is everything okay?" The officer asked

"Yes, why do you ask?" Jack replied, as he analysed the policeman's body language

"We received a report by one of the neighbours of several suspicious characters hanging about, the neighbour thought that a burglary was in progress," the officer said, as he unclipped his holstered revolver.

"Nothing like that has happened here, perhaps the neighbour sent you to the wrong address," Jack replied calmly.

"Our information I believe is quite accurate; I think I had better investigate under the circumstances, would you mind accompanying me Father and helping with my inquiries?"

"No, not at all my son, Yvette you can stay here, it won't take long."

"I would prefer the young lady to accompany us sir," the police officer stated quite emphatically

"Very well then come along Yvette" Jack said as he took her hand and pretended to play along.

Yvette looked at him sideways. He could detect the anxiety and confusion in her eyes. He winked at her as a sign that everything would be okay. Jack and Yvette led the way. The policeman followed closely behind. As they approached the house Jack suddenly pretended to lose his footing on the pebbled pathway and fell violently backwards, hitting the back of his head on the policeman's face. There was a crunching sound as the policeman's nose broke and he fell backwards whilst Jack managed to maintain his balance. Jack apologized profusely as he turned around. "I am terribly sorry, how careless of me, this has never happened to me before. Officer, officer are you okay?"

The policeman lay on the ground, blood all over his face and appeared unconscious.

"Oh my god Father, what have you done, have you killed him?" Yvette gasped.

"Not intentionally my child let me see if he is still alive." Jack checked the officer's vital signs.

"He's alive, just out to it. I will use the police car's radio to call for help." Jack said and then quickly walked over to where it was parked, whilst Yvette stayed with the officer. He picked up the two way radio and called headquarters.

"Hello, this is car 246 reporting on the disturbance at Saint Pious Presbytery. Everything appears to be in order, over." Jack said in a voice that was meant to resemble the policeman's

A young female voice answered, "Charlie is that you? Thought you signed off at 3:00pm and gone home, what are you doing there? You are not supposed to be on duty in any case, no code has been logged for that address."

Jack terminated his side of the call.

"Hello Charlie, hello," she continued to transmit.

Jack went over to where Yvette was kneeling.

"Come Yvette, let's go."

"But Father, he's hurt, I must attend to him." She conscientiously pleaded

"Not if you want to get killed." Jack coldly replied

"Pardon?" Yvette answered rather surprised at Jack's matter of fact statement

"I will tell you in the car, come now." He firmly said in a no nonsense manner

Yvette obeyed and together they drove away in search of a safe place.

"Why would these people break into our Presbytery Father?"

"I don't know if you overhead the Matron when she said, 'they don't like your kind in this town'. That makes me suspicious and even more so, when an off duty policeman turns up and wants to investigate, especially when both neighbours are away. I think he was on their side and came to finish the job."

"Which was?" Yvette asked becomingly increasingly aware.

"Of either scaring us away, or making me disappear all together and that makes me wonder what they are hiding."

"Me too," Yvette added. "What do you think will happen when the drunken sailor comes to?"

"He'll probably want to know what happened to him and then if one of the hippos hasn't crushed the other, he will set them free."

"And the policeman….?"

"Oh, he is quite alright. When he wakes up, all four of them will probably plot another attempt at us which means that we are not safe in this town." Jack concluded

"Can't we go to the police?"

"We don't have enough evidence."

"Surely a priest's word is good enough." Yvette naively suggested

"That's if you are a priest." Jack replied almost giving away his true identity

Yvette luckily did not grasp the meaning of his statement.

"I think our best bet is to go to another town for the time being. Do you know of one?" He asked

"Yes I do Father. But since it is almost 9:30pm, my parents will worry about me, I need to contact them."

"Very well, here use this." Jack passed her his one of a kind custom made Ericsson mobile phone. Yvette made contact and explained the situation. Her parents understood and realized that she was in safe hands. She then gave Jack the appropriate directions to reach the next town.

Yvette proved to be a good navigator. As they drove through Newburn Jack sensed that they were being followed. To confirm his suspicions, he executed a series of road changes and evasive manoeuvres.

"That's the wrong way Father." Yvette said a little surprised that Jack had taken a different route

"I know, but we are being followed."

"Are you sure?" She asked as fear and anxiety started to fill her mind

"Most certain of it…." Jack confirmed as he looked into the rear vision mirror

"What shall we do now?"

"Pray for guidance my child." Jack flippantly replied

Yvette as was her habit produced her rosary beads and started praying as she looked behind.

The car that followed was a low slung hearse with modified suspension, exhaust and souped up powerful V8 engine. It was painted in customary black colour and two heavily built sinister characters sat in the front seats. The black hearse followed about five car lengths behind. It slowed and indicated that it was about to park. The road ahead was full of parked cars. A tow truck sped past and overtook Jack and Yvette, apparently on its way to an accident. One hundred metres down the road it screeched to a halt, and with wheel lift down, started reversing towards Jack's white Ford at breakneck speed. Its movements distracted Jack so that he did not see that the black hearse had caught up to them. Now it was alongside them, boxing the Ford in. Behind them and moving up very rapidly towards them, was an ambulance from Longevity Plus.

'Oh how I miss you, my lovely lady,' Jack thought, as he calculated his next move.

"Yvette, hang on," he yelled, as he slammed on the brakes to momentarily halt the car.

The black hearse forged slightly ahead of them. Jack then floored the accelerator, turned the steering fully to the right, released the brakes and slew the car around the hearse. Within seconds he performed the opposite manoeuvre and deliberately drove the white Ford into the hearse's rear right hand tail light assembly, at an angle that pushed the hearse forwards and around. The hearse spun uncontrollably around and crashed sideways into the reversing tow truck. The wheel lift automatically engaged, lifting the car up and over. The ambulance could not stop in time and crashed into the two other vehicles. Jack in full control of the white Ford spun the wheel to the right, straightened the car and sped away.

"Brilliant guidance thank you Yvette." He jokingly said as he flashed a devious smile.

23

CHANNELS OF DISCOVERY

"Mathrem' really produces an extra-ordinary force field," Brendan said to the priest as he looked for a way out of the dissecting room.

"Does not work that way," replied the priest.

"Then how does it?" Brendan asked as he continued to search for clues.

"The word makes your outer electrode magnetic mantle more aware of its capabilities so that it can interact with all levels of consciousness."

"What are you saying?" Brendan asked seeking clarification

"That everything is alive; everything is an expression and experiment in life. But everything is not the same in terms of consciousness. Everything that contributes to everything that exists is at a different level of consciousness to everything else."

"So?"

"As your impostor thought, it is like that attracts like. When your assailant threw the scalpel and other projectiles at you, your consciousness and its consciousness interacted. They knew they were not meant for each other, so repulsion occurred and the objects went back to their proper owner."

"Why is it that they responded to my commands and allowed me to heal him?"

"They responded to your consciousness of caring, they realized that their intention was to help, not damage, and so they forgave themselves of their sin and left. You need to realize that everything constantly evaluates and calculates its position in life, with a view to making itself perfect."

"But in the process of perfection and evolving it causes man to think that religions and their dogmas and the histories of them were filled with contradictions," Brendan correctly suggested.

"Exactly and so you are beginning to understand not so much the mystery of life but how it is seeking its own perfection, all of your gifts are universal to all and do nothing more than interact with life itself and allow it to express itself."

"So, life is a gift," Brendan said.

"Precisely not one to be abused but one to be played with so it can realize and express its own creativity"

"I wish this room wasn't so white" Brendan sighed as he tried to adapt his eyes to the brightness

"Follow the cold." The priest whispered

"Pardon?"

"You heard me, follow the cold," the priest said.

Brendan walked around the room and detected a cold draught. He pushed the wall at that spot and it clicked open. As he entered the adjoining room, the lights automatically switched on and revealed….
"A huge mortuary," he said

"Unusual for a hospital with such a success rate for curing the incurable, don't you think?"

"You're saying all of the drawers are empty?"

"Take a look." The priest prompted Brendan

Brendan reluctantly took hold of a drawer handle and hoped that he would not see a corpse, as funerals were never his strong point as a priest. With his eyes closed he slid the drawer open and held his breath

"What you expected?" asked the priest.

Brendan opened his eyes and saw box upon box of pharmaceutical products Pethidine 100mg ampoules, more pethidine, venlafexine ampoules, more venlafexine.

"The drawer is full of the stuff and it's not for here, it is destined for elsewhere. It arrived here and now it appears it is being re-directed" Brendan said as he examined the various boxes and their address labels.

"Quite so," said the priest, "and now the time has come."

"For what?" Brendan asked.

"For you to hear my confessions so that I may be released from my earthly bounds and be allowed to continue my cosmic journey Come Brendan, please hear my confession?"

"Very well." Brendan replied even though he didn't think it was the most appropriate place to do so

The priest knelt in front of Brendan and made the sign of the cross.

"Bless me Father, for I have sinned." He solemnly said

"And what is it that you have done wrong?" asked Brendan.

"I have kept silent for too long and have allowed continuous suffering to rain down upon my fellow man."

"How did you manage to do that?"

"I was the assistant parish priest at Saint Pious for many years and enjoyed the glory of supposedly healing people, especially those at Longevity Plus and I cherished all of the money bestowed upon me as gifts in appreciation of my 'work'. "One day the local pharmacist came to confession. I recognized him by his voice, he was very distraught and started crying, telling me he could no longer live with his conscience and the immorality of it all. He told me in explicit detail how he would order massive amounts of drugs for the hospital. He would chemically alter pethidine and venlafexine, using high intensity ultrasound and elevated temperatures, to produce a new generation of designer drugs that were so addictive they literally captured their market. What was so good about these was their pharmaceutical purity. The original drugs never reached the patients because the patients were never sick in the first place and so all of the cures that I and the hospital performed were fakes. I didn't believe one word he told me because I held his staff at Longevity Plus in such high regard. Largely because of their eminent reputation and the rumour that the pharmacist was having marital and mental problems because of his much publicised affairs with one of the very attractive theatre nurses at the hospital. In any case, that pharmacist was found dead the following day. His death made me think twice about what he had told me. I confronted the parish priest about it; his reaction was very guarded, if not offensive. I had never seen him so angry about anything, so unproven. It was as if I had exposed the rawest of nerves. The next day at Sunday mass I consumed poisoned altar wine and here I am," the priest very painfully and regretfully said

"That is quite a confession, but to me it sounds as though you are passing me the buck," Brendan replied.

"You know that is not true, I in my form cannot influence any human, I am powerless. At the most I might scare a few. I needed to tell someone who was highly evolved, so they could remedy the situation. After years of waiting, you finally appeared and there was no doubt in my mind that you were my salvation."

"So you propose that I am the one." Brendan almost scoffed

"Yes, you are and you know it. Look at what you are capable of."

Brendan stood quite still pondering.

"That was an incident involving only two men, but you are talking about organized crime it seems to me," Brendan put forward.

"So?"

"What do you mean so?"

"Nothing is impossible and you are very well equipped my son, goodbye." The priest hurried said and without wanting to engage in any further discussion faded from view, and as he did so, Brendan could hear him happily saying, " It's finally here I can see it the light…. here I am… I am coming."

Brendan knew he was now alone, left to his own devices. Was this the task that his entire life was leading up to? Was it similar to that of Jesus Christ of Nazareth?"

If he did not face it, what would be waiting for him? Would it be more difficult? How much suffering would he cause if he didn't face the challenge and how much would he endure if he did? Would his rediscovered gifts ever desert him?

The sound of a door opening shook Brendan out of his train of thought. I wish I could be unnoticed he thought as he held that vision. Two orderlies dressed in white each pulling a hydraulic goods trolley behind them entered the room. Having read their clipboards they busily assembled the respective orders quite oblivious to Brendan's presence as he stood out in full view. They walked about opening the different drawers, placed packages on the trolleys, walked past him and around him and said nothing. Once they had finished Brendan decided to follow them out. No one paid any attention to him, neither patients, visitors, nursing staff nor security guards. It was as if he wasn't there at all. The orderlies took the pharmaceutical quality drugs, now neatly packed into laundry bags, to the enclosed undercover loading area and left them to be loaded by armed drivers into laundry trucks. Brendan watched and took a mental note of the signage on the trucks. It read Add – Dictive Laundry Company – once you've tried us, you never go anywhere else.

Brendan glanced at his watch; it was 8:00am. Where had the time gone? He needed help. He sat down on the loading bay, intoned OMRA and mentally searched for Jack Stern, as a remote viewer would do.

After the attempt to highjack them, Jack suggested to Yvette that they should go to another town, different from her original choice.

She suggested a rather elegant Swiss hotel, Chateau Alpine, run by two chic middle aged ladies. The chateau was located at the edge of a national park, northeast of Newburn. Yvette had often gone there to enjoy the cuisine when she overcame the guilt of spoiling herself

"Father, you do understand that it will be difficult for me to stay at this place."

"Yes, but do not be overly concerned, after all, you are in the company of an honourable gentleman, who won't be sleeping in the same bed as you, my child."

"Are you sure you are a priest?" asked Yvette.

"You are very persistent with that thought," Jack replied.

"It is because I am used to the 'holy types.'"

"Oh those well if you want to know about my self defense and driving skills, I learnt those early in my life. I made up my mind to be well educated in all aspects of life. No one is immune to violence and everyone should know how to survive under all conditions. As for those 'holy types', always look beyond the social person I say."

Yvette looked at Jack quite confused, but confident that her intuition was proving to her that the man of her dreams was in her company, tantalizingly so. If only he was not a priest, how that would change everything. As they drove they discussed the events that had occurred. Jack wondered if the car was electronically bugged with a homing device. It seemed to him that it was worthy of consideration. Either that or the attempt on their lives had been carefully planned with the two backup attempts which they had skillfully eluded.

The drive took them less than ninety minutes. During their time, Jack could feel that he was becoming more drawn to Yvette. There was something about this girl that fascinated him. It was more than her external beauty and more than the innocence that she be held. He concluded that it was the elements of truth. She possessed that elusive something that would make him complete. It was that strain of love that had escaped him in all of his pursuits of the opposite sex. Not one of his relationships had ever presented to him what Yvette possessed. What made her even more fascinating to him was that it came naturally to her, like the breathless beauty of a rare rose that defied the rules of nature in creating its own magnificence. Yvette was certainly intelligent. She used her foresight and telephoned the chateau ahead of time. Luckily two vacancies existed; however, they were not acceptable to Jack, as they were not adjoining rooms. He suggested that they share the same room and that he would sleep on the couch for security and for the same reason would adopt a different name, say Jack Stern, someone he knew from long ago. Yvette agreed with the proposition.

The chateau was easily found following Yvette's directions. It was located two kilometres along the exit road into the national forest. The light of day would show that it was a delightfully beautiful building full of sparkling colour in the Swiss tradition. Flower boxes bursting with red and white geraniums adorned every conceivable window which reflected the gaiety of the gardens.

Jack parked the Ford at the rear of the building. He removed all priestly paraphernalia, made himself look civilian and taking Yvette by the arm walked through the main doors into the foyer to be greeted by a friendly balding male clerk who sprouted a very large bushy moustache. The man's eyes immediately sparkled as he recognized Yvette.

"Ah Fraulein, a pleasure to see you again," he said in a strong Austrian accent. "I see you have company tonight, very unusual for you, always alone and elusive, yes?"

"No, more shy than anything else, as you should know." Yvette replied as she tried to hide her embarrassment

"Ah, that is what you girls always say. And who is your gentleman friend?"

"Guardian actually" Yvette politely corrected the male clerk

"Looks like a lady's man to me," the desk clerk said grinning mischievously.

Jack nodded and smoothly said, "Yvette rang ahead some time

ago, we have a reservation."

"Ah yes, two separate rooms."

"Could we change that to one please?"

"Ah, but of course, which one would you like, the one with the queen or king size bed?" he asked with a devilish smirk.

"The queen will do and is room service available?" Jack answered

"It is late, but I am sure we can satisfy your wishes," he said, continuing to smirk and wink at Yvette who by now had begun to blush.

Jack noticed her embarrassment and concluded that she was still a virgin.

"Thank you." Jack replied with a smile

"A pleasure and now, would you fill the sign in sheet please?"

Jack attended to the formality and where it said sign here, filled in Virgo. The big moustached Austrian reached across the counter, took Yvette's hand, kissed it and gave her the room keys.

"To my heart you know??" He said as Yvette's blush deepened.

"Thank you," she whispered shyly as she waited for Jack to finish.

"You certainly have him eating out of the palm of your hand," Jack stated as they left for the room.

"It's not like that, I rarely come here."

"He gives me the opposite impression." Jack teased wanting to determine how many suitors she actually had

"I wish you would believe me."

"I do," replied Jack, somewhat assuredly.

Yvette found room 312 situated on the upper floor. It was located in the middle of the hallway. On opening the door and switching the lights on, they were greeted with a bright happy environment, tastefully decorated with fresh flowers and pictures of Switzerland. The suite had all the customary luxury features, television, DVD player, bar fridge, telephone, fax and computer for internet buffs all located in the main entertaining room.

The bedroom with its own balcony lay to the left, whilst the rest area comprising bathroom and toilet lay to the right. Jack asked

Yvette to make herself comfortable as he picked up the phone and asked for room service.

As he waited, he looked across at Yvette who was reclining on the couch.

"You must be starving, correct me if I am wrong, you probably haven't eaten since lunch time."

"Sort of, I had a glass of milk around 4:00pm." Yvette answered

"Would you like to freshen up while I order? Anything you fancy in particular?"

"Anything will do," she said quietly.

"Very well."

Yvette went into the bathroom and attempted to wash away the cares of the day. The cold water stimulated her facial skin causing it to glow even more. She could not help but realise that she was a woman in love, but for all of the wrong reasons, it worried her to such an extent that guilt set in.

"I have suddenly realised something," Jack said once Yvette rejoined him

"What is that?" she replied feeling a little fresher

"We only have the clothes that we stand in."

"Yes what of it?"

"Would you not like a fresh change for tomorrow?"

"It doesn't matter." Yvette answered as she was used to such things

"Oh Yvette, you are very sweet, come sit down next to me, let us have a chat." Jack said as he appreciated her humble nature

Yvette obeyed and together they spent time on the coach side by side verbally fumbling with each other until the waitress interrupted their intimacy by rapping on the door.

Jack let her in thanked her by giving her a generous tip and then proceeded to serve dinner. The aroma of the food wafting from the trolley was captivating. Yvette was hungry and yet she was not. Love had a way of satisfying all of her needs.

"Let me do that," Yvette softly said as she stood up.

"It is my pleasure. Surely it is time that the tables were turned," he said as he placed a plate of veal cordon bleu with mushroom and pepper sauce, accompanied by peaks of mashed potatoes, and cauliflower topped with bread sauce before her.

"It looks wonderful Father."

"But of course, and now for the drink," he said, as he poured cold fresh milk into a tall glass and set it before her.

"Milk!"

"Yes, a very good vintage, brilliant white colour, soft on the palate, light buttery taste, caresses the taste buds, smooth finish with a velvety aftertaste."

Yvette laughed.

Jack joined her sensing her transformation. As they ate, talked and laughed, he continued to witness the change in her from a shy, quiet, reserved devout young girl into a happy blossoming young lady.

When they had finished, Yvette took the dishes into the bathroom and washed them.

When she returned Yvette went up to Jack and said, "Father, I am very tired, thank you for everything, good night." Unable to control her feelings any longer, she blurted out, "It's a pity you are a priest," and then she ran quickly away into the bedroom and shut the door.

This left Jack pondering when and where he should tell her of his proper identity. Not now, he would not take advantage of the situation. He realised that he needed to prove to her and to himself that he was the man she that she sought.

With his mind buried in these thoughts he automatically went about the room making certain that everything was secure, he locked the door, turned off the lights and then once he had found the spare bedding Jack attempted to find a comfortable position on the sofa.

As he gently lulled himself to sleep his mind began wandering, about the many things that might have happened to Brendan O'Reilly. How was The Infirmary? How were the girls? How was his office managing?

As sleep gradually overtook him, suddenly before him stood the image of Brendan who was vigorously miming "Where are you?"

24
CONTACT

As hard as they could try, neither Jack nor Yvette could wake up at 6:00am as habits dictated instead both of their minds mutually agreed that rest was the order of the day and that they should both sleep longer. At about 8:00am they both began to stir. Yvette was naked except for her panty briefs and Jack was still in the same clothes from the previous day. The phone rang with total disregard to the peace and serenity that they both were enjoying. Jack out of a sense of duty lazily reached for it.

"Hello..I mean good morning" He warmly answered.

"Is that you Jack?"

"Yes, who is this?" he asked not immediately recognizing the caller's voice.

"Brendan." The handsome priest abruptly answered

"How did you know I was here?" Jack asked becoming increasingly alert.

"You told me last night."

"So, I wasn't dreaming." Jack replied as he remembered the vision just before he fell asleep the previous night but nothing after that

"You certainly weren't in fact you were quite explicit. Can I come and see you straight away, it's pretty urgent?"

"Of course, take a taxi, I will pay the driver when you arrive," Jack said, sensing the drama in Brendan's voice and concluding that something serious had probably happened to him.

"Very well see you soon."

Jack cradled the phone and stood up to see if Yvette was awake. He went and stood in the bedroom's doorway.

"Good morning Yvette, Hust du slaffen gutt," he asked in an over accentuated German accent.

"You speak German," she said laughingly.

"Only the swear words."

"Oh, you are very funny indeed. Who was that on the phone?"

"My friend, Jack Stern, he is coming over. Isn't that rather strange, haven't heard from him in such a long time, then all of a sudden he calls."

"I'll get ready and make breakfast, whoops," Yvette put her hand up to her mouth and giggled. "Sorry Father, I forgot where I am."

Jack nodded in agreement. "Easily done….. Breakfast is down-stairs would you care to partake?"

"I think we will need to straighten out our clothes." Yvette said as she looked at Jack in his crumpled mess.

"I need an iron," he agreed as he examined his shirt. "I am sure there is one in the wardrobe. I will leave you to shower and prepare yourself"

Yvette waited for Jack to leave before she threw back the sheets and wrapped herself in one of the bed coverings and then went into the bathroom, passing Jack at the wardrobe on the way. Jack out of the corner of his eye admired the outline of her curvaceous body as he unfolded the ironing board.

While Yvette showered, Jack stripped down to his underwear and attended to pressing his clothes as best he could. Satisfied with the result, he then attended to Yvette's and hung these on a coat hanger. He hurriedly dressed himself and handed Yvette her clothes discreetly through the bathroom door. After a few moment s Yvette emerged looking quite radiant.

"Your turn Father," she said

"I might have to do it later."

"Why?"

"No shaving gear, no toothbrush."

"They have a kiosk down stairs, can't have you going out looking scruffy."

"You don't like the idea of beauty and the beast?"

"I've been in the company of enough of those, thank you and you don't even come close," she sweetly remarked as she disappeared through the door.

Jack shook his head and grinned.

Once she had gone, Jack took advantage of her absence. He stripped down once again, and took himself into the shower and enjoyed the warmth of its water and the fragrance that she had left behind.

Yvette returned within ten minutes, she brought with her tooth paste, a toothbrush, shaving cream, disposable razors, a reasonable aftershave, a comb and a deodorant that both of them could use. She laughed at the sorry state of Jack's crumpled clothes and set about pressing them again, but this time, as only a woman knows how to do.

Jack emerged from the bathroom with a towel wrapped around his waist. Yvette looked up at him and was surprised by his physical stature. Jack was quite muscular, defined in an athletic sort of way with a perfectly proportioned body. He was tall; approximately 183 cms in stocking feet.

"Your needs are over there," Yvette ambiguously said as she pointed to the plastic bag. "What sort of sport do you play, Father?"

"Only the interesting ones"

"Such as…?"

"Tennis, skiing, chess and other mind games," he replied as he collected the bought items and returned to the bathroom.

When he re emerged she handed him his clothes, which he briefly smelt, satisfied that a deodorant would keep them reasonably fresh for the next twelve hours. He got dressed.

"Breakfast time," he said "Ready to go?"

"Certainly am."

The Chateau Alpine was serving a continental smorgasbord in its indoor outdoor restaurant. It was always well patronised. People came from near and far to experience its delights. Being late in the morning, there were quite a few vacant tables. Yvette suggested a romantic setting overlooking the rose garden. Jack agreed and it seemed to him that they were on their first date.

As they sat down he suggested in a low whisper, "Yvette, whilst we are away from Saint Pious, could you refer to me as Jack Stern please?"

"Yes, but when the real Jack Stern arrives, what shall I call him?"

"We will work something out."

"All right, can we eat? I'm famished." She replied without even sitting down.

"Let's go," Jack said as he stood up to join her.

The array of food was extensive; there were different types of continental sausages to choose from, fried bacon, crepes, fluffy scrambled eggs, Swiss style muesli, fresh and canned fruit and an assortment of fish, roasted tomatoes with herbs and a large assortment of cakes and pastries. All of this was presented in a garden setting of flowering geraniums in theme with the rest of the building.

"One of the women running the hotel is a mixture of French and Swiss that is why the food is so good. She has, in her own way, blended the best of both of these cultures and cuisines," Yvette pointed out, as she carefully positioned an assortment of food on her plate.

"You're very patriotic," Jack observed.

"The French are very chic, artistic and imaginative. They do things just for the love of life. It is not patriotism, but an appreciation of their passionate approach."

"I agree, I've had my share of French experiences." Jack commented as he remembered many of his previous sexual encounters

Yvette looked at Jack sideways, but thought nothing of his innuendo

"Here, try some of these petite sausages, oh and you must have the Swiss meatballs and some of this and some of that," she excitedly said as she pointed to the various dishes that bore a sexual reference.

Jack obeyed and soon found himself seated before an enormous mountain of food.

"Oh Father, didn't you know that gluttony is a sin?" She playfully said.

"Shall I put it back?" Jack replied as he pretended to appear embarrassed.

"Oh no, that won't be necessary, it is not as bad as it looks, it's quite light and delicious, you will be surprised." Yvette answered letting Jack off the hook.

Jack suddenly realised something. "You have an accent, which I hadn't noticed before, not very strong, in fact it is subtle and very mysterious."

"Sure it's not the surroundings Father, I mean Mr. Stern."

"Quite sure"

"Then you must be taking more notice of me." Yvette said as she continued to flirt.

Jack cautiously avoided the comment; he smiled and nodded and continued with his meal. They sat in relative silence as they ate and enjoyed their food; both contemplated their own individual situations with respect to each other. They made eye contact frequently and both overhead the same conversation from the adjoining table which caused them to react negatively.

"It's absolutely horrendous, how could such a thing happen?"

"I agree, to think that such a holy man was shot and killed, who would think."

Jack and Yvette turned in the direction of the two ladies

discussing the front page report of the morning's daily newspaper. The headlines read 'Catholic Priest Shot Dead'. Underneath it in bold letters 'Archbishop's life hangs in the balance'.

"Excuse me Yvette," he said as he stood up abruptly and briskly walked to where the ladies were seated.

"Excuse me, may I?" He politely asked.

"Yes, of course," one of them replied as she handed him the newspaper.

Jack glanced at the front page story and unemotionally digested its contents. Yvette appeared at his side and let out a muffled cry as the shock of the story hit her. Tears flooded her eyes and trickled down her cheeks. Sensing her anguish Jack produced a clean white handkerchief and dried her tears. The ladies looked on and admired his tenderness.

"Oh, what a wonderful gentleman," one of them said.

"Thank you Madame," he replied as he allowed Yvette to cry on his shoulder.

Once settled, he guided her back to their table.

"Do you think what we went through last night was related to what happened at the Archbishop's palace?" she asked as she walked with him.

"I don't know, I hope not, but one never knows, I am only the locum priest, I shouldn't think so."

"Perhaps your sermons about finding the power within upset someone," Yvette suggested "Perhaps a religious crank, maybe someone at the hospital, after all, it was the Matron and some of the security guards who came after you"

"Are you suggesting that they had something to protect?" Jack asked in an attempt to uncover Yvette's depth of understanding.

"I've heard nothing Mr. Stern." Yvette's tone of voice was convincing.

"All right then, we may have to be very careful, no telling what might happen next. No point worrying about it either. Let's finish breakfast and then plan our next move."

Yvette somewhat distant, lost in her own world of thought, reluctantly agreed. The remaining food on their plates had by now grown cold. They decided to finish the meal with pastries and coffee. What the newspaper story destroyed in mood the pastries restored, light seductive and addictive, they returned the sparkle back into the morning. Jack and Yvette both held a cup of hot coffee in their hands as they gazed into each other's eyes and reflected on the events of the previous days. The morning slowly dragged on, Jack broke the mood and looked at his watch, it was fast approaching 10:30am.

"More coffee Yvette…?"

"No thank you, I am quite full, perhaps later, however, I need to go to the toilet, if you would excuse me."

"But of course," he replied as he stood up in a gentlemanly fashion.

Within minutes of her departure a handsome young man entered the hotel, asked directions for the whereabouts of the restaurant and made a beeline for it. Jack recognised Brendan as he approached the waiter's station.

He gestured to Brendan and asked, "How much do I owe the taxi driver?"

"I have already taken care of it thank you."

"Have you had breakfast?" Jack asked in a caring tone of voice.

"Come to think of it, I haven't eaten for 24 hours, so yes, that would be a good idea."

"Better hurry, looks as though they are starting to clear things away."

Brendan hurriedly grabbed a large plate helped himself to what was left over.

Yvette meanwhile returned.

"Miss me?" She asked.

"Of course I did, we have company." Jack warmly replied.

"Your friend Jack Stern is here?"

"Yes, he is over there," Jack pointed to where Brendan was standing

"He is very handsome, how will I choose…"

Jack remained somewhat neutral and ignored the invitation to flirt.

Brendan returned. "I'm sorry I didn't know you had company."

"Yvette, may I introduce you to errr… Brendan O'Reilly," he said, hoping she would grasp the situation quickly.

"A pleasure Brendan," she said as she extended her hand

"And you might be?"

"Yvette, I am the housekeeper at Saint Pious."

"Really that's nice also a pleasure" he said as he accepted her hand and held it tenderly. He continued, "You must be one of the most attractive women I have ever seen."

"Have you seen a few?"

"In my travels…."

"What sort of work do you do?"

"I am a consultant to those seeking to improve their lives you could say." Brendan replied as he placed his breakfast on the table and pulled up a chair from an adjoining table.

Yvette looked at the real Jack Stern and secretly wished that he and the real Brendan O'Reilly could be switched around.

"So you are working in the area?" she continued.

"I have just finished a contract in Newburn, but I encountered a spot of trouble, that's why I am here, to ask Jack from some assistance," Brendan explained as he dug into his breakfast with relish.

"Speaking of trouble," interrupted Jack, "have you heard of the Monsignor's assassination?"

The shock of the word 'assassination' stopped Brendan eating momentarily. He quickly regained his composure and tried to make out that it had no effect on him. Yvette concluded otherwise.

"No I haven't, I've had my own survival to deal with, tell me more."

Jack described the reported events and then went on to tell, in graphic detail, of the attempts on his and Yvette's lives. They had caused Yvette some grief, yet she remained surprisingly unshaken by all of it.

"Considering what happened to me, I conclude that all of these events, including mine, are not isolated, but interconnected." Brendan replied and then he described the violent events that he had experienced in detail, except that he did not include his intercourse with the phantom priest, and the process of attunement and the gifts that he had discovered. That was better left for another day, if not by practical demonstration.

"Well then, I am sorry to say, it appears as if we are dealing with a Mafia style operation involving blackmail, money and drug laundering. Unfortunately it appears to involve high up members of the Catholic Church. The questions are: how big is it? Can we correct things? How far do we expose it bearing in mind the consequential ramifications?"

"You are not suggesting engaging in politics are you Mr. Stern?" Yvette asked. "If you are, that is wrong. Being of French stock I would say that it is freedom that must be satisfied, nothing else. People must not live a lie, shouldn't you act what you preach in your sermons, expose everything and everyone, the people have a right to know?"

Jack sensed a degree of moral anger in her voice. "I was only speaking out of concern for the church and all those whose faith may be shattered as a consequence."

"The church will not fail Mr. Stern she like the human body will cleanse itself of its parasites and continue on living, totally renewed, it is your duty to help with this process, what do you say?"

"That I am swayed by your argument."

Yvette was pleased by Jack's response

"But it will be very dangerous and I think it better if you were not involved. A fair maiden like yourself should be kept safe at all times." Jack then said

"I agree," Brendan said without any hesitation

"Very well then we had better sit down and work out some sort of strategy so to speak." Jack suggested and with that the trio left the restaurant and returned to the hotel suite.

25
DIVIDE AND DISGUISE

In the relative safety of the hotel suite for the next two hours, Jack, Yvette and Brendan discussed ways of saving all of the innocent bystanders that they had encountered. Brendan decided that it was his duty to rescue the ladies at The Infirmary as he had grown very fond of them, whilst Jack understood that it was his task to set the flock free from those conducting their aberrant business at St Pious. Both concluded that each had a duty in destroying the origins of the evil that prevailed at Longevity Plus.

"We cannot for one moment trust the police force, no telling how many of its members are involved. Therefore, matters become difficult for us under the present circumstances," Brendan concluded after weighing up all of the available evidence.

"Then you both need a disguise," suggested Yvette.

Brendan and Jack looked at each other and laughed together.

"Did I miss something?" Yvette asked rather perplexed as she was oblivious to their private joke.

"No, nothing at all," replied Jack, "but you are quite right, we need to stay very vigilant and as unrecognisable as possible."

"Where is the nearest town from here that has a store which

stocks theatrical makeup?" he asked.

"About 20 kilometres there is a very good magic and fancy dress shop that caters for such things."

"Excellent, we should aim to be there by lunch time."

"And miss out on the cuisine here, no Father, I prefer that we eat here, then we go," Yvette replied quite defiantly.

"Very well in that case, I suggest that you stay whilst Brendan and I go together."

"Well actually Father, I would prefer to stay here with Yvette, the thought of the fine food has seduced me." Brendan replied.

"Okay as it is almost lunchtime, off you two go. I need to make several telephone calls, might grab a bite before I go, so see you downstairs later," he said waving them away.

Once they had vacated the hotel suite Jack activated his phone and dialled out.

"Hello is Miss Sutton there please?"

"One moment sir….." An office worker at Global Balancing Act answered and put Jack on hold.

"Good morning." Julia Sutton professionally answered a minute later.

"Yes, it is still morning." Jack flippantly answered in a different tone of voice.

"How may I help you?" Julia asked unable to identify the caller.

"Miss Sutton, charming as always, how are you?" Jack responded in his normal voice

"Mr Stern I didn't recognize your voice what a marvellous surprise, we have all missed you sir."

"Is everything alright?"

"Yes sir, apart from two nasty looking gentlemen." Julia replied with a slight tremor in her voice

"Explain."

"They were here a few days ago and caused quite a scene. They were demanding to know your whereabouts." Julia replied as she relived the event in her mind

"Did you tell them anything?"

"How could we sir." Julia truthfully asked

"You couldn't because I didn't tell you…listen can you please do me a favour?"

"Yes sir of course I will you know that."

"Go to my private drawer and punch in the following code." Jack gave her a code number to key in that would deactivate the secured desk drawer and then he said "Once you open it retrieve a file marked 'Devious Disguise.'"

"Very well sir, give me just a moment." She politely answered

Jack could hear Miss Sutton's movements as she carried the cordless phone and obediently executed his instructions to the letter

"I have it sir."

"Excellent. Now see if you can find a photocopy of the Federal Health Department's Inspector Certificate."

"Yes, I have it."

"Excellent …. Can you fax it to me on the following number?" Jack asked and gave her the appropriate telephone number.

"Consider it done Mr. Stern anything else Sir?" She asked wishing that he would ask her out to dinner

"Nothing at all, thank you Miss Sutton, hopefully I will see you soon, goodbye."

Jack rang off. Miss Sutton sat at her desk, blissful at having spoken with her handsome boss whom she admired terribly but disappointed that her desire for romance had been ignored.

Meanwhile Jack telephoned the next number.

"Good morning, Archbishop's residence," greeted the priest on duty.

"Good morning Father, this is Father Brendan O'Reilly, whom can I speak to now that Monsignor is dead and the Archbishop critically ill?"

"Bishop Hoxley has stepped in during the emergency Father."

"May I speak with him?" Jack asked

"What parish are you from?"

"Presently at Saint Pious I was assigned here whilst Father Kelly went away on sabbatical."

"I will put you through, one moment please." Jack tuned his ear to pick up any whisperings that indicated the phone line was tapped.

"Good morning Father O'Reilly, Bishop Hoxley here. I believe we may have briefly met some time ago," The Bishop said in a rather distinguished well cultured voice.

"Yes we did," Jack replied bluffing.

"I hear you had a spot of trouble at Saint Pious?"

"The reason for my call Bishop, I believe it was a deliberate attempt on my life."

"Seriously?"

"Yes. I have chosen to go temporarily into hiding, can you help me?"

"Of course my son, we are well aware of your situation and have already sent people down to St Pious. Your voice sounds different to what I remember." The Bishop answered

"Probably the stress Bishop," Jack continued to bluff.

"Tell me my son, where are you calling from?"

"I am at the local police station."

Sensing that things were not quite right Jack terminated the call reflected for a moment and then he dialled the next number.

"Good morning, The Infirmary, Christina speaking, how may I help you?"

"Yes, my name is Isaac Rumplestein, I am wondering if Mr Jack Stern is available?"

"No I am sorry sir he is away on business you may speak to either Mr. Badcock or his secretary."

"Mr Badcock will do nicely thank you." Jack replied

"One moment please." Once again, Jack tuned his hearing to pick up any whisperings on the telephone line.

"Good morning Mr Rumplestein, Louis Badcock here, how may I help you?"

"Well, Mr Badcock, I heard on the grapevine that you were looking for suitable clients for your line of business."

"That might be the case."

"Well depending upon what you can offer, I might be persuaded to bring in a group of my colleagues for some R and R."

"Could you explain further?"

"Of course I will" Jack obliged. "I arrange medical conferences on all sorts of topics, I am thinking of holding one not far from Newburn. As a treat for my doctors who attend, especially those who are sexually frustrated by their wives lack of attention in the bedroom and other circumstances, I thought that your establishment could provide them with some extra-ordinary after dinner sweets."

"We can certainly do that. Have you seen our extensive menu?"

"The very reason I thought of you," replied Jack

"Excellent, the deal will include incentives for you which I cannot discuss over the phone. We can only do that in person, when can we meet?" Badcock greedily asked

"How about tomorrow afternoon....?"

"2:00pm suit you?"

"Yes that will be fine," Jack answered as he visualised Badcock rubbing his hands together.

"Before you go, I take it you know where to find us."

"I certainly do see you at 2:00pm Mr Badcock?" Jack dryly replied and then without any warning he disconnected the call and went downstairs to the restaurant.

Yvette was right the smell of the food was intoxicating to say the least. But Jack was strong there was a duty to perform, no time for procrastination. A quick bite to eat was all that he was prepared to allow himself no time for a long lingering luncheon today

Jack found Brendan and Yvette seated at the same table at which they had breakfast.

"Faaa…" Yvette stopped and corrected herself. "Mr Stern, I am terribly spoilt today, twice in one day I eat here, that is naughty, yes?" she said in an accent that was becoming increasingly inviting.

"And why not, I take it the food is better than you expected." He replied

"It is absolutely divine," interrupted Brendan.

"Here, try some" Yvette said as she offered a spoonful to Jack who willingly accepted it and thought that perhaps he should stay.

A waitress appeared by the table. "Will you be staying for lunch sir?"

"May I have a club sandwich and some coffee please?"

"But of course sir," she smiled as she took down his order.

"Well, what did you discover?" Yvette asked in a whisper as she bent forwards.

"That the Catholic church acts quickly, they have already sent a replacement to Saint Pious and want to know my whereabouts," he said, keeping the rest a secret.

"What did you tell them?"

"That I was safe at the police station." Yvette giggled whilst Brendan sat quietly.

"Police station, how outrageously funny," she continued to giggle

The waitress returned and placed Jack's order in front of him.

"I ordered a club sandwich not the Matterhorn," he said as he counted the number of layers in the carefully constructed sandwich.

"It will keep you going."

"That it will."

An hour later Jack was in Brendan's Ford motoring to the magic shop. Before he left, he had taken the precaution of altering the car's number plates with the use of black electrical tape.

As Jack drove he activated his mobile phone and punched in a number that illegally accessed the police radio channel. He had discovered previously that all communication systems, whether radio or telephone overlapped, and the degree became stronger as a result of advances in microwave technology. It was merely a matter of mathematics to connect the two. The police channel buzzed with all sorts of activity. A hunt was on for a couple who had broken into Saint Pious Presbytery, abducted the priest, and violently assaulted Longevity Plus' Matron and her boyfriend. Furthermore, the couple then attacked an off duty policeman and in their escape, rammed an ambulance and a tow truck whilst on an emergency call. A description of the car was being broadcast as well as the description of the likely culprits. Police are nothing more than a bunch of trouble makers Jack thought as he kept all of his senses on full alert. He then wondered if the media had started to sell the story. No mention in the morning paper, so perhaps it wasn't major enough or the police had asked to keep it hush hush; a matter they wanted to deal with quietly in their own way. Jack realised that the best way of not attracting attention was to act confidently and be out in the open which he thought was always the best place to hide.

The town of Spring Meadows was an enchanting midsized town. Its buildings' architecture reflected a very strong Scandinavian influence. It didn't take Jack very long to find the magic shop thanks to a combination of Yvette's directions and his extra-ordinary homing ability he was outside of the store within minutes of entering the town. A police car was parked on the opposite side of the street. The police officers were in the hardware store conducting personal business.

The multi-coloured sign on the magic store's windows read 'Mischievous Mayhem' indicating a shop seemingly filled with magical delights. Jack opened the door and stepped into a world of childish imagination with the exception that all everything was real and where thoughts became reality without limit. He made his way about the aisles choosing his needs and when ready, paid by credit card and left. From there, he made his way to the largest department store in the town and once he had located an appropriate changing room, created his new identity

Yvette and Brendan meanwhile once they had finished their meal had some spare time to occupy which they spent roaming around the vast national forest. Yvette showed Brendan some of her favourite meditation spots which she believed gave her the best opportunity of being as close to her god as possible. One of these was a clearing in the middle of the forest through which a stream fed by mountain snow ran.

"This is a very special place for me, look at the grass, it only grows here, see how soft it is and how velvety green it is. The four leaf clovers grow in perfect harmony with the other plants. Around the clearings edges grow the most beautiful wild flowers that blossom at all times of the year springtime is especially spectacular with berry bushes providing masses of fruit, it is a place to rejuvenate the soul and feed the body from nature's bosom" Yvette softly said as the sunlight caressed Yvette's blonde hair adding sparkle to it.

Brendan felt her childlike sensitivity and smiled.

"And you know what else grows here that no one seems to have discovered, a most unusual wild rose that produces a flower that only lasts one day. Its petals are intensely red in the middle and brilliantly white on the outside, its fragrance is a joy for the nostrils to behold, a mixture of rose and lily of the valley."

"Where is this bush?"

"Over there," she replied pointing to an empty spot.

Brendan saw nothing.

"Can't you see it?" she asked

"Not really."

"Then try this," she said, as she took a square piece of purple cloth from her pocket

Brendan looked at her quite confused.

"Stretch the cloth, look through it at the sky for about ten minutes and then look back at the spot."

Brendan felt quite silly, but nevertheless, did as she requested.

"Times up, now look at the spot." She said after counting for 10 minutes

Brendan stared in disbelief, there in its entire glory was the rose bush bearing unopened buds.

"When does it flower?"

"When you want it to."

"Pardon."

"It seems to me that it only flowers when it appreciates its true beholders," Yvette suggested

"Does that apply to all of the other bushes?"

"Wonderful….so you can see those as well, see I told you this was a magical place."

"How did you discover it?" Brendan asked feeling rather privileged for being taken there

"I followed my heart when it told me to explore the forest and this is what I found, but I think it is only beautiful if you have the proper heart and the eyes."

"How does the purple cloth work?" Brendan asked.

"I think it changes the makeup of your eyes so that you can see into the ultra violet." Yvette explained.

"So the world is fuller than I ever imagined" Brendan concluded.

"It certainly is by a factor of at least twenty times" she agreed.

Brendan had just learnt another lesson about life and completeness.

"I hope you now understand what it means to open one's eyes and ears and really discover the world in all of its magical glory."

"You certainly are a rare rose amongst women," Brendan commented.

Yvette thanked him for his compliment and when he had enough they walked back to Hotel Alpine.

26

GERIATRIC INVASION

Jack entered the lobby of the Chateau Alpine and hobbled towards the reception desk dragging his luggage behind him.

"Good morning," bellowed the big moustached desk clerk, in a strong Austrian accent, as he looked Jack up and down and grinned at his obvious struggle with his belongings.

"And to you to," replied Jack in a croaky voice as he stood slightly stooped over.

"Staying for a day or two sir?"

"Not quite, I am looking for a gentleman by the name of Jack Stern and his lady companion Yvette."

"Ahhh the exquisite Yvette, room 312 upstairs," the Austrian uncaringly answered as he played with his moustache and pointed to the stairs.

Jack nodded thanks and as he turned he muttered under his breath 'may your hairy lip be infested with a thousand fleas and scabies'

Jack disappointed the arrogant Austrian by avoiding taking the stairs and finding the elevator around the corner. Once upstairs, he walked briskly along the empty corridor to the suite and let himself in. It was empty, no signs of his colleagues.

He dropped his shopping by the settee, sat down and closed his eyes and proceeded to visualise the events of the next day in his mind, going through each one of them step by step with a sense of confident achievement. It was as if he had commanded the universe to obey his will and time to stand still.

"Excuse me, who are you?" asked Brendan as he stood in the doorway with Yvette by his side.

Jack stood up and turned to face the handsome priest, slightly stooped over he extended his hand ever so slowly.

"Pleased to make your acquaintance, my name is Isaac Rumplestein, the desk clerk let me in. I told them I was a personal friend of yours and your charming companion."

"He had no right to do that, I don't know who you are and I am pretty sure Yvette doesn't either," Brendan snapped back.

"Then perhaps you have a short memory and perhaps you should take a closer look."

Brendan looked at Yvette seeking guidance. "Yvette, do you know this man?"

Yvette gingerly stepped forward and cautiously looked intently at Jack. "No, I can't say I do," she replied

Jack stared at them and without any warning dug his fingernails into his face and started to rip away his disguise. Yvette yelped with fear as she watched the bizarre scene unfold before her, but when she finally saw who it was she happily applauded. "Absolutely brilliant, who did it for you?"

"I did." Jack unassumingly replied

"How absolutely wonderful, who taught you may I ask?"

"I encountered excellent makeup artists and teachers during my university years when I was studying drama."

"You're quite the actor then," she inferred.

"You could say that," Jack replied looking away.

"And so I suppose you want me to do the same." Brendan asked

"That's the general idea," Jack agreed as he went into the bathroom to wash his face and remove all traces of makeup.

"Supposing I told you I could go anywhere unnoticed." Brendan replied acting as though he was super smart

"I'd believe you. But how long can you can you keep it up for?" Jack ambiguously answered

"What do you mean?" Brendan asked a little despondent

"Only the masters know their true capabilities, a fledgling like you may fall before he can fly."

"Whom have you been talking to?" Brendan asked feeling a little insulted

"No one in particular, just expressing an opinion based on my extensive reading. In any case, let's not take any chances. Whatever gift you have, I suggest that you use it only in short bursts until you become proficient and that you rely on the disguise in the interim period." Jack replied in a manner not wishing to hurt the priest's feelings

Brendan thought about it for a while and agreed. He wondered whether Jack Stern was similar in nature to the phantom priest at St Pious a master soul of sorts but not letting on.

For the rest of the late afternoon, leading up to dinner, Jack demonstrated his makeup skills by expertly transforming Brendan's appearance into someone else with Yvette looking on and giving a suggestion here and there.

The trio decided to eat in by ordering room service. During the course of the meal they agreed that it would be safer for Yvette to stay at Chateau Alpine whilst Jack and Brendan conducted their recon-naissance the following day.

"I am sure the Austrian bell-hop will have something in store for you, I mean something for you to do around here while we're gone" Jack said as he stared deeply into Yvette's eyes.

"I told you, I am not that sort of girl, however if they do become short staffed I will certainly lend a hand It will be better than sitting around here and doing nothing."

"Speaking about lending a hand, I almost forgot, where did you intend sleeping tonight Jack?" Jack asked Brendan.

"I was going to book an adjoining room for a few days." Brendan genuinely replied not wishing to be an imposition

"I am willing to share my bed," Yvette innocently said "but which one of you would I feel or be the safest with, the priest or the handsome businessman?" She asked in a manner which suggested that although she wished to preserve her virginity she wanted to have some fun as well.

Early the next morning straight after breakfast Jack and Brendan, fully disguised, set off back to Newburn. The first port of call would be Newburn's Feel Good Pharmacy. Jack suggested its name was probably for the benefit of its owner and all those connected with him, rather than the recipients of its dubious goods that it flaunted as being beneficial to one's health and well being. Their journey was uneventful. Along the way, Jack did notice several unmarked police cars on patrol, but then he wasn't quite sure whether they were police or Mafia, it certainly was a thin line separating the two.

The pharmacy was smaller in area than Jack had anticipated; nevertheless it was packed with its traditional junk plus a smattering of supermarket lines making it very appealing to the gullible public. The best selling line it seemed was toilet paper, a veritable mountain of it, and better than supermarket prices. Keep your arse clean and you will never get sick. Now there's a good motto, thought Jack, as he surveyed his surroundings.

"It's early in the morning and already there is a long queue of brain washed people or should I call them sheep just busting to get their quota of magical bullets. Little do they know how much harm these so called medicines cause them, all they do is blow holes in your health system" Jack cynically whispered out of the corner of his mouth into Brendan's ear as they entered the pharmacy.

The heavily disguised pair walked slowly together towards the main serving area and waited patiently their turn to be attended to. A young freckle faced girl with a mass of vibrant red hair approached them.

"Good morning, welcome to Feel Good Pharmacy, how can I help you?" she asked bobbing her head up and down as though it was attached to her shoulders by a spring.

"Is the owner in?" Jack slowly asked in a deliberate and authoritative voice.

"He is, but he is very busy I don't think you can…"

"He may have to change that." Jack interrupted her midsentence

"Pardon…..?" She replied a little taken aback

Jack produced a business card which had printed upon it in bold letters 'George Striker, Chief Investigator Pharmaceutical Section Federal Health Department'.

"Show him that will you, it might just change his mind" he said as he feigned a smile.

The young girl faltered, took the card and ran into the dispensary.

Jack observed the owner furrowing his brow as he received Jack's official greeting card. He looked up and then suddenly disappeared into the adjoining storage room as though he was running away from something. The young girl not knowing what was going on came down and apologised.

"Mr. Sandrino won't be long."

"Neither will we" Jack calmly replied

He looked at Brendan who telepathically confirmed that he knew what he was expected to do.

A few minutes later Sandrino emerged from the storage area looking a little ruffled nevertheless he came down to attend to his unexpected guests.

"Good morning Mr Striker and…?"

"Mr. J Backhouse," Brendan answered in a monotone voice.

"How can I be of assistance?" Sandrino asked as he forced a downward smile.

"We are here on a routine check." Jack coldly answered

"I've just had one just weeks ago." Sanrino answered questioning the need for another unnecessary inspection.

"That might be the case however; we are the real auditors who audit the auditors if you know what I mean." Jack unemotionally replied as he stared at Sandrino who appeared somewhat uneasy

Sandrino nodded nervously that he understood.

"May we?" Jack asked, as he manoeuvred himself behind the counter, with Brendan following closely behind.

The trio stepped up into the elevated altar like dispensary. Two dispensing assistants continued on with their work, neither one daring to look up. Sandrino tried to hide his anxiety as he shuffled about vetting completed prescriptions.

Brendan and Jack stood in the middle of the dispensary and idly made notes. Jack then checked the dispensing books, measuring and weighing equipment whilst Brendan calmly slipped away and disappeared into the storeroom.

Once there he stood quite still, and after intoning OMRA, mentally used his new found vision to scan the walls of the room but did not detect anything unusual.

A young female shop assistant walked past him, oblivious of his presence. Brendan watched as she entered the female lavatory. After a while she emerged and walked into the staff common area, again, nothing unusual.

He checked to see if the male toilet was empty satisfied that it was he let himself in and found nothing unusual Brendan then cautiosly entered the female toilet that the female assistant had a moment ago used. In contrast to the male toilet it was large and spacious with four cubicles and a generous makeup area. A mirror stretched along the entire wall facing the cubicles. Brendan peered at the mirror and saw faces on the other side. Behind the mirror was a large rectangular room with no windows, nor apparent doors. In the centre was a long stainless steel table with a conveyor belt upon it. This ran through a large box with dials indicating temperature and frequency settings and measurements of a monitoring kind. The conveyor belt had trays of ampoules on it and it moved quite slowly at about 2cm per minute. Brendan calculated it took 20 minutes for the vials to go through some sort of alteration process. Once cool, each vial was taken out of their tray and placed into packets of tampons. These were then packed into cartons and neatly stored in a corner of the room.

To Brendan's surprise a young lady emerged from the end cubicle, which had previously been empty, she walked past him without taking any notice. Brendan waited for her to vacate the toilet and then he entered the cubicle from where she came. There appeared to be nothing unusual about it, he fiddled with all of the cisterns' buttons, but nothing happened. He toyed with the toilet roll holder, still nothing. Then as he leant against the door closing it he accidentally touched the coat hanger and the back of the cubicle came to life. The cistern fell onto the floor, the wall flipped up, lights flashed in the darkness of the opening alerting staff to incoming persons. Brendan hesitated to advance, he did an about face and left.

"Who's there?" one of the chemists loudly asked as he walked towards the open toilet seeing nothing, he activated the internal security switch which closed the opening. "Probably a malfunction," he mumbled once he was satisfied that no one was there.

Brendan rejoined Jack who was involved in an intense investigative discussion with Mr Sandrino who appeared to have all the correct technical and regulatory answers.

Jack turned to Brendan and asked, "Everything that you looked at in order?"

"It would seem so sir."

"Right then, Mr Sandrino and his operation here appears to conform, except for a few minor irregularities that I detected and which I am sure he will be willing to rectify."

Jack then faced Sandrino and said, "Isn't that right Mr Sandrino?"

"Yes, it is." Sandrino replied glad that his ordeal was about to end

"Good then We'll finish up here by checking out the shop."

"Be my quest" Sandrino answered and remained in the dispensary

"Very kind of you," Jack replied, as he and Brendan stepped down into the shop area.

They examined the shelves behind the counter that were stocked with numerous poisonous substances otherwise known as so called medicines, and then they looked at the freestanding gondolas. Brendan became preoccupied with the condoms', pregnancy tests and personal lubricants' section but stopped what he was doing when a familiar gruff voice behind him rang out.

"Excuse me."

Brendan stepped forward and made way. From the corner of his eye he identified the voices owner as being none other than Louis Badcock who went up to the counter and asked to see Sandrino who came down in an instant

"Mr Sandrino, two cartons of tampons please on our account."

Brendan initially didn't know what to do, but then decided to act normally so as not to attract any attention. He also walked up to the counter and stood next to Badcock.

"Yes sir?" the shop assistant asked.

"A packet of sugarless chewing gum please," Brendan asked, as he stood next to Badcock, who seemed to have regained most of his arrogant aggressiveness since their last encounter. The only bruise to his ego it appeared was his heavily bandaged hand.

"Looks nasty," Brendan said in a raspy voice.

Badcock grunted a reply of sorts that had nothing to do with his injury.

Brendan looked at him in the eye as he accepted and paid for his gum. Badcock reacted almost immediately his eyes narrowed, his pupils constricted and his mouth tightened as though he had recognised a foe.

Sandrino meanwhile returned with the two cartons of tampons as requested by badcock. This distracted Badcock which allowed Brendan to slip away and find Jack without further delay.

"Who is that old man?" Badcock asked noticeably rattled.

"He is from the Federal Health Department, didn't quite catch his name. The main guy is G Striker."

"Any problems?"

"Not at all the operation's too tight and too clean always kept that way for the likes of them." Sandrino answered in a shifty tone of voice

"Excellent." Badcock said in a distant frame of mind

'You seem perturbed."

"I think I know that guy," Badcock said feeling a little uneasy as he nursed his injured hand and remembered how the injury happened.

"Probably an old customer from way back."

"No much more recent than that something about his eyes."

"Considering what you have been through similar looking eyes will most likely cause the same a reaction, that's all it is."

"You're probably right," Badcock agreed as he put the parcels under his right arm and thought no more about the incident.

Back in the car Brendan told Jack about the clandestine operation that he had discovered at the back of the pharmacy.

"Why do you think Badcock collected two boxes of the mysterious ampoules?" Jack asked

"I hope it is not for the girls," Brendan replied a little concerned about their safety.

"I shouldn't think so, in any case, did any of them exhibit any sort of strange behaviour when they were sexual therapists?" Jack asked

"Not at all." Brendan answered

"Badcock may be using the substances either himself or on someone else or simply trafficking them. We need to obtain a sample so that we know what we are dealing with. Pity you didn't do that back at the pharmacy."

"Guess I became a little scared." Brendan freely admitted

"That's normal in the beginning."

"You seem to know a lot about this. Let me guess, it's from your readings."

"Exactly how are we doing for time?" Jack answered changing the subject

"11:00am."

"A good time for brunch and costume change you need to lose at least 20 years old man." Jack teased the handsome priest

"You should talk."

Jack laughed at his response as he started the car and drove it to the next stop namely Longevity Plus

"Why are we going there?" Brendan asked out of frustration "I can understand the pharmacy and in any case what are we going to do once we find out what their up to do we alert the authorities?"

"Not quite. I thought that we might shut them down ourselves."

"Are you crazy?" Brendan asked as he tried to grasp the magnitude of the situation.

"Should I be? Where is your faith? What about the story of David and Goliath?"

"It's only a story." Brendan fired back

"You mean it's not fact?" Jack flippantly replied which caused Brendan to become increasingly confused and frustrated.

"How can two ordinary men?"

"Who says you're ordinary? Will you finally accept and recognise who you are and what you are capable of doing" Jack answered in a strong tone of voice

Brendan remained silent. And brooded for a minute

"How does it feel to be a criminal on the run?" Jack then asked.

"I'm not a criminal." Brendan defiantly said as he crossed his arms across his chest.

"The law says you are."

"Where did you get that idea from?"

"From this," Jack replied, as he produced his mobile phone and connected it to the police channel.

Brendan listened for a moment and said. "It's all lies what are they saying."

"Jack Stern, the owner of The Infirmary, is sought on charges of aggravated assault, possibly attempted murder. He is extremely dangerous, Federal Authorities have also been alerted" The police channel barked.

"What did I tell you!" jack remarked without a care in the world and obviously loving the attention.

"How can they?"

"It's easy; they make it up as they go along. Don't you know what man-made law is all about?"

"No." Brendan replied naively.

"Bully tactics."

"Imagine if there were no man-made laws, there would be no criminals." Jack comically said.

"How would you control the people?"

"With love Brendan I believe that everyone is born good and innocent, it is law that makes them bad, whether it is civil or church it does not matter and furthermore, it depends upon where you live and in what country of the world you live and, what religion or beliefs you have been exposed to."

The reality of Jack's dialogue hit Brendan hard "Wonderful philosophy, but where is it going to get us?" he asked.

"The answer you are seeking lies in the meaning of the word 'philosophy'."

"Which is?"

"Dealing with the truth, when you understand that concept, you will be free to act without reservation and no problem or challenge will ever seem impossible. So think about it, come up with a solution to the task of freeing all those that you care for in Newburn."

Brendan dwelt on Jack's words as he drove for several streets and then turned into the parking lot of Newburn's central shopping centre.

Jack spied a police car parked in a disabled bay and decided to position his car in the empty space next to it.

"What are you doing?" Brendan asked.

"Hiding us, why?"

Jack turned off the car and got out with Brendan following gingerly. Jack led the way to the food hall and went directly to the Japanese counter selling sushi.

"May we have two deluxe sushi trays and two servings of seaweed please" He said to the man behind the counter.

"Ah yes sir," replied the Asian shop assistant, as he grabbed the pre-packed trays from the refrigerated glass display cabinet. "Chopsticks sir?"

"Yes please."

"Ahh, thank you. That will be $36 please."

Jack paid the man and with trays in hand, led Brendan to a relatively quiet table in the middle of the eating area.

"Now enjoy."

Brendan looked at his meal and then at Jack who was already relishing his food. Brendan copied Jack's every move, poured a little soy sauce from the supplied sachet, then applied a flake of ginger and then put some green stuff on top. He grabbed his portion of sushi awkwardly with his chopsticks and somehow managed to find his mouth, much to Jack's amusement who watched with anticipation of Brendan's reaction. Brendan's nostrils instantly flared, his eyes watered, he momentarily stopped breathing, his mouth was on fire, he was speechless and yet the tortured look on his face said it all.

"Been wasabied my friend, not a good idea to drink water, makes it worse, try the seaweed," Jack said containing his laughter.

Brendan quickly obeyed and consumed a copious amount of the seaweed. He closed his eyes and waited for the assault on his senses to subside.

Jack meanwhile left and purchased a carton of milk and on his return offered a glass of it to Brendan.

"This will also help. You were very adventurous with the Wasabi my friend. Let me show you how it is done. Obviously you haven't come across this before and I thought you were a priest of the world."

Jack then demonstrated the safe underpowered approach of eating it which Brendan quickly mastered, enabling him to enjoy the remainder of his meal.

"Quite satisfying and yet it isn't, if you know what I mean," Brendan quietly deduced once he had finished eating.

"Quite so, a Japanese enigma one would say."

"So what's for dessert?"

"There's plenty to choose from, a chic patisserie over there, waffles and cream from the Gelare shop, or chocolates from that exclusive Chocolatier."

"I could enjoy this life." Brendan freely admitted without feeling any guilt or shame

"There is nothing wrong with it, in fact I don't think for one moment the good lord wants us to be poor considering the wealth the world has to offer."

"Can I have waffles and cream and chocolate," Brendan asked, like a little boy completely captivated by the excitement of it all.

"But of course." Jack answered and accommodated the priest's request and then allowed Brendan to thoroughly enjoy his dessert uninterrupted. Afterwards while they were both partaking of chocolates and cappuccino coffees he asked, "Have you given any thought to the challenge at hand?"

"No, but I think that all I'll need to do is ask for divine guidance."

"Very well, I am relatively happy with that idea. Would you like anything else or are you finished?" Jack asked as he dismissed Brendan's suggestion as being nonsense in his mind.

"Just about I've got another two mouthfuls to go"

"Good, after that let's go to the public toilets and change our appearances." Jack suggested

They emerged thirty minutes later looking quite different in all aspects, face, hair and teeth

"It's getting on Brendan" Jack said as he looked at his watch "I think we should split up for now. I'll drop you off at Longevity Plus where you can obtain samples of the vials that you saw at the pharmacy, I'll meanwhile visit Badcock at the Infirmary and wet his appetite with the prospect of delivering a big bunch of new clients and then we'll meet up at the pharmacy after you have obtained samples of the vials that you saw being treated so that we can estimate the size of their operation"

"That sounds great, but how will I get back to the pharmacy?"

"Walk of course, it's not far, about two kilometres at the most, should only take you about half an hour." Jack almost cold heartedly replied

Brendan reluctantly agreed and with that they both departed.

27

WINE INTO WATER

Jack drove Brendan's white Ford into The Infirmary's crowded parking lot. Busy time of the day, he thought, as he looked for a vacant parking bay. Poor girl, he thought, as he spotted his timeless lady standing alone looking quite forlorn. He wished he could whistle to summon her as one would do with a well trained horse, there was no doubt she was obedient, but to respond to a whistle, perhaps that was going a little too far into the realms of fantasy. But then again, one really never knows, especially when some aficionados claim that a Ferrari has a heart and soul. The girls were not the only ones that needed rescuing.

Jack parked the car, locked it and went over to say hello to his timeless lady he was oblivious of the fact that he was being watched from an upstairs window by a dark sinister figure.

"Won't be long," he whispered, as he ran his hand over the left front fender. 'A little dirty maybe, otherwise she looks good shape and appears to be raring to go' he imagined.

"Lovely car, is it yours?" asked an elderly gentleman, who was beaming with sexual satisfaction as he walked past.

"Unfortunately not, like you I'm just admiring it." Jack convincingly fibbed

"Going indoors for a bit?"

"Sort of" Jack once again fibbed

"They're extra good today; don't know whether it's them or something I ate or drank, I feel like I could do it again and again, not bad for a 70-year old, hey what."

Jack nodded and walked away. Not wishing to hear any more as he did not have any time for men boasting about their sexual conquests.

"Strange fellow," muttered the satisfied stranger, as he adjusted his sexual apparatus and felt it stir again.

Jack meanwhile entered The Infirmary through the rear door and casually made his way to reception.

"Good afternoon sir, I shan't be a moment," the young lady said as she adjusted her head-set and made eye contact with Jack Stern.

"Yes, we can certainly do that, please ring us on the day to confirm numbers Thank you for calling The Infirmary and have a nice day." She said after which she clicked off and removed the telephone headset.

Jack cleared his throat. "I am here to see Mr Badcock."

"You will find him upstairs on the first level. Take the elevator, his office is easy to find."

"Thank you," he replied as he looked upwards in the general direction of the office and then clumsily went through the motions of pretending to be a stranger to the complex.

Brendan meanwhile had arrived at the gates of Longevity Plus and had already assumed invisibility.

"Come in sir, are you Mr Rumpelstein?" Badcock's secretary asked as Jack appeared at the office door.

"I am," Jack answered "somewhat early I'm afraid." He apologised

"That doesn't matter" Badcock's secretary warmly replied. "Louis is eagerly expecting you," she added, and she ushered Jack into Badcock's plush office. It was more lavishly appointed than Jack remembered. On a side table fresh coffee was brewing and a plate of pastries awaited selection.

"Come in Mr Rumpelstein please sit and make yourself comfortable"

"Thank you" Jack replied in an elderly voice as he sat down. Jack peered at Louis Badcock over his glasses and looked beyond Badcock's flamboyant dress and his nakedness. The soul of a greedy, ruthless and sadistic man was clearly evident and with it came its own distinctive smell which assaulted jacks nostrils.

"Coffee and pastries…?" Badcock asked as he pointed to the side table.

"That would be nice."

"Sugar and cream in your coffee….?"

"Two sugars please, thank you."

Badcock attended expertly to Jack's request. Jack looked about the office as Badcock placed the tray before him. Jack took a sip of his coffee

"Okay?"

"Rather good, tastes of a fine Columbian Mocha blend."

"Your taste buds are very accurate Mr Rumpelstein or may I call you Isaac?"

"Please do."

"Your medical colleagues that you mentioned on the telephone how many do you have to cater for?"

"At this stage between 50 to 100 and it will probably be closer to 100."

Badcock licked his lips and asked "What sort are they?"

"Oncologists actually, I've arranged a symposium on a unique pharmaco-pharmacognosy approach to the treatment of various aggressive cancers."

"How interesting"

"Many of the doctors are sexually frustrated as you may appreciate, working ridiculous hours being married to socialites who flaunt their husbands' reputations and money only a handful remain faithful and fit the description of the loyal suffering husband. I thought that although some may already have girlfriends on the job or on the side, they were entitled to after dinner treats, especially the ones that your fine establishment has on its menu"

"When did you intend bringing the boys over?" Badcock asked with a greedy smile.

"Within 48 to 72 hours. Firstly, I have to make certain personal discreet approaches and then organise the appropriate transportation. I don't think they want to arrive en masse, most will prefer some form of heavily disguised non- descript private taxi. Also there would not be any meals involved; it would be straight down to it with measures taken to ensure that their identity remains anonymous and is kept secret at all costs."

"No problem," Badcock assured Jack who remained unconvinced.

"That remains to be seen Louis, for although I have heard of this place, I need to check it out personally."

"Very well, the girls are coming up to their lunch break. I shall arrange a personal tour to confirm our discretionary capabilities."

Quite the polished pimp thought Jack as he then drained his cup of coffee and dusted the crumbs off his clothes. "Shall we go then, no point wasting any further time?" Jack asked as he stood up

Badcock jumped to his feet at the suggestion and escorted Jack out of the office to the girls' working area. As they walked he explained the procedures that would be followed. Jack listened as he took careful note of the building's electronic security. They went up to the next level by the staircase. Badcock glanced at his watch. "They are probably in their common room having a bite to eat."

"Are they ever let out?" Jack asked insinuating that in some respects they were treated no better than captured animals.

"Once in a while if they are good otherwise they live like caged pussies, helps to bring out the animal in them, the clients like that. We usually take them on group outings and let them go home twice a year, if they have a home to go to that is."

"Quite sad" Jack genuinely replied

"No sentiments please Isaac, they are well looked after as you will find."

They reached the working girls common room door. Badcock didn't bother knocking he simply barged in. The girls, conditioned by his rude behaviour didn't even pause to look up; they continued to eat in silence until Jack entered the room. Then they paid attention to him.

"Stay seated ladies, I am just showing this customer around the complex," Badcock roughly said in a firm and loud voice

Jack used his customer privilege and stepped in front of Badcock and to introduce himself.

"Hello ladies, I am Isaac Rumpelstein, how are you today?" he asked in a gentle voice.

"None of your business you stinking Jew!" Naomi and Felicity both hissed out of disrespect.

Badcock who was near nearby raised his hand and was about to violently slap both of them in the face.

Jack quickly interrupted and said "Not Jewish."

"With a name like that you certainly are," they hissed again.

"I understand your assumption. I may have a name suggesting it however, my mother was a Christian and my father was only part Jewish, I never practiced nor was I expected to adopt that religion"

"Then change your name, you might find life easier as so many cunning Jews have cleverly found out."

"Perhaps one day I will if and when I meet a crazed Arab intent on killing me."

"Isaac, girls, that's enough interaction for now, we're not here to discuss politics nor religion, girls get on with your meals" Badcock abruptly said as he took Jack's arm and forcibly escorted him out of the room.

Badcock's actions gave Jack a chance to ascertain Badcock's strength something which he would remember for future reference.

"Spritely lot, quite vicious with their tongues, obviously good at oral," Jack commented as he walked briskly away from the girl's common room.

"The best there is." Badcock as a matter of fact bluntly answered

"Are they medically checked on a regular basis?"

"Every month to the day."

"Excellent."

"Anything else you want to know?" Badcock roughly asked looking quite annoyed.

"Not really, only how much you intended charging."

"That depends upon what level of experience you want your doctor friends to have."

"Explain."

"We have at our disposal a modified pharmaceutical grade drug when given at the correct dose heightens sexual pleasure."

"Which one might that be?"

"That's rather secret but if you must know, considering your background, a combination actually of altered pethidine and venlafexamine. The chemist who discovered this was brilliant, too brilliant and sadly took his own life."

"That's terrible, so how does it work?" Jack asked as he pretended to show sympathy

"It appears to be based on the fact that pethidine causes euphoria, and the altered venlafexamine produces the right amounts of brain neuro-transmitters in the right parts of the brain dealing with sexual response, whammo, huge orgasms." Badcock explained in simplistic terms

"Congratulations. Sounds like a world first; a veritable gold mine in the making and highly addictive I would imagine. What if you increase the dosages does it cause still bigger whammos?"

"No quite, in fact a different response. So M.r Rumpelstein now you know why our establishment is so highly regarded and sought after by our clients."

"What about adverse drug reactions, especially those allergic to opiates?"

"We checked that out, every client is given a questionnaire which they must complete before the fun starts."

Badcock produced a sample of it from his jacket's side pocket and handed it over.

"Very professional indeed I do think that we can do business." Jack replied as he examined the piece of paper

"There is something else Mr Rumpelstein you might like to consider."

"And that is?"

"Besides giving you a commission for your generous support, there is another activity that we are involved in, perhaps we could go back to my office and I will explain it to you."

"Very well, I am all ears."

Badcock and Jack walked together in silence back to the office. Once they reached it Badcock locked the door behind them and walked towards the window overlooking the car park. He stood with his hands behind his back. Jack decided to stand next to him.

"Isaac," he said and paused momentarily to clear his throat. "This fine establishment, besides the obvious, is also a recruiting station."

"You want to recruit me?"

Badcock ignored Jack's flippant query.

"My instincts tell me," Badcock said as he looked at Jack with a steady gaze "that as we constantly recruit doctors to help us with Longevity Plus you might be interested in assisting our endeavours."

"How?"

"By asking them to refer their patients to take advantage of Longevity Plus's excellent health facilities; so if you could put forward some names, we will take it from there and reward you handsomely with a spotter's fee even if nothing comes of it."

"What makes Longevity Plus better than other hospitals?" Jack asked playing along

"Its record of cures."

"Really?"

"Yes, the names we are looking for are not specialists, but ordinary GPs who would refer cancer patients or other serious conditions to our team of experts."

"For the patient's benefit?" Jack quickly deduced

"But of course." Badcock smugly replied

"I can't give you an answer straight away based on face value and the love of money. It needs my careful investigation and consideration; after all, it is people's lives that we are dealing with as well as the doctor's reputations."

"Well said, perhaps I misjudged you, here take some literature, it will help you to decide," Badcock replied, as he produced an impressive folder dealing with Longevity Plus' world-wide reputation.

Jack gingerly accepted the material and pretended to look slightly disturbed. "On the other matter if we could come to an agreement on price I can then leave and contact you as I previously indicated within 48 to 72 hours with the confirmed numbers."

As they haggled to and fro Jack continued to act as though he was disturbed was gave Badcock the impression that he was a somewhat genuine gentleman. Jack wished that Brendan had been present there with him.

It was becoming increasingly easier for Brendan to access and maintain his gifts and with this, came the realisation that through the process of attunement, he could access other abilities as well.

Jack's wish came true; the events with Badcock effortlessly transmitted themselves to Brendan who received them without surprise.

The images enabled him to describe his course of action in a seemingly divine way. The air at Longevity Plus was still quite still, not a leaf, nor blade of grass moved. The guards were also lethargic and not entirely observant. However, you would have had to be blind to miss the movements of the mysterious Brendan as he meandered his way into the side entrance of the complex that led to the storehouse of drugs.

The fallen leaves, and the other dead matter that lay on the ground, scattered before him as he went and then they returned to their original positions once he had passed.

The artificially sick people who were outdoors witnessed the events and thought themselves crazy and the guards who were alert thought themselves to have sunstroke. Brendan sensing their reactions giggled. Inside the complex his movements went totally unnoticed even the opening and closing of doors by him did not attract any attention. Soon he found himself in the empty mortuary. No bodies there, only drawers full of boxes of pethidine and venlafexamine. He opened one and looked at it intently and perceived that it was different in vibration to those that he saw at the pharmacy. These are unaltered, he concluded. But why he questioned in his mind. The pharmacy alters them and some find themselves at The Infirmary, but these here get picked up by a laundry truck and go where? Is there a black market for these drugs? Are they being used for some other purpose? I wish I knew. In any case, what better way is there, of finding out who may be involved, than by doing this? He then opened all of the drawers and proceeded to stand in the middle of the room.

Brendan summoned all of his confidence and continually intoned OMRA following by TORHOR as he opened out his arms and closed his eyes. With intense concentration he visualized being not so much in command of the ampoules' contents, but rather in sympathy with them, and accordingly attracted their attention and obedience. It is not proper, the use for which you are intended, and therefore I ask of you to change your form and return to your base elements. The molecules considered, analysed and obeyed rendering themselves into a soup of carbon, hydrogen, oxygen and nitrogen all harmless in their primordial state.

Brendan thanked them for their consideration and waved the drawer shut as he heard the door handle behind him turn.

The same orderlies that Brendan had once seen before came in and proceeded to load the boxes of ampoules into empty laundry bags. Once completed they took these out to the laundry truck and whisked them away, except this time Brendan decided to accompany the truck by walking next to it, as it drove slowly towards the main gates. Once there, the duty guards waved it through, oblivious of Brendan's presence as he walked past both of them completely unnoticed.

The truck's signage changed as it rounded the corner. From the top of the side panels a canvass unrolled itself to display 'The Gourmet Fruit and Vegetable Company, Head and Roots above the Rest'. Rooted would have been more appropriate, Brendan thought. Oops, did I really think that, oh well, welcome to the real world. "Hope you enjoy the water," he sniggered as he waved them goodbye.

On the same road but in the opposite direction a white Ford driven by Jack Stern came towards the handsome priest. Seeing the invisible Brendan standing by the road side Jack flashed the car's headlights and stopped near him.

"How did you see me?"

"With my eyes," Jack innocently replied

"I am supposed to be invisible."

"To most people you are."

"Let me guess, it's from your extensive reading that you can see me."

"Did you get the samples?" Jack asked without giving any further explanation.

"No."

"But I thought that we had agreed that you would." Jack replied a little irritated by the priest's lack of action

"Yes, I know, however, I discovered that the ampoules in the hospital were unaltered."

"That's interesting, they must have two distribution drug networks going, and by not keeping all of their eggs in the same basket, they're conducting a good business practice called diversity," Jack concluded

"I wouldn't know," answered Brendan.

"Come on Brendan the Catholic Church acts in the same way it is one enormous business, the best that there is, you should know differently."

Brendan reacted in a hostile manner. "We've discussed this before and in any case, what do you mean or should I ask hinting at?"

Jack looked Brendan in the eye, "It runs on feeding its customers guilt, fear and empty promises, quite sporting isn't it. Now if it taught the Christ principle properly then that would be different."

"What do you mean, 'the Christ principle'?"

"Oh come on, you should know what I am talking about. I have taught this before. Jesus was a Christ and he came to teach the principle."

Brendan looked at Jack blankly.

"For god's sake Brendan, you have that ability within you."

"I thought they were simply supernatural powers."

"They are, but they have a name. Look my friend think about it. In the sense of what you have been able to do, put them all together and what do you have?"

"That reminds me." Jack looked at Brendan steadily and said "Yes"

"I changed all of the ampoules into water."

"Brilliant, absolutely brilliant, what a clever idea that should flush them out seems like you have completed our work here let's go and see how Yvette is doing."

"Wait a minute, now that I know what I have, can we please stop by the pharmacy for a moment? In the true missionary spirit, I need to do more conversions."

28

SUBSTANDARD GOODS

At Longevity Plus the small dark sinister figure answered the call to attend Longevity Plus's surveillance room at 3:00am in the morning.

"What's the problem?" it shouted as it almost kicked the door open.

Startled by its violent entry one of the guards on duty nervously answered. "We have observed strange goings on in the mortuary earlier today. The videotapes are ready to go if you would like to have a look."

"Go ahead," it whispered in a low growl.

The picture of the mortuary room formed on the monitor. All was still and then the door mysteriously opened and closed it itself then nothing.

"That's it?" the small dark figure roughly asked.

"There's more, fast forward to 12/41," the security guard answered. The monitor showed all of the cadaver doors opening to their full extent again it seemed by their own accord and then nothing.

"Probably a malfunction of some sort," the small dark figure barked.

"I don't think so, look what happens at 12/81, all of the drawers shut simultaneously."

"So what do you think that we have here, ghosts? It is a malfunction nothing else," The small dark figure answered annoyed at being summoned so early in the morning

"I am not so sure," the security guard answered and was about to put forward his own theory when the phone rang.

"Hello, control room," the other guard answered. "Yes one moment, I will hand you over. For you," he gestured as he handed the cordless phone to the small dark figure.

"Hello, what do you want? What do you mean nothing?" It violently barked

Silence pervaded as the small dark figure listened intently to the chemist on the other end of the line. The small dark figure became pale and then reddened with rage, slamming the phone down almost breaking in two as it shouted "Get out get out now! I need to talk in private."

The security men left hurriedly. Making no apologies for its action the small dark figure continued with the telephone conversation.

"This not only means that will we lose big dollars and have supply problems, but that the new contract is in jeopardy as well, damn it, did you check everything?"

"Yes" the chemist flatly replied

"And…" The small dark figure coarsely said as it sought further information

"As you know, the pethidine and venlafexamine are crucial to the process even though they account for less than one percent of the total content. It's the chemical molecules that they supply which makes the final product what it is, namely the best hallucinogenic substance there is. For each batch to fail simply means that there would not have been any pethidine or venlafexamine in the ampoules. We had some left over so we checked and found nothing but water."

"So what are you saying?" The small dark figure asked.

"Someone has decided to become greedy and sold out to another competitor or we have been sabotaged."

"Whom do you suspect?" the small dark figure asked as it decided in its own mind who in its circle of business associates the likely culprit or culprits were likely to be.

"I think we need to look at the source and all those involved, including storage and transport."

"I agree, you check from your end and I will check from here," the small dark figure replied and signed off abruptly.

At 5:30am, whilst it was still dark, the telephone rang at the residence at Newburn's Feel Good Pharmacy's owner, Mr Sandrino. His wife stirred out of her blissful sleep and answered the call.

"Hello, who is this?" she asked lazily. "One moment please," she replied as she shook her sleeping husband.

"Wake up darling, it's the police."

"Huh, what did you say, police?"

"Yes, they are on the phone," she said as she passed the handset to her bleary eyed husband

"Hello, Sandrino here."

"Good morning Mr Sandrino there has been a disturbance at the pharmacy, we need your attendance right away."

"Oh, very well, I will be there as soon as I can."

Sandrino cradled the phone, shook the cobwebs out of his head, and made for the adjoining bathroom.

"Anything serious?" asked his wife.

"Don't know, shouldn't think so, the pharmacy is very secure as you know but they still want me there God knows why," he bitterly replied, as he washed his face and surveyed his unshaven features. "Looks like I had better go."

"Don't be long," she said lovingly.

"Be back before breakfast, promise," he replied, as he walked back into the bedroom and looked for his clothes from the previous day.

"In any case, it's probably some electronic fault, something very simple. God knows why the security company couldn't attend to this, unless they don't have their set of keys," he continued to grumble, as he put on a pair of casual slacks and a thick cotton jumper.

He slipped on a pair of worn out joggers, grabbed his car keys and then gently kissed his wife on the cheek and swiftly departed.

"Now longer than half an hour?" she indirectly wanted him to promise.

"Okay, see you soon."

The Feel Good Pharmacy had certainly been good to him and would continue to do so providing he obeyed. He enjoyed a very rich lifestyle, complete with all of its trappings. Thanks to his university degree and more importantly to his shady connections. As he drove his top of the range Jaguar automobile he wondered why his presence was at all required this morning, it was most unusual the next ten minutes would reveal all.

The pharmacy appeared deserted as he drove up to it. No obvious police presence at all. The building appeared intact. He parked the car, armed it electronically, and approached the pharmacy's main entrance.

The doors simultaneously opened and a voice commanded, "Come in Mr Sandrino, close the doors behind you and follow me, the small dark one is expecting you."

Sandrino completely free of any guilt or fear followed obediently into the dimly lit secret laboratory situated behind the female toilet.

"Good morning Mr Sandrino," growled the small dark figure.

"A pleasure to see you again," he happily responded

"I cannot say likewise," it acidly replied as it stared menacingly at the unsuspecting chemist

"What seems to be the problem?" Sandrino asked a little uncertain of the circumstances.

"It seems someone has decided to become very, very greedy and tamper with our joint operation."

"That's news to me."

"Are you certain of that?" the small dark figure asked in a threatening fashion.

"I am"

"We're not so convinced, Franz tell him of your findings."

Franz cleared his throat. "All of the ampoules picked up from Longevity Plus were nothing but water. The altered ampoules from here are nothing but water, and yet the ampoules retained as batch samples are okay, so the question is, who switched the goods?"

"You want me to help find out?" Sandrino asked quite innocently.

"We have already done that," snapped the small dark figure.

"And what have you found?" Sandrino asked not expecting to be implicated.

"That you have been feeding far too well and it's time to put an end to it."

With that, the small dark figure moved its hands slightly, and immediately its heavies bounced into action.

They grabbed Sandrino by each arm and thrust him onto the laboratory's conveyor belt and strapped him down firmly.

"What are you doing, are you mad, this could kill me?" Sandrino shouted as he struggled fruitlessly to break free

"You have acquired too much sudden wealth and you will now pay the price, how dare you bite the hand that feeds you" the small dark figure retorted.

"What sudden wealth?"

"$750,000 in cash"

"Bloody hell that was a windfall from an insider trading deal on the stock market"

"Likely story, where's your proof? What about the water ampoules, here, next you will be telling us you are a victim of circumstantial evidence."

"I'm innocent," Sandrino cried, as the conveyor belt started moving slowly towards the high intensity ultrasound chamber.

"Gag him; I don't want to hear any more lies from this finocchio"

The conveyor continued its merciless journey.

"You're a distant cousin to the family blessed with a degree that we needed. You have been constantly monitored in minute detail, something you must have worked out or became incredibly slack. In any case, you got away with some minor things, but this is in-excusable and unforgivable. We don't know what you did with the ampoules and we don't care, all we are concerned with is that we have stopped the leak." The small dark figure slowly said and smiled sadistically before it nodded for the operator to commence the torture session.

Sandrino's struggles were in vain. Everyone present donned highly protective earmuffs. Darkness filled Sandrino's mind as his head received a burst of microwaves and ultrasonic sound waves which caused him to lose consciousness.

Mrs Sandrino's beautiful dream of places that she had never visited before was broken for the second time in the morning with the incessant ringing of the phone. She didn't want to answer it, the dream state that she was in was far too embracing, but the telephone just wouldn't go away and so she relented and reluctantly picked up the bedside hand piece.

"Hello, Mrs Sandrino, who's calling please?"

"It's Officer Glen Parker Paramedic from the Newburn's Ambulance service."

"Yes?"

"Your husband has been found collapsed at the pharmacy, I am afraid he is in a serious condition, we are taking him to County General Hospital, would you like to meet us there?"

"Straight away," she automatically replied, and slammed down the phone.

In a state of numb shock she dressed, not bothering with what goes with what, or whether one should wear makeup or not and then she raced out of her bedroom and hurriedly knocked on her daughter's bedroom door.

"Veronica, Veronica, can I come in?" she stammered.

"Okay Mum, I am already awake come in what is the matter you sound completely distressed?

Mrs Sandrino flew to her daughter's bed and fell onto it sobbing uncontrollably.

"Mum, what's happened? Mum, Mum, tell me?"

"It's your dad he collapsed and is being taken to hospital."

"Where did this happen?"

Mrs Sandrino continued sobbing as she answered "At the pharmacy."

"What was he doing there?"

"Answering a police call. Now he's in an ambulance on his way to County General; I've got to get there."

Veronica remained relatively calm. A study of ancient Greek Philosophies and metaphysics had prepared her for such a situation. She quietly took control.

"You are in no condition to do that, here, give me five minutes and we will go together, I'll drive."

"What about the pharmacy?"

"Damn the pharmacy, I will handle it later leave to me I'll do everything by phone."

Mrs Sandrino comforted by her daughter's words settled down and she patiently waited on the bed as her daughter dressed even though it seemed like ages to her.

Within minutes they were on their way to the hospital, after they had locked their luxurious three storey house, complete with all of its extravagant fixtures, fittings and furniture. Veronica sped along paying no attention to speed limits in her series 7 BMW. They flew past numerous police cars without incident; it was as if they all knew what had happened. Along the way she telephoned staff members at the pharmacy to advise them of what had happened and after a series of unproductive contacts, managed to find a suitable locum pharmacist to satisfy the legality of the situation. This took up the entire thirty minutes of their high-speed drive to County General Hospital.

Mr Sandrino had already been admitted into the emergency ward and was being assessed by the duty doctor and a consultant neurologist.

Veronica had hardly stopped the car when her mother rushed out of it and ran into the main reception area. Veronica decided to leave the car where it was and quickly followed behind.

Mrs Sandrino was allowed into the emergency ward where her husband lay quite still, oblivious to all life about him.

"Oh my god is he dead?" she gasped, as she looked at his limp body and grey features.

"Not quite, but very close," the neurologist grimly answered.

"What happened to him?" she asked. The consultant was about to explain when Veronica joined them.

"You must be Veronica, pleased to meet you," he said as he offered his handshake which Veronica ignored.

"I was about to tell your mother that I believe your father has suffered multiple strokes in the brain, something that I have never seen before, I can't tell what will happen to him until we can do further detailed investigations. For the moment his body is coping very well, heart, lungs, liver and kidneys all seem to be performing. As for his brain, well, it must be in extreme confusion to say the least. There is no need to put him into intensive care, but we shall nevertheless hook him up to a series of monitors in case something goes wrong, that is all I can tell you for now."

"How long will he remain in this state?" Veronica asked.

"Depends on the individual, his regenerative powers and the will to live, it could be weeks, months or forever, I can't tell you. As I have just said before, he has had multiple strokes in the brain, that's what we know at this stage according to the x-ray evidence."

Mrs Sandrino swallowed hard and asked. "Can I stay with him?"

"Absolutely, it is probably the best medicine of all, namely to have a loving individual next to you."

Veronica put her arms around her mum. They stayed with Mr

Sandrino and observed him as he struggled to find his way back to conscious reality.

Meanwhile the neurologist advised admissions to make a private suite available for Mr Sandrino, and gave explicit instructions as to the duty of care he expected from the nursing staff and the various diagnostic tests that he wanted performed which included an MRI.

Later that morning, whilst Mrs Sandrino and Veronica were sitting in silence at Mr Sandrino's bedside the neurologist presented his findings.

"Mrs Sandrino, Veronica I have had a look at the results of the various tests that I requested. The MRI tells us the most, it is worse than I expected."

Mrs Sandrino gripped Veronica's hand with fear as she braced herself.

"There are literally dozens of very fine aneurisms that have exploded in your husband's head. Under these circumstances there is no therapy available. To open up the brain and try to perform some sort of microsurgery is a waste of time. To implement some sort of chemical treatment is also a waste of time. The only course of action is unfortunately to wait and see what will happen. I can offer no hope."

The prognosis escalated Mrs Sandrino's grief to such an extent that she almost became comatose.

Veronica sensed this and started talking to her mother. "Mother, listen to me, Dad will be alright, he is a fighter he will come through."

"Didn't you hear what the doctor just said, there's no hope."

"Mum, there is always hope, always, believe me, here take my rosary beads, pray, I am sure someone will hear you." Veronika urged her mother as positively as she could.

Mrs Sandrino accepted the beads, stared into space and started to mumble incoherently.

The neurologist feeling somewhat inadequate and useless clenched his lips into a forced downwards smile, nodded and left.

29

REVERSAL

On their return from Newburn, Jack and Brendan in the company of Yvette enjoyed a good night's sleep at the Chateau Alpine.

In the morning after they had detailed and exhausted all of their previous day's exploits as conversational material they focused on fine tuning their proposed rescue of The Infirmary's working girls and the exposure of Longevity Plus various criminal activities.

"Your drug conversions will work brilliantly to our advantage," Yvette confidently said after hearing what Brendan has done to the stores of pethidine and venlafaxamine, "I think we should alert a good investigative journalist to cover the story."

Jack nodded in agreement whilst Brendan half listened as he turned on the television set to view the early morning news.

"Do you know of any reporter we could approach?" Jack asked Yvette

"I think it has to be someone national with a good measure of clout, no good bothering with the locals they won't get us far," Yvette replied

"Good god," exclaimed Brendan as he turned up the television set's volume.

Jack and Yvette both stopped talking and listened to the televised news story that had grabbed Brendan's attention.

'Local police are investigating the circumstances surrounding the discovery of Mr Sandrino's collapsed body outside his pharmacy this morning. At this stage it is thought he might have been the victim of a bungled burglary. Mr Sandrino has been admitted to County General Hospital and remains in a critical condition. Now for today's weather'

Brendan switched off the television via the remote control.

"Doesn't sound right," he muttered.

"Just another official police story, is that right Brendan?" Jack cynically asked the handsome priest

"I am learning fast master. I hope I haven't accidentally caused this tragedy. I need to find out,"

"And if you have?" asked Yvette.

"Then I am responsible for his misfortune, something that I didn't think would happen. There is nothing worse than innocent people being hurt."

"What makes you think that he was innocent? You saw the operation he had going in the back room, he is guilty as hell." Jack said without any doubt in his mind.

"I know what you mean, but what I am trying to say is…"

"That you don't approve of the consequences of your actions," interrupted Jack, "and yet this is the way it is. What this event tells us is that if Mr Sandrino was disciplined then there are other people involved besides those that we have encountered and therefore we have to be extremely vigilant." Jack further concluded

"Can I at least go and visit Sandrino and see what I can find out?" Brendan asked in order to pacify his mixed feelings

"If you wish but please be very careful. Yvette and I will stay here and see who we can get interested in investigating Longevity Plus."

"Thank you," Brendan replied as he hurriedly grabbed the car keys to the white Ford sedan and then without saying another word he rushed off to right the wrong that he thought he had caused.

"He is like a little boy with a new toy," Yvette said once he had left.

"What makes you think that he is grown up?" Jack asked

Yvette laughed at the thought.

At Newburn's Feel Good Pharmacy the locum pharmacist settled into his job nicely. The staff members although in a state of shock were very accepting of the situation and went about their duties efficiently in the belief that life goes on.

The shop was busier than normal with an influx of well wishers bringing in get well cards and bunches of flowers. Mrs Sandrino's daughter Veronica arrived at noon to see if everything was running smoothly. She left her mother at County General Hospital to attend to her husband in the best possible way by sending lots of loving energy to him and praying unceasingly to anyone that might listen.

Veronica finally went up into the dispensing area after being delayed by every staff member who wished to hug her intensely and express their feelings.

"You're not Jeff," Veronica said with a worried frown as she looked at the rather odd looking relieving pharmacist.

"No I'm not," the stranger replied coldly. "My name is Mr Spanitsa; Jeff couldn't make it so he arranged for me to fill in for him."

Veronica became rather suspicious as she had not been informed of the substitution. "May I see your credentials please?"

Spanitsa stopped what he was doing and withdrew his wallet from his back pocket. He produced his current driver's license complete with photographic identification, and his current pharmaceutical license to practice, also complete with photo ID.

Veronica took them from him and went into her father's private office and checked him out.

Spanitsa remained calm throughout and smiled when Veronica emerged after 20 minutes.

"Everything appears to be in order, although I am puzzled how Jeff managed at the last minute to become involved in a freak car accident that also landed him in hospital,"

"Strange things happen," Spanitsa replied even though he knew all of the details leading up to the freak accident and who had orchestrated it.

"I am sure they do, at this stage I don't know how long we will need you, it might be days, weeks or even months, so if you could advise me on you availability we can…….."

Spanitsa interrupted, "I have no other commitments."

"Very well, what we offer is the standard rate for a manger, plus 25% loading as a casual"

"Quite acceptable" Spanitsa replied although the money was not important to him

"Then we will leave it at that until further notice. This place runs smoothly by itself, all you will have to do is fit in."

"Very well" Spanitsa eagerly replied as he appeared satisfied with the arrangement

"Any questions?"

"Not at all" He replied

Veronica shook Spanitsa's hand to seal the verbal contract and then she returned to her father's private office to telephone the hospital. "Hello mum it's Veronica, how is Dad?"

"No change darling, I will just keep praying."

"Have you had lunch?"

"No," she faintly whispered as she was already emotionally drained.

"Mom that's not good, look everything here is okay, we seem to be in capable hands so I will come back now."

"Okay darling, see you soon bye," Mrs Sandrino replied and put down the phone.   ·

Once Veronica had left Spanitsa waited until the appropriate moment came. He left the dispensary by excusing himself to go to the toilet and then satisfied that all was clear, let himself into the ladies toilet and then into the concealed laboratory. The warning lights flashed, the chemist stopped what he was doing and peered at the intruder.

"Ah it's you Spanitsa, everything going okay?"

"No problems."

"I told your bosses years ago that this pharmacy should have been mine."

"You know what they're like, family comes first."

"Bad choice…..you're far better off with strangers."

"Yeah."

"So what are you doing?"

"Nothing much until you arrange for more stocks of pethidine and venlaflexamine," the chemist replied.

"I'll check on it, perhaps I'll order a little more."

"No danger in that, it all goes to a good cause," the chemist chuckled.

Brendan's determination caused him to neglect taking notice of his car's speed. He was well and truly over the speed limit. Unlike the Sandrinos his excessive speed would not escape the attention of the police patrolling the roads and highways if he didn't slow down. Unfortunately his intense preoccupation with Mr Sandrino's well being prevented him from taking any notice until the sirens and flashing lights came screaming up behind him and assaulted his senses.

Damn it, he thought, not exactly the time and place for this sort of annoying thing.

"This is car 253 in pursuit of a white Ford sedan exceeding the speed limit by 70 kilometres per hour on highway W40 over."

"Car 253 acknowledged."

"Come on mister pull over, I've got your arse" shouted the police officer as he targeted Brendan's car.

Never panic, thought Brendan, only extend your talents to their maximum limits and beyond, he suggested to himself. If I can go unnoticed why can't I extend that talent and encompass the car he surmised. Brendan began to repeatedly intone OMRA as he visualized the car becoming part of his personality fade from view and blend into the scenery.

"Headquarters this is car 253 again, we have a situation here, that white Ford…"

"Yes 253."

"Has…"

"Yes 253."

"Disappeared…"

"253 are you alright?"

The police officer braked his high powered pursuit vehicle to a screeching halt and sat quite still as he rubbed his eyes in sheer disbelief and stared into the distance.

"Car 253, respond please."

"253 here cancel that call, returning to base, over."

Brendan looked in his rear vision mirror and congratulated himself on another dimension learnt, chameleon ability extended to inanimate objects. At the speed he was travelling, and with the roads almost empty, Brendan was at County General Hospital within a short time. He parked his car in the staff car park and proceeded to find Mr. Sandrino's room. It was not difficult for him to do so at all. The door was ajar, he peered through the opening and saw a very sad and distraught Mrs Sandrino seated next to her husband who had all sorts of monitors attached to him.

Brendan gently pushed the door open as he commanded the window curtains to flutter creating the illusion that a draught had caused the door to open. Mrs Sandrino hardly stirred and remained in her intense meditative state.

Brendan approached Sandrino and stood next to him on the opposite side of the bed to that of Mrs Sandrino. He observed both of them and his heart became filled with sorrowful compassion. He took hold of Sandrino's hand and felt the life force coursing through his body in a confused fashion. Brendan remembered the text of a book called the Infinite Mind he had read some years ago. In it was contained the suggestion that all beings interacted on a soul or outer electromagnetic level even before they relied on things like speech or body language. In the present circumstances this was the only available avenue that Brendan had available to 'talk' with Sandrino. He closed his eyes and mentally intoned OMRA as he breathed in deeply through his nose, held his breath and exhaled slowly through his mouth, while searching in his mind for Sandrino's soul personality. Slowly the mist cleared. Before him stood the clearly defined Mr Sandrino, looking quite distressed as he realized that he was suspended between conscious physical reality and the spiritual world, with no road map to show him the way home. A look of shocked surprise filled Sandrino's face as he saw Brendan.

"Are you God?"

"No." Brendan gently answered

"An angel?"

"No." Brendan once again gently answered

"Not the devil."

"Hardly."

"Who are you then?" Sandrino asked as he became increasingly worried.

"My name is Brendan O'Reilly I am a Catholic priest. In fact I am standing next to your body and holding your hand."

"Did my wife call you? Are you going to give me the last rites? Is it all over for me? Oh god, I didn't want my life to end like this."

"None of this; your wife doesn't even know that I am in the room."

"How's that possible?" Sandrino asked.

"That doesn't matter for the moment, it is more important that we get you home."

"Can you?"

"Yes, it is entirely possible; however, I need your help."

"To get me back," Sandrino wished and pleaded.

"No, to tell me all about the pharmacy drug operation."

"I'm just a puppet whose misfortune it was to be a distant cousin of one of those who runs the business, their name is Ricci. They simply used my qualifications to keep the operations running and provided I kept an informed blind eye, paid me a percentage. The money overcame any pangs of conscience I had; I never told my wife or daughter what was going on. They believed that the pharmacy was the sole source of our income."

"Is that all you know?" Brendan asked.

"It is."

"Are you sure there is nothing more, because if there is and you haven't told me then I might fail in bringing you back."

Sandrino's image looked increasingly disturbed.

"There is always a small dark heavily disguised figure overseeing the entire operation. I was always answerable to it, I could never find out who or what it was. I believe it is part of the Ricci family but I didn't know who it is. I heard that Mr Ricci died so it can't be him."

"How does Louis Badcock fit into all of this?"

"Badcock had some sort of altered drug delivered to the brothel. He worked out a suitable dosage that, combined with other drugs, gave mind blowing orgasms. He then distributes to other brothels far away so as to not compete with his. This is the way he ensures a good clientele that keeps coming back. The drugs that go to Longevity Plus are unaltered, I believe they are genuinely used there for medical purposes, I can tell by the way that the prescriptions are written for the hospital patients," Sandrino said rather embarrassed by his past.

"If you knew that the drugs delivered to Longevity Plus went into making designer drugs of addiction, would that have changed your mind when you were offered the pharmacy?" Brendan asked.

"I don't know. You see, all the legal drugs that pharmacists sell are addictive. There is no difference between legal and illegal stuff these days, all that separates the two is who manufactures it."

"Do you think that the dark figure you spoke of lives in Newburn?" Brendan enquired.

"I don't know, but I feel very bitter towards it for destroying my body, especially when I told it the truth,"

"Mr Sandrino, once your health is restored what will you do?"

"I don't know, run I suppose, change my identity and hope for the best because once the Mafia marks you it's for life, there is no escape,"

"Having said that, what is your choice, return to consciousness or enter the spirit world?"

"That is such a difficult choice to make, here I feel safe in a timeless location, but devoid of love. If I return then I shall have love again but also fear and anxiety to complement it. I suppose I could risk it, can you bring me back, can you, please?" Sandrino earnestly pleaded

Brendan acknowledged his plea and focused all of his attention into healing Sandrino's brain.

Again it was the process of talking to each one of Sandrino's ruptured cerebral blood vessels, and asking them to return to their original place, as he had done with the altered pethidine and venlafexamine materials. Brendan tried to achieve this by mentally intoning OMRA KAHE as loud as he could but to no avail, the only option was the audible one.

Brendan then left Sandrino and returned to the physical world. Still invisible he was greeted with the sight of Sandrino's wife and daughter discussing what they would have to eat for lunch as they left the room. Brendan waited for a brief moment, politely commanded the door to lock by itself and then conducted the healing process as it was meant to have been done. It was just a matter of minutes before Sandrino re-entered the world of physical consciousness. As he opened his eyes, he breathed an immense sigh of relief. His ears picked up the noises of the monitors that were attached to him and confirmed his existence or otherwise. To him the room was empty, not a soul about, was it a dream that he had experienced when he saw Brendan O'Reilly or was it an optimistic hallucination bordering on a near death experience for now it did not matter, he was alive and he wanted to stay that way for as long as possible.

Brendan, invisible to Sandrino, watched and listened to his thoughts. Once the dark figure learnt of Sandrino's recovery how soon before it gave orders to silence him forever. Brendan had revived him, but was it his responsibility also to keep him alive and fully protected? Not even his beloved god did that in the sense of keeping all of his creatures physically alive. How could Brendan? Christ certainly didn't. At least Brendan had given Sandrino a second chance it was up to him now to make his own new choices in life.

Sandrino pressed the alarm buzzer at the side of his bed signaling that he needed the duty nurse as soon as possible. As he waited he falsely concluded that the small dark figure hadn't intended killing him, but was rather more intent on teaching him a lesson by causing him permanent bodily harm.

"Yes Mrs Sandrino, you buzzed me?" the nurse automatically said, as she walked into the hospital suite.

"No, I did," replied Sandrino.

The nurse stood aghast.

"What's the matter?" Sandrino asked. "Seen a ghost?"

"The doctor, judging by his case notes, didn't – didn't expect you to survive, it's a miracle," she said as she made the sign of the cross. "Wait until I tell him; I will call him straight away."

"Could you page my wife first please, if she is in the hospital?" he asked

"But of course sir," the nurse replied as she made for the phone.

Within ten minutes the room was filled full of joyous pandemonium as Mr Sandrino's wife and daughter hugged and kissed him. The nursing staff looked on in complete awe, even the normally composed neurologist admitted to shedding a tear at the sight of the miraculous recovery. The event rekindled his belief in divinity, something that medical science had over the years progressively stolen from him.

"It certainly is a miracle," mumbled the neurologist.

"That it surely is," Mrs Sandrino replied as her way of confirming and emphasing his conclusion "My belief in prayer always works," she proudly said as she smiled from ear to ear

"Mum, I did say someone was listening didn't I?" Veronica said even though she had to secretly admit to herself that she only said that to give some measure of hope.

"That you did my capable daughter that you did."

30

IS NO ONE SAFE?

Brendan remained quite still and unnoticed in the corner of the room observing all of its activities, until he sensed that Sandrino somehow felt his presence by continually looking towards his location and straining his eyes. Concerned that his power was weakening, Brendan decided to leave and drive back to the chateau and tell his friends of his findings.

Meanwhile, Yvette and Jack, after Brendan had left earlier that day, had gone their separate ways. Yvette wanted to spend some time reflecting in the forest at one of her favourite spots. There was a genuine pressing problem that needed urgent attention. Jack on the other hand was quite relaxed and knew that everything would ultimately fall into place. He decided to stay in the hotel room and was determined to find a good investigative journalist. They had morning tea together before Yvette left. It was hard for her because the more time she spent with Jack the more she became drawn to him. It was the same for Jack, except that his dilemma, considering the number of women he had had in the past was convincing himself that this was indeed true love and not another passing infatuation.

As Yvette walked from the chateau into the forest she was

oblivious to everything and everybody around her. She constantly thought of Jack and cursed herself ever so politely for her sinful nature made worse by falling in love with a very handsome priest. This was a mortal sin by thought alone and could it be that by this process she would lead Jack to commit adultery. After all, he was sort of married having taken a vow of celibacy, the same way that married people sort of take the same oath by remaining celibate outside of their marriage. Her love for Jack, unfortunately, had become as intense as that for her parents and the Blessed Virgin Mary and was now firmly established. Irrespective of what the future held, Yvette would never forget Jack; he was a permanent part of her makeup so the idea to walk away from it all would never work. She could devote herself to him as his lifelong housekeeper and in the process, follow him wherever he went, but this would only cause tongues to wag and eventually destroy his holy reputation by gossip alone. She did not have the right to do that. Yvette decided to allow her subconscious to run around the maze of this dilemma and find a way out that would satisfy all aspects and people both moral and divine. She walked on automatically until she reached her sanctuary. She made the sign of the cross and with hands in prayer position fell to her knees.

"Such easy prey," whispered the big moustached Austrian as he lustfully watched from behind the forest undergrowth.

"Just like a female deer," his two Asian companions replied in low voices as they contemplated their attack

"So, like we planned okay, you hold her down and I will go first then we keep swapping around until we are all drained."

The Asians nodded eagerly, grinning like two jackals on heat just waiting to savour their sexual delights.

The trio slowly crept forward and encircled their prey. Yvette's deep meditative trance made it very easy for them to approach unnoticed. All of her senses were turned inwards as she remained oblivious to their presence.

The excitement of the pending attack filled the trio's bodies with adrenalin drying their mouths and throat, flaring their nostrils, quickening their heart rates and pumping more blood into their already fully erect reproductive members.

Yvette's head and shoulders hit the soft grass with a thud as the two Asians pounced on her and forcibly held her down.

'What is this, who?' her mind screamed as she desperately struggled to break free whilst she tried to identify her assailants.

"So Miss Perfect in all of your glory, how long did you think you could get away with teasing us, hey? Always playing so hard to get, so aloof so prim and proper, well we'll show you, come on boys, time to fill her up with some meat, the sort she's wanted and craved for" the Austrian roughly said as he towered menacingly over Yvette.

She was shocked to see that it was him and then realized the serious nature of her predicament. She was going to be raped repeatedly. If she struggled she would most certainly end up hurt one way or the other, but if she just lay there, that might also incite them further. Confusion and terror filled her mind. How could this be happening to her, a devout Christian, always praying, working solidly in the Church, attending to people's needs, always obedient, unselfish, what was this a punishment for, surely not for falling in love with a priest?

The Austrian grinned sadistically as he savagely pushed his body between Yvette's legs; he remained kneeling as he unbuckled his belt, dropped his trousers and forced down his underpants to expose his erect penis that demanded satisfying. The two Asians sniggered and shouted, "Go for it man, hammer her hard, fill her up, we just love watching, go man go, stick it in, look man she wants it."

The Asians sexually explicit words caused Yvette's heart to thump harder and harder, her breathing to become increasingly labored and erratic, her eyes widened and everything around her became excessively magnified. This was not how her life was meant to be. She caught sight of the Austrian's ugly penis and images of unwanted pregnancies and sexually transmitted disease assaulted her mind. The Austrian urged on by the demonic Asians grabbed at Yvette's cotton underwear and started to rip it apart. The Asians cheered him on.

"Hey man, this is better than watching those X-rated videos," one of them coarsely said

"Yeah, we could be the next porno studs, did you bring the video camera?" the other asked in broken English as he yearned to have a digital copy of their sexual adventure.

Yvette closed her eyes, her body refused to accept her fate. She tried desperately to kick and push off her assailants but they were far too strong.

"Excuse me, you do know you are about to enter a holy temple," a voice from behind asked.

The Austrian stopped what he was doing and looked around.

"Huh," he grunted, as he looked at the priest standing a couple of metres behind him.

"What are you doing here you sick bastard," he shouted angry now that he had been disturbed

"Like I said, do you know you are about to enter a holy temple? If not, then you should at least perform the necessary..."

"Clear off, you religious freak," the Austrian shouted, interrupting Jack mid sentence.

"Oh dear me, you really should listen, otherwise..."

"Look, I've had enough of this," the Austrian said as he stood up to face Jack, not realizing that his trousers were still around his ankles and that he had fully exposed himself.

Jack looked at the Austrian's erect engorged penis and with a straight face asked, "Are you threatening me with a dangerous weapon?"

The Austrian remained silent whilst the two Asians stayed where they were and awaited further instructions. The Austrian looked back at them and nodded. Both Asians produced flick knives and waved them with malicious intent.

Yvette tried to see who was challenging the Austrian, but could not, as he was standing directly in her line of sight.

"Either you leave or we carve you and the girl up into little pieces." The two Asians threatened

"Well, if we have to fight dirty, I might as well defend myself," replied Jack, as he took his crucifix from around his neck and held it up to represent a small sword. "Clever don't you think? A cross normally but inverted it becomes a little petite sword just big enough for a fairy."

The Austrian was becoming increasingly outraged at this mockery, plus he was well and truly sexually frustrated with all of his glandular secretions demanding to be discharged then and there he didn't have time for this nonsense.

Jack sensed his impatient anger and took advantage of it by making the first move. He swung at the Austrian with his crucifix and its chain in hand. The crucifix missed its mark but the chain didn't and it whipped across his face severely lacerating it. The Austrian howled with pain and he instinctively reacted rather violently by lunging at Jack in an attempt to punch him to the ground.

Unfortunately for him the Austrian forgot that his trousers were still tangled around his ankles and as he lunged forward he tripped over them and fell forwards crashing his erect penis head first into the soil. His torso and head followed, the resultant pain was so intensely overwhelming that he immediately lost consciousness.

Yvette gasped with relief at the sight of Jack. The two Asians leapt to their feet releasing Yvette in the process. With knives in hand they ran screaming towards Jack who looked coolly at them and said, "Two kitchen hands, Yuck A Moto and Sushi Lu."

When the timing was right, instead of retreating Jack took two steps forwards, jumped onto the back of the Austrian and used him as a spring board. The Asians by now were on each side of him. Jack pushed himself off the Austrian's back, propelled himself upwards into the air twisted and quickly brought his arms down to his body and which made him spin around twice. The move temporarily confused his would be assailants.

They stood momentarily stunned, Jack allowed his right hand to depart from its position and release his crucifix and its chain, which sliced through the air and with the utmost precision zeroed in on the assailants' weapons shattering them into small pieces. It then changed direction and flew up and hovered stationary over Jack's head. The two Asians, stunned at the loss of their weapons, looked at each other and then at the unconscious Austrian and then at Jack who stood triumphantly on the Austrian's back. Yvette by now had moved away into relative safety.

"Well my yellow skinned kitchen hands, what to chop, chop karate style?"

The crucifix and chain continued to whirl around Jack's head. Frightened by its appearance, the Asians ran away and disappeared into the depths of the forest.

Yvette meanwhile re-arranged her clothes to cover her partial nakedness and restore her modesty. All of her anguish had completely vaporized thanks to Jack's intervention. Her faith in her belief was restored.

"You were absolutely amazing, are you ex marine?" she asked.

"Not at all"

"How did you do that thing with the crucifix?"

"The mind does strange things when it is frightened," Jack replied "All I did was perform a few pseudo martial arts moves to frighten them off"

"Are you sure?"

"Absolutely."

"But I swear I saw you dressed in priest's clothes and now you are as before a civilian in casual clothes. Your crucifix hangs loosely around your neck," she said a little confused.

"Look, like I said, the mind does strange things in moments of great distress."

Yvette reluctantly nodded as a sign of accepting his explanation but deep down she knew what she had seen and she would wait patiently for the moment to arrive when the truth would be told

"More importantly, are you alright?" he asked, as he put his arm around her as a sign of protection and comfort.

"Yes I am, thank you," she replied, cherishing the closeness of his body.

"I knew he fancied you, but this."

"Yes, it comes as a surprise to me as well. How did you know I was in trouble?" she asked

"Something I've picked up over the past two days." He replied

"I have always been very wary of big moustached men; they always appear to be cowards to me bullies and violent types in fact that mistreat women. When you left this morning for the forest I watched you leave and noticed the three of them leave shortly after you heading in the same direction, I feared the worst, that's why I came," he explained.

"I'm glad you did," she replied. Their eyes met and Jack smiled he lent forward and was about to kiss her fully on the mouth when the noise of a man approaching them stopped him from doing so.

"What are you two strangers doing and why is that half naked man doing lying face down on the ground?"

Jack and Yvette giggled slightly in response to the Forest Ranger's questions

"He'll explain everything when he wakes up," Jack said without any further explanation as he took Yvette's hand and headed in the direction of the chateau.

The Forest Ranger looked at them suspiciously as they walked away and he then applied first aid.

When all of the commotion had subsided within the walls of the private hospital suite, and they had been finally left alone, Mr Sandrino turned to his wife and whispered, "We have to leave as soon as possible."

"You have just recovered from a very serious injury and you want to leave, no my darling, you have to rest like the good doctor ordered," Mrs Sandrino lovingly replied.

Sandrino swallowed hard and forced a downward smile. A shadow of fear and shame descended upon his face which forced him to partly explain in fits and starts his shady business dealings in Newburn during which he struggled to look at his wife and daughter in the eye.

"Darlings, if I stay they will certainly kill me this time, we have to leave right now and get away from here as quickly as possible. We can't even go home in case the house is being watched."

"What are you talking about?" Mrs Sandrino asked completely beside herself with overwhelming anxiety.

"The family is involved in the pharmacy." He finally admitted

"Yes I know our family, you, me and our daughter." She replied

"No, not this family, the family"

"You are not being serious," Mrs Sandrino said completely floored by his revelation. "How did this happen?" She further asked fearful of the likely consequences.

Sandrino hesitated briefly and then went on to painfully describe how he came to 'own' Newburn's Feel Good Pharmacy and how the profits were made. As he did so the gravity of the situation finally hit home. Veronica, the calmest of all of them made the following intelligent suggestion

"Dad, firstly are you sure that you're 100%?"

"Yes, no doubt about that and if I were to tell you how it came about you probably wouldn't believe me."

"I agree," Veronica paused, reflected for a moment, and then said "Since you think we are being watched, it would not be a good idea for all of us to leave at once. Whoever is the head of this organization probably thinks you won't return anyway and won't think of killing you in the hospital. So you might be safe here with Mum for the time being. If I came and went checking on the pharmacy and going home that behaviour would seem perfectly normal. I cannot risk attracting attention by leaving home with heaps of suitcases so I suggest after I leave here I return home, ring the pharmacy to check on things, go shopping and collect the necessary financials and leave within a reasonable unattractive period of time, probably early evening. So Dad, tell me, where is it stashed and Mum the same please."

Mr Sandrino and his wife looked at each other with reddened faces that suggested they had been found out.

"Come on you two, tell me."

Sandrino signalled for Veronica to sit on the bed close to him. He then whispered into her ear all the information that she needed to know which she committed to memory. Mrs Sandrino meanwhile looked on making out that she was unaware of what he had just revealed.

"You should have told me about this years ago Father" Veronica said quite disgusted.

"If I had, it would have ruined your teenage years. I kept it from you so as to protect you," Sandrino genuinely responded.

"But it almost cost you your life Dad," Veronica said holding back a few angry tears

"It isn't like that, what I did could not have caused this to happen. All of this has been brought about by someone who I believe is a vigilante of sorts and wants to expose the racket that is going on. Perhaps that is something that I should also consider doing."

"And lose your life once and for all."

"I may have already done that," Sandrino replied solemnly.

Veronica looked at him intensely and reflected on his statement.

Meanwhile Mrs Sandrino approached her husband from the other side and took hold of his hand.

"I will always support you my darling, no matter what you've done or what happens."

Sandrino squeezed his wife's hands in appreciation and forced a smile.

"Thank you," he whispered as he drew his wife closer to him.

Veronica's heart softened as she watched them comforting each other

"I'll be back later tonight," she softly said. "If that is okay with you… Dad…. Mum"

"Promise me you will take extreme care and watch your back," Mrs Sandrino pleaded as she turned to face her daughter.

"I will Mum," Veronica answered assuredly as she stood up. She kissed her mother and father on their respective cheeks and quietly left.

Her parents waved her goodbye in the hope that she would return unharmed at the agreed time. Veronica walked down the corridor to the lift doors with the intention of being as observant as possible and mentally recording everything she saw. At the same time she was also very intent on interpreting everyone's body language as accurately as possible, making certain that whatever pathway she took it would be to her advantage. The walk to the car was uneventful. Hospital staff remained pleasant and unobtrusive. Nothing happened that would alert her of any imminent danger. The car didn't appear to have been tampered with. Veronica drove out of the hospital grounds, passed several cars that were parked on the verge outside of the hospital property, and then accessed the main road back to Newburn. She constantly monitored the traffic ahead, to the side and behind her. If she was being shadowed then it was being done very well, if not, then whatever surveillance she was expecting might be waiting for her at home.

Veronica decided to visit her father's pharmacy instead of calling it by telephone. Within the hour she had parked the car outside of the Feel Good Chemist. Once inside she was warmly greeted by its staff and customers who all wanted to know how her father was recovering. Not wanting to give anything away she simply remarked, "He is in a stable condition. It will be some time before we know the final outcome."

That seemed to satisfy everyone's caring nature. Mr Spanitsa looked very busy in the dispensary attending to all matters with a vigorous attitude, which suggested to the casual observer that he already assumed that the entire operation belonged to him. It dawned on Veronica that Spanitsa was most certainly a family plant. She was relieved that she hadn't given anything away about her father's recovery and she hoped that the hospital was secure and that no family allies worked there.

Veronica went through the motions with Spanitsa on the day's activities and ended by picking up some necessary toiletries. Cheekily she said, "Just put them on my account," as she hurriedly packed them into plastic carry bags.

The journey home was uneventful. No one followed her. Veronica stopped at the nearby supermarket. She bought an assortment of goods that were consistent with weekly food requirements and then she drove home. The street in which they lived was quiet; no unusual cars parked on the verge anywhere. Their house also appeared secure. Veronica unlocked the front door, disarmed the security system and then brought in the shopping. Once she had put everything away she went upstairs into her spacious bedroom and changed into a tracksuit. Veronica then took her large sports bag and went about the house retrieving all of the essential financials that her father had talked about. Luckily the stashed monies were in $100 note denominations, so the odd $200,000 fitted neatly into the bag as did the other documentation, personal bank and cheque books, credit cards and passports. What took Veronica by surprise was the abundance of secret hiding places that her parents had built into their house. Most of these were right out in the open. Satisfied that she had attended to everything she made a number of random telephone calls and then headed for the squash courts. As she closed the door behind her she did not bother with the house security, her own was much more important. The street outside was as before nothing untoward.

Once inside the 7 series BMW she subtly congratulated herself. She drove the car along a much longer convoluted route rather than the direct one and arrived at the sports centre within twenty minutes. She made doubly sure that she had not been followed and she even made certain that there were no suspicious characters about the complex. With bag and racket in hand Veronica went through the main doors and turned right to go upstairs. She sat in an available seat in the viewing gallery overlooking a court in which two rather energetic young men played a very competitive game of squash. Sensing that she was in no danger Veronica left the sports arena and drove back to County General Hospital.

Mr and Mrs Sandrino were discussing their probable futures when Veronica stepped into the private hospital room.

"Thank god you're back," her mother gratefully said as she set her eyes upon her precious daughter.

"A promise is a promise," Veronica replied.

"Was everything okay?" Sandrino asked.

"Like you said Dad" She replied as she pointed to the large sports bag that she had with her.

"Excellent. I think we should make tracks."

"That's not a good idea Dad; we should wait for the opportune moment and escape in a synchronized fashion rather than leave all at once."

"What do you suggest?" he asked

"It is presently 8:00pm, visiting hours finish about 10:00pm. I brought you a simple disguise a wig, a bushy moustache; a change of clothes and a pair of cheap reading glasses."

Sandrino smiled at the thought of it all

"At around 9:45pm or when the nurse visits you last, I will leave for the car and you can change and follow on, leaving Mum to bring up the rear."

"Sounds good," Sandrino said as he placed his entire safety in his daughter's hands.

Mrs Sandrino nodded in agreement.

The time went by quickly as they discussed where they were going and what they could do. Considering Sandrino's involvement with the family all of its members had to be avoided at all costs. The 9:45pm departure did not go according to schedule. The station nurse called in followed by the registrar and then the neurologist. It was 10:30pm by the time the window of opportunity arose for them to leave. Veronica left by the elevator followed by her father in disguise some nine minutes later and then her mother within another four. They were all safe within the confines of the BMW. Veronica drove slowly out of the car park and once away from the hospital grounds, gunned the engine and quickly accessed the main highway to freedom. About ten minutes down the road there suddenly appeared a detour sign indicating road work in progress. The lanes converged into one. There were no workmen to be seen apart from one directing the traffic to take the detour, which meant taking a side road and then connecting up with the main highway five minutes later.

"This doesn't feel right," Veronica said as her intuition went on full red alert

"You are just being paranoid," Sandrino suggested.

Veronica wasn't sure about that, however, she reluctantly agreed and turned off thinking the side road would be a smooth run. Within a kilometre another detour sign appeared, this time causing the traffic away from the side road onto a gravel track that headed into dark and semi mountainous terrain

"Still think this feels right?" Veronica asked

"Sort of," he replied hesitantly. But within five minutes they were the only ones on the road, which was devoid of any lighting. Veronica switched the high beam lights on which stretched into the darkness revealing an eerie almost deathlike atmosphere.

Mrs Sandrino, sitting in the back seat, took out her rosary beads and began to pray. A blaze of light flooded the cabin of the BMW blinding everyone inside of it temporarily.

It seemingly came from all directions accompanied by the roar of several high powered engines. Veronica put up her hand to shield her eyes. Once she had become accustomed to the light she was able to distinguish three off road vehicles complete with rows of high powered spotlights and fitted with battering rams coming at them from each side and one from behind.

Mrs Sandrino muffled her scream as the three vehicles of destruction descended upon them. Not one to submit to fear or terror Veronica calculated their position with respect to the available power of the BMW and floored the accelerator as she changed from automatic to manual drive mode

In second gear the engine screamed in response, driving the rear wheels into an absolute frenzy, spraying up the loose gravel directly into the windscreen of the up and coming 4-wheel drive. The stones splattered and bounced off the windscreen causing it to crack and craze. The driver braked hard. Veronica continued to pump the BMW for more power, shifted into third gear hoping that she could avoid being squashed by the two monsters attacking from the sides. The loose gravel was not the most co-operative surface to try and escape on. Finding no real adhesion the wheels spun in frustration. One bang followed the other as the two off-road vehicles struck. Luckily the damage inflicted was behind the rear wheels allowing them to continue working. Veronica eased off the power, shifted down into first gear and pushed forward. It worked; the BMW was free. In the lower gear it found its feet and surged forwards. The gravel continued to be a very demanding surface, almost mischievous, pulling the BMW this way and that in an erratic fashion. Veronica met the challenge turning the steering wheel violently in response and blending it with a mixture of acceleration and brakes. The menacing 4-wheel drives followed closely behind, their larger knobbly tyres found more grip which enabled the 4 wheel drives to catch up progressively.

"I don't think we can outrun them Dad?"

"Take evasive action," he shouted.

The road ahead started to veer to the left, the BMW's high beam headlights picked up a track to the right.

"Dad, that road ahead, do I risk it?"

"No, might be a dead end" Sandrino screamed back. "Press on, this road has to come back to the main highway somewhere," he added

"They're almost upon us" Mrs Sandrino screamed from the back seat

Her husband looked back to see the first of the three truck just metres from the BMW's damaged rear end.

"Wish I had my gun" Sandrino grunted

"Here Dad, is this what you want?" Veronica answered as she opened the centre console.

Sandrino grabbed the weapon, a gift from the family, released the safety catch, powered down his passenger window, positioned himself and while he held onto the car's door frame he shot the gun at the drivers in the pursuing vehicles. The bullets hit two of the windscreens; one found its mark and buried itself deep into the driver's chest. Burning pain filled his thorax, he struggled for breath, but lost the battle and slumped over the steering wheel, losing control of the vehicle which, given its freedom, spun around into the path of the following vehicles. One driver was quick enough to react and steered his 4-wheel drive out of the way; the other wasn't so responsive and suffered a crash head-on. The remaining driver cursed profusely; he activated his walkie-talkie and screamed several incoherent orders to his fellow assassins whist he continued his pursuit intent on crushing the BMW and its occupants. Sandrino having emptied his gun of bullets ducked back into the passenger seat and reloaded. No sooner had he finished than the following vehicle slammed into the rear of the BMW. The impact caused the boot to fly open, severely limiting Veronica's rear-view visibility. Mrs Sandrino screamed, "Oh my god, save us."

The safety belt system strained to keep her in place. Veronica made every effort to stay calm but the threat of dying fuelled the seeds of panic deep inside of her. The 4-wheel drive struck again this time mounting the rear bumper bar and causing the BMW's front end to lift up. Veronica pumped the accelerator to pull away, with the extra weight, the wheels responded and the BMW broke free. The front came crashing down; Veronica was at her wit's end to keep in control as the car snaked on the gravel. Sandrino incensed at the assault on his family was just about to once again shoot at the 4-wheel drive when two shots rang out and blinded the BMW.

"What's happened?" screamed Mrs Sandrino

"They've taken out our lights," shouted her husband.

"The truck behind has also switched off his lights," Veronica added.

Now in complete darkness, the Sandrino family faced a hopeless situation. The pursuing driver however was in complete control; he had donned his night vision goggles. A third shot then rang out from a high powered rifle.

"That missed us," Sandrino said as he nervously laughed.

"Afraid not Dad, temperature gauge is rising."

"Damn it."

"The engine is going to seize."

"We're done for."

Veronica refused to accept defeat. In the pitch-blackness her eyes strained for a way out. She looked to the right, straight ahead and left and managed to catch sight of lights intermittently peeking through the trees. Not knowing where they stood she took a chance and threw the BMW into their direction.

"What the hell are you doing?" her father shouted.

"Trying to save us," she retorted as she forced the car along.

The engine groaned with pain, the suspension yelled 'stop' as the car tried to obey its driver. It was not built for this terrain.

The 4-wheel drive however had no trouble and was about to firmly engage in more intimate contact with the Jaguars rear end almost as if it wanted to mount it doggystyle. Veronica had driven onto a bush track and headed the car towards the salvation of flashing lights. She drove on convinced that help was at hand. The lights became brighter, bigger, until they were upon them and then the awful warning flashed before their eyes – Danger, Road Out. The 4-wheel drive, with full traction on increased speed and with an almighty strike, hit the BMW with a force that pushed it through the danger sign into the beyond. Silence filled the Sandrino family's ears as the BMW floated through space. The 4-wheel drive stopped at the edge of the precipice; the driver watched and waited sadistically as he counted the seconds to the anticipated climax. A few moments passed, which seemed like an eternity to the Sandrinos, and then the explosive sound of a high velocity impact filled the air. Twenty seconds later the crash site erupted into a ball of flame as the ruptured fuel tanks and other devices attached to the underside of the car by friends of the family exploded.

"Wonderful things tracking devices," the triumphant hired assassin whispered to himself as he watched the burning inferno.

31

BACK IN TOWN

As they walked back to the chateau Yvette was pleased that she was holding Jack Stern alias Father O'Reilly's hand. It gave her a sense of protection.

"Do you think it is still safe for us to stay at the chateau?" she asked

Jack considered her question for a moment as he watched his step. "I think your admirer is a coward and therefore it is probably not safe, especially for you to stay alone any longer. Also I don't quite know what his next moves are likely to be; certainly his pride and penis have definitely been insulted, so I am more than certain that he will try revenge of one kind or another. We cannot report this incident because the police are looking for us and in any case, some of them are crooked, as we have both found out. Once Jack Stern returns we'd better make tracks."

"Where to?"

"I have often said that the best place to hide is out in the open Newburn's 'Hotel Large' is to my of thinking the perfect spot"

Yvette's eyes sparkled at the suggestion. She gripped Jack's hand more firmly as she erased the morning's frightening events from her memory forever. Yvette reminded herself that out of all things something good always happens.

When they reached the chateau both of them sensed that the staff attitude towards them had changed. Yvette and Jack were now viewed with an air of caution, if not passive aggression. "Something's happened," Yvette said in a low voice

"I know what you mean, I hope Jack's not far away."

"So do I" She whispered

Yvette and Jack felt as though they were under constant surveillance and that at any given moment they would be pounced upon. Not wanting to portray any air of guilt they nonchalantly made their way back to their hotel suite to find Brendan waiting for them.

"Jack, I don't think we are safe here anymore," Yvette hastily said. Brendan looked rather surprised at her comment.

"But why?" he asked.

Yvette looked at Jack and said, "Will you please tell him?"

Jack forced a smile and told of the ordeal that Yvette had survived. Brendan's reaction was one of fury.

"Surely you are going to report this to the police," he blurted out

Jack looked at him in a questioning way.

Brendan, realizing his mistake corrected himself and said "I think we'd better move on."

"Where to?"

"Hotel Large, out in the open no better place to hide, but before we go, I have to tell you about what I did today," he said, sounding very excited.

"Yes my son, what saintly things did you do today?" Jack said as he cocked his head to one side

"Well" Brendan started off by saying and then went on to detail the his extraordinary achievements during the morning

"Does this mean you could make people in intimate contact with you disappear as well?" Yvette asked out of curiosity.

"I suppose, why do you ask?"

"Because that would be the perfect way of rescuing the girls at The Infirmary all you would have to do is hold hands, stay close together and leave as one group."

"That is absolutely brilliant," remarked Jack, as he looked out of the windows at the grounds below.

"Do you really think so?" Yvette asked.

"I certainly do, and you know what?"

"No."

"Jack will have to try it out right now."

"Why?" Brendan asked a little confused.

"Because the police have arrived and that Austrian desk clerk is talking to them right now. Think you can do it Jack?"

"I guess I will just have to." Brendan replied with a degree of confidence

"That's my boy" Jack said in a congratulatory fashion.

"Collect your stuff and put it into that bag over there. I'll don my disguise and together we will leave in four minutes flat."

While Jack attended to his disguise Yvette continued to observe the intercourse between the Austrian and the police down below and whilst she was doing so another unmarked police car pulled up next to them manned by two plain-clothes policeman.

"My admirer is a coward," she cursed. "He must have spun a good story; probably told them something bizarre."

"Like you are a sexual pervert," whispered Jack in his old man's disguise.

"What, how did you change so quickly?"

"Years of experience." Yvette frowned out of disbelief. 'There was more to this man than meets the eye' she thought

"Come now children, let us escape."

Brendan took Yvette's hand and intoned OMRA with a view to making them one and invisible. Jack shuffled his way out of the suite with Brendan and Yvette one step behind. At the end of the passage the elevator indicated that it was on its way up. Jack decided to take the stairs and hoped that the foyer would be empty. Yvette and Brendan followed closely behind stepping lightly, so as not to arouse suspicion. Jack realized that their means of escape was partially thwarted. They could not take Brendan's car, as they would surely be apprehended.

When they reached the bottom step, Jack with walking stick in hand, approached the reception desk. He cleared his throat and asked, "Excuse me sonny, do you know where Mr Jack Stern and his companion are? They don't seem to be in their hotel room."

"The police also want to know that sir," the clerk on duty answered as he pointed to the plain-clothes detective madly running about the reception area.

"Are they alright? Not hurt I hope. They are such a wonderful couple you know."

"Not from what we have heard sir."

"Pardon?" Jack asked pretending to be old, frail and partially deaf.

"I said, not from what we have heard," the desk clerk reiterated firmly.

"What have they done?" Jack asked.

"I am not at liberty to say, except that our Austrian duty manager did state that he had been sexually assaulted by them in the forest, along with two of our kitchen hands."

"Never," Jack replied in an astonished tone of voice.

"Believe what you may, but those are the facts."

"Well, looks as though I came out here for nothing. Could you ring a taxi for me please?"

"Very well sir, where would you be going?"

"Back to the bus depot in town"

"Very well, they usually take about fifteen minutes to get here."

"Thank you," Jack replied as he handed the desk clerk a $5 note for his trouble.

"You are very generous sir, sorry about your friends."

"So am I," replied Jack.

"Perhaps you could ask the detective for further information," the desk clerk suggested.

"That won't be necessary, they were only business colleagues, not real friends, it doesn't matter, I'll just keep going I suppose," Jack said looking most despondent. "Thank you anyway," he added as he turned and shuffled towards the main doors.

By now there were four marked police cars and two unmarked ones in attendance. Got nothing better to do, Jack cynically thought, as he watched the police scurry around like dogs looking for a lost bone.

The taxi arrived within the specified time. The driver seeing all the commotion and police presence drove his vehicle cautiously down the driveway and looked for his fare. Jack signaled for the driver with a wave of his stick. He picked up his bags of samples and approached the taxi, opened the rear door and threw the bag into the back seat leaving the rear door open, allowing Brendan and Yvette to seat them-selves. He then opened the passenger door and was about to step inside the cabin when he realized what he had done and apologized.

"I'm sorry, I have left the door open, one moment."

Having closed the rear door he sat in the passenger seat and asked the driver to take him to Newburn's bus terminal and then sat in relative silence making the odd meaningless comment now and then until the journey was over.

At the deserted bus terminal Jack paid the fare and included a generous tip. Once again portraying a rather forgetful elderly gentleman, he opened the left hand back door, walked around to the rear of the taxi, opened the rear right hand door and retrieved his bag. He thanked the driver and walked away mumbling to himself.

The driver was about to drive off when he saw both back doors still open.

"Silly old fool," he cursed as he alighted to close both of them

As he walked back to his seat he saw Jack in the company of Brendan and Yvette and flittingly thought, "Where did they come from?"

"Well, that went extremely well," concluded Jack. "We will just wait for the taxi to drive away and then let's change direction and walk to the hotel which isn't too far away."

"What if we are noticed?" asked Yvette "They will most likely call the police." She then said answering her own question

"No chance of that, here, put on these disguises," Jack replied, as he handed over two wigs, glasses and a moustache.

"Where shall we change into these?"

"Out in the open of course; if anyone is about they will think that we are going to a fancy dress do or are involved in something prankish."

Yvette and Brendan looked a little sheepish as they donned their temporary disguises.

They were at the hotel within twenty minutes and attracted no attention from anybody as they walked through the streets.

"Okay my good friends, time to disappear again."

"What do you mean disappear again?"

"I'm checking in by myself, but stay close."

Brendan and Yvette held hands and disappeared from view.

Once inside the hotel Jack approached the concierge desk and pretended to look quite distressed.

"I say my good man, I am in a spot of bother, I am stranded here for a few days due to circumstances beyond my control and I need some emergency lodgings. Could you accommodate me?"

The hotel duty manager stopped what he was doing and glanced at Jack analysing him in the process.

"We are rather full sir. It really depends on what you wanted and are prepared to pay. All of our less expensive suites are fully booked."

"Then I suppose I will just have to make do with one of the more expensive ones, hey what," Jack said as he produced his platinum American Express Card from his breast pocket.

'Mr Jack Stern' the duty manager said as he read the card's details. "You must be quite important sir; I haven't seen one of these in ages."

"Not really," Jack said in his elderly voice.

"Will the executive suite do sir? It is unoccupied and will remain so until the end of the week."

"That will be fine."

"Excellent, I need some details, could you fill in this form for our records please." Jack readily obliged and attended to duty manager's request.

"Quite extraordinary"

"What's that?" asked Jack

"Well, in a short period of time, we have had two Jack Sterns staying here at the hotel; the only difference being the home address and the dates of birth."

"As you said, 'extraordinary' perhaps I will get to meet the other Jack Stern while I am here."

"That would be quite spooky sir," the manager said as he raised his eyebrows.

At that instant Brendan sneezed and he and Yvette instantly appeared before the duty manager's eyes and disappeared again. The duty manager shook his head in disbelief and rubbed his eyes.

"Something the matter?" asked Jack

"Will you need some help with your bag sir?" he replied in a slow and deliberate fashion as he ignored Jack's previous question.

"Not at all, as you can see, I travel very light, I only have the one. Thank you for your assistance" Jack said as he took possession of the key.

"The room is situated on the 4th floor."

"Yes, I can still read, thank you so much."

The duty manager grunted a reply and went about his duties as his mind tried to fathom what he had just seen.

The executive suite was much more lavish than Brendan had enjoyed on his previous stay at the hotel. Even Yvette commented on its décor after she contained her laughter.

"That was so funny, what you did Jack," she giggled.

"It wasn't intentional," replied Brendan a little annoyed at losing his power.

"We will have to be doubly careful and make certain that you don't have a profound sneezing attack otherwise we will all be caught," Jack rightfully cautioned his friends

"I wonder what set you off; it was probably cheap perfume or dust I suppose." Yvette speculated adding to the conversation

"You're not prone to hay fever are you?" Jack asked

"Not at all," Brendan replied.

"Look at the bright side, you regained your visibility quickly, that's all that matters, so don't worry about it," Jack said. He made certain that the room was secure and that they had not been followed, and looked out of the windows that faced the street below.

"In any case, I think that I have a plausible explanation," he said as he faced them.

"And that is?" Brendan asked.

"A sneeze in physiological terms is a nasal orgasm."

"W-w-what did you say?"

"A nasal orgasm closely, if not perfectly, approximates the same neuronal discharge as a sexual one."

Brendan blushed at the thought.

"So men are capable of multiple orgasms!" Yvette comically deduced and then cheekily said "But only if they have a sneezing attack"

"Quite so," Jack confirmed and continued, "as you may gather, the sexual aspect robs you of power and that is the reason why so many strict religious orders advocate celibacy."

"And that is what attracts women to priests" Brendan suggested as he remembered the many women who had recently flaunted themselves at him

"Pardon"

"Think about it, those highly evolved mystic monks with all of that power imagine what sort of incredible energized lovemaking they are capable of. No wonder black trackers exist," Brendan subtly argued.

Yvette looked away and avoided looking into Jack's eyes. The suggestion of black trackers tore at her heart. This was something she was not, she was simply a woman in love; it was the opinions of others that tormented her.

"Are you okay Yvette?" Brendan asked sensing the change in her mood.

"I was thinking about the girls at The Infirmary. With all that sexual energy, I wondered how much suffering they've endured, and whether they've serviced a priest or two and experienced the mystical power you spoke of."

"There's only one way of finding out – we'll ask them," Jack replied. "And tonight is the time to strike!!!!" he boldly announced.

"But why so quick. We're hardly prepared!" Brendan replied

"Ah, that's where you're wrong," Jack corrected the handsome priest "I've managed to get a few people interested, all it needs is for us to act and act quickly. Now, how developed is your power of telepathy?"

"I don't know, why do you ask?"

"Because when we strike we will have to be in intimate contact with each other."

"What about Yvette?"

"She will stay here and we will collect her later. To play safe I have obtained some miniature radio transmitters," Jack said. He went to his bag and produced two sets containing wireless ear pieces and microphones. "These are state of the art capable of transmitting over a distance of about 200 metres. One for the ear to hear with and a microphone disguised as a stick pin for the label to catch your voice."

"Father, how do you know about things like this?" Yvette asked.

"From my theatrical days at university we had to learn about such things for authenticity. We once produced a spy drama for the stage so we learnt about these gadgets. In those days they were quite cumbersome, not as small and sophisticated as today's equipment."

"You're very different to other priests," Yvette concluded.

"Absolutely I joined relatively late in life so I am more experienced in a variety of avenues than those who entered the seminary straight from college."

Yvette seemed satisfied with his explanation and asked, "Will you still adopt my suggestion for rescuing the girls?"

"Providing Jack here doesn't experience a sneezing attack," Jack replied, looking directly at Brendan who remained silent and was not amused.

32

SILENT STRIKE

Jack picked up his mobile phone and selected The Infirmary's telephone number from its memory. Yvette and Brendan looked on.

"Hello, this is The Infirmary, Christina speaking, how may I be of assistance."

"May I speak to Mr Badcock, please?"

"It's rather late sir, I'll check if he's still in, just one moment." Jack patiently waited until the call was transferred.

"Louis Badcock here"

"Ah, Mr Badcock my name is Mr Rumplestein; we met a few days ago. I've decided to partake of your establishment's facilities. My clients are more than interested. However, they want me to give them feedback from my first-hand experience before they dive in so to speak."

"That will be our pleasure Mr Rumplestein. Yours will be on the house of course. When can we expect you?" Louis Badcock greedily asked.

"This may seem strange but my preferred time for lovemaking is usually about 1am. I don't sleep very well and sex really helps," Jack said in his elderly voice as he thought up a convenient excuse

"That's nothing to worry about we get all sorts of unusual requests," Louis answered.

"One other thing"

"And that is." Badcock asked

"I would prefer to be the last customer and have the girls all to myself so that I can give my clients the appropriate recommendations if you know what I mean?"

"I'm sure you'll find them equally good, but to make certain, I'll give them an hour's rest and a shot of vitamins before you arrive, so they're up to it. Tell me, once you're satisfied with the service, what sort of client numbers can we expect?" Louis asked, as he mentally calculated the potential profit he was about to make

"At this stage I have thirty five confirmed professionals some of the others are playing hard to get but I somehow think are not going to pass up this opportunity" Jack replied sensing Badcock's greed.

"Excellent I guarantee you that we will give them the time of their lives."

"That remains to be seen, Louis." Jack knowing full well how the evening would turn out

"I have no doubts." Louis thought for a moment and then asked. "What time can we expect you?"

"Midnight tonight."

"Until midnight" Badcock signed off and cradled the phone

Jack switched off his phone and said, "Phase one over Badcock's expecting me at twelve o'clock midnight tonight."

"Let's hope that everything goes smoothly," Yvette said.

"One thing" Brendan asked a little uneasy of the task ahead

"Yes?"

"If I manage to get the girls out safely, where do I take them?" Brendan asked

"That's up to you, surprise me! Remember you've got the talents, make something happen," Jack responded openly inviting the priest to be wildly creative.

Brendan remained silent as he cast his mind into the murkiness of the future, seeking solutions. Yvette stood by his side and also remained silently pensive.

Later that night at 11.45pm Jack disguised as Isaac Rumplestein and Brendan completely invisible took a taxi from the hotel to The Infirmary.

The duo arrived completely unnoticed as The Infirmary was bustling with activity. The restaurant was almost three-quarters full, much to Brendan's disgust; however, Jack saw it as an advantage. Badcock was milling about with some of the perfectly satisfied, if not exhausted patrons, sharing a smutty joke here and there as he sipped on his Bacardi and coke. As soon as he saw Jack walk in he excused himself and ran over to Jack and broadly smiled, before he had a chance to say anything Jack verbally attacked him in a loud voice.

"What's this Mr Badcock?!!! I thought you quite clearly told me that you would give the girls a rest before I had my ways with them. The restaurant is almost full and it would appear full of sexually-charged bulls needing immediate relief It's 12 o'clock Mr Badcock!!"

Badcock swallowed hard, not knowing what to say. Greed had got the better of him; he had indeed double booked both the restaurant and the girls.

"I've made a terrible mistake Mr Rumplestein. I shouldn't have arranged for you to visit tonight without checking the bookings. I'd lost your details so I had no way of contacting you. What can I say but I'm very sorry, the girls will finish up about 2.30am, so how about it then?" Badcock said, most apologetically, hoping that it would cool his adversary down.

"Like I said Badcock, I want them all to myself, fresh as daisies not shagged out!!! Otherwise I might have to take my customers elsewhere!!"

Badcock was becoming agitated at Jack's tone of voice, and at the prospect of losing his valuable clients, not only for himself but for Longevity Plus as well.

"Mr Rumplestein, perhaps we could sit down and talk about this over a cocktail or two," he said as he looked around rather embarrassed and hoped that the other patrons had not taken any notice of the scene that Jack had just created.

"Look Badcock, I have a hard cock and I want some tail. I'm tired, grumpy and need some sleep. I have a clientele of doctors whose sperm-counts are going through the roof and if they do not receive professional attention within 48 hours God knows what will happen. Do I make myself clear? Can't you create some sort of emergency to clear the house out?"

Brendan who was standing close by all the time latched onto the content of Jack's outburst and slipped upstairs.

"Mr Rumplestein, please relax; come sit down. I'll try to do my best. Please have a drink on us. Please," Badcock desperately pleaded.

Jack feigned a softening of his heart and pretended to reluctantly agree. Badcock led Jack alias Mr Rumplestein around some tables to a quieter part of the restaurant and summoned a waitress. Brendan meanwhile had reached the red light section of The Infirmary. The last thing he wanted to see was the girls doing it; even though it was a natural act it didn't appeal to him at this stage of his evolution.

He stood at the end of the corridor mindful of the security cameras. He'd been caught once before, a valuable lesson for him as it taught and showed him the powers that he possessed. Brendan stared at one of the cameras and with a flick of his finger dispatched its lens straight into the ceiling to record nothing but white. Then grinning to himself, he visualized all of the building's fire system, namely the water sprinklers, located in the ceilings becoming very, very hot so hot that they burst and sprayed water everywhere extinguishing all of the imaginary flames that had engulfed The Infirmary all of which he achieved without mentally intoning OMRA Brendan had ascended to the next step of his capabilities.

The reality of his thoughts expressed themselves through the mixture of sounds that reached his ears. Water gushed and splashed all around him, girls screamed, some as they threw off their clients and the others just for the sake of it as the alarm bells relentlessly shouted 'evacuate, evacuate the building'

Everyone ran into the corridor seeking escape, fearful of being caught in a burning inferno. Brendan stepped forward and opened a door to a room that was empty. He stood by the door and as each girl tried to run past he grabbed her by the wrist and flung her into the room much to her unexpected surprise. In a matter of thirty seconds he had gathered all of them closed the door and revealed himself to be alive and perfectly dry.

"Oh my god," they cried

"We thought you were dead," Felicity said blissfully tearful.

"Badcock told us you met with an unfortunate accident," Naomi confided

"I did," replied Brendan, "and in the process I discovered my true self, but, enough of that, I've come to take you all away."

"Where do we go? None of us have a home."

"Then I'll find you one, trust me," Brendan assured them. The girls clung to his every word, in their hearts they cherished his love for them and the fact that he had returned to rescue them. Brendan signalled for them to stand nice and close next to him.

"My beautiful ladies, we are going to walk out of this place totally unnoticed."

"Thanks to the commotion" Naomi guessed.

"Not quite, you will all become invisible providing you do one thing and one thing only without letting go for one second and that is, hold hands."

"How...why," many whispered.

"I can't explain how it works, it just does, so line up behind Felicity, stand closely behind one another, join hands and follow me. Remember never let go of anyone's hand no matter what happens. Walk softly; don't make a sound and never let go, okay?"

They all nodded even though they were afraid and fearful

"Excellent Felicity give me your hand" Brendan said as he mentally intoned OMRA just to be sure and with a confident sparkle in his eye opened the door and led the girls out into the corridor. It was empty, the sprinklers continued to merrily dump water everywhere. The fire alarms had gone berserk and the deafening noise they made flung itself around the walls all over the place.

Down the stairs Brendan and the girls went, slowly, stealth fully, in harmony. They did not see a soul until they almost reached the bottom floor where the restaurant was located. Some of Badcock's thugs came rushing up the stairs and Brendan pressed himself against the wall. The girls instantly copied his movement and held their breath in total fear of being detected. The thugs passed by and brushed their bodies against some of the girls leaving behind a stench of murderous intent.

Brendan and the girls continued down the stairs until they reached the restaurant floor. Brendan looked around and saw that the area was deserted freedom it seemed beckoned just metres away through the main doors, but then Louis Badcock emerged from the kitchen with six of his henchmen. Badcock signalled for the main front doors to be locked and barred for he believed that his prized tools of the trade namely his girls were still somewhere in the building and he did not want to lose them. If anything he would be the one to decide who could stay or go and how they would do so, either dead or alive. The thugs that had previously rushed upstairs returned via the same route.

"Nothing upstairs Boss, it's all clean no fire, no girls, no nothing!"

"Did you check the penthouse suite?"

"Nothing Boss!"

"They must still be in the building, no one saw them leave, they must be hiding somewhere, but where?" Badcock loudly said as he squinted and wiped the water away from his eyes. "Check everything again, cupboards, rooms, lockers!" he ordered and waved his thugs away.

"Yes Boss!" his thugs and henchmen answered as they turned to leave.

"Damn water! Some fire system! Doesn't know when to stop! I'll catch my death of cold! Where's that damn fire brigade?" he bitterly complained as he started to shiver

"I can hear the siren's Boss. They must be just around the corner," one of his fat thugs said

Brendan and the girls heard the same and made their way to the centre of the restaurant – and waited. Once the fireman arrived it would allow them the opportunity of finally escaping. Badcock's thugs and henchmen had not gone very far when one of the girls started to sneeze. They all turned to see where the noise had come from. It was contagious. Several of the other girls sneezed as well and then Brendan, not wishing to, let out an enormous one. His entire troupe stood out completely visible, looking extremely wet and afraid except for Brendan who looked at Badcock and waved as if to say, 'Helloooo, I'm back!!!!!!!!'

Badcock drew out a silver revolver from beneath his coat's breast pocket and pointed it at Brendan and the girls. His action prompted his thugs to react in similar fashion. The sound of clicking revolvers surrounded them causing the girls to shiver more from fright than from the cold.

"Well Mr Stern, I don't know how you managed to defeat us last time, but now it's different! How fast are you? Faster than a speeding bullet? Or bullets coming at you from different directions!!" Badcock said in a loud clear and deliberate voice, as he stared at Brendan whilst he squeezed his revolver ever so tightly.

Brendan assessed the situation and could not imagine how he could protect his cherished ladies. Granted he could extend his power to make them invisible, but to guarantee their safety against a barrage of bullets, that was quite another thing.

"Well!! Answer me!! What's the matter? Finally met your match? You didn't think that you could defeat me and the family did you?"

Brendan remained motionless and speechless.

"Didn't your mother ever tell you not to play with guns? You naughty boy!" a voice rang out next to Badcock who turned and was startled to see the real Jack Stern, alias Mr. Rumplestein materialize before him. Before Badcock has a chance to say or do anything Jack Stern quickly continued, "Let me introduce you to my biblical friend 'able cane'. With that Jack crashed the cane across Badcock's gun hand inflicting instant excruciating pain, causing Badcock to drop the weapon and bend forward exposing his buttocks. Jack then whipped the cane against Badcock's protruding posterior inflicting even more grief. Badcock stiffened back not knowing which one was worse, his hand or his backside

"Hate seeing an animal in distress," Jack said as he struck one final blow to the nape of Badcock's neck.

This gave enough time for Brendan to restore his invisibility and that of the girls. He signalled for all of them to fall flat along the floor. Badcock collapsed in a heap whilst Jack stepped forward twirling the cane in both hands

"Anyone else want to rumba?" he teased his stunned onlookers

The thugs responded by wildly shooting at him. The bullets whizzed past Jack crashing into the wall and fixtures behind him.

"Nasty things guns….!!!" Jack said as he disappeared from view.

The cane remained spinning in mid air. The thugs stopped shooting their revolvers and stepped forward from their various positions. The others came running down from upstairs with guns in their hands. Once Badcock's militia had passed them by, Brendan and the girl's got up and crept towards the main doors. Badcock lay on the floor with the cane hovering above him spinning on its imaginary axis. His thugs looked on not knowing what to do, police and firemen burst in through the main front doors.

As the commotion spread throughout the bottom floor Brendan and the girls discreetly left.

The street outside was congested with fire brigade vehicles, police cars and onlookers. Brendan looked around for suitable transport but saw none in the confusion of flashing lights and bodies running to and fro. He cursed himself for not being prepared. Thoughts of taking a chance on the open streets crossed his mind but then he steadied his focus to find his master within and asked for guidance. Within moments the voice of his intuition suggested he try The Infirmary's car park where Jack Stern's 'lady' was waiting.

Brendan guided the girls through the outside chaos and walked steadily towards the red Ferrari. In the distance he could see a figure standing by its side. As they came closer Jack Stern, devoid of his Mr Rumplestein's disguise, could clearly be seen.

"Glad you could make it Mr Stern," Jack flippantly said. "How are you girls?" he added.

"Fine once you arrived. Tell us how did you do that?" one of the girls thankfully answered

"What are you talking about?"

"That thing with the cane." The same girl asked

"Oh that, just a magical levitation trick I learnt at university."

"Okay, enough! Brendan, tell me once and for all!" Brendan demanded to know

"Tell you what?" Jack answered blank faced and quite flippant.

"You have the power, correct!"

"Well this might answer your question," he replied, as he disappeared from view and reappeared behind Brendan.

"Satisfied?" he asked Brendan who turned around to face him

"Just to make completely certain, watch this," he said as he snapped his fingers and the cane that was part of his Mr Rumplestein's disguise came flying through the air and hovered before him

"When will you tell Yvette?"

"In good time and I suppose it will have to coincide when you tell yourself."

"What!"

"Your proper destiny"

Brendan frowned in confusion at this and said nothing more. Suddenly noises started to invade the relative peace of the car park. Badcock had come in hot pursuit with his band of thugs in tow to look for his girls and their rescuers.

"We better leave now," whispered Jack as he observed Badcock and his posse marching towards them

"Very well, let's run," Brendan suggested.

"Too slow, we'll take the Ferrari."

"It's a two seater with little or no room in the back!" Brendan snapped back as he thought that Jack's answered was completely absurd

"Only in your reality," Jack retorted. "Look, heaps of room, come girls get in," he said, as he opened the passenger door and pushed the seat forward to reveal a cavernous back seat. All of the girls without hesitation leapt in. Jack pushed the seat back into position, gestured for Brendan to get in and then seated himself.

Badcock and his armed men advanced through the car park and searched everything and everywhere. They stopped and assembled themselves in front of the Ferrari.

"At least they didn't get away with this," Badcock grunted. "It'll pay for some of my losses."

"Invisibility please maestro!" Jack whispered as he observed Badcock from inside of the cabin

"But Boss!!" one of the thugs exclaimed.

"Yes you buffoon, what do you want?" Badcock angrily barked frustrated at not having found his girls

"The car"

"Is very nice, I know!"

"No it's gone!!!"

"What!!!!" screamed Badcock as he looked at the empty bay. "It was j-just th-there!!!!" he stuttered.

"Accelerated motion please" Jack softly coaxed his 'lady's' motor to spring into life and then he gently released the handbrake and floored the accelerator. The car responded with complete obedience, not a flutter, the rear wheels brutally dug into the compound's bitumen, his 'lady' proudly pushed her chest forward and sent all before her sprawling to the ground

"Where to now" Brendan gasped as Jack sped the Ferrari away.

"Let's collect Yvette and then I'll take us to a safe house that I've arranged." He replied as he concentrated on the road ahead of them.

"How did you get all the girls into the back seat," Brendan asked a little more relaxed now that he got used to the fast speed at which they were travelling.

"It's all a matter of perception, understanding and hidden knowledge."

"Explain."

"Everything that exists has its own level of consciousness capable of reacting to all other levels of consciousness, but limited only in its ability to create." Jack abstractly replied

"So?"

"This Ferrari, believe it or not, is alive by virtue of its consciousness and therefore can adapt to suggestion if it thinks that it can coincide with the suggestion's concept of reality. In this case it agreed that there was more space than material, therefore it simply pooled all of the space together and generated a giant void capable of transporting all of the girls."

"Amazing," Brendan replied indifferently having heard this explanation before.

"No, more like understanding, my friend," Jack corrected the handsome priest

"Then you have this Christ principle as well and it appears are much more advanced than me."

"I suppose you could say that." Jack said without giving it much thought

"You knew from the beginning, but how?"

"By your aura, it's pure white and brilliant, quite extraordinary. It would have been a profound shame to let you go uninstructed when I first met you at the roadside café." Jack explained as he remembered their chance encounter

"You took a chance."

"Sort of" Jack replied

"Have you seen the same aura in other people?" Brendan asked, as he became increasingly fascinated by this newfound knowledge.

"Now and then"

"So what did you do?"

"Nothing I'm sorry to say." Jack admitted

"Why?" Brendan asked, feeling somewhat disappointed with Jack's reply

"A gut feeling telling me, either they weren't ready or that circumstances weren't right. In your case it was the opposite so I let it happen. Aren't you glad I did so?" Jack asked with a smile

"It certainly has changed my perception of…"

"Religion?" Jack interrupted Brendan mid sentence

"And the rest"

"That's why it's very important for you to find your true destiny," Jack warmly asserted.

"I'll have to meditate on that," Brendan answered truthfully.

"You won't have to do that; it will come to you very quickly if it hasn't already done so."

Brendan forced a smile and thought for a while.

"Almost there," Jack said. He turned the corner of the street that led to the Hotel Large, and parked the Ferrari in a 'No Standing at All Times' loading bay, directly opposite the building.

"Keep it invisible my boy!" Jack said as he was about to leave the car

"Yes Master," Brendan replied as he snapped out of his train of thought. "Wait, she's not in there they've abducted her!"

"How do you know?" Jack asked.

"I can hear her. She's in that fruit and vegetable truck over there."

Brendan said with a sense of concern as he pointed to the vehicle

"Head and Roots above the Rest," Jack muttered sarcastically as he read the truck's signage.

"It's the transport they use to ferry the drugs from the hospital to where ever."

"What an exciting morning! Rescue Yvette and discover the location of one of their major depots, if not manufacturing labs. Jack you see, how right I was, you're absolutely brilliant!!" Jack heartedly congratulated the handsome priest

Brendan nodded in agreement. He looked back to see how the girls were doing. They were all asleep. Content that they were finally safe once and for all.

"Do we follow with or without the girls?" Jack asked as he continued to observe.

"It depends on the truck."

"Let's follow it and see."

"Okay" Brendan replied as he sensed the adventure that lay ahead.

33

INTELLECTUAL INTERCOURSE

The interior of the Ferrari felt similar to that of a chapel during vespers. Both Jack and Brendan lowered their voices to a whisper out of respect for their precious cargo as they drove along.

Brendan glanced back at them and remarked. "They look so innocent; one could hardly imagine what sordid experiences they've been put through."

"Sleep does that to you."

"What's that?" Brendan asked softly

"Returns you to your innocence," Jack replied, as he concentrated on the truck's movements. He went on to say, "You will observe, irrespective of an individual's outer appearance and personality, they will always look so peaceful during sleep and the reason for that is, their soul travels back to the realm where all things are at peace with each other."

"Is that how you define innocence?"

"Precisely" Jack relied knowledgeably

"So, you are saying that if the outer personality can mirror or be one with their soul, they will always be innocent in the 'awake' state."

"Yes."

"Hmm, that is a hard concept for me to grasp."

"No it's not; think about it in a metaphysical way and you will grasp its concept, take the opposite approach and you reduce everything to a mechanistic scientific approach which is doomed to failure."

"So is that what is wrong with the scientific world?" asked Brendan.

"And the religions one as well," Jack replied with authority.

"Explain."

"If you read the modern world history, going back about 2,000 to 3,000 years, and I am sure you may have studied this during your seminary days."

"Only what the tutors expected of us," Brendan interrupted.

"Well, you will find that many of the so called witches, and even catholic saints were hunted down and killed by various means including burning, crucifixion, or being ripped apart by animals. These people were in fact misunderstood for one simple reason, they were above and beyond superstition and they were dedicated metaphysical investigators. They learnt of the laws of the universe and put them into practice; it enabled the world's human population to advance by degrees to higher levels of understanding by the most obscure means of propagation.

So you see all of these individuals discovered this Christ principle. That is why the most venerated master soul, Jesus himself, realized that it was not restricted to him alone and it led him to state that many would follow that would achieve even greater results."

"Do you think that was true?"

"Certainly, however their records are hidden in the secret schools of learning and in the most remote monasteries, irrespective of their religious faith. So you see metaphysics has no religion."

"So how does one acquire these talents?"

"By the simple process of discovering and learning from the master within, who will come knocking on your door through the voice of intuition, which the majority of people ignore; otherwise, a sufficiently evolved soul once connected to its outer personality and purely innocent in nature, can achieve all of its wishes without the need for instruction."

"Is that me?" Brendan asked shyly,

"It is," Jack once again answered with authority

"If what you are saying is so good for the world, why then would these enlightened souls be persecuted?"

"For two reasons, firstly most humans when they do not under-stand something become afraid and that fear causes them to destroy the very thing they should have embraced. Secondly, the present world as we know it runs on deceit, a terrible disease that opposes enlightenment in all of its aspects. This disease delights in instilling and feeding on the fear of humans it has been so successful that the majority of humans are completely obsessed with it and promote it continuously."

"Let me guess," Brendan asked.

"Go on," Jack consented.

"In law making and in publishing bad news"

"You've got it."

"So what is the solution?"

"To re-educate the masses and make all of them aware of the power that lies within." Jack explained

"What about deceit?"

"That entity can only exist on fear. The very fear of taking the plunge into a whole new world of thought strengthens it

"Momentarily I suppose, so it won't just disappear." Brendan guessed

"It can't and won't because we are not all at the same levels of spiritual evolution."

"So it continues?" Brendan sadly concluded

"I'm afraid so."

"Where does that leave us?" Brendan asked and then paused for a brief moment to collect his thoughts and then he suggested "Would the proposition that the only world we can change and thoroughly enjoy is the one inside of us, and perhaps in the process introduce others to it, for their advancement and ethereal joy."

"Well said I'll make a proper priest of you yet." Jack laughed quietly as he complimented the handsome priest

"There's one thing that still bothers me."

"And what's that Brendan?" Jack asked in a fatherly fashion

"I have come across the philosophical sayings 'so above as below' in my readings. If what I experience here on earth is below, does that mean above is the same?" Brendan asked sounding a little confused

"Only if you take it literally; remember this is a metaphysical statement. To give you a glimmer of the truth what it properly implies is that once an individual discovers this Christ principle, he or she can engage in creating physical realities from the responsive unseen."

Jack's explanation satisfied Brendan to some degree but it caused him to think of other things. "Even though deceit is everywhere, surely my beloved Catholic Church is not all bad, look at all of the charitable good it does."

"I agree, but only if the charity does not satisfy deceitful purpose and only if it's limited."

"What do you mean by limited?"

"One cannot continually support the poor or give to those who pretend to be poor. It is better to teach these people to create their own wealth; otherwise we become part of deceit's web. So make me a promise, whatever you do in your life, whatever you encounter, always look at the percentage hold that deceit has and act accordingly. Furthermore, never be afraid or allow fear to enter you again."

Brendan stared at Jack and resolved to do his best.

"Enough lesson time, let's rescue Yvette," Jack suggested.

"Where do you think we are?" asked Brendan.

"Somewhere in a farming belt I should think. Let's confirm it on the GPS system for future reference."

Jack activated the dashboard computer to display the co-ordinates. He kept one eye on the truck ahead and one on the screen.

"It's slowing down," Brendan observed.

"Shall we follow it in and rescue her now?" Jack asked as he also slowed his car

"I feel like a hound dog," replied Brendan.

"Very well pup, let's go and fetch."

The truck slowed to a crawl and then turned left onto a road marked Private. It stopped and flashed its headlights in a pre-determined pattern. Up ahead a single blue light flashed once and a set of heavy gates previously unnoticed by all slowly opened. The truck rumbled through, followed by Jack's Ferrari. Armed guards stood at each gate.

"What can you see?" Jack asked as he surveyed the area.

"Lots of fields full of corn, wheat, scarecrows, eerie figures and shadows. Then of course there are the buildings ahead, which include the farmhouse, machinery shed, looks like some animal quarters and a series of glass hothouses. That's as much as I can see in the moonlight and you?"

"Just the same, except to the right of the hothouses I glimpsed a long row of reflectors in the ground, which suggest a private landing strip."

Brendan looked in the same direction and came to the same conclusion. The truck drove up to the machinery shed and parked parallel to it. The driver and his associate sat in the cab with left the engine running. Jack pulled up next to him. Everyone was oblivious of their presence.

"What now?" Brendan whispered.

"Go and get her is the order."

Brendan stepped out of the Ferrari and looked at the side of the truck realizing there was much more space than solid matter. He re-arranged things to suit the purpose, all of the matter streamed to the perimeter of the wall, exposing the interior's contents with Yvette seated on a crate looking very lost. Her face was covered with many bruises, the result of putting up a fight and resisting her captors. Brendan decided to avenge her injuries before taking her out of the truck. He walked back to the driver's door and permanently fused its locking mechanisms with his mind and then he remotely turned the cabin's radio up to a volume setting beyond its capabilities. The noise was deafening. The driver and his mate went crazy and no matter what they tried they could not turn the radio off or get out of the cab. They even tried to break the windscreen without success. Brendan watched with sublime satisfaction.

"That should give you something to think about you nasty, nasty men." He thought

The noise from the radio could be heard everywhere. Lights soon came on in the farmhouse and elsewhere. People started shouting, "Turn the f...ng racket off."

The truck's occupants couldn't do anything more than suffer the pain. Armed guards came running in from the fields. Brendan quietly walked away and through the opening in the truck's sidewall took Yvette by the hand and led her out. She shed a tear of joy at the sight of him and lowered her head to hide her injuries. Brendan gently lifted her head and stroked her face, instantly repairing her wounds. Guards milled around the truck shouting obscenities. By now the driver and his mate were faint with exhaustion, their hearing was permanently damaged. Brendan and Yvette entered the silence of the Ferrari and they sped away.

"Are you alright?" Jack asked.

"Yes, I am fine now," Yvette answered, feeling safe once more

"That's quite a show you put on Jack."

"It is what they deserved," Brendan answered feeling no quilt for his actions

"Forgotten about Christian virtues already?" Jack teased the handsome priest

Brendan remained silent.

Jack looked at Yvette and asked, "I thought you were safe in the hotel?"

"It was that damn hotel desk clerk; he must have recognized us when Jack lost his power momentarily during his sneeze. I was asleep in bed when he and that policeman who we encountered at the Presbytery burst in with two other nasty men."

"Did they…?" Brendan asked fearing the worst

"No, I resisted as best I could, but the policeman hit me in revenge for what happened to him that night at the Presbytery. He threatened that they would deal with me good and proper at the farmhouse. I was supposed to be dessert for all of his farmhands," Yvette said with courage.

"Well, just as you suspected," Jack said as he looked at Brendan.

"Can I go back and…?" Brendan asked as clenched his teeth and tried to conceal his rage.

"No you have done enough for tonight."

"Yes Jack my other dashing knight in shining armour listen to the man"

Brendan blushed at the thought of it. Jack meanwhile steered his obedient lady towards the main gates, which had been left open and drove through.

Back at the farm, the farmhands and the guards tried their hardest to extract the driver of the truck and his offsider both of whom were unconscious by now. Nothing worked. They could not even open the doors or smash the windows. They managed to open the bonnet and disconnect the battery and fuses, but that had no effect and the deafening noise continued.

Jack looked back at the scene in his rear-view mirror.

"What exactly did you do Jack?" He asked Brendan

"When I saw what they had done to Yvette I thought that they should be taught a lesson. I instructed the doors and windows to resist all evil, and I asked the radio to cleanse the cabin's occupants with its sound, that only it could produce itself by self transition."

"Sounds like a nuclear process," Jack suggested.

"It has the desired result," was all that Brendan was prepared to say

"Well gentlemen…" Yvette started to say before she looked behind "how did you get all of the girls in here?"

"That's an involved story," Jack replied.

"Why don't you go and join them, there is more room back there," Brendan suggested.

"Okay, but where to now?" Yvette asked feeling a little tired after the day's strenuous events

"To the safe house," Jack replied as he pointed the Ferrari back onto the main country road.

34

DARK FORCES

Brendan O'Reilly's determination to cleanse The Infirmary of its sins and wicked people namely Louis Badcock and his cronies by magically activating and freezing the fire sprinkler system lasted until 7:00am the following morning. The fire department was at a loss as to how to stop the torrential flow of water through the building that was constantly fed by its fire sprinkler system. The outside pressure valve regulating the supply had been difficult to locate and when it had been it was found to be immoveable. It required the services of the local water corporation's emergency crew to solve the problem by shutting down the main supply to the street in which The Infirmary was located. From the time that Brendan and Jack escaped with the girls, to that when the water flow was stopped, the immediate area surrounding The Infirmary looked like a circus of frenzied activity. Badcock was distraught throughout the ordeal to say the least.

"My business is ruined," he was heard to have bitterly cursed

"The girls are gone and even if I got them back, where would I start again? There is nowhere, damn, it will take months to clean this mess up. Damn it, and damn that f….ing Jack Stern."

Badcock walked about the building grim faced. His waterlogged shoes either squished with his every step or they waded through deep water in rooms where it hadn't drained away.

The captain of the fire brigade that had attended the emergency approached him and stated, "Mr Badcock, we've looked around the building as best as we can it's our duty to submit a report on the extent and nature of the damage incurred. As you are aware, there was no fire, simply a malfunction of the sprinkler system. The building has suffered major water damage throughout with flooding at all levels. The fixtures and furniture in most areas are ruined. The bottom floor appears to be all right as it is made from concrete, the upper levels being constructed from timber are all suspect. It is difficult to draw a conclusion at this stage, time will tell as to the extent of structural damage caused by material distortion. We will probably have to call in the city engineers for their opinion and then work hand in hand with your insurance company's assessors. At this stage I would say that It looks as though The Infirmary is completely incapacitated," he said with a smirk on his face.

The captain being a born again christian had never approved of the establishment.

Badcock stared at the fire chief and mentally dismissed him as being a non-event. If anything, his comments made him more determined to resurrect The Infirmary in a bigger and better way than previously. His only concern was that of his superior, whom he assumed would not be pleased. Perhaps his explanation and future vision would placate the beast. Badcock's mobile phone vibrated in his jacket pocket followed by a muffled ring tone.

"Hello, Badcock here."

"I've heard of our misfortune Louis, can you tell me anymore?" the small dark figure asked.

"Not over the phone, we need to meet urgently. I will call you when I have arranged everything." Badcock abruptly replied and without any warning disconnected the call.

The small dark figure was not amused by Badcock's sharp tone of voice or his rude telephone manners but in a quaint way respected him anyhow

By 9:00am that morning Badcock had orchestrated all those that he thought would once and for all rid him of any further annoyances caused by Brendan O'Reilly whom he knew as Jack Stern and his associate Jack Stern whom he knew as Mr Rumplestein.

The meeting was held in the medical conference room at Longevity Plus. As usual, the small dark figure sat in its favourite dark corner deciding to listen before making any comments.

Badcock had assembled the best of his henchmen plus the Harsh Man who was still nursing his bruised ego following his encounter with Brendan. The Ricci girls were also present. Everyone was seated around the conference table looking rather nervous.

"We have a big problem, as you all know. Mr Jack Stern is a particularly annoying man who swindled the Ricci's father out of their ownership of The Infirmary with the assistance of his old sidekick Mr Rumplestein. He has now stolen our prostitutes and almost destroyed The Infirmary. The manner in which he did this, leads me to conclude that he is no ordinary individual. He appears to be a master of illusions. I would call him a magician with a gifted criminal mind. What he is up to is anyone's guess. He might be working for another organization or he might be bent on setting up his own. It does not matter which, we have to stop him and stop him fast. Our friends in the police department are on the job now as I speak and will alert us once they locate him dead or alive. The former I would prefer and I have instructed them to shoot on sight I don't think finding Mr Stern will be difficult, there are not too many red Ferraris around here."

The small dark figure spoke. "What will you do if you find him alive?"

"Waste him of course."

"How do you intend doing that when you have previously failed miserably?"

"Who told you that?" Badcock asked looking quite enraged.

"Our colleagues the Ricci girls who witnessed the events of your first physical encounter with Mr Stern that is how you came to injure your hand isn't it?" Louis avoided the question.

"So what do you propose?" Badcock asked, once he had regained his composure.

"Like you said, we are not dealing with an ordinary man. Unlike you Louis, I have been doing some research of my own and taking into account what happened to you and the Harsh Man over there, and the manner in which our pharmaceuticals have been switched or altered. I think we are dealing with someone who is super human and is on some sort of super hero ego trip. It is my guess that he has trained for decades with some sort of hybrid Zen masters. This would account for some of his talents, especially in the art of warfare, deception, invisibility and all that. So your idea that he is some sort of magician is vaguely correct. However, what he does is for real and the only way we can defeat him is by finding someone who has greater powers and is attracted to our way of thinking. As you know our organization has vast resources thanks to the diversity of our operations. There is nothing that we can't do. This Mr Stern is not even a fly in our ointment. He is a meaningless speck, but he must not be allowed to become anything more. I have contacted our arms' division and instructed them to find us an operational D-Man who have existed for thousands of years and have been recorded in history under different names. They delight in instilling fear into people as a means of control and defeat. Their methods are limitless, in terms of being able to deal with one person or a multitude, and in being able to induce all magnitudes of fear. Their power is such that one small glance from them can reduce any person to ashes by the process of self-destruction induced by the body's own unstable thermodynamics system."

A deadly silence pervaded the room.

A satanic smile spread across the face of the Harsh Man, he was already savouring his deathly revenge on Jack Stern.

Badcock swallowed hard, his voice reduced to a harsh whisper, "These D-Men, are they devils? Will we be safe?"

"As long as you genuinely support and believe in our cause," the small dark figure answered.

"What do you mean?" Badcock asked, becoming increasingly concerned as to what others thought of him

"They have an uncanny ability of knowing who is loyal and who isn't, and no, they are not devils in the true sense of the word, but they represent everything demonic or damaging that starts with the letter 'D'."

"How quickly can you get this guy over here?" asked the Harsh Man as he was rather impatient to get things moving

"Our organization has one on stand-by all of the time he is on his way right now."

"Excellent!" everyone present responded.

"We need to lay a trap if we are to rid ourselves of this nuisance," the Harsh Man suggested.

"Precisely," the small dark figure agreed. "What do you suggest?" it asked

"We must take advantage of Mr Stern's super hero ego by anticipating his next most likely move I Think that sooner or later he will come back and want to destroy the pharmaceutical drugs at Longevity Plus that is where we should be waiting for him." The Harsh Man put forward

"I am one step ahead of you, good suggestion however."

The Harsh Man frowned, a little disappointed at being under minded by the small dark figure's cockiness

"I have taken steps to install electromagnetic detectors in the hospital storeroom. These are high tech devices obtained from the air force and used by NASA themselves they detect all life forms, so if our Mr Stern thinks he can enter our premises undetected, he will be in for a real shock."

Just then the phone rang.

The Harsh Man who was sitting close to it, picked it up and answered

"Hello, yes, I will hand you over." The Harsh Man gestured to the small dark figure and handed over the cordless phone.

It listened intently and then exploded by shouting, "What, not again, damn him," and it violently slammed the phone down.

"What happened?" one of the Ricci girls asked taken aback by the small dark figures outburst

"That was the farm, they can't explain what happened or how it happened, but that Yvette girl has disappeared and our most trusted and reliable drivers have met with a freak accident in the truck that they used it appears that they are both permanently deaf. No one saw anything, no one knows anything; it has to be that damn interfering Jack Stern character."

"We'd better install the detectors at the farm as well," the Harsh Man quickly suggested.

"Better do everything," Badcock loudly blurted "not just that, double up the guards, put those high tech detectors in the pharmacy, and tighten up everything. There's too much money involved here, we can't afford to lose any more shipments. What really bothers me is that I wanted to have that girl and raffle her off as a prize virgin."

"Perhaps if you are a really good boy I will give you that opportunity once again," a gravelly voice said as it reverberated around the room

They all looked around to see who had spoken.

Some of Badcock's henchmen drew their weapons in anticipation that it was Jack Stern

"There is no need for that," the invisible voice suggested as it swept the guns from their hands.

"What the hell," the startled henchman shouted many of whom momentarily lost their balance and fell off their chairs whilst some of the others scrambled to retrieve their weapons.

"Don't even think about it."

The Ricci girls looked frightened; they thought they were re-living the incident that saw Brendan O' Reilly dispatch the Harsh Man and Louis Badcock. They looked at the door and thought of running out of the room.

"No need to do that," the voice roughly told the twins.

"I am not whom you think I am," it said as the form of the D-man materialized before everyone's eyes.

"You got here quickly," Badcock said as he smiled.

"Quicker than you thought," the D-man answered.

"You've been here all along," the Harsh Man deduced.

The D-man nodded as Badcock and the rest of them surveyed his makeup. He stood 190 cms tall with an extremely athletic body; muscular and taut. His face was not unusual, ordinary in fact, but the most striking features about him were his nails and hair. They appeared metallic in nature as though they were intended for some sort of electrical conduction. His glance was terrifying and when he smiled his teeth magnified the terror he instilled in others. They swallowed hard, not knowing whether to be glad or fearful that they had him as an ally and as a means of disposing of unwanted nuisances.

The small dark figure stood up and walked over to the D-man.

"Well, do you know what to do?"

"Of course," he answered. "I have been fully briefed."

"So what will you do?" asked the Harsh Man.

"Play the waiting game, time means nothing to me."

"And then...?"

"When he appears, I shall use these to crucify him," the D-man replied as he displayed three highly luminous long pin-like objects in his hand that he had retrieved from his coat pocket.

35

SAFE HOUSE

The drive to Jack Stern's mountain hideaway was uneventful. Yvette although pure in nature did not have any airs about her she did not judge others nor compare herself to them and therefore had no difficulty in getting on with the girls once they had woken up. Their dubious past did not cause a problem. In fact, she considered them to have remained pure even though their bodies had been physically violated. Yvette explained to them who Jack Stern was namely, Brendan O'Reilly, the locum parish priest at Saint Pious and that he and the real Brendan O'Reilly, were to her understanding, close friends although in reality it was the other way around.

As Jack's Ferrari drew closer to its destination, Yvette recognized the countryside and asked, "Aren't we near the Hotel Alpine?"

"Actually we're on the other side of the National Forest."

"I didn't know there were private houses around here," she said.

"Just one," Jack replied

"Which is?"

"Jack's grandfather lived on the verge of the forest line before it was designated a National Park. He did not much care about the value of his property, for him it was more about the remarkable location, so he came to an agreement with the authorities over the land area when they repossessed his property. Somehow he found a legal loophole in the legislation that entitled him to a percentage of his original property. After much bickering, treats and negotiation that involved high brow lawyers he was allowed to stay after receiving compensation for the land that was taken away from him. In order to keep the bureaucrats quiet, he agreed to living beneath the ground so he constructed an underground hideaway. He got a bit carried away and tunnelled beyond his borders into the face of the mountain and discretely constructed a multi-layered retreat. It is quite impressive. He even devised a series of cleverly disguised windows in the mountain face, to give him a panoramic view of the horizon below and went to the extent of inventing a complex reflecting mirror system that re-created those images inside his hideaway so you can sit with your back to the window and still see outside."

"It's the perfect retreat for meditation," Brendan commented even though he had never been there.

"Is that right?" Jack asked as he knew that Brendan had no prior knowledge and was therefore bluffing

Jack pulled the Ferrari off the main road and steered it down an overgrown dirt track. He drove his timeless lady gently out of consideration for her delicate suspension and out of a desire to leave the track unmarked. The girls in the back seat sat up to admire the scenery which was made up of tall trees, majestic mountains and wildflowers that had arranged themselves in a dazzling array of colour and form. As they drove along the mountains in the distance drew closer and closer until they represented a solid impenetrable wall.

"Stop," the girls shouted thinking they were about to crash into them

Jack took no notice and drove the Ferrari straight into the mountain face. The girls braced themselves for a crushing impact but none came. Instead, the Ferrari drove smoothly through the mountainside and entered a very secret cave sufficiently large enough to accommodate two other vehicles.

"What happened?"

"I just parked the car." Jack dryly replied as though nothing had happened

The wall" One of the girls inquired completely confused by the event

"Optical creation, didn't I tell you Jack's grandfather was brilliant?" he answered.

"It looks so real, doesn't it ladies?" Jack asked as he studied their astonished faces and went on to further explain "He achieved the effect by multi layering the images. In that way, the final image that he created was almost alive by changing character with the time of day and the seasons. It has remained undetectable for decades."

"I'm not surprised," said Brendan. "I suppose he had some special powers as well?"

"Not quite, but he did think and read a lot. Acquired a lot of insight into the nature of some things," Jack explained.

Jack turned the engine off and proceeded to step out of the car.

Brendan followed and in true gentlemanly fashion, helped each one of the girls out of the rear seat. Jack led the way through the complex, which consisted of the original underground lodgings, now converted to a cellar for food storage, the ground floor for vehicle use and then a staircase that made its way through three other levels. The first was a heart of complex where all of the cooking and washing was done. The second was where the creative aspects of life were pursued and the third where communication in all of its modern day forms was conducted. Jack took them up to the third level and allowed them to admire the national park's scenery below before he cheekily asked tongue in cheek "How good are you girls at cooking?"

Yvette sensing his doubt quickly came to the rescue after seeing their shy and evasive reactions and took charge of the situation quite enthusiastically.

"Come along Mademoiselles don't take any notice of him, follow me," she merrily instructed them and led them downstairs to gather the necessary provisions from the cellar. She like the others was amazed to find a large array of canned and fresh produce and an upright freezer full of frozen fish, meat, breads, pastries and ice-cream confectionary. After consulting with her newly acquired 'sisters', she made the appropriate selections and went upstairs with them to cook up a storm, instructing them as she went. As they worked diligently to prepare a mini banquet, Yvette could not but notice how silent all of the kitchen appliances were, and deduced that it was very sophisticated equipment driven by advanced solar generated electricity. The girls watched her with a mixture of loving admiration and gratitude.

Each one in her own heart wished that her life could have been different so that she could have enjoyed her virginity for longer.

Jack and Brendan remained upstairs in silence and studied the projected landscape in detail.

"Jack, do you think we are safe here?" Brendan asked.

"I wouldn't have brought us here if I knew otherwise," he truthfully answered.

"You look quite pre-occupied."

"I am." Jack answered

"What's on your mind?"

"A number of matters"

"Such as?" Brendan asked wondering how serious they were.

"Well, I am afraid I might hurt you in discussing them."

"How?" Brendan inquired

"By telling you certain truths, are you ready?"

"I suppose."

Jack produced the copy of the Douay-Rheims version of the Holy Bible that he had found at Saint Pious presbytery and held it in his hands

"Do you remember back at the chateau when you learnt of the assassination of Monsignor Monahan and the attempt on the Archbishop? We shared our experiences and I suggested that certain members of the church might be involved in money laundering, if not worse, and furthermore they might be involved with those who are involved with Longevity Plus and The Infirmary. I didn't expand on it, but now that we are safely out of harm's way, it is time to detail what I have found and also to warn you about the dangers associated with your talents. Before I show you, do you know who the brothers in black are?"

"It is not a religious order that I am aware of, or even a nickname for one," answered Brendan. "Why do you ask?"

"Because in this biblical ledger it makes reference to them," Jack said as he pointed to the page that was open.

Brendan looked at the reference and pondered a while.

Sensing his loss for suggestion, Jack proceeded.

"It doesn't matter for now, what I want to share with you is how this represents a financial record of the church's involvement with The Infirmary. As you know prostitution in this state is illegal, therefore, a number of people I think have been paid to look the other way."

"Certain authorities," Brendan interrupted.

"The clergy, lobby groups such as anti-corruption, anti-prostitution, the police, both local and federal and who knows who else."

"Quite a list to support" Brendan deduced

"Most of these I think are paid cash in hand, but others run on bank accounts for taxation purposes, for one simple reason."

"And that is…?" Brendan asked

"To prevent being audited; as long as the government receives its share, it will leave you alone."

"Why do you think that the church is involved?" Brendan asked.

"Two reasons, greed on the part of individual priests and tax minimization purposes. Gives you an idea of what your destiny might be," Jack bluntly answered

"Maybe" Brendan awkwardly answered

"This Bible gives us an insight into how it all started." Jack insinuated in more ways than one

"How do you mean?"

"Well, suppose we believe that the Old Testament is arranged chronologically. Then the first book, namely that of Genesis, deals with the establishment of The Infirmary and Longevity Plus. Look at chapter one the numbers 15, 7, 8 and 1 are highlighted. If you arrange these numbers you find the date the 15th of the first '87, which is when both of these businesses came into being. The very words of these verses support that idea. Verse 7 and 8 relate to the firmament, meaning bricks and mortar, and called it heaven. It is certainly heaven making love with a woman as it is to behold that you have beaten a life threatening disease."

"What else?" Brendan asked becoming increasingly interested

"Well, each of the chapters thereon represent some sort of encoded bank deposit, a date with a reference made to cash amounts which I suspect are multiples of $10,000. These were probably not done at Newburn, but at different banking locations using different banks."

"Any idea which ones?"

"Sort of, if you look at the bank of the Bible you will find a summary of the historical and chronological index to the old testament. Here you have highlighted in different colours numbers and names, which again stand for dates, banks and account descriptions. I have names such as Dan Amran, Gad, Azarias, Zacharias, Bocci and many others. There are even references to possible points of banking. A notation 'semborn' is highlighted. This probably stands for the town of Seaburn and salmon is probably Salmon Harbour. I think that Zacharias Bocci being a high priest is the Archbishop."

"Never" Brendan replied refusing to accept Jack's deduction

"I am sorry Brendan, but it all points to it."

"And I suppose you intuitively reasoned who the others stand for?"

"As best I could. There are of course people that I could not ascribe code names to. The problem with this information is that it is insufficient as evidence for a prosecution, but it is sufficient to start an investigation."

"What about the banks?"

"I think these may fall under certain names which contain the letters that represent the banks' abbreviated title. For example, OC in the Kings of Urad I believe is a Swiss Bank and Obed in the line of Judas represents a German Bank."

"Rather complicated then," Brendan surmised.

"And that's why we need to obtain a very good computer hacker who could help us trace the documentation and expose what is going on."

"But if so many are being paid off, won't they go to great lengths to protect their interests?"

"Precisely"

"Who can we trust then?"

"Those who are far removed from this area"

"Otherwise, we are sitting ducks," Brendan said.

"You guessed it," Jack replied and paused to allow Brendan to dwell on it. He then said "That brings me to the next area of concern, namely your safety."

"I've taken care of myself when I have faced grave danger; life threatening it was," Brendan proudly asserted.

"I understand that, but what I want to instruct you more about are the dangers it may bring, especially of the world of deceit."

Brendan looked at Jack and realized that he was being deadly earnest.

"Our last spiritual master, namely Jesus, as I and others have discovered, came to teach the power within and the ways of accessing this and the infinite creative energy fields that are associated with it. He learnt this from the age of twelve onwards when he journeyed into the countries of India, Pakistan and Tibet where he learnt the basis of it all. It was through his own meditation that he fine tuned his abilities into some of the events that were recorded in history. There was much more however, and that was handed down in the secret mystical schools that he founded, which unfortunately became fragmented with time. His discoveries posed a threat to the world of deceit. He taught the principles of harnessing creative energy into bringing about one's physical reality in all respects, and therefore represented a real threat to those who ran the world of materialism, using the concepts of induced physical and mental slavery shackled with and by money. Christ's world was one of intelligent thought and he understood that the power that he had was not fixed, but constantly flowing, for that is the way of the universe. He was betrayed as you know, but what are not written are the reasons for his crucifixion. If you study carefully some religious pictures you will see that light is shown as emanating from Christ's hands an exaggeration to some, who view it simply as a symbolic item, but to the learned, they understand that the reactive power found its way into Christ's body through his feet and exited in the charkas of his palms. The only way to stem this process was to drive metallic objects into his hands and feet, thus shutting down the flow. The metal was unique in character made up of a mixture of rare elements and held by the masters of deceit."

"But surely Christ could have prevented this happening to him," Brendan interrupted.

"Do you remember in the New Testament where it was written that a woman with an issue touched Christ to heal herself and he felt the power go out of him?"

"Yes," Brendan answered.

"Well, there is more to the story. This woman was actually an agent of the world of deceit and was sent to gauge the extent of his power. She knew where to touch him and what to use. Otherwise, she would not have made any impact unless he desired it."

Brendan nodded to show that he understood.

"The message here is to keep all of your enemies away from you, at least at arm's length."

"So what you are saying is that for Jesus to have been caught, his charkas would have had to be shut down."

"Precisely," Jack confirmed.

Brendan looked at his palms in anticipation of seeing light coming from them.

"You won't see that happen until your eyesight adapts itself."

"Like Yvette showed me in the forest you mean?" Brendan said.

Jack visibly reacted to this statement.

"What do you mean?" he asked.

Brendan then described how Yvette showed him how to 'see' the rare rose in the forest.

"I knew she was special but I didn't realize that she had abilities beyond the norm. Typical woman, hiding things and remaining mysterious," he laughed, as he reverted back to his original topic of discussion.

"Coming back to you, what I am telling you is to be very careful from now on. I think you have done so much damage to the world of deceit that it may well and truly attack you. Jesus realized that once an individual discovered the power, he or she should keep it to themselves otherwise, they will be hunted down as witches by the ignorant deceits."

"Surely the world needs to be liberated," Brendan said.

"It does, but just look at the world 2000 years on. What progress have we really made in teaching the world the real principles of life?"

"Limited I suppose," Brendan admitted in hindsight

"Then the knowledge must be kept relatively secret," Jack said as he reached for his mobile phone.

"What are you doing?" asked Brendan.

"Contacting my computer hacker friend to see if he can open up the secret world of banking"

Brendan studied the outside surroundings as he waited for Jack to conduct his telephone business.

"Hello Stanley, Jack here. How have you been? Marvellous, excellent, are you very busy. Feel like doing some spy work? Yes, excellent! Could you find out everything possible on the following names? Yes, banking especially."

Jack gave Stanley a list of names and possible associated banks and then as he was about to end the conversation he turned slightly pale at the news that Stanley had for him.

"When, was anyone hurt? I didn't know, no matter, I will sort it out, thank you, I'll be in touch."

Jack, then without any delay dialled the next number.

"Hello, hello." No answer then a recorded message. 'The offices of Global Balancing Act are presently closed due to unforeseen circumstances. Please ring again in two days time or you may leave a message after the tone, thank you.' The beep signalled the electronic answering machine was recording.

Jack dialled the next number.

"Hello Miss Sutton?" Jack asked hoping that it was her

The voice on the other end of the line trembled, "Is that you Mr Stern?"

"Yes it is are you alright?"

"Pretty badly shaken," she replied, "how did you find out?"

"From Stanley a few moments ago precisely, what happened?" Jack asked full of anger and concern

He waited patiently as Miss Sutton mustered up the courage to describe the events of the morning.

"About 11:00am they arrived. They said they were official government agents. They flashed some sort of identification and then smashed up the office good and proper. There is almost nothing left intact."

"What were they looking for?" Jack asked as his mind searched for answers.

"They wouldn't say; they were extremely rough."

"Did they hurt you?"

"Just a few bruises some of the staff were cut by flying glass and three suffered broken bones."

"Did you call the police?"

"Household security came down but they were powerless to act.

When the police finally arrived the thugs had left."

"Did they take anything?"

"Nothing at all"

"Very well, stay put, do as the message says stay away for a few days. I will handle everything."

"Thank you sir" She meekly answered

"I am sorry this has happened Miss Sutton," Jack said, again quite genuinely.

"It's alright sir," she paused and then softly said "Sir?"

"Yes Miss Sutton?"

"Does this have anything to do with that Ricci deal?" She asked

"I can't answer that question, but I will let you know, goodbye."

"Goodbye sir." She answered in a fragile and frightened voice

Brendan sensed Jack's anger as he asked, "What happened?"

"My office has been trashed by federal impostors."

"Looks and sounds like Badcock is really mad then"

"I don't understand why, he has never met me in my normal state, and I conducted the purchase of The Infirmary in the safest possible way, leaving no trails leading to me at all."

"Dinner is served gentlemen," Yvette cheerfully disrupted Jack's somber mood as she stepped into the room. "Come and enjoy a feast inspired by your lovely ladies."

36

INFORMATION HIGHWAY

Yvette took both of her handsome men by the hand and led them downstairs. She sensed that all was not quite right with either of them. The real Jack, although outwardly happy, was pre-occupied with something besides the issues at hand. The real Brendan felt uneasy with his personal security.

"I am sure you will enjoy the fabulous food; the girls have been very creative," she said, lightening the atmosphere.

"Well, that remains to be seen Yvette, your efforts at the presbytery were just okay," Jack replied in a playful manner.

"You will be surprised Father, it may even be better than what you have eaten at the Archbishop's palace."

"Who says he eats well?"

"Rumours, Father, just rumours." Yvette brightly answered

Brendan remained silent, not wishing to engage in the conversation.

The trio reached the eating area. The girls were already seated waiting patiently for Yvette, Jack and Brendan to join them. They had left three chairs vacant at the head of the table out of respect.

Jack cast his experienced eyes over the array of food. He clapped his hands repeatedly and applauded their combined efforts "Yvette, ladies, you deserve a standing ovation. If it tastes as good as it looks, then I shall have to pronounce you master chefs."

Yvette and the girls giggled.

Brendan forced a smile but remained silent and took his seat.

Jack walked behind Yvette waited for her to be seated and gently pushed her chair in. He then proceeded to act as the waiter and served everyone around the table in a gentle and pleasing manner.

"Father, you shouldn't be doing this," Yvette mildly protested with some of the girls nodding in agreement

"And why not I am nothing more than a servant in many respects it is my duty to minister. Please let me continue with my duties," he said in a most frivolous way, as he bowed at the waist, waving one hand in the air as he did so.

The girls laughed at his theatrical antics and continued to fill their plates

When all had been suitably attended to, Jack looked around and commented, "Yvette my darling, you have one vital element missing, the wine."

"I couldn't find any Father," she replied excusing herself.

"That's because neither Jack nor I told you of its secret where-abouts," he replied as he walked towards a seemingly solid wall, tapped it three times and stepped back. The wall came alive and a section of it swung out revealing a selection of fine wines and liqueurs. The girls applauded in amazement.

"Now my lovely ladies, which wine would you like to compliment your meal with?"

Those who had some fleeting knowledge gave their preferences as Jack read off the labels, whereas the rest trusted their choice to Jack who did not fail them.

The mixture of food, wine and above all safety, produced a very happy environment. It allowed everyone to relax and cast aside any previous worries they might have had.

"Tell me Father how did you and Jack get to know each other" fabulous Felicity asked half way through her meal.

"Quite by accident," Jack replied.

"How's that?"

"We met at an ecclesiastical affair."

"A fund raiser"

"Aren't they always," Jack cynically replied.

"And then what?" Brandy asked.

"We sort of hit it off and developed a friendship. But the truth of the matter is, the church was very worried about Father Brendan's shady exploits and I was instructed to clean up his act," Brendan explained.

"You're not a paedophile are you?" Brandy frowned as she analytically looked at Jack Stern who simply flashed an innocent smile.

"Not at all," Brendan replied on Jack's behalf. "In fact, his biggest problem was his devilishly handsome looks."

The girls studied Jack's facial features to decide whether Brendan's explanation was plausible.

"Yes I would agree with you Mr Stern," one of the other girls said. "Especially in a priest's outfit, but how did that pose a problem?" she asked.

"Well, it is all a matter of perception. Too many people started rumours that he was having affairs with parishioners' wives." Brendan whispered as though he was spreading idle gossip

"OOHHHHH."

"So in order to overcome that, I was called in by the church."

"And so was I," countered Jack.

The girls looked at him quite surprised.

"To correct him and his business interest in the brothel after all, even though he contributed to church coffers, the money was tainted if you know what I mean. Can't have that, can we?" Jack said with a mischievous grin.

"So what are we going to do with the brothel?" one of the other girls asked.

"Forget about it, you are never going back there, those days are well and truly over and done with," Jack adamantly said as he looked each one of them in the eyes.

"In fact Brendan and I will help you to find new lives." Brendan convincingly said

"Okay, but surely Badcock will want revenge of some sort?" the same girl asked

"He is not the problem." Jack replied and handed over to Brendan to report on their discovery at Newburn.

"Brendan and I have found out about the way Saint Pious and Longevity Plus and The Infirmary were linked to generate new drugs, launder money and entice more people into their nasty web. We even think that besides the local police force others, including certain health authorities and perhaps federal agencies are involved. It is quite a monster. We would like to expose it and let the media do its job as a way of shutting down the satanic operation but is a matter of knowing whom to trust."

The girls all sat grim-faced on hearing this news except for one fresh faced girl who suddenly blurted out, "If you ever want to know everything about anything, just ask your call girl, 'cause we know it all."

Her unexpected and spontaneous statement caused an immediate ripple of laughter.

"She is right you know," Felicity confirmed "We have had quite a few crime bosses come through the brothel to check it out. They even chatted us up; paid for sex never had any and very discreetly left us their phone numbers in case we wanted a change of scenery. Never had a chance though, Badcock's security was too tight, plus the constant reminder of what would happen to us if we did."

Brandy nodded as tears welled in her eyes and trickled down her cheek.

"I do miss her so," she sobbed, as she remembered the death of her close friend.

"How did these crime bosses tell you how to contact them?" Jack asked as he observed the ex prostitutes display their past psychological traumas.

"Like this," replied Felicity as she dug into her bra briefly fiddled with her breast and then produced a number of business cards.

The first had DDS Inc printed on it. The initials stood for Double Delivery Systems. Below it was the name of the company's president Mr Laurence Carpenter plus his private contact number. The next card was from International Lifestyles Importers, Mr Johan Bliss was its director and the last business card was Electrical Ecstasy, its motto being, 'We'll really switch you on and get you buzzing'. Mr Ramsay Toggle was the Operations Manager.

Jack and Brendan studied them briefly before passing them to the other girls for their perusal.

"Felicity, you did say that these crime bosses paid for sex and had none?"

"Yes I did."

"It doesn't make sense, because I was led to believe that drugs were introduced into client's food and drink, which would make them horny as hell and also would be instrumental in giving them enormous orgasms at the appropriate time," Jack said.

"Mr Badcock as you have guessed has links to the federal police. There would be a photograph in the computer of anyone suspected of being a criminal, which Badcock was given access to by his friends in law enforcement. As soon as anyone suspicious came into The Infirmary they would be photographed by the surveillance cameras, and their image sent to his personal computer, which then checked them out by relaying the information to the police computer. Anyone with a criminal record however minor would not have received any drugs at all. Mr Badcock is a real fox, leaving false trails covering all of his bases and keeping his back doors closed."

Brendan looked at Jack

Felicity then asked Brendan, "How was it then that you managed to buy The Infirmary?"

"Mr Ricci was the legal owner and sold it because he owed a lot of money to the organization. Over the years he had embezzled a great deal of money and lost it on a very bad stock market deal. He panicked and was forced to sell sold it in hurry. The constant anxiety of worrying about the debt and the fear of being hunted down and tortured before being cut up into little bits while he was still alive was too much for him and he died of a massive heart attack."

"So, the rumours were true and I guess Badcock didn't know what to do with you until you started messing around with the business"

"I suppose." Brendan answered much relieved that he had got the story conveniently correct.

Jack was impressed with Brendan's explanation. It was obvious to him that Brendan was continuing to evolve by picking up people's memories and reporting them accurately.

Meanwhile the business cards found themselves in Yvette's possession who after a while said out loud, "Which one do we go with, a carpenter who delivers, a clown who makes you laugh or a sparkie that gives you a zap."

"Most importantly, what can they offer us?" Felicity asked.

"Will we be going from the frying pan into the fire?" Brandy questioned.

"Father, what are your thoughts?" Brendan asked Jack.

"If you propose that we contact one, two or all three of the unsavoury characters, then what will we say to them? Come, take over everything, or should we be clever, sell them the information and keep the money for the girls."

"Sounds like a good idea, let's try it," Brandy said enthusiastically.

"Later ladies, later, let's enjoy dessert first," Yvette firmly motioned "Come on, let's clear the table and treat ourselves to some delicious ice cream."

This time Jack restrained himself and allowed the girls to do the fussing. Yvette and the girls very quickly assembled a glorious display of rich dairy ice cream and Italian Gelato of various flavours. It had been a long time since the girls enjoyed such simple pleasures. The Infirmary's atmosphere in the past had always been oppressive and it seriously dampened their sense of taste making meals times nothing more than a necessary chore.

"Eat up gentlemen, the ice cream is excellent for caressing the taste buds, soothing inflamed tissues and stimulating the brain," Yvette bubbled.

"Sounds kinky," Brandy giggled.

Yvette blushed at the suggestion. "Just now you suggested that Badcock would seek some form of revenge."

"That has already happened," Jack said.

"I thought so," Yvette replied regaining her composure.

"I learnt earlier from Jack that his office was ransacked by bogus federal agents. They didn't take or find anything."

"I think it is a sign of Badcock's madness," Jack explained.

"All the more reason to call these people and take the focus away from us," Felicity concluded, and then she moaned "mmmmm this Tiramisu Gelato is just divine."

"Never take anything seriously," Brendan quipped.

"All right then, let's have some fun" Jack said, as he fumbled to find his phone in one of his jacket pockets

"Eeny, meeny, miny, moe, which one be a go," he said, as he chose one of the business cards that lay face down before him. "Well, hello sparkie."

Jack carefully punched in the mobile number and received a call diversion message. He waited until a voice answered, "Who's that?"

"Robert Adolfson, Mr Toggle," Jack said feigning a Norwegian accent.

"Yes, what of it?"

"A girlfriend gave me your card; she said you are always looking for new business ventures."

"Maybe, what are you offering?"

"Information."

"On what?"

"One of your competitors."

"Who?"

"Louis Badcock, he runs The Infirmary."

"Yah, I know, small time crook, no competition to us."

"So you won't be interested in what I have to offer?"

"Not at all."

"What about illegal drugs then?"

"Don't touch them, not interested, too dirty, too dangerous, only like the girls, much safer, okay."

"Yah, okay, bye then." Jack clicked off.

The girls remained silent.

Naomi piped up and suggested, "No 2 please."

Jack turned both cards over and studied their respective owner's names.

"Which one sounds more of a crook, Mr Laurence Carpenter or Johan Bliss?"

"The first one," remarked Brendan. "The latter is an international drug dealer not interested in the local market."

"That is quite some insight you have Jack," Jack said most impressed by the priest's conclusion.

"Let's see if you are right." Stern punched in the telephone number of the posh sounding Laurence Carpenter.

"DDS Incorporated, Shelley speaking; how can I help you?" was the greeting.

"Hello, may I speak to Mr Laurence Carpenter please?"

"I'll check sir, one moment. Whom shall I say is calling?"

"Mr Robert Adolfson," Jack said in a Norwegian accent.

"From?"

"Information Highway and Company."

"Thank you."

"Carpenter here, how can I help you Robert?"

"It may be the opposite Mr Carpenter."

"How is that?"

"Well it depends upon whether my girlfriend got it right."

"Go on," Carpenter replied.

"She used to work at The Infirmary."

"Say no more. Jot down this number; it is my private secure line."

Jack complied and wrote down a series of digits and hung up. He then punched in the new number.

"Is that you Robert?"

"It is."

"Good, what did your girlfriend tell you?" he said in a meticulous drawl.

"Only that you might be interested in hiring her."

"Yes, and what else?"

"That perhaps you might be interested in the workings of The Infirmary and its associated side lines."

"Which are?"

"The production of exclusive designer drugs all made from pharmaceutical grade narcotics and anti-depressants."

"I thought The Infirmary was only a brothel."

"That's the deception."

"Tell me more."

"I can't."

"Why?"

"Because it is worth a lot of money and I mean a lot of money"

"Look, let's say that I'm interested, how much do you want?"

"You make an offer. All I can tell you is that it is definitely a business in the 8 figures category."

"Very interesting, what do I get in return for my investment?"

"The locations of the central depot, manufacturing labs, the technical know-how to continue running the operation and the entire distribution network."

"I need proof."

"It doesn't work that way."

"Why?" Carpenter asked.

"Because once I show you I won't have anything to sell."

"Okay, besides whetting my appetite with imaginary cheap talk, is there anything concrete you have to offer me?"

Jack looked at Brendan who had tuned into the conversation all along. Brendan reached into his pocket and produced a number of ampoules.

"Samples of the drugs do?"

"Certainly, when and where?"

"By post," Jack suggested.

"Very well, by tomorrow."

"Not possible, perhaps the next day, address details please." Jack wrote these down and signed off by saying, "I'll be in touch."

"He is our man, question is, how big is he?"

"Probably a four foot midget," replied Brendan, to which the all the girls except for one laughed.

The odd one cleared her throat and said "Give me a computer and I will find out for you."

Jack turned to face her and said, "Very well then, Brenda, got some hacking skills, have we? That should be to our advantage, we shall start after coffee,"

37

BOGUS HACKER

"Well Brenda, you appear to be a girl of many talents," Jack said as he escorted her to the third level.

"Yes I am."

"Now there's confidence for you. Not only are you a gifted relief expert, but you have acquired certain computer skills as well."

"That's right," she replied with a sly grin.

"Well, I'm impressed. Exactly when did you have time to do all of this?" he asked.

"In between customers, I have a laptop."

"Badcock allowed you such luxuries?" Jack said rather surprised.

"He was always good to me provided I performed to his satisfaction."

"I see, well, here we are," Jack said, as he walked into a pocket of the third floor that contained an array of sophisticated computer equipment. He turned to look at Brenda. "Before I let you loose I will need a few moments to activate the system, perhaps you could browse around while I boot up."

Brenda nodded. She casually walked around admiring the internal and external protected views, while Jack busily pressed all sorts of numbers and letters necessary to activate his electronic genius. After a few minutes it was merrily humming away.

"It's all yours Brenda," Jack said smirking as he stood up.

"Thank you," she replied as she took her seat.

"Tell me when you have something."

"Shall do," Brenda replied as she studied Laurence Carpenter's business card.

Jack went downstairs to find Brendan and some of the girls carefully washing the dishes, whilst Yvette and the others were deep in conversation, becoming better acquainted with each other.

"How's Brenda doing?" Felicity asked when she saw Jack step into the room.

"Quite well I think. She should have some very interesting data for us to examine once I return."

"From where?" Brendan inquired wondering why Jack was leaving

"The postal box, I have decided to post off Mr Laurence Carpenter's samples that I promised him, can I have them please?"

Brendan passed them across and said, "You give me the impression that this hideaway has just about everything necessary for anyone to survive."

"One could say that," Jack replied as he accepted the ampoules.

"Where will you post them?" Yvette asked.

"As I previously hinted, there is a mail box on the main road about an hour's walk from here. It serves the local community of forest rangers. I thought it best if I go alone in disguise."

"Good decision, be careful won't you?"

"As always," Jack replied, as he descended the stairs that led to the garage.

Once there he accessed a secret room and went inside to change into his hobo disguise and prepare the ampoules for posting. He left the complex by another route, a corridor that meandered its way inside the mountain and exited on the northeast face of the escarpment.

Jack emerged from the opening only when he was more than

certain that the coast was clear. He made his way down through the heavily scented pine trees and onto the sun drenched plain. After taking a few moments to find his bearings, he made a beeline for the mailbox through the thick carpet of flowering shrubs and perennials. He walked slowly taking careful note of the scenery and paid meticulous attention to what the insects were saying and the music that they created. Although seemingly abstract in nature, it was the same as the musical phrases and sketches that the great composers had captured on paper, and enlarged through the brilliance of their imaginations.

Every encounter with nature and her creatures was another stepping stone in Jack's journey towards ultimate knowledge. Jack understood that the living dead were those who refused to learn continuously by whatever means possible and he felt very sad for them. Conscious life was after all learning in the physical realm that was one of its purposes for existence and so it was that Jack totally preoccupied and immersed in such philosophical thoughts slowly approached the vicinity of the mailbox. There were a few people about, all talking with each other about local political issues, and the complete lack of action taken on various aspects of National Parks Management. No one took any notice of Jack, the old decrepit hobo, as he shuffled towards the mailbox. He fumbled in his pocket to retrieve a small package and then he pulled the handle to open the chute. The mailbox hungrily accepted his donation with an almighty snap of its lid.

"Dangerous things, no wonder they are painted red," he muttered, as he counted the fingers on his hand. The locals who witnessed his dangerous encounter with the mailbox laughed at him and shouted "What's the matter old man, not quick enough?"

Jack simply looked away in disgust to face the walk back home.

Several satanic-looking black cars sped past in a frenzied hurry and violently threw dust into Jack's face. The locals laughed again. Jack wiped away the annoying debris as the back draught caused by the cars continued to swirl about him.

"Sinister lot," he mumbled under his breath as he stared down the road.

A truck blared its horn behind him startling Jack into moving quickly. It was the postal van, come to collect the mailbox contents. Jack glared at the driver who refused to make eye contact. The locals laughed again.

Jack thought twice about disciplining them. Instead, he momentarily stood transfixed and surveyed the scenery before him, switching his focus to that of a bird's flight, the insects that he had noticed before played music of a different kind, one of fearful alarm as the bird's feeding frenzy was upon them.

Jack watched as the battle for survival raged. As he did so, he caught sight of what he thought was an injured black crow sitting on a tree branch. As he approached it, Jack deduced that it was probably deformed from birth and yet it was still alive. The question was why?

The answer came to him as he patiently stood still and observed. The bird sat alone. It was constantly visited by different members of its flock, who would either bring it food or keep it company, during which time an audible discourse between the two would invariably take place. The deformed crow was not a fledgling, it was a mature adult, so what was the point of its existence and why was it so important?

In this case the concept that, only the fittest survive in nature, was quite wrong. There was a social security system of some sort in action but once again for what purpose? Then it dawned on Jack that this deformed animal was the flock's teacher, a master soul of a kind, not pre-occupied with food and water, its entire life was devoted to the higher levels of consciousness and learning which it shared and taught with those who sought its wisdom. He further postulated that such enlightened life forms find a pathway to the spiritual evolution of their souls. Jack stirred out of his trance to see if there was anything or anyone unusual around him, or in fact observing him before he took the pathway towards the safe house's secret entrance. There was nothing. Two and a half hours had elapsed and the walk and the rejuvenating sunshine had done him the world of good. In a few more minutes he would add what Brenda had been able to find out to his discoveries.

Once inside the lower ground secret room he divorced himself of his derelict old man disguise and then contacted Stanley on his ultra secret telephone line. He then went upstairs and found all but two members on the third level. Brenda was still seated at the terminal pretending to hack away, much to the amazement of her onlookers.

"Found anything darling?" Jack asked, as he entered their intimate circle.

"Quite a lot actually."

"Well, show me," he asked. Brenda produced fifteen sheets of printed material dealing with Mr Lawrence Carpenter's business affairs.

"Impressive to some, but not to me," Jack said as he shuffled through the papers.

Brenda's face reddened in defiance. "It's good stuff" she defensively said.

"To the amateur, but it is not what we wanted is it dear? It tells us nothing of his illegal operations or of his illegal contacts does it?"

"Well, it does sort of."

"Where?"

"Right here," she said pointing to the screen.

"That's nothing," Jack retorted as he intensified his attack on Brenda's self proclaimed ability.

"Yes it is," she angrily answered back.

Jack stared at her briefly with a penetrating glare, giving her a chance to properly explain. The other girls looked on rather uncomfortably.

Brenda flicked to the next page on the screen and cleared the lump out of her throat. "This page shows us which companies he deals with, two of which we have business cards for, namely Mr Johan Bliss of International Lifestyles and Mr Toggle's Electrical Ecstasy."

"So, Ramsay Toggle was lying when I rang."

"So it appears," Brenda said with a sigh of relief.

"But he wasn't the only liar was he Brenda?" Jack firmly asked

"What do you mean?"

"We have a traitor in our midst."

The girls looked at each other suspiciously each one afraid to point the finger at one of the others. Jack allowed them to settle down and then said, "You didn't think for a minute I would allow anyone to use my computer without taking the necessary precautions did you?"

Brenda's lump returned to her throat.

"All the information you acquired, in fact, all of the information you sent, that's right, sent, went through to two separate filtering stations. One of these is located at my hideaway residence and the other at my hacker friend's computer with whom I have just spoken not very decent of you Brenda to email Badcock and his cronies and tell them of our whereabouts."

Brenda sat there totally submissive, looking somewhat sorry.

"Well ladies, forget the electronic surveillance equipment, your complete kit was and is Brenda. Let me guess, you loved your work, is that right?"

Brenda's head hung low as she nodded.

"You're a nymphomaniac?"

"Yes," she mumbled.

"Otherwise, you wouldn't have liked the job. What is your relationship with Badcock?" Jack asked as he continued his intense stare at Brenda.

"I was his brother's mistress; I had an affair with Badcock. His brother was going to kill me, but Badcock smoothed everything over. Part of the deal was to make me work in the brothel and bring him information."

"Otherwise?" Jack demanded.

"He, that is his brother, was going to kill me."

"But what do you know about the brothers in black?"

Brenda sensed that she had to tell all for her own survival. "It's actually brother with blacks. Badcock's brother is responsible for the distribution of the orgasm enhancing drugs used in brothels. It was Badcock's vision to have The Infirmary's concept franchised nationally. He already has six outlets opened under different names. The Blacks are priests within the Catholic Church who effect distribution by using St Vincent De Paul charity trucks. You will find a clothing bin always close to any one of the brothels, except for The Infirmary. The shipments are deposited in the bin when it is empty and then the brothels sent the St Vincent De Paul trucks later to collect it."

"Everything happens so innocently," Jack remarked. "So tell us the names of his brothels?"

"Bliss 1, Rest Now, Hips of Services, Real Dreams and True Fantasies."

"That's absolutely correct Brenda" Jack said as he produced a printed sheet from his back pocket.

"This is what my friend found out. Unlike you, he is a real hacker, so you see Brenda your little trick to alert Badcock did not work and although you have given us some information, I don't think we can trust you completely. So what I think we should do..."

Jack was stopped mid sentence as Brenda leapt out of her chair, pushed him aside and fled down the stairs.

"Aren't you going after her?" shouted one of the girls.

"No need," replied Jack as he pressed a few keys on the computer's keyboard. "She won't go far. By the time she has reached the ground level all will have completely changed. She won't know where she is." Jack sensed that the girls didn't understand. "The bottom floor where the cars are stored is a system of shifting corridors and walls. It only allows access to the above, if you are a friend, bearing the correct entry codes, otherwise it recognizes you as a foe and frustrates you, confuses you, after many long hours, you find yourself out in the middle of the

National Forest, the entry into the complex also changes and remains eternally secret.

Brendan came up onto the third floor with one of the other girls. "How did Brenda go?"

"Away," Jack dryly responded as the girls in his company laughed

"Did I miss anything?" Brendan asked.

"Sort of, you might say that the hacker hacked off."

Brendan frowned, as a sign of not wishing to be left out of the private joke.

"Okay, we will explain." Which Jack did so over the next 15 minutes with the aid of the information that Stanley had sent him.

"It appears that Lawrence Carpenter is an independent and may well be interested in taking over the entire operation. He has faced many federal investigations over the years, but has always managed to come out unscathed with no charges pressed."

"He must have a very good accountant," suggested Felicity.

"I think he is our man and the best plan of attack will be to sell The Infirmary to him and with it, the infrastructure, namely the pharmacy and the farm that Jack and I located."

"Quite a neat saleable package," Naomi concluded.

"Precisely, we will give Carpenter about 24 hours to receive and then test the samples, and then we will contact him with our proposition."

"Even if you do sell him The Infirmary, won't Badcock still come after us and try to kick Carpenter out?"

"I suppose, but considering that Carpenter has been around longer than Badcock and the Ricci Family I dare say he might be better equipped."

"I just hope you are not underestimating him," Brendan cautiously replied.

"Time will tell; meanwhile what about some fun and games," Jack playfully asked

The girls looked at each other as if to say, 'we thought that was all behind us'.

"Not what you're thinking girls, come with me."

He took them to the second level and introduced them to the games room neatly hidden away from view. The room was another secret hideaway, very large and tastefully arranged to accommodate table tennis, snooker, wall climbing, trampolines, floor mats and some gymnasium equipment.

"Is there no end to this complex?" Brendan privately asked Jack as he stood next to him.

"Not really," Jack replied. "The building has ears and thinks for itself, so if there is something that you would like to be added, all you have to do is say it out loud and my grandfather will do the rest."

"What do you mean by do the rest?"

"Oh, didn't I tell you."

"No, my grandfather's ghost inhabits the place."

"Oh, not again," sighed Brendan, as a woman's scream pierced the air.

38

GHOSTLY FRIENDS

"Where did that scream come from?" Yvette asked wondering if Brenda was in trouble

"Sounds like it came from downstairs," Felicity accurately replied as she also wondered what had happened to Brenda

"Our hacker has probably encountered Jack's grandpa," Jack said quite happily.

"Sounds like she has received a rather good measure of penance," Brendan said of the cuff

Jack smiled in a devilish way and nodded in agreement.

"Is it true that your grandpa's ghost is here in this hideaway?" Yvette asked Brendan.

"He is."

"What is he doing here?" Yvette wondered.

"I can explain that for you" Jack said as he found a comfortable chair to relax in.

"Come and join me and I will tell you what I know."

The other girls overheard this part of the conversation and decided to abandon their activities and join in as they all enjoyed listening to a good story come fairytale.

"Over the years, Jack's grandfather's antics in here and about the National Forest, have conjured up all sorts of bizarre stories dealing with frightening ghost encounters some of which it was claimed resulted in personal injury. So much so, that most people are afraid to come anywhere near this place unless they are thrill seekers. In the process, he has made this location safe and isolated. It is my understanding that one of the reasons that ghostly individuals remain earth bound is the fact that they don't know that they are dead or they are pathologically attracted to materialism or simply they have a karmic debt to repay."

"In my grandfather's case..." Brendan interrupted, "he simply wanted to be around helping out wherever he could. I think, based on my experiences with him, that he is new breed of ghost."

The girls looked at Jack and Brendan with a blend of awe and nervous anticipation.

"You mean like Casper the friendly ghost?" one of them asked.

"More advanced than that I would suggest. It is like he has one foot in the physical world and one in the next dimension, a sort of go between with a twist. He only relays his knowledge to those he loves and those who are receptive to him. Unfortunately, or fortunately, should I say, fear has restricted his followers to a few family members."

"Does he speak?" Yvette asked.

"I will let you discover that once all the screaming stops," Jack replied at which point it suddenly did.

"Almost on cue," Brendan remarked, and then the surrounding peace was shattered with an almighty sound of exploding rocks.

The vibration shook the entire complex without causing any damage at all. For everything contained with it moved fluidly in unison to the shock's vibrations.

"What the...?" the girls exclaimed frightened that they had experienced a profound earthquake and were expecting the ceiling to fall in.

"Grandpa's doing alterations," Brendan calmly explained

"I think he has got a bit carried away with his latest idea of creating another indoor swimming pool fed by one of the natural springs that flows through here."

"So what you are saying, given enough time, he will literally transform the entire interior of the mountain," Yvette quite correctly assumed.

"Will he kill Brenda?" Felicity asked changing the subject back to the trauma associated with ghostly encounters

"The answer is no, he does not have the power to do that, but I am certain he will teach her a thing or two."

"Do you think he could do it quietly, I think we all need a good night's sleep," Naomi said as she was exhausted by the day's events.

"I am sure that can be arranged," Jack replied, as he picked up a squash racket and gestured for Brendan to join him in a game

Although uneasy about a ghostly presence, the girls gingerly returned to their previous activities of playing games and kept an eye out for anything unusual. In a matter of hours it was surely bedtime. The group retired to level 1 to share the sleeping quarters. Jack, ever mindful of the girls' modesty, drew a series of curtains to separate the girls from the boys. Each had a double sized bed complete with soft eider down quilts and the finest Egyptian cotton for bed linen.

Using a master control panel that was located near his bed head, Jack programmed the lighting and internal environment to reflect one that resembled the forest floor. Within a matter of moments after he had silently conducted the evening prayer and a blessing of his newly acquired flock, the lights automatically gradually dimmed as a series of mirrors and upward channels came into play and bathed the room with natural night light, casting heavenly stars all about them and letting in the freshness of the mountain's morning breeze. The soft warmth of their beds lulled them into a deep sleep. All except for Jack who stayed awake for his ghostly grandpa who appeared once he was satisfied that all had passed him on their way to the plain of dreams.

Grandpa stood next to Jack's bed

"They are all beautiful souls. You have done very well my son."

"Thank you Grandpa, it wasn't me you know it was Brendan who rescued them."

"Oh, that is what you always say. I noticed that there is an exceptionally beautiful soul amongst them."

"Do you mean Brendan?"

"I can't say; you know how it is."

Jack sensed that his grandpa was playing with him, not wishing to let on.

"How's Brenda?" Jack asked.

"Hysterical, but she should calm down soon. I got most of the blackness out of her. I don't think she is going back to where she came from in a hurry.

"That's good, so when can you tell me about the placements for the girls?"

"After you have finished your work I can't do it beforehand; the future constantly throws up countless possibilities, every time you do something, it changes."

"Only the end result doesn't."

"Quite so," agreed Grandpa. "I will leave you to get a good night's sleep, good night."

"Good night," Jack replied mockingly.

"Idiot!" Grandpa snapped back. "You know very well that we don't sleep!"

As Grandpa faded from view, Jack studied the night sky and allowed his heart to look for home. The next morning as habit would have it, Jack awoke at 5:45am. He immediately sensed that this would be a day of achievements and in order to ensure this, he mentally went through his early morning mystical rituals. When he had finished his body felt rejuvenated and his soul further advanced. The morning air was heavily scented with the fragrance of dew studded rose petals and was surprisingly warm. Jack slipped out of his bed and without making a sound stealthily crept up the stairs to the top level. His Chopard wristwatch displayed 6:25am, just the right time to contact Stanley one of his secret operatives.

Jack took his custom made Ericcson phone out of its recharge unit and selected the appropriate code from its memory. The phone had only rung once before Stanley pounced on it.

"Good morning sir, I was expecting your call," Stanley said, quite chirpily considering he had been up all night. "How did it go with Brenda?" he asked.

"As I suspected, I gather you have been successful," Jack said.

"Very, and I must say it happened quite mysteriously."

"How do you mean?" Jack asked sensing that Stanley had obtained some outside help.

"I tried the usual approaches and was partially successful, but then I started running into all sorts of resistance, cyber walls some pretty nasty cyber warriors if you know what I mean."

"I do," Jack confirmed.

"Well, I just sat there expecting my computer to melt down as there were a massive number of explosive spikes heading my way. I wished and wished for some sort of cyber hero to come to my rescue. All of a sudden, this strange looking figure appears on the screen. I thought it was the end; none of my diffusers worked, I was truly cooked. Then this thing started darting about the screen and the craziest thing happened, Tchaikovsky's 1812 Overture starts playing. Cannon going off, left, right and centre and explosions all over the screen; man it was really weird. This figure runs around chopping up all these spikes, man it blew me away."

"And then…" Jack asked quite amused by Stanley's childish description.

"The screen goes blank. The figure appears large as life, winks at me, gives me the thumbs up sign and disappears."

"And then…" Jack asked.

"It was a piece of cake after that, I could go anywhere, do anything, man I could have accessed the most secret…"

"Yes, I hear you," Jack said, cutting Stanley short

"Sorry man, now for your stuff."

"That would be appreciated."

"Okay, now if you wanted the data for criminal or smut purposes, then I have to print up hundreds of pages, carefully notate and cross reference all of these and detail who is who."

"Meaning all those involved are using fake names," Jack sharply concluded

"They do, but they make the mistake of using the same initials.

"So Louis Badcock is…?" Jack asked.

"Probably Lionel Banner," Stanley deduced.

At that moment Grandpa appeared by Jack's side beaming quite happily.

Jack looked at him as if to say 'can't you see I'm busy'

Grandpa nodded to say that he would wait patiently.

"In summary, what can you tell me now?"

"The organization includes members of the Catholic Church, with links to the Ricci Family, runs a very complicated paper trail that involves a lot of cyber companies. The major banks that hold all of the monies are Swiss and German. The same sum of money is shifted about via invoices and electronic payments between 10 to 15 companies and finally finds its home in one of the banks. The reason for the movement is to wash and filter it, making it pristine, and in the process, zero dollars are paid in tax. In fact, the very clever way in which invoices are written for fictitious stock, causes the government to lose money in paying back sales tax on exported goods."

"Very clever," Jack commented.

"More than that, they will have to pay off tax officials if any one of them is lucky enough to accidentally crack the operation."

"Can you keep working on it?"

"Shall do," Stanley eagerly said.

"Then I will be in touch in good time, goodbye," Jack signalled off and looked at his grandpa.

"You should have been there, it was just fantastic."

"You make it sound so real," Jack said.

"But it is, people don't realize what they have created in the Internet, it's a whole new world out there."

"How real is it?" Jack asked.

"As real as the physical"

Jack tried to comprehend what Grandpa was on about.

"Shall I explain it sonny?"

"That would be nice."

"Do you remember when you were a young lad and I taught you how physical events became recorded in the ether?"

"Yes I do," Jack replied as he reflected on his past.

"The electronic machines create a similar situation, except what has happened in this case is that the events are not merely recorded, but go on to create 'living entities' within the web and in the ether, at a vibratory level different to that created by the physical world. The reason why they are living is of the energy that the net constantly supplies in addition to the energy that humans feed them by their thought processes."

"So?"

"One day these entities will take a leap to becoming human."

"So this is another avenue of life begetting life? So are you guilty of murder?" Jack asked referring to his grandfather's role as the cyber warrior.

"No, only guilty of becoming a transformer," Grandpa answered very pleased with his handiwork

"So you have changed them from distinct beings into amorphous random energy," Jack suggested.

"Precisely."

"These beings, do they live in the ether?"

"No, they constantly flitter from the ether to the confines of your computers and their means of communication; they are very mischievous – in fact, downright destructive at times, causing all sorts of havoc to the artificial minds of the computers. That is why your computer experts will never ever build a problem free model."

"Largely because they don't know what they are dealing with," Jack summarized.

"Precisely,"

"Would you like to stay for breakfast?" Jack asked.

"Okay."

"Then let's get started," he suggested as he made his way downstairs to the kitchen.

"Still know how to make things move around?" Jack teased. "Good, once we are in the kitchen you can beat the eggs nice and fluffy and I will prepare the rest and remember, keep it quiet."

Grandpa gave Jack one of his mischievous smiles and said nothing. Together they produced a rather elegant breakfast of scrambled eggs, waffles, French and plain toast, canned fruits, a variety of jams and percolated dark Columbian coffee. Once complete they summoned all to partake of the early morning feast. Grandpa sat at the head of the table as visible as he could be. Both he and Jack admired the girls as they assembled around the table, each one including Brendan, exuded a heavenly glow after their good night's sleep. No one thought anything unusual about Grandpa's presence until Yvette asked, "Who is your friend Brendan?"

"Ladies, meet Grandpa," he answered. Their reaction was not as he had expected. Instead, they all remained calm and began to engage in conversation with him. Grandpa became quite amused at their willingness to talk with him and voiced his approval.

"Good morning Mademoiselles, a pleasure to make your acquaintances. Apologies about last night, I hope my renovations did not disturb you too much I got rather carried away."

Jack looked at his Grandpa and thought since when has he been able to speak. Sensing his curiosity, Grandpa sent Jack a mental message. "Since I learned the ability to agitate the air's molecules as sounds do."

"What do ghosts live on? Naomi asked.

"Different forms of cosmic energy, there are about 144 sorts, each one providing a most needed frequency for well being, almost like vitamins and minerals," Grandpa explained.

"Do they taste good?"

"In their own way, but nothing like we experience as mortals which I can now appreciate" Grandpa said in a pathetic way. The girls sensed his sorrow.

"Perhaps, next time." Yvette suggested as she believed in reincarnation Grandpa forced a smile and nodded.

"Your package is with Mr Carpenter." Grandpa announced

"That was quick, I suppose you saw to it personally," Jack asked.

"Absolutely, it was my pleasure, anything to help."

"And?"

"He is buzzing," Grandpa remarked.

"Good, then I will contact him later today. Things are moving along quite nicely. How's breakfast by the way; ladies may I ask?"

"Excellent, delicious, mmmmm," they all replied. "Quite French and not bad for a man"

"The music is good," Yvette said in an obscure way which caused Jack to made eye contact with her and wonder if she was the beautiful soul that Grandpa had seen.

39

RELUCTANT BUYER

The Strauss composition Tales from the Vienna Woods which filled the air and created the happy atmosphere that Jack and his newly acquired friends enjoyed over breakfast was in contrast to a malevolent mood that the small dark figure was in.

It wanted its organization to flow as smoothly as the orchestra that played the celebrated music. Those two impish men, namely Father Brendan O'Reilly and that Jack Stern although gone, still poised a serious threat in the small dark figure's mind and they would continue to be so until they were rendered dead and dissected.

Its organization was not out of the woods yet even though its overall security had been tightened, extra guards called in, plus at great expense and speed the most advanced electromagnetic detectors installed at Longevity Plus Mortuary and at the Feel Good Pharmacy's manufacturing facility. If any enemy attempted to penetrate these facilities, the D-Man would be there in a flash, ready to annihilate them once and for all. The small dark figure contacted in turn Louis Badcock and then various key staff members at the Pharmacy, the hospital, the farm and lastly the Ricci girls to make certain that all was in order. Not content with the answers it received it sent out a covert distress signal only known and recognized by those in the deep underworld to attract the D-Man's attention who responded at the drop of a hat.

"You wanted to see me?" he asked as he came into view.

"I am growing impatient, any progress with those two trouble-makers?"

"Not immediately."

"I have sent out many experienced scouts, but also nothing." The small dark figure bitterly stated

"These guys are good, very good; I tried to locate them on a field of dreams and did so once but could not follow them back."

"Why didn't you just destroy them then and there?" The small dark figure impatiently asked

"Because they are indestructible," the D-Man coldly replied as he brushed aside the small dark figures ignorance. The small dark figure looked away in disgust.

"There was an exceptionally beautiful soul amongst them." The D-man continued

"So what of it?" The small dark figure asked once again demonstrating its ignorance

"I haven't seen one like that for at least 2,000 years."

"It is probably that Jack Stern," the small dark figure said, sounding increasingly irritated.

"I am not sure, it was so beautiful that it even made me think twice," the D-Man said quite ashamed.

"You had better remember to what side you belong."

The D-Man's metallic nails and hair crackled at that reminder, sparks flew chaotically about them.

"That's better, now go and find them."

"Yes sir," the D-Man responded sharply and snarled as he disappeared from view.

Meanwhile, Louis Badcock wishing to improve his position within the organization was also conducting his own search and destroy mission.

Brendan and Jack, although quite insistent that they would wash the breakfast dishes, were firmly dispatched from the kitchen by the girls' 'don't you dare think about it attitude'.

Both retreated to the third level whilst the girls individually went about their personal chores.

Grandpa continued to entertain the girls by demonstrating his extra-ordinary powers, which, as he instructed them, are not limited to the spiritual world.

"Grandpa did say that Laurence Carpenter has the samples and is suitably impressed," Brendan said opening the conversation

"And my friend Stanley couldn't find any link with him and the organization, therefore, I think we can safely proceed as planned," Jack replied as he picked up his phone and connected it to an external speaker.

"Might as well let you listen in, two pairs of ears are better than one."

Jack dialled Carpenter's direct line and the phone rang eight times before he picked it up.

"Who's that?" Carpenter answered abruptly.

"The man who is going to make you a fortune"

"Really I've heard this before sorry but I don't have time for crank calls, go away."

"What's the matter Mr. Carpenter not impressed with the samples that I sent you?" Jack sublimely asked in a business like no nonsense fashion.

On hearing this Carpenter's brain switched tact and he suddenly recognized the caller.

"My apologies Mr Adolfson," Carpenter gushed.

"Well?" Jack asked in his Norwegian accent.

"Oh yes, the samples arrived early this morning, we have already tested them and they do appear to have some sort of effect." Carpenter said in an understated fashion

Brendan looked at Jack who returned his gaze to indicate 'he is toying with us'.

"One moment Mr Carpenter, I have another call coming in," Jack said as he put Carpenter on hold.

"Quite a changed attitude since yesterday" Jack observed

"Playing very hard to get, probably wants everything for nothing," Brendan suggested which he knew was typical of the super rich

"Would you like to negotiate the deal?" Jack asked giving Brendan the opportunity to act tough

Brendan thought about it for a while.

"Quickly now he won't wait forever," Jack said with some sense of urgency

"Okay then," Brendan replied accepting the proposition and he held out his hand to receive the telephone.

Jack activated the phone and allowed Brendan to continue with the conversation. "Mr Carpenter, I am Norm Difluca an associate of Mr Adolfson, I am sorry to say that his other call needed his immediate attention therefore he has asked me to act on his behalf."

"Very well Mr Difluca that's understandable as far as we are concerned it is early days for us, the samples you sent appear to have some effect, but not enough for us to become excited about or for us to become involved with at this time. Perhaps you can give me a call when things change?" Carpenter said smoothly.

"Very unlikely, under the circumstances I think we had better take our business elsewhere, thank you for now" Brendan stoically replied and was about to disconnect the call when Carpenter hurriedly said, "Hang on Mr Difluca, perhaps I was…

"Trying us out yes it was glaringly obvious. Mr Carpenter, we know how damn good our drugs are, and it would not come as a surprise to us that you are probably trying to analyse these right now as we speak, but may I inform you that without the correct know-how, you have no chance in heaven or hell of copying these, capisce?"

Carpenter remained silent and then reluctantly replied after a moment, "I do."

"Well, that's just fine, but under the circumstances, I don't know if we will want to do business with the likes of you."

"I congratulate you Norm, you have seen right through me, how can I remedy the situation?" Carpenter falsely replied as he toyed with Brendan

"Perhaps with a sign of good faith how about $20,000 in cash up front as a down deposit" Brendan bluffed as he tried to gain the upper hand

"That is an awfully large amount." Carpenter replied

"Not for a man with your considerable wealth Mr Carpenter," Brendan countered and paused to view the mental game of chess that they were playing.

"Very well, but I want something in return." Carpenter said almost ruthlessly

"I'm listening."

"I heard on the grapevine that Badcock has lost all of his girls."

"So?"

"I need to inject some fresh blood into one of my clubs."

"How much would you like?" Brendan asked pretending to play into his hands.

"Two or three would be nice."

"I am sure we can accommodate you Mr Carpenter." Brendan answered giving him the impression that he had access to them and would most likely deliver as requested

"Excellent, jot down the following location," Carpenter instructed

"Wait a minute Mr Carpenter, what makes you think that we are close by?"

"Jot it down anyhow and tell me when you can make it." Carpenter replied avoiding the question

"Okay," Brendan answered as he wrote down Carpenter's directions.

"Have you got that?"

"Yes, I'll ring you back once I have everything you asked for and make suitable arrangements, goodbye." Jack looked at Brendan quite surprised.

"You are going to hand over three of our girls?"

"Not at all, I thought we could turn up together with three girls, collect the money and disappear." Brendan nervously answered

"Just like that?" Jack asked thinking that the handsome priest was a fool

"Yes," Brendan said quite naively thinking that everything would be alright.

"Suppose he takes the girls drives them away, makes you wait for an hour or two so he can check out the merchandise and then gives you the money."

"Then, that would not be very nice."

"Since when are organized crime bosses nice?" Jack acidly asked the priest as he stared at him

"To their own families"

"Come on Brendan, you have got to do better than that. We can't use these girls like that now that we have rescued them."

"I've put my foot in it, haven't I?" Brendan ashamedly asked

"You certainly have, but the good thing is that Carpenter doesn't know who we are what we look like, where we are, how to go about making the stuff or whether we are coming or not, so we still have the aces."

Brendan gave a sign of relief.

"In essence, so far you have done very well" Jack said in an almost sarcastic fashion.

"What do you suggest we do?" Brendan asked as he had no idea how to proceed next.

"Start worrying my son," Grandpa said as he suddenly appeared and dropped a small black item on the table in front of them.

"What's this?" Brendan said as he picked up the object.

"A transmission device, a beeper, tells people where you are – I found it attached to the underside of the Ferrari."

"That explains those horrid black cars on the highway," Jack said as he recalled the events at the mailbox

"That's right, they were looking for you."

"Will they find us?" Brendan asked as he peered out into the landscape and feared the worst

"Not a chance. For one thing, I have disarmed this little black menace and secondly, this home of ours is very secure, I designed it that way and then there is me."

"Okay Grandpa, that's quite enough." Jack said

"What's the problem sonny?" Grandpa asked Jack even though he knew that Jack disliked his inflated ego at times

"Laurence Carpenter's attitude," Brendan said changing the subject

"That's nothing," Grandpa said confidently.

"Alright then, we will explain the situation and you provide us with a solution." Jack challenged his ghostly relative

"I'm listening," he replied.

Brendan described the telephone conversation he had earlier with Mr Carpenter while Jack made use of the powerful telescope that sat unnoticed in the corner of the room adjacent to the window.

"Lots of activity out there," Jack mumbled as he focused on the numerous black vehicles and their sinister occupants.

"Want the heat taken off sonny?"

"Pardon" Jack asked

"They think you are still around here."

"I suppose." Jack reluctantly agreed and cursed himself for not previously checking his vehicle for such devices

"Well, let's re-activate this little monster and send it elsewhere, be my pleasure to help."

"Okay, do it Grandpa." Jack freely accepted his offer

Brendan watched as Grandpa picked up the device, re-activated it and disappeared from view

"Now I suppose we will have to wait until he returns to work out the Carpenter problem," Brendan sighed.

"That won't be long, he moves very quickly," Jack replied and as soon as he had done so, Grandpa re-appeared.

"There, all done, now to the Carpenter problem."

"That's just what I said," Brendan said astonished by the speed with which Grandpa acted

"So where is the device?" Jack asked knowing in advance what the answer was likely to be.

Grandpa's ghostly outline took on a purplish hue as he exploded into a fit of laughter.

Some of the girls came running upstairs to see what all the commotion was about. The room echoed with his ghostly laughter. He appeared to be unable to stop himself from laughing.

"Tell us what's so funny," they asked.

"What, what, I, I, I did with, with the homing device."

The girls looked at Brendan and Jack to see if anyone had any sense about them but they saw they hadn't. Finally, Grandpa was able to bring under control his hysteria and calmly replied, "I put it on a police car that was on the other side of the mountain near the Chateau Alpine."

"Absolutely brilliant Grandpa," Jack happily congratulated his relative on a job well done

"That will keep them guessing for a while now what about Carpenter?"

"That's easy too; I have seen him playing with the stuff. He is only too keen to get his hands on the whole operation, typical gangster, wants everything for nothing."

"So what shall we do Grandpa?" Jack asked as he acted out the question. The girls that had come upstairs remained and waited to hear his proposal as they thought it might concern them.

"I don't want the girls involved, they remain here. We bring along one girl, me myself and I or is it three."

"Oh Grandpa, you're such a beast," Naomi howled.

"Didn't you know that I was a cross dresser."

"In a former life or just for now in which case there's a new one for you, a cross dressing ghost. Wow now that's different," Naomi continued to howl

"We change locations for the meeting, we choose, not him. It must be out in the open, but discreet." Grandpa cleverly said once the excitement of seeing him in drag had quieted down

"And we bring along Brenda," Jack suggested. "She's still lost in the tunnels I take it?"

"Yes, happily undergoing her purification," replied Grandpa with a gleam in his ghostly eyes.

"Which I trust will include a memory component," Jack suggested.

"You mean, she will forget this place?"

"Yes."

"Put it this way, I can't erase it, you know that is impossible, I will just relocate it, making it hard to find."

Jack appeared satisfied with grandpa's solution.

"Where did you intend meeting with Mr Carpenter?" Brendan asked.

"The location he suggested is three hours drive from here, Salmon Cove, is that right?"

"Yes." Brendan replied as he looked at the address that he jotted down

"He's based in a fishing village," Naomi concluded. "Does that mean that he imports the drugs concealed inside the catch of the day?" she asked.

"That's old hat, probably a bit more innovative than that, more likely to be in the rope."

"Pardon?"

"Cotton strands are excellent for absorbing drugs."

"More of your extensive reading I suppose is that right Jack?" Brendan asked as he looked at Jack in an amicable way.

"But of course."

"I know a nice spot on the coast, used to go there often, peaceful, great fishing spot and lots of ruins to explore. O'Flattery's Point, that's the place to meet." Grandpa carefully suggested

"No one lives there, off the beaten track," Grandpa then said very satisfied with his choice. No one made any comment. Grandpa took it as a vote of approval.

"Right then time to contact Carpenter and tell him of the new location and revised meeting time"

Brendan obeyed and in a matter of minutes; the future it seemed was sealed.

"Well, I suppose you better set off, down to the Ferrari gentleman. Grandpa will fetch Brenda," Jack said as he stood up.

"Didn't you want to go by the fast route?" Grandpa asked. "Much safer you know," he added.

Jack looked at Brendan, who sensed he was about to receive another lesson in the Christ principle. Yvette could tell that their presence was not wanted so she urged the girls downstairs.

"I've had one spiritual master so far and he left to go home, I suppose you're his replacement," Brendan said almost guessing as he looked at Grandpa

"Not at all sonny, I'm his master. In the scheme of things I am more elevated than he is."

Brendan forced a smile to show that he understood.

"Come then laddie, lesson time." Grandpa said as he donned his spiritual regalia.

40

WHAT IS THIS PLACE?

Brendan sat like an obedient schoolboy; his innocent eyes looked about the room as he waited for his ghostly teacher to begin the lesson.

Many thoughts filled his mind and they all converged into one inescapable conclusion and that was that none of what had happened to him recently had been by chance, it was all pre-determined. In essence it represented a wakeup call to find himself and his true destiny.

Brendan's mood quickly changed from that of a naïve eight year old to that of an accomplished graduate, possessing a doctorate of philosophy with honours. Then in a second he shattered that thought and returned to his innocence once again.

"A very wise decision sonny."

Brendan looked at Grandpa.

"You knew what I was thinking?"

"The languages of the brain are not the words of the spoken kind. Instead, they are of a nature that is easily seen in the aura. You must never let your abilities make you arrogant for your powers will diminish."

"What is this place?"

"Where heaven and earth meet," Grandpa replied.

"Such places exist?"

"Always have done."

"Anywhere that I know of"

"Yes, the pyramids of ancient Egypt."

"Please explain" Brendan respectfully asked as his intellect thirsted for that knowledge.

"Our earth is alive. It is fed by the energy of the 12 horizontal and vertical lines that transect it. Each one of these has an associated fascicle of seven force lines that in turn breaks down into seven lesser important lines. It is by the geographical and architectural patterns that the vibrations called 'genius loci' concentrate. The pyramids were built in such a location and fashion as to create this hinge between the finite and infinite."

"Are they still active?" Brendan begged.

"No."

"Why?"

"Because as the earth moves through the cosmos the position within the grid of energy changes," Grandpa explained.

"And so does the position of the 'genius loci,'" Brendan concluded.

"Precisely, and that is how the folk-lore story about finding a pot of gold at the end of a rainbow came about, except it was not gold, but something more precious. Gold can be destroyed, the knowledge of the universe cannot."

Brendan quietly considered this revelation.

"Once the genius loci shifted, so did the fertility of the soil and its people. The region would revert back to its normal state as determined by its climate and the advanced civilization would crumble."

"But there is nothing extraordinary about this place."

"Only its location, remember, it needs an architectural masterpiece to focus and disperse the energy of the genius."

"I can see a connection to people," Brendan said.

"How?" Grandpa asked.

"Each one of the great musical geniuses was a biological architectural masterpiece that focused and dispersed the energy, and in doing so, created for our benefit the beauty of its nature, whether it was in music, painting or any other creative pursuit."

"But never destructive," Grandpa finished off the statement.

"Does the opposite exist, does a moron loci exist?"

Grandpa laughed and said, "Only the world of deceit that makes every attempt to prevent individuals from discovering not only the genius loci that exists here, but their own within."

"This concept has far reaching consequences doesn't it?"

Grandpa sat silently allowing Brendan to theorize.

"It explains the rise and fall of civilizations all over the world in a temporal sense and even why nations vary in their wealth and why people prosper or perish by virtue of their location on the earth. I like this process of attunement, quick, let's start building a pyramid."

"I'm afraid that won't happen here. The world of deceit has a very strong hold, the genius loci is restricted to those who can feel its presence within this great national park."

"That's why the rare rose grows here."

"You've seen it."

"Yes I have, it is exceptionally beautiful."

"Well, if you have seen that, then you are ready to learn fast travel," Grandpa concluded.

"Faster than the Ferrari?" Brendan teased.

"How does the speed of thought grab you?"

Jack meanwhile sat quite amused as he listened to their conversation.

"How does it work and can I take others with me?" Brendan excitedly asked.

"I'm glad to see that you are eager. Let the process of travel begin then. Whenever you want to travel in body simply close your eyes and intone the words Spiritus Ruah, Latin for travel, seven times, visualize the place and the co-ordinates you want to be at whether

317

alone or holding someone's hand and with a bang, you will be there."

"Surely it can't be as simple as that," Brendan queried.

"It is; however, it requires your absolute belief and desire for it to work. Once you have mastered visualization you can then program your mind so that all you have to do is think about body travel and you will do so without hesitation. Let's try it shall we?"

Brendan gingerly nodded.

"Close your eyes and think about being next to the Ferrari downstairs, good, see yourself touching the paintwork, feel it, good, intone Spiritus Ruah and you're there."

Brendan followed in detail and when he opened his eyes he stood before the Ferrari.

"What happened to the bang?" he said very disappointed that it hadn't occurred.

"You're highly evolved like a V 12 engine that's why it went so smoothly. Come on, let's find Brenda," Grandpa explained as he led Brendan through the secret corridors.

"Can't I experiment anymore?"

"No need, like I said, you're highly evolved. Come on she is quite near I can hear her sobbing."

Brendan struggled to keep up with Grandpa as he floated merrily through the air, lighting up the corridors as he went.

They found Brenda sitting by what appeared to be a disused well. It looked as though she was contemplating suicide. Grandpa disappeared and allowed Brendan to attend to her mental anguish.

"Brenda?" Brendan softly said as he quietly approached her. "Are you all right?"

She looked at him very afraid and distraught.

Brendan cursed Grandpa.

"It is not what you think," he could hear Grandpa saying in defense of his actions.

"What's the matter child?"

Brenda sobbed as she related how she had spent the hours re-living her past and how ashamed she had become of it. She thought that death was the only solution available to her.

"Everyone deserves many chances in life. That you feel shame and sorrow means that you want to make amends. Come child, let me help you."

"She is only fooling you," he could hear Grandpa telling him.

"Go away; I know when someone is lying."

"You'll be sorry," Grandpa insisted.

Brenda accepted Brendan's hand and allowed him to put his comforting arm around her.

Grandpa in his own invisible way led them back to where the Ferrari was parked.

Jack was waiting for them. Grandpa stood nearby dressed as a woman. He wore a latex rubber face mask and latex gloves, sunglasses hid his lack of physical eyes, all in all, he presented himself nicely as a well attired blonde.

Brenda looked at him and said nothing. They all remained silent until Brenda could contain her curiosity no longer.

"Who are you?" she asked of Grandpa.

"Just another working woman looking for a job," was his reply.

Brenda sensed that she was no longer staying at the safe house.

"Where are you taking me?"

"For a job interview," Jack replied.

"But I want to stay, I have changed my ways, I promise I have," Brenda sobbed as she resisted going into the car

"I think she means it," Brendan suggested.

"Then she will have the opportunity to prove it when I introduce her to her new employer," Jack's unemotionally replied as he held her firm but she continued to resist

"Look Brenda, you have a choice, either you come with us or I will return you back to the corridors to face your final fate which one will it be?" Jack menacingly asked as he towered over her

Brenda lowered her head and nervously pondered her situation she looked at Jack's steely gaze and realized it was futile to resist. "After what I have been through, I think I had better come with you." She meekly answered

"A wise decision, take Brendan's hand and I will look after this lovely lady' okay, let's go." He firmly said and then the trio simultaneously intoned Spiritus Ruah and in a matter of seconds the foursome appeared at the ruins of O'Flattery's Point.

41

LAND, AIR AND SEA

Whilst Brendan, Jack and Grandpa had no difficulty with their fast travel, for Brenda it was the opposite. Hers was a frightening ordeal of distorted images and sounds before she even landed with a spine jarring bang.

"Where am I? How did you? What are you some sort of witches, devils? Oh my god," she asked totally confused as she erratically stumbled about not knowing in which direction to run.

"Oh do be quiet, all you have done for the past hour is scream, rant and rave, just stop it and settle down," Grandpa hollered at her .

"Err," Brenda stammered looking at him directly.

"You heard me. Now stay put like an obedient dog, and do not give us any further trouble, otherwise I promise you I will reduce you to ashes if you even whimper."

Brenda grimaced at Grandpa's authority and instantly calmed down as she thought that he was a powerful demon who was good to his word.

Brendan was not very happy with the situation. He didn't like seeing women being mistreated. In this circumstance however, he accepted it, as he wanted to see if Grandpa's suspicions were correct.

Jack familiarized himself with their surroundings. Grandpa was correct about the location. It looked the ideal fishing spot completely abandoned, not a soul in sight, old dilapidated buildings of various dimensions were scattered about the promontory perfect for the fisherman who wanted to get away from the maddening crowds. There was an abundance of rock walls and rickety jetties and judging by the diversity of the birdlife the clear greenish waters were certainly rich fishing grounds. It did not make sense that the area was deserted.

O'Flattery's Point had probably acquired some sort of bad reputation concocted by land developers or drug runners to keep people away, he postulated.

The warm sun caused Jack to reminisce of days gone by, when he would sit, fish and idly pass the time of day, studying the hypnotic patterns cast by the restless waters below.

"What are you thinking about?" Brendan asked as he approached Jack.

"Not much, how about you?" he replied.

"Bit confused about Brenda, and a bit concerned how things will go this afternoon."

"I'm sure everything will be fine."

"Boys, hello boys, I think we have company," Grandpa shouted as he pointed out to sea.

Jack and Brendan turned to see three high powered speed boats heading in their direction from a distance.

The sound of their loud outboard engines soon became muddled moments later, with that of helicopter blades beating the air as the aircraft approached from the right.

"Air Force and Navy; I wonder where the Army is?" Jack asked somewhat sarcastically.

"Just over there," Brendan pointed to a cavalcade of stretch limousines that was headed towards them.

"Snipers in the rooftops," Jack observed as he pointed to the flashes of light that appeared sporadically from the surrounding buildings.

"Did you bring your sling shot?" he jokingly asked.

"Do I look like David?" Brendan replied understanding that Jack was making a biblical reference to David and Goliath.

"No, far too handsome by the way, I like your new shirt."

"Pardon"

"Moving red polka dots suit you. Buy it in Hong Kong in some novelty shop did you?" Jack continued to quip.

Brendan looked down at his white shirt and saw red dots moving about.

"If you want to know, they are laser targeting lights from high velocity rifles. Becoming nervous?" Jack flippantly asked.

"Not at all, the challenge becomes more interesting," Brendan replied, as he observed the trail of cars nearing them.

The two high powered all terrain vehicles in the front and the two that brought up the rear were painted matt black, whilst the centre vehicle in total contrast was brilliant white.

"Well, what do we have here, perhaps it is the good surrounded by the bad," Jack suggested as he tried to make sense of it.

The cars came to a screeching halt and their occupants remained seated until they were satisfied that the area was secure.

Brendan could hear numerous foreign voices barking over hand held walkie talkies. Once the dust had settled the order to alight was given.

Eight heavily armed bodyguards exited from the each of the two forward and rear vehicles, each group fanned out in a well trained pattern. Each member was equipped with a telescopic eyepiece, advanced personal radar device, automatic weapon and bullet-proof vest. The manoeuvre was intended to visibly unsettle and instill morbid fear into all of its onlookers.

"Frightened anyone?"

"I am," Brenda freely admitted and almost hysterically screamed as she started to tremble and shake uncontrollably

"Shoosh, you don't want to make them nervous," Jack cautioned the distraught hacker. "Remember, those guns have hair triggers, if they think for a moment that you're a threat, no thinking what they will do."

Brenda wasn't able to contain herself and was about to start screaming hysterically.

Grandpa who stood next to her placed his hand firmly on her shoulder and applied pressure to certain acupuncture points causing her to immediately fall asleep.

"It's okay," Jack shouted to the armed guards. "She has just fainted, all too much for her."

The guards maintained their positions. The centre door of the white limousine facing the foursome opened, and Mr Lawrence Carpenter, or should we say Colonel Lawrence Carpenter self proclaimed modern day evangelist of organized crime alighted. He was dressed in a resplendent white suit complete with white silk shirt and tie. His cufflinks were fashioned out of pure white gold, as was his tie clip. A chrome plated six shooter complete with white pearl handles was holstered on his belt. Everything about Mr Carpenter was white, including his hair, eyebrows, fingernails and sparkling teeth.

"Good afternoon allllll," he said in a Southern style accent.

Jack responded by extending his hand and politely introduced himself, "Mr Carpenter, pleased to meet you, I'm Robert Adolfson, the gentleman to my right is ..."

"Norm Difluca, is that right?" Carpenter interrupted jovially. You must be wondering about the accent, is that right?"

Jack and Brendan nodded.

"Always put my voice through a filter to modifier it on the phone."

"Keeps your competitors guessing I take it" Jack said making light conversation but then he changed his tone and asked, "Bit over the top, this army of yours isn't it? Just whom were you expecting?"

"I have many enemies Mr Adolfson, especially one Louis Badcock. We believe that he might be the one behind several sabotage attempts on our organization and even behind a failed assassination attempt on me, so when I heard about what you boys were offering, I wasn't sure whether it was a set up or not."

"Nothing of the sort Mr Carpenter we like you want to see an end to Badcock," Brendan explained.

"Why is that boys?"

"We have our personal reasons." Jack replied tight lipped without giving any further information

Carpenter looked at each one of them analytically and after a moment said, "I accept that, now where are my lovely ladies?"

At that point Brenda had woken up. She realized what was about to happen to her and what lay in store for her so she attempted to run away from the group, shouting as she ran.

"I don't want to go, you can't force me, I don't want to do it again."

"Leave this to me Mr Carpenter," Grandpa said in a high pitched voice and gave chase.

Within twelve seconds he caught up to her and pacified her as he had done previously.

"Quite the reluctant virgin," Carpenter satisfyingly said as he enjoyed ravishing resistant women. "Put her in my limo boys I'll deal with her later," he instructed two burly guards who stood nearby.

When they had executed his orders Mr Carpenter withdrew a bulky envelope from his inside breast pocket and presented it to Brendan

"$20,000 I believe was the deal as a sign of good faith, correct gentlemen," he said pretending to be angelic in nature.

"Correct," Brendan confirmed.

"Very good, now what figure shall we settle on for the nitty gritty info?"

"$250,000 I believe is a fair amount considering what you and your clients are likely to reap in return," Brendan said in a business like fashion

"And that is?" Carpenter asked seeking monetary clarification.

"A heavenly experience," Jack replied leaving Carpenter to decide what his answer meant

"In hard copy gentlemen I expect a hard copy do you understand" Carpenter firmly said and repeated his statement twice more. "Until that is affected I'm taking you Mr Adolfson hostage just to guarantee our delivery. You got any problems with that Mr Difluca?" Carpenter asked, changing his voice from angelic to demonic

"Not at all," Brendan a little flustered replied sensing Carpenter's change of mood.

"We are only too willing to oblige," Jack politely said un-phased by Carpenters actions.

"Butttt," Brendan stuttered.

"But what Mr Difluca you're not by any chance nervous about being unable to deliver are you?"

"Not at all," Brendan said confidently.

"I'll await your phone call then," Carpenter said, as he waved a series of hand signals to his bodyguards suggesting that it was time to depart.

Jack and Grandpa were escorted to the front black vehicle leaving Brendan to ponder his and their fates. He watched as Carpenter's military might dispersed, leaving the surroundings as peaceful as when Brendan and his group had first arrived. Brendan then walked about the deserted village fishing for ideas. When he'd had enough of wandering he decided to return to the safe house in the mountain. Brendan had spent two hours searching for a dose of inspirational courage that would see him through to the next stage of his development.

Grandpa was right, all he had to do was think about a place and he was there in a flash.

His mind had been permanently programmed to execute thought travel. It would prove useful in times of extreme danger, especially when other measures failed to protect him from harm.

One thing continued to bother Brendan. In all the time that he and the others were at the Point, he felt that someone else besides Carpenter's men was intensely watching them.

42

REUNITED

Colonel Lawrence Carpenter, in the luxurious comfort of his limousine's cabin, allowed a smile to spread across his face as he looked at Brenda who was seated opposite him.

Carpenter opened a console next to his seat and flicked the necessary switches that made his part of the mobile retreat completely private and sound proof. Another flick of a switch and his seat extended itself into a comfortable bed, big enough for two. He signalled for Brenda to join him which she did obediently and without any hesitation, shedding all items of clothing as she slowly moved across.

"You're quite the actress. How I missed you," he whispered, as he placed his arms around her naked waist and drew her warm and responsive body towards his.

Brenda reacted passionately by kissing him fully on the mouth and exploring his tongue with hers.

Carpenter's manhood responded immediately and Brenda gave it the attention it richly deserved.

It had been a long time since they had made love; Carpenter had out of respect remained celibate, the tension in his penis clearly demonstrated that. It took all of his mental effort not to discharge then and there. Instead, he shifted his body's focus by reaching for a jar of his favourite climax cream, one that he had personally researched with meticulous attention to detail.

Sexplosion was a blend of essential oils that guaranteed to give mind-blowing orgasms in both men and women. It was flower power at its best.

Brenda's nostrils reacted immediately to the scent of the product, her mind flooded with images of glorious lovemaking and the promise of sexual ecstasy. Her genitals eagerly responded by producing an abundance of nectar like mucous, her nipples and clitoris became engorged and erect.

Lawrence Carpenter very erotically massaged the cream into all of the right acupuncture points, the nape of the neck, the small of the back, the nipple line, the soles of the feet, the insides of the thighs, lastly the labia and clitoris. The combination of smell and touch fed and stimulated Brenda's rapid ascent to cerebral orgasm. As Lawrence finally applied the cream to her clitoris with a feather-like touch, her head exploded into a kaleidoscope of sexual pleasure. She collapsed by his side and realized that Lawrence was indeed a sexual master. Her nymphomania was never satisfied, except by him, and he had used this to his advantage. Lawrence patiently waited for his moment of pleasure. He slowly undressed until he was fully naked and then introduced his penis into her eager mouth. In a matter of moments she tasted the oysters of his seminal fluid. Lawrence lay beside her exhausted drained as she maintained his erection then rode it to satisfy her hungry vagina. They caressed each other in the afterglow of their lovemaking.

"Lawrence," she purred, "please don't send me back I want to stay with you, please. I never want to have sex ever again with that horrible brother of Badcock's. God, how I hated being his mistress, I was really afraid for my life when he suspected that I was having an affair behind his back. I only wanted to be with you darling. You know I would do anything for you."

"That's alright my precious pussy cat, I'm sorry I put you through it," Carpenter pretended to apologize.

"How I despise Louis, I don't ever want to be around him anymore."

"That depends on what you have discovered so far, and also what Badcock believes has happened to you. In any event, you are not the only one that hates him," he replied.

"What do you mean?" she asked, as she looked into his eyes searching for the truth.

"I hate them as well."

"Because they are business rivals"

"No."

"Why then?"

"Because of what they did to me when I was young."

That statement puzzled Brenda. "I don't understand."

Carpenter realized that what he was about to say would injure her deeply; however, she deserved a thorough explanation.

"Louis and Jacque are my step brothers."

The statement hit Brenda hard. "You're sick bastard, you sent me to have sex with your step brother?"

"It wasn't like that; I didn't mean to hurt you."

"No of course not, you used me to further your means to an end, God you're sick. Didn't you think for one minute that I had feelings, you brothel owners, you are all the same, use and abuse, that's what you are all about, never give a damn about us girls," Brenda bitterly replied as she considered lashing out and digging her fingernails into his face.

"Can you give me a chance to explain please?" he quickly asked "I didn't realize you were in love with me, I thought you were just eager to satisfy a sexual appetite, that's why I sent you. Look, I'm very sorry for what I have done." This time Carpenter answered with some sense of genuine emotion.

"So what's the big deal about them hurting you?" Brenda asked still visibly hurt.

"My dad had two wives, the first was their mother and the second was mine. Both women died young and mysteriously. Dad's business was very obscure, I never knew how he made his money, however, I do remember meeting many strange people. Our dad also died mysteriously leaving us three boys to be raised by our uncle who favoured Jacque and Louis, but not me. They treated me like an outcast. You could say I was a modern day male version of Cinderella. Instead of being rescued by a fairy godmother, I ran away from home at 15 years of age, and carved a way in life for myself."

"So your name is Badcock?"

"Not any longer. I took the name of my benefactor when he died.

Louis Carpenter was very good to me. He was a lonely man whom I met in the park one day whilst I was employed as a gardener's assistant. He admired the way that I took care with seedlings and started a conversation with me about the subject. One thing led to another and I began to visit him at his home after work. His house was a shambles, the garden a disaster. I offered to tidy things up for him and he reluctantly agreed. Within three months I transformed it into a showpiece, it was simply magnificent. Mr Carpenter loved it so much that he spent all of his time in his surroundings, and began to understand the health benefits of being with plants. Sadly it came too late, Mr Carpenter had terminal cancer and died peacefully shortly after. In his will he left everything to be equally shared between me and a girl that turned out to be his prostitute. We went on to become rather good friends and lovers for a brief moment. She taught me how much money was to be made out of prostitution, especially if you looked after your girls. She was murdered some months later by a jealous client, leaving me the whole operation to run. It is quite ironical that my stepbrothers were in the same business. They inherited it from our uncle whom I believe was in partnership with our father. Mr Carpenter was also in on the business as a backroom director. There was an ongoing feud between the Badcocks and Carpenter over territories, which was made worse once I took over. The beauty of the situation is that no one in the opposition ever knew or saw Carpenter so they did not know whom they were dealing with. Now that I am here I am intent on taking personal revenge and destroying their empire."

"So you will use anyone as a means to achieve that end" Brenda snarled, as she realized that he had no love for her at all. "Well then, if information is all you want out of me, besides convenient sex, I suppose I'd better tell you what I know and leave," she abruptly said.

"That would be helpful," Carpenter coldly replied much to Brenda's disgust.

"The two people that you have taken are both freaks. One is a ghost dressed up as a woman, and that Robert Adolfson is really a priest, Father Brendan O'Reilly."

Carpenter sat there in sheer disbelief.

"What an absurd story, what the hell have you been sniffing? What utter nonsense," Carpenter disbelievingly said as he pushed Brenda away and retreated to another seat and pre-occupied himself, with other business matters.

Brenda remained tight-lipped and said nothing more. She cursed herself mentally for thinking that she loved this man. This was not love, it was a physical attraction, fed and driven by her sexual appetite.

Carpenter the prostitutes' evangelist was just another Badcock feeding off the misery of his workers. Okay, perhaps he provided better working conditions, but in all other respects he was not different to any other madam. Brenda resolved with dogged determination to escape her present lifestyle, even if it meant death.

Grandpa and Jack Stern meanwhile sat like obedient schoolgirls in the cabin of vehicle in which they were held prisoner, which was following Carpenter's white limousine.

The journey to Carpenter's lair took about 90 minutes. It was situated in a valley, and much to Grandpa's and Jack's surprise, was a horse riding school with a difference. The name of it was White Stallion Riding Academy 'The ride you want is right here', was its apt slogan.

The Academy was spotlessly clean, set up complete with multiple barns, outhouses, paddocks, hurdles and training courses. All of the horses were white and needless to say, beautifully groomed. The place exuded professional friendliness, the sterile type that one receives in any stereotyped retail establishment.

Grandpa and Jack both took careful note of everything as the convoy drove through the main entrance and headed towards an immense barn situated at the rear of the complex. The cars entered one by one and drove up circular ramps, which took them to a multi-layered complex. The bottom floor was a parking lot split into two sections, one for customers and the other for staff. The fleet of automobiles parked in the latter.

Jack and Grandpa were forcibly dragged out of their car and forcibly ushered upstairs into Carpenter's plush quarters.

"Did you see another storey?" Jack asked as he walked beside Grandpa.

"No, it obviously uses advanced reflective technology, a hologram to disguise the building."

"Do you think we have seen enough?" Jack asked.

"Nah, let's stay, I am having too much fun."

"Won't it be hilarious if they take your clothes off," Jack suggested.

"Depends on how desperate they are, doesn't it sonny."

"You're not suggesting spiritual sex?" Jack asked.

"There's a new angelical fetish," Grandpa replied.

"Blasphemy?"

"Not at all."

"Do they do it?"

"Who?"

"Spirits."

"Do what?" asked Grandpa.

"You know, have sex."

"I'm not telling, I'll let you find out when it's your time."

Jack was tempted to say, 'I can hardly wait', but he knew that it was dangerous to tamper with fate.

A similar situation existed in Newburn. Badcock was tempting his own fate by engaging in an overheated discussion with the small dark figure in the penthouse suite of the Large Hotel.

"So far you have achieved nothing," Badcock screamed.

"Look here Louis, you are in no position to criticize."

"Yes I am. I've lost The Infirmary and it's your fault. If you had kept an ear and eye out, the sale of The Infirmary would never have happened."

"What's happened has happened. All we can do is remedy the situation but what you need to realize is as I have told everyone before, we are dealing with Zen Masters."

"I have at least tracked down the culprits to the vicinity of the great national park."

"Yes, I've heard about that, what was it again a tracking device found on a police car! You fool, can't you see that they are smarter and wiser than you. Do you think for one minute that they are going to be easy to defeat. Wake up Louis; they are making you out to be a clown!"

Badcock seethed with rage at the small dark figure's comments and violently retorted, "Well, what about your freak D Man?"

"You called?" a voice erupted from the corner of the room.

Badcock froze, hoping what he said had not been overheard by the demon

"So you think I haven't been doing my job. Sounds like you are losing faith Mr Badcock. Perhaps you should be taught a lesson," the D Man said, as he bristled with electrical excitement.

The small dark figure sensed his desire for a kill but did not give the order. Instead, it softened its mood by asking, "What have you to report?"

The buzz of electrical energy subsided and the D Man answered, "One of my scouts, the keeper of the point contacted me."

"Yes, which one are we talking about?" the small dark figure asked.

"O'Flattery."

"Very interesting, that is one of our major drop-off points."

"I know."

"Who was there?"

"The priest O'Reilly, Jack Stern, Brenda, a new girl and a small private army of body guards that patrolled land, air and sea."

"Who were they protecting surely not the priest."

"Not at all the man's name was Lawrence Carpenter. He made himself out to be a modern day evangelist of sorts all dressed in white."

"What happened?"

"After a brief discussion Carpenter took three of them away, leaving Stern behind, who after a couple of hours wandering about the ruins then disappeared. What do you want me to do?"

"Nothing, just keep me informed of any developments for now" the small dark figure replied.

"Very well," he answered and disappeared.

Badcock breathed a sigh of relief, which the small dark figure disregarded.

"Wellllllll," Badcock courageously started to say "It appears that he has made some progress after all."

"So it would seem. I'm rather curious about Carpenter though. How would they have found out about him?"

"I've heard nothing. As far as I am concerned, he is just a small time operator, no threat to us. His claim to fame is that ridiculous flower power cream of his."

"Even so, he could be plotting something," the small dark figure suggested.

"He doesn't stand a chance. We are too strong for him."

"Damn it Badcock, didn't you just hear, he had a small army out there. All we need is a gang war to attract attention to ourselves. If that happens, all the guys that you pay off will have to be seen to be doing their job. That means investigating all of us and shutting us down, even if it is temporary!"

Badcock understood the ramifications of the situation. "What do you propose?" he asked.

"We must put our trust in the D Man and the Harsh Man. They will remedy the situation."

Badcock reluctantly agreed even though he had his doubts

"Very well, but if they fail…"

"Enough of that," the small dark figure angrily shouted. "Just go about your business and get The Infirmary operational again."

Badcock backed down and reluctantly obeyed it seemed, but not entirely for in his subconscious which was merrily plotting away he knew that he would have an opportunity sooner or later of avenging himself.

43

LET'S GO FISHING

Brendan returned to the safe house and was promptly greeted by all of the girls who were extremely anxious and eager to learn how it had all gone. They bombarded him with a thousand questions before he had a chance to say anything eventually he managed to calm them down and went on to describe what had happened at O'Flattery's point.

"That was not Lawrence Carpenter," Felicity emphatically stated without any shadow of doubt on her part on hearing Brendan's evidence.

"I Think it must have been one of his employees masquerading on his behalf" Naomi suggested as she also supported Felicity's deduction

"Obviously he wants to remain totally obscure. I even think that his going out dress was a clever disguise," she continued.

"At least he was true to his word," Brendan sheepishly said as he displayed the $20,000 in cash.

"Hardly sufficient for all of you however with the promise of a further $250,000 that should give each one of you a relatively good new start in life." He optimistically suggested

"More importantly do you think Brendan is safe and what will happen if and when they discover that Grandpa is a ghost?" Yvette asked more concerned about their safety than the promise of money.

"I suppose they will get the shock of their lives," Brendan replied as he smiled at thought of Carpenter's men undressing Grandpa

"What does Carpenter want in return for the $250,000?" Felicity asked as she secretly cherished and welcomed the opportunity of a new start.

"Carpenter wants me to provide him with a hard copy of the exact manufacturing process of the sexually enhancing drugs, as well as the location of the farm and Badcock's distribution network."

The girls looked at each other questioningly and then at Brenda who swallowed hard.

Yvette looked at him directly and asked, "Will you be able to do that?"

"The farm location is easy; I can easily obtain that information from the Ferrari's GPS memory. The method of drug preparation is not difficult as I can retrieve that from my mem…"

Brendan stopped as he sensed the girl's skepticism. Their collective body language shouted, 'Yeah, who can possibly do that. We can hardly remember what we did yesterday, never mind recollect in minute detail a sophisticated and highly technical chemical process!'

Even though the girls had recently experienced many extraordinary events in the company of Jack and himself, they were not ready as yet to fully accept his supernatural abilities.

"What I meant to say was that I would use the notes that I took from the pharmacy to furnish that data."

This explanation was more acceptable to the girls.

Brendan then realized that real knowledge was in the hands of a select few who kept it to themselves. They only propagated it when the time and the recipients were right.

"As for Badcock's distribution, that presents a challenge, I honestly don't know where to begin looking."

"You can't go back to The Infirmary. I am sure all of the records there have been destroyed," Naomi said.

"I suppose," Brendan sighed looking genuinely lost.

"Perhaps Brendan's friend Stanley could help," Yvette suggested.

"I'm sure he could, but I don't have his contact details."

"Oh dear, wait a moment, I think some information came through on the fax." Naomi suddenly remembered

Really, let's take a look then," Brendan said as he went in search of the fax machine

It was not a fax, but emailed material that the computer had automatically printed.

Brendan picked it up scanned it thoroughly in an attempt to find an address or contact number of sorts, but no luck. Although very detailed, the information dealt with the issues that Jack had discussed with Brendan before namely the financials of all those involved in the nefarious on goings in Newburn.

"Not much help I'm afraid," he reluctantly said.

"Ohhhhh," the girls sighed despondently.

"Don't worry," Yvette reassured them, "there is always a solution to every problem, I am certain you will work it out."

Brendan looked at Yvette's angelic countenance and thanked her for her encouragement.

"I need to be alone, could you excuse me?" he said as he made his way to a quiet corner of the safe house.

"Come girls, let's go downstairs, perhaps we can work this out," Yvette suggested, leaving Brendan all alone to ponder.

He sat staring into space as he reflected on the fact that he had lied to Jack about the drug samples taken from the pharmacy. Brendan had another two ampoules set aside for a rainy day, which it appeared, had just arrived. He retrieved them from the hiding spot near to where he was sitting and studied them intently. Brendan's mind quickly intoned the mystical words which cast him into the three dimensional molecular world contained within one of the ampoules that he held in his hand.

He saw himself standing next to the sexually enhancing drugs which he abbreviated to SED, which when spelt backwards became DES, short for Desmond, and as it was the opposite of SED, Brendan thought that DES was in all probability more than likely a poor sexual performer

"That's not funny," Brendan heard one of the SEDs say

"Pardon?"

"You know what I am talking about."

"I don't, I'm sorry."

"Yes you do, you know very well that you can't tell how good a person is in bed by their name."

"Really the numerologists have got it wrong then have they?" Brendan mockingly answered

"Insolent upstart."

"What do you want here?" another SED grunted. Brendan looked at the herd of identical SEDs. They appeared as stylized multi coloured self animated stick figures.

He quietly and politely replied "I've come to ask you if you know how you were put together?"

"Of course we do, you silly fool."

"Could you tell me then please?"

"Why should we?" one of the brighter SEDs arrogantly shouted. Brendan thought it strange that such simple life forms were demonstrating specific emotional traits.

Was it here at this level of life that such things found their origins, he asked himself.

"Well, what are you waiting for?" the same arrogant SED impatiently asked as Brendan had not offered an explanation.

"I need your help to rescue a friend of mine."

"That is none of our concern," another even more arrogant SED shouted.

"Well it is, for it is because of you that my friend is being held hostage and will be killed unless I deliver the formula."

The SEDs looked at Brendan suspiciously. They visibly started angrily chatting amongst themselves and debating the issue at hand until they reached common ground. The one that had the most conversation with Brendan approached him, whilst the others shuffled behind.

He looked at Brendan and explained.

"The arrogant aggressive side of us is made up of one part pethidine and the rest, which is the softer modifying element, is two parts venlafaxine. We come together through the process of heat and vibration, which bear the numbers 101.3 and the quadruple of that to the fourth power of 10 all strictly confirmed. Do you understand?"

"Yes, I do," Brendan nodded.

"Good, then you can go."

"One last question"

"What is it now," the same SED replied, looking quite disgusted

"How do you work?"

"As lock and keys"

"Meaning"

"We run around the human body searching for the locks that we can undo."

"All located in the brain?" Brendan asked wanting to understand more fully

"Fool, did you not listen, I said the body, all of it."

"The sexual response is not isolated in the brain?"

"Not at all, it is an entire body involvement to the point of…"

"Spiritual ecstasy?" Brendan guessed.

"Correct, now leave us alone."

Brenda drifted back to normal reality and carefully wrote down the manufacturing in precise detail.

"That is two things attended to, now for the third, but where do I start," he thought to himself

As he mindlessly looked around his eye caught an old tattered paperback book entitled 'Supernature' by Lyall Watson . Thinking it applied to him, and that it probably contained all of the information that Jack knew, Brendan picked it up and began reading.

It was a science book that dealt with specific topics from a slanted viewpoint that provoked the mind into thinking obscurely and in so doing immersed the reader in a sea of radical thought. It was not until Brendan reached the section dealing with water that he realized the significance of Jesus a Christ. Water it was written, at any given time whilst in the liquid state, existed in all three phases continuously, that is gaseous, liquid and solid. If that was true, Brendan postulated to himself that the miracle of Jesus walking on water was due to his ability to summon all of the solid particles to interlock and form a stable bridge. He remembered that the Bible reported Jesus as saying, "I am the living waters" Brendan's eyes widened and his heart raced when he began to read that water has a memory. In that moment he realized where he would find Badcock's records.

The Infirmary had been flooded throughout with water; everything in the building was saturated with and drenched by the liquid. As it did its work, it recorded everything that it came into contact with and it flowed away with all of that information. All that Brendan had to do was obtain a sample of that water to access the data which he sought.

With a song in his heart he waltzed down the stairs to the next level and found Yvette and some of the girls discussing the contents of Stanley's email.

"Found anything interesting?" he asked.

"Very complicated Mr Stern, it would all make sense if we knew who all of the different people are."

"Yes it would, keep working on it; I came down to say that I shall be away for a little while."

"Okay, off you go, we will continue studying these documents."

"No, I'm sorry, what I meant to say is that I shall continue contemplating, but I shall do it while I walk around in the bowels of the mountain."

"Of course, Jack, we're quite happy here. Tell us when you would like a cup of tea or something to nibble on," Yvette replied taking no notice of what Brendan was rambling on about

"I shall" Brendan's almost whispered before he made his way downstairs leaving Yvette and the girls to continue working on Stanley's material.

Once he had reached the lower ground floor, Brendan went over to the Ferrari and made certain he could retrieve the farm's location from the GPS system which he easily did satisfied with this result he proceeded to visualize The Infirmary, and in no time at all he was there. The site was a hive of activity. Badcock he sensed had not wasted any time in restoring The Infirmary. A team of building surveyors, architects and builders were presently examining the damage. They were deciding as to what could be repaired and what needed replacement. It was not as badly damaged as the fire chief had previously reported. Obviously he was a staunch opponent of The Infirmary and wanted it out of town.

Brendan assumed invisibility and carefully walked about the building. There was no shortage of water to choose from and luckily it had neither rained nor had the reticulation system been used.

Brendan determined that the best places to take a sample would be from the drain or soak wells in the street outside the main entrance to The Infirmary. He looked around for a suitable container and wasn't sure how big it should be. Would a teaspoon of water contain all that he required or was it more, Brendan did not know. He went to the rear car park as he remembered that there were several rubbish bins there, which in all likelihood would contain an empty bottle or two. His hunch was correct and he picked up an empty screw top 250ml glass Coca Cola bottle. It was a little dirty and full of dead ants. "This can't be good for you," he mumbled as though he was talking to the ants then he unscrewed the lid and prepared to wash it out with water from a nearby tap.

There was a certain peace in the garden and Brendan enjoyed

the trees talking amongst themselves in the way that trees do. In the middle of it all Brendan could detect an unusual frequency of sound, it was clearly beyond the normal hearing range of human limits, situated at about 27,000 hertz, he guessed. It was not continuous, but rather erratic in its makeup, resembling a fly buzzing around looking for a suitable place to land. It bothered Brendan because he thought that he was the prey. With bottle upside down in hand, he quickly walked back to gather his source of water , consciously aware of the sonic search light which became louder as he drew closer to The Infirmary's building. The drain on the opposite side of the street looked to be the best place to draw a sample. There were plenty of parked cars providing ample camouflage. Brendan knelt down and immersed the Coca Cola bottle. As the water filled the bottle, and he was about to replace the cap, the car next to him exploded into a thousand pieces. The force of the explosion flung Brendan's body up and over a six foot security brick wall of the adjacent house and he landed heavily. Severely dazed he shook his head to see if he was still intact, his vision was blurred and his ears rung loudly but otherwise he was in good shape

'A terrorist attack of sorts,' he thought as he picked himself up and tried to orientate himself 'probably a gang's reprisal.' He continued in the same line of thought as he stumbled about a little unsteady on his feet. Then suddenly without any warning the brick wall in front of him exploded. Bricks flew in all directions and hurtled towards him. In the fractions of seconds that he had at his disposal Brendan's mind very quickly intoned the mystical words taught to him by the ghostly priest at St Pious and the bricks bounced off his anatomy, rendering no harm at all.

He glanced up and saw the origin of what had caused the massive destruction. On the roof of The Infirmary stood a figure dressed in black, juggling balls of intense light; the figure hissed with satanic energy. Sparks flew from the figure's hair, nails and teeth. Brendan realized that he was the prey and was being hunted with a view to becoming exterminated. There was only one way out and that was to escape to a different location.

His mind automatically chose the safest place he had known in his life namely the Archbishop's private cathedral. Within moments Brendan stood at its main altar, a magnificent handcrafted marble edifice built to God's glory. Brendan breathed a deep sigh of relief as his mind raced to comprehend the ferocity and suddenness of the attack upon him. If this was Badcock's revenge, then full credit had to be given to him in finding such a capable assassin. The question was what sort of sophisticated military weapon did the assassin throw at him? Was it a new breed of compact thermo nuclear device that one could hold in the palm of one's hand? The question was answered in a flash of blinding light and thunderous noise as the altar exploded. This time Brendan suffered no adverse effects at all even though he was violently thrown against the cathedrals wall. His body was attuned and firmly locked into its defensive mode.

He gathered his senses, scrambled to his feet, looked intensely all around him determined to escape once again just before he watched in horror as a devilish figure excreted itself out of the Sacred Heart statue.

The D Man stood 20 metres to the right of Brendan and juggled two balls in his left hand as he asked, "Well Zen Master, you have survived these attempts on your life, I see you are most accomplished in your discipline. Which school did you attend?"

Brendan looked at him squarely and not even blinking once, replied, "A catholic one of course."

The D Man un-amused continued to stare at Brendan.

"Do not toy with me, I know your type, I have eliminated all of you over the centuries and yet your kind wishes to persist, how unrelenting of you. Tell me to whom do you belong."

Brendan had not the faintest idea what the D Man was raving on about. Instead, he carefully studied him in an attempt to know his enemy and find his weakness. Then he truthfully replied, "To God."

"Which one?" the D Man shouted.

HIs question confused Brendan, and he thought best not to answer, as it would be to his advantage. Instead, he thought of Christ at the synagogue and in a flash was transported to the local Jewish church.

Brendan's presence set the alarm bells ringing. The synagogue had been heavily secured after the threat of terrorist action by anti Semitic groups sympathetic to the Palestinian cause in the Middle East. Security guards rushed in, the internal floodlights came on and focused on Brendan who stood innocently on the cherished altar.

"Come down at once," the guards commanded as they approached him with pistols in hand.

Brendan did not move he did not know which one of the guards was the D Man in disguise. One of them raised his gun and was about to fire a warning shot when the guard behind him shot him in the back. The image of the D Man flowed out of dead guard's body and he threw the remaining destructive balls towards Brendan. The remainder of the guards panicked and started shooting wildly at the D Man. The bullets simply fused into his anatomy causing no harm at all which brought a smile to his face. The D Man retaliated by casting a sinister look into the face of each guard who in turn crumbled into a twisted heap of broken arms and legs.

The two balls raced past Brendan towards the walls of the synagogue and burned ancient hieroglyphic symbols into them.

Brendan instantly thought of the Egyptian pyramids and was there.

He sensed the D Man's imminent presence and concluded that his choice of location was being accurately tracked by him. Brendan took one last chance and changed his tack. He closed his eyes and desperately thought of Yvette.

"You snuck in unnoticed and unannounced," Yvette said as she lifted her head from her work.

"Yes I did, didn't I?" Brendan answered completely flustered and almost out of breath. He nervously looked around to see if the D Man had followed him.

"What's the matter?" she asked, sensing his distress.

"I can't definitely say, but I think I've just experienced a profound vision of Badcock's revenge."

"Tell us about it?" Felicity said as she also detected Brendan's overwhelming anxiety.

Brendan collapsed on the floor and lay on his back to calm himself down, after a few minutes he sat up and described his horrendous life threatening experience in a surreal sort of way.

"Sounds like you had quite a vision down there. We'll check the news on the computer later to see if it has been reported. Come on let's have a cup of tea, it will soothe your jangled nerves," Naomi suggested after hearing Brendan's rendition of the events

"Sounds rather good," Brendan replied as he took a seat and waited.

It didn't take long to prepare the infusion; the tea was a soothing blend of peppermint, chamomile, passionflower and hops. Just what Brendan needed to clear his body of lingering anxiety, and prepare for his next task, namely the reading of the waters, but where had he left the sample. He thought that he had lost it during the D Man's onslaught. Damn it, he would have to return to The Infirmary and obtain another sample, however, that was not safe. That strange noise that he detected was most certainly some sort of sophisticated detection device that the D Man used.

"Has any one of you seen a Coca Cola bottle with water in it anywhere around here?" he asked.

The girls laughed at his question.

"What's so funny?" he asked feeling his face redden

"It's in your pants pocket," Naomi answered. "We didn't know what you had in there until we saw its shape," she added.

Brendan's face reddened even more.

"Well, the man of the world is embarrassed."

"Even the most experienced has his moments," Brendan replied, as he raised an eyebrow in defense. He then stood up and took his leave retreating back to the third level of the complex. Once there he took the bottle out of his trouser pocket and looked around for a suitable container to pour the water into. He found it on one of the numerous tables that adorned the level. Satisfied that it was adequately clean he poured the precious liquid into it, took a deep breath and attuned his mind in the same way that he had done with the drug ampoules. Brendan expected to find small entities to deal with because water was made up of three molecules. Instead, he was surprised to discover the opposite. They were large, Crystalline and in a constant state of activity.

"Excuse me, can anyone help me?" Brendan politely asked as he gazed about.

Not one of the Crystalline beings answered, they were too pre occupied with their intermingling.

Brendan watched mesmerized by the goings on, not knowing where he was in the scheme of things. Was he on top, in the middle, or on the bottom of the bowl? Had anyone of them even noticed him?

"You look lost," said one of the waters as it sped past.

By the time he had time to reply, it had disappeared completely.

"Could someone please possibly help me?" he shouted.

"Can't, too busy, too much input, can't do anything until we are cleansed of all the needless emotional baggage that we are carrying," some of them voiced back.

"How do you get rid of it?" Brendan shouted into the seething mass.

"The sun and the wind do it for us," was the reply.

"How long does it take?" Brendan asked.

"Depends where we find ourselves in the ocean, if we are on top it can happen quickly, if deep down maybe years"

Brendan understood and took himself back to the normal world.

Obviously he had to initiate the cleansing process and return when the waters were less murky.

Gently does it, he concluded. Otherwise he might strip them of all of their information. He searched his mind for possible solutions and then it struck him that the oceans were nothing more than one enormous mixing bowl. With that thought in mind he sped downstairs to the kitchen area and found a clean handheld mixer. He dashed back eager to try his idea. He plunged the mixer into one of the available power points, inserted the twin rotors into the water, switched on the device and selected the slower speed. The rotors spun into life beating the waters and aerating them at the same time. After three minutes Brendan thought that they surely would have had enough. He switched off the mixer, withdrew it and allowed the waters to settle. Once again, he immersed himself into their world and found it decidedly different.

The Crystalline beings were no longer on top of each other they were more or less evenly separated with room to move.

Aerating had created space and a sense of freedom. A group of Crystallines, who appeared wiser than the rest, greeted Brendan. "Now that we are no longer weighed down, we feel better and are able to assist you," they said in unison as they bowed towards him.

Brendan returned the gesture and said, "I thank you for your gentle assistance."

"What is your desire?" one of the Crystallines asked, shimmering with light as it did so.

"I understand that you absorb the memory of everything that you come into contact with."

"That is correct, but it is not permanent, otherwise water would have no use on this planet."

"How is that?" Brendan asked.

"We; that is the service of water, washes away the negative emotions of all people, and carries it to the ocean where it is stripped away."

"But what about memory?" Brendan asked, afraid that he had wiped away the precious information that he sought.

"That is different," they replied.

"How so"

"We discard old memory when we come into contact with something new."

"So it is transient?"

"Yes it is, but remember depending upon where we find ourselves at any given moment, whoever samples us may obtain knowledge dating back years, even centuries, especially in waters that have been locked away."

"Are you suggesting that the secrets of the world can be found there?"

"We are," they replied.

"What happens to all of the negative emotions that are washed away from you in the oceans?" Brendan asked smiling at his use of the word 'wash'.

"They influence the weather."

"Really"

"Oh yes, if too many people harbour these destructive energies, the wind becomes enraged, and as you are aware causes all sorts of havoc."

"People's feelings influence the weather?"

"They do, and if and when you become enlightened as to how all things are linked, you will appreciate the miracle and complexity of life."

Brendan bowed his head humbly and softly said, "Thank you, for now I understand why it is important for each one of us to love one another."

"Because it ensures your happy survival in all respects," the waters answered

"Can you help me with a problem?"

"If we can, what it is that you request?" they asked.

"You recently washed The Infirmary, and I was wondering if you retained a Mr Badcock's business dealings?" Brendan respectfully asked.

"Give us a few moments to find those who were there."

"Very well," Brendan replied as he continued to appreciate the beauty of the Crystallines.

Their shape was designed in such a way to allow them to easily interlock with each other from numerous angles, thus facilitating the Omni directional spread of hardness. He wondered if this was their way of self propagation and held that thought until it was interrupted.

"Excuse us sir, we are ready."

Brendan held his breath in anticipation.

"We have found a few who have a recollection of what you desire; they are on their way. They will be here shortly."

"Thank you," Brendan replied, as he drifted back to what he was previously thinking about. It became obvious to him that the world of crystals was more than highly polished reflective surfaces and angles. It was practical in all respects.

"Your information is here sir," the Crystallines announced as they bowed towards him.

"How would you like it sir?"

"Pardon?"

"In black and white or colour?"

"Colour please."

"Very well," they replied, as they assembled themselves into a particular shape.

Brendan looked puzzled and then became aghast as images were projected from a screen of assembled Crystallines. He searched for the origin of the picture, thinking that it was similar to a movie projector. But then he saw that the assembled screen was in fact more like a digital television screen, with each Crystalline contributing to the picture with its own separate information. When the show had finished, the wise Crystalline said, "Is that what you were seeking?"

"Yes, thank you very much."

"Good, we believe that you may have had some difficulty in remembering all of it, so we entrust to your care a concentrate of it. Guard it well, and if you need to recall what you have seen, simply fill a fountain pen with it and it will do the rest," the wise Crystalline said as they handed over a clear vile of what appeared to be warm solid ice.

Brendan accepted it, expecting it to melt then and there in his hands. The elder sensed this and corrected his fear

"What you hold is a crystal of water, it will not melt. In fact, when we form ourselves into liquid immoveable objects we need not separate or melt, if it were not for the laws that we agreed to eons ago."

"And which laws were they?" Brendan asked.

"Those that deal with life"

"I don't understand."

"Life wanted to be able to impart unlimited voluntary movement into each one of its creations. It pleaded with everything to help and that is what we did, help, but some remained stubbornly immoveable. There is a twist; much to our mischievous joy we can still exist in any form we wish to at any given temperature."

"Why?" asked Brendan.

"To demonstrate our unique independence"

Brendan understood, bowed and thanked his gracious hosts and returned to his physical world.

The Crystallines were indeed correct. He had experienced information overload and required the assistance of his newly acquired watery gem.

Brendan searched the level in the hope that he could find a refillable fountain pen. In the middle right hand drawer of an old fashioned oak desk with leather inlay, he found a collection of some fine looking writing instruments, which were in keeping with the scholarly pursuits that the real Jack Stern had alluded to. Brendan avoided the gold painted and solid gold pens and selected a plain one.

He unscrewed it and examined it thoroughly for signs of dried ink or dust. Satisfied that it was clean, he inserted the water crystal into the ink compartment, reassembled the pen, placed writing paper from the top drawer on the table top and proceeded to write. The movement of his hand activated the crystal, which omitted a bluish light and took over the pen. It started writing of its own accord, nothing verbose or lengthy, just names, locations and dates, short, simple and to the point.

44

ACCIDENTAL TRUTHS

Brendan did not relate any of his 'watery' experiences to Yvette or the girls as he thought it wise not to. Instead he allowed them to present their findings on Stanley's email data which he contently listened to and discussed with them over dinner during which time he wondered how each one of their lives might have been different had they been given better opportunities prior to landing up in The Infirmary, but then he thought that perhaps it was not the lack of these, but rather the absence of intuitive insight in not recognizing what was good for them or was it. Of all the girls at this point in time Yvette in his mind was clearly the most intelligent and he enjoyed listening to her immensely irrespective of the topic of conversation. Later that night when all was said and down and they had settled down for the night and the girls slept peacefully in the soporific environment of the safe house, Brendan could not. His mind was relentlessly pursued by the events of the day and it felt to him as though the D Man had invaded his inner sanctum and was pursuing him even as he slept. Brendan awoke every hour on the hour drenched in perspiration out of fright and the fear that the D man was inside the safe house. He could not settle himself until he finally remembered the words of his first spiritual master at St Pious and it was only then that he dreamed of reversing the tables. Now Brendan was the aggressor, the conquering hero who chased the D Man hither and thither with a sword fashioned out of love and a battle axe crafted from the thorns of a thousand red roses.

He awoke the next morning feeling completely exhausted and he reflected on the meaning of his dream and concluded it was symbolic, an omen of things to come. The time was 7:30am. Brendan turned to admire the angelic faces of those who slept around him. Not wishing to disturb any one of them, a boyish smile spread across his face as he entertained the ambitious idea of single-handedly cooking breakfast for everyone. After all, time was nothing more than man's feeble attempt to compartmentalize exerted and non exerted natural forces. Do away with the silliness of putting everything into a box, become part of the flow and in doing so, achieve miracles in the process. It was as simple as that he realized.

In the blink of an eye a sumptuous breakfast lay before him. Everything cooked and presented to culinary perfection. With the absence of time each dish remained unaltered in freshness and temperature. In another blink of the eye the scene changed to that of Yvette and the girls happily sitting around all together and relishing the food.

Brendan could see that breakfast was going to be a drawn out affair which did not fit in with his plans of setting out early that day so he politely excused himself and collected all of the information that Carpenter had asked for. Not knowing where to find him, Brendan focused on Carpenter's image, his telephone number and his line of work, in the hope that his mind would easily locate him. Within a few minutes Brendan found himself in an old dilapidated house, thinking that his powers had deserted him, Brendan sought a way out, only to be confronted by an elderly gentleman.

"What are you doing here?" the old man harshly snapped as he approached the handsome priest.

"My apologies sir, the door was open," Brendan hastily replied knowing full well that what he had just said was not the truth.

"What nonsense, all the doors and windows are bolted shut, you would have to break them down to gain entry," the old man angrily retorted.

"Now tell me; what are you doing here?" he demanded to know as he produced a small revolver from his pocket.

"I am actually looking for Mr Lawrence Carpenter; I think I have lost my way."

"What is your business with him?"

"I'm delivering a package." Brendan replied

"I see nothing like that on you."

"It's small."

"How small?" The grumpy old man asked

"Well, it's an envelope actually."

"Show me, hand it over, quickly," the old man demanded as he pointed the revolver at Brendan's heart

Brendan obeyed and waited as the old man tore open the letter and browsed through its contents.

"Come with me," the old man signalled with the barrel of the gun. Brendan reluctantly followed and walked towards a seemingly ancient door. Brendan grabbed hold of its handle and turned it clockwise but it resisted.

"Turn it the other way and step back," the old man instructed the handsome priest as he stood next to him

Brendan obliged watched and waited until there came the sounds of rusty old cogs meshing with each other as springs and levers snapped into action. The door was hinged at the top and flung forward revealing a room that was full of old world charm and extreme beauty. It was obvious to Brendan that this old man had an appreciation of the fine arts. The walls of the apartment were covered in paintings featuring masters such as 'Van Gogh, Monet, Picasso, Rembrandt and Pissarro' to mention a few. The furniture was made of oak turned by master craftsmen. The woollen carpets were thick and luxurious woven by hand into intricate patterns. The lighting fixtures were ideally located to accentuate the intermingled beauty of all the works of art.

"Take a seat Mr…" the old man warmly said as he put away the gun.

"Brendan O'Reilly sir."

"Well Brendan what are you, informant, private detective, spy?"

"Neither sir, I'm simply seeking to buy back the freedom of my friends."

"And who might they be?"

"Jack Stern and his grandfather"

"And why is Mr Carpenter holding them?"

"In exchange for information"

"About?"

"The dealings of a one Mr Louis Badcock"

"Interesting," the old man said as he played with his unkempt hair.

"And who might you be?" Brendan asked.

"The man you are looking for."

"Pardon" Brendan replied rather surprised by his answer

"I am Lawrence Carpenter," he replied smiling.

Brendan looked at him and frowned deeply, revealing his suspicious doubt.

"Oh, I understand, you have met the other younger Samuel Badcock, alias Lawrence Carpenter."

"I have?"

"Yes you have. I thought as much. Let me explain the situation Brendan, but before I do that, would you care for a drink?"

Remembering what had happened to him with Jack Stern in that roadside café, Brendan thought that the safest thing for him to do would be to partake of something similar to altar wine, perhaps a sherry that had been made from a specific grape according to ecclesiastical standards. Accordingly he requested, "Perhaps a sherry."

"I thought as much, now let me see what I have," the real Lawrence

Carpenter said, as he shifted through his collection of fine liqueurs located on a nearby drinks trolley.

"Will a Portuguese Olorosso do?"

"Ah yes, thank you very much sir," Brendan replied not knowing what that was

"This is a particularly fine specimen, I think I will join you," he said as he poured out two generous portions.

Brendan accepted the glass and savoured its contents. The wine burst onto his taste buds, drowning them with a mixture of honey, burnt raisins and oak flavours. He nodded indicating his sublime pleasure, and sat quietly contemplating the origins of the wine, as the real Lawrence Carpenter sat down opposite him and detailed the true story of the relationship between him and Samuel Badcock.

Everything was the same as what Brendan had heard previously, apart from his death and that of the prostitute, and this led Brendan to ask, "I gather you are using Samuel Badcock as the decoy."

"That is correct, but I may have made a bad decision, because for some time now I have suspected that Samuel is a little too ambitious. The information that you showed me confirms this. Obviously he wants to branch out on his own and what better way than to take over his step-brother's operation."

"Do you think he will succeed?"

"Of course not, he is driven by greed and hatred, not very clever thinking emotions. Besides, Louis Badcock has the Ricci girls and other Mafia types involved with him. Samuel is doomed."

"But the army?"

"Oh, that's mine; I give the final orders if necessary. Here, take your papers back, give them to that fool Samuel, it won't do him any good, but at least it will get your friends back."

The real Lawrence Carpenter paused and then asked out of curiosity "Is he giving anything else in return?"

"Yes, $250,000"

"Generous, ambitious little swindler"

"I hope you don't do anything before I rescue my friends." Brendan almost pleaded

"Don't worry, I won't." Carpenter answered in a quasi reassuring manner

Brendan looked at him and did not know whether to trust the real Carpenter or not. Carpenter sensed this and said, "I will prove it to you, let's ring Samuel and arrange a meeting between you and him."

Brendan agreed and watched as the real Mr Carpenter reached for an ornate reproduction French telephone, dialled a silent number and then handed over the hand piece to Brendan.

"Carpenter?" the voice answered.

"Norm Difluca."

"Yes."

"I have your information."

"Excellent, shall we meet at the same place, say 2:00pm?"

"Very well and the money?"

"Don't worry; I will bring that along, you will only receive it if I am satisfied with the info."

Brendan remained silent.

"Did you hear me?" the fake Carpenter asked as he thought that Brendan was being evasive.

"I did."

"Well, is everything in order?"

"It is." Brendan calmly replied not letting on that he met the real Lawrence Carpenter

"2:00pm then."

"Agreed and see you then." With that Brendan cradled the phone.

"What is your proper name?" the real Lawrence Carpenter asked as he stared at Brendan

"The one I gave you," Brendan truthfully replied.

"Are you sure it isn't Jack Stern?" Carpenter persisted.

"What makes you think that?" Brendan asked.

"My sources tell me that there was trouble at The Infirmary before the accident, it seems the new owner decided to revolutionize its concept and make it into a sex therapy clinic. There was an attempt on Jack Stern's life after which he disappeared, then he appears at O'Flattery's Point with the intention of selling highly confidential information to Samuel Badcock, I think you had better come clean Mr Stern."

"You've found me out Mr Carpenter" Brendan replied pretending to play into his hands

"That's better, it makes it much easier to do business," Carpenter said as he moved about the room.

He stopped for a moment, paused, thought and then pointed a finger at Brendan. "You will go to the meeting Mr Stern, but the information you sell will not be exclusive, do you understand?" he said looking most businesslike in a cunning sort of way at Brendan.

"Yes, I do. Where is your copying machine?" Brendan asked as he opened the envelope containing the vital information

"We'll use the fax machine over there." Carpenter said as he took the sheets from Brendan hands

Brendan watched as Carpenter went about duplicating the data.

"There, that should do it, I have a copy to sell to whoever I wish and you have a copy for Samuel's purposes." Carpenter deviously said as he congratulated himself

"What will you do with yours?" Brendan asked.

"I thought you would have worked that out Mr Stern. The most important part of this information is that dealing with the drug manufacture, the rest is useless to me or any other hard-core drug dealer. Prostitution is a sideline these days, not as much money in it anymore. By the time Samuel has his copy I will have sold the formula ten times over and made a small fortune."

Brendan wondered if he had done the right thing, because through his actions the spread of this drug would reach astronomic proportions. I can't change the world, he thought. Then he saw a glimpse of a future in which the ultimate act of terrorism occurred that liberated humanity for all time.

"If you have nothing more to say we can part company," Carpenter said, shattering Brendan's pensive mood.

"Ah no, nothing at all sir."

"I still can't work out how you managed to enter my house."

"You could say, I came through the walls." Brendan honestly said

"I'm not amused Mr Stern, do not joke with me."

"Very well."

"Come then, I will show you out." Carpenter roughly said as he ushered the handsome priest out.

Brendan wondered how quickly the real Carpenter would act on the drug information that Brenan had provided and if it would jeopardize his chances of obtaining the $250,000 from the fake Carpenter. Carpenter took Brendan out of the old world room by an alternative route and showed him the street outside. It was the same street that the Archbishop's palace was located in. Brendan wondered how well the Archbishop was doing and at the same time hoped that the D Man had not followed him.

"You are looking much better today Your Grace," the perky young nurse said to the Archbishop, as she added notes to his medical chart.

"Very glad to be out of intensive care," he softly replied as he was still quite weak.

"Well I suppose you will believe in miracles even more. What did the doctor say? One more millimetre and the bullet would have not only hit your heart but ruptured your aorta as well?"

"Yes I believe that is so."

"Okay, open wide, that's it, don't bite will you," the perky nurse said as she inserted the thermometer into his mouth

"Pulse rate is good and strong. Judging by the way the bed sheets are going up around your groin area, I think your strength is returning; might need to give you a little silver spoon treatment if you don't behave yourself."

The Archbishop remained still and was not amused by the innuendo.

The nurse continued with her cheerful disposition and attended to the intravenous drip making certain its flow rate was correct.

"Another twenty-four hours and you should be off this," she said sounding quite positive. "See you in another four hours, unless you need me more urgently," she erotically purred with a wink of her eye. She signalled to the man at the door. "You can come in now,"

"Good morning Father Sierra, I am very glad to be able to see you," greeted the Archbishop

"Likewise, Your Grace."

"How have things been?"

"Not good, Your Grace."

Before Father Sierra could say any more, there was another knock at the door.

"See who that is will you Father?"

"Of course, Your Grace," Sierra replied as he took five steps towards the door

"Ah Father Rigoli, please come in."

"Thank you Father, Your Grace," Father Rigoli replied as he entered the private hospital suite

"Make yourself comfortable; is there anything I can get you?"

Father Rigoli thought for a moment "I've just had morning tea, perhaps a drink."

"And for you Father Sierra?" the Archbishop asked.

"Is there a menu," he enquired "this place feels more like a hotel than a hospital."

"It's on the table by you." Father Sierra found it and browsed through it's contents.

"Cappuccino would be nice, thank you."

"And a flat black for me," Father Rigoli requested.

The Archbishop attended to their respective wishes by telephoning room service. "So, what do you have to tell me?"

"Father Sierra and I have analysed the situation and implemented some appropriate measures."

"Yes," the Archbishop said, listening intently.

"The assassination of Monsignor Monahan, and also the attempt on your life, was as a result of Father Monsignor Monahan's greed. It seems he had cleverly helped himself to some of the funds and our business colleagues discovered this anomaly after doing their monthly audit. They were most unhappy and acted in their typical irrational manner. We have spoken to them and smoothed things over. In their own way they apologized for shooting you, again it seems that they acted on impulse rather than exact knowledge. They assumed that you knew of Monsignor Monahan's actions and that you had approved of them. Everything is back to normal, except we have, that is, we have all experienced a drop in revenue due to events that have occurred at The Infirmary, the pharmacy and the farm. Most things have normalized themselves with the quick actions of our brothers in black, although The Infirmary will not be operational again for at least six months."

"Very good, what else?" the Archbishop asked.

"It was not a good idea to have sent Father Brendan O'Reilly to Newburn. Reports suggest that he has become somewhat of a renegade, teaching all sorts of weird and wonderful ideas about the power within and that sin is nonsense, amongst other things. Without a doubt, he represents a real threat to our integrity and all that the church has built up over the centuries. We don't need a second coming of Christ or some fool telling us that you can achieve the same results as Christ did that will rob us of our hard earned power. Luckily he has disappeared and we don't know anything about his whereabouts."

"Sounds to me as though the sexual pressure he was exposed to got to him and he finally cracked," the Archbishop suggested.

"I think you might be right Your Grace," Father Rigoli agreed

"If I may continue," Father Rigoli then said

"But of course."

"The replacement priest is handling the matter very well until the parish priest returns. However, we feel that as a result of Father O'Reilly's preaching, he may have incited some fanatics within our congregation who have taken responsibility upon themselves to re-structure religion."

"What are you saying?" the Archbishop asked, looking somewhat confused.

"There have occurred military style terrorist attacks on three different locations. A car bomb went off outside The Infirmary, your beloved Cathedral's altar was bombed and the Synagogue has also been desecrated. The media has reported it as being the work of religious extremists who are focusing on the Judeo-Christian religion."

The Archbishop appeared very disturbed at this news and he turned white.

"There is more Your Grace. Our intelligence tells us that although eye witness reports are sketchy; it appears that Brendan O'Reilly is responsible for or at least has had some involvement with these attacks."

"Oh my god, the man has truly cracked," the Archbishop moaned.

"Well and truly," both Father Sierra and Rigoli answered.

"What are we to do?" the Archbishop asked.

"We have instructed our own people to apprehend him, otherwise the various police agencies are on the lookout."

"What a pity, I suppose we are to blame in some respects, using him the way we did. However, one was not to know the outcome."

Father Sierra and Rigoli nodded their heads in agreement.

In Newburn the Archbishop's colleagues were also discussing similar matters.

"And what do you have to report?" the small dark figure asked of the D Man.

"That everything is working extremely well, your device caught that Jack Stern outside of The Infirmary and I was there in a flash."

"Good."

"He was doing something strange; it appeared to me that he was taking a sample of water from the drain."

"How curious, perhaps he has switched jobs from that of a brothel owner to one of a Health Inspector," the small dark figure joked.

"I don't think so."

"Why and what happened?"

"I attacked him with spheres packed with unstable entropy that normally vaporize everything, unfortunately for me he somehow survived."

"What?" the small dark figure said in disbelief

"The car that I targeted was reduced to minute particles, but he escaped unscathed."

"You're joking. What happened then?"

"He hid behind a brick fence which I blew up and then he fled to a Cathedral foolishly thinking that he would be safe inside. But I easily found him standing on the main altar. I hid in one of those ugly Christ statues and attacked him from there."

"This time you killed him?"

"No."

"Why not?"

"Because as I suspected, he appears to be a highly evolved Zen Master, in fact he is exceptionally talented. I can't guess from whom he learned, I thought I had previously eliminated all those who posed a threat to our world of deceit." The D Man painfully explained

"Continue," the small dark figure, said becoming increasingly angry.

"He survived that attack and he tried to elude me by changing tact and fleeing to a Synagogue but I followed him and once there I killed a guard and then tried to frighten him by writing ancient text on the walls, but all it did was make him flee to the pyramids of Egypt, which makes me suspect that his origins lie there. He might be a descendant of those Atlantean Arians. They possessed immense knowledge and who knows he may have even re-discovered it and taught himself."

"Are you telling me that Zen Masters originated from the Atlantean's?"

"It is a possibility."

"So, where is he now?" the small dark figure impatiently demanded to know.

"He realized I could track his thoughts about locations, so he has changed his mind and started thinking about people. It was too much for me and I couldn't follow as they freely move about in no fixed location. The entire chase did teach me the extent of his powers so that the next time we meet I will know how to disable him."

"Something tells me that that can't be too far away." The small dark figure smirked as it rubbed its hands together

45

WATER, WIND, EARTH AND FIRE

As Brendan walked down the street in which the Archbishop lived, memories of past days that were simple and carefree filled his mind. All that bothered him then was his awakening sexuality, and the conflict it produced within him which was caused by his unwavering obedience to the church's unnatural law of celibacy. Brendan admitted to himself that he was all of a sudden profoundly interested in the opposite sex and that becoming a priest had created a huge void in his life. What was it that he had once read, A Woman Makes a Man Fertile , question; was this only restricted to the reproductive sense, or was it broader in context suggesting that a woman's ideas or ideals were brought into fruition by a man's actions. Perhaps the religions that allowed their pastors to marry were indeed better. Brendan reflected on the memory of meeting up with a fellow student from the seminary some time ago. Now, also a priest, he was more liberal in his approach and viewed his vocation as being nothing more than a job. Brendan thought it disrespectful at the time, but now was not quite sure. He began to see the merits in both sides of the argument.

His friend had also stated quite liberally, that one does not join the navy but rather the priesthood to see the world. As he approached the gates of the Archbishop's palace, he suddenly felt that it was not safe to be there as it was probably being watched by unseen eyes and he desperately hoped for his own safety that it was not the D Man who was doing the watching. Brendan decided then and there to vacate the premises and to return to the girls and see how the real Lawrence Carpenter fitted into Stanley's financial jigsaw puzzle. In the blink of an eye Brendan was back in the safe house and on finding the girls told them of his discovery. His revelations both confused and shocked them all the more.

"How many Lawrence Carpenters are there?" Felicity frowned.

"We've seen one, you've seen two, which one is the genuine one? Or are they all crooks trying to feather their own nests?" she went on to say.

"I really do think that the last man I met was him," Brendan gingerly put forward.

"Trust no one I say," Naomi suggested and went on to cynically explain "In this business, they are all creeps trying to accumulate as much money as they can by whatever means they can think of" .

"But his story sounded convincing. I really do believe that he is the genuine Carpenter," Brendan defensively said.

"So what of it, is he going to protect you or hand over money for all the suffering we have endured? No, all he is going to do is make a fortune out of selling that drug formula that he bluffed you into copying for him."

"Do you really think that I would easily hand over one that would make thousands of people hopelessly addicted?" Brendan snapped back.

"What are you saying?" Yvette asked in a gentle voice, sensing his anger and noble spirit.

"By now all of you are well aware that the world that I Brendan and Grandpa live in is a little different to the norm."

"We had guessed that and are comfortable with it, right ladies," Naomi gestured to all around her. They nodded in agreement.

"We don't know whether you are an angel or a good warlock, it doesn't matter, you mean us no harm and therefore we accept the situation. So tell us, what you have done and tell us the truth, not like before pretending to have had visions etc."

"Very well," he answered, glad that the girls were aware of his powers

"This may be a little hard to comprehend; even a little weird," he said and paused midsentence. "Everything, it appears, can respond to thought commands, so instead of handing over a proper formula I handed over one that would be correct with the first batch only and then would change itself step by step with subsequent batches causing each one to fail."

"Could you explain that a little more fully?" Yvette asked wishing to satisfy her chemical curiosity.

"What I did was to ask the chemical symbols and numbers to alter themselves, either by changing their magnitude or altering their position in terms of their relationship to eachother," Brendan explained.

"That would only work on the original," said Yvette.

"Not quite. When the document was copied so was the instruction, I made sure of that."

"So what you are saying is, when the crooks test the formula it will work once only to satisfy them and then after that it will not, and if they decide like your supposedly real Mr Carpenter to sell the formula…" postulated Yvette

"It would already have altered itself," Brendan said completing her sentence.

"Which creates a very nasty situation for Mr Carpenter because everyone he sells it to will be after his blood," Yvette grimly proposed.

"And hopefully not mine," Brendan optimistically replied

"Well done Jack," the girls applauded.

"I have one last thing to do and that is deliver the information to

Carpenter who is willing to pay us the $250,000 and get back Brendan and Grandpa safely," he said.

"Well you had better get on with it, time is of the essence young man," Yvette urged.

In a blink of an eye Brendan was gone again, leaving the girls to rest and play.

He did not take himself straight to O'Flattery's Point; instead he deviated to the place within the forest, where the rare rose grew. On this occasion there was no need for him to use any special prior preparation such as viewing through a piece of purple cloth. A solitary rose bush stood before him in all of its magnificent splendour heavy with blossoms and heavenly fragrance. As he concentrated his gaze there appeared a nebulous body that floated about the bush administering to its needs, touching it here and there, making certain that all was well. Brendan watched in amazement as the rose bush and its angelic gardener lovingly interacted with each other. He wondered if Yvette had seen this before and if she had ever considered herself to be a human version of that bush. There was much symbolism here, but little time to grasp it all, it was fast approaching 2:00pm, the false Lawrence Carpenter or otherwise, would already be waiting at O'Flattery's Point, genuinely eager Brendan hoped to affect the exchange.

Brendan arrived in a flash. His entry point was out of the way, discreet and undetectable. The scene before him was as before, an army of bodyguards strategically distributed to ensure Carpenter's security. Jack Stern and Grandpa had found themselves a shady spot beneath a tree and were talking about nonsensical things. Carpenter was busy on his mobile phone. He stood next to his pristine white limo with Brenda inside giving off hostile vibrations. Brendan assumed invisibility and walked unnoticed towards Lawrence Carpenter. Only Jack and Grandpa saw him.

"Where's my boy, Norm Difluca? He's late," bellowed Carpenter resplendent in white. Numerous guards shook their heads indicating their ignorance.

"I'm sure he will be here soon, in fact, he is probably standing next to you," Jack yelled.

"Yeah, you are one funny man Mr Adolfson."

"Were you looking for me Mr Carpenter?" Brendan said as he became visible

"What! Where the hell did you come from?" Carpenter asked rather startled by Brendan's sudden appearance

"I was here all the time."

"Yeah that's very funny." Carpenter acidly replied

"No, it's true, the sunlight," Brendan gestured. "What about it?"

"It's very bright, as you are. I was hidden in all of its brilliance."

"Trying to flatter me Norm?" Carpenter said a little stirred.

"Not at all just stating the obvious" Brendan said in an attempt to flatter Carpenter

"Got the info I wanted?"

"Depends on your financial position Lawrence," Brendan replied forcing a smile.

"Boot," Carpenter commanded.

The limo's driver obeyed and activated the boot to open revealing a light brown suitcase on its floor amongst other things. He gestured for Brendan to examine the suitcase which was unlocked and its contents which he casually did.

Satisfied that the agreed sum of money was all there Brendan produced his side of the bargain and very causally awaited Carpenter's response.

"Nothing happens, no exchanges until I check this out. Why don't you go and talk to your friends." Carpenter barked and waved Brendan away

"Very well," Brendan calmly replied and he walked towards Jack and Grandpa. Carpenter whisked the information inside the cabin. Brushing Brenda aside he dialled a silent number on the limo's telephone and waited, "Yeah it's me, got the info, ready for transmission? Good," Carpenter said in staccato fashion.

He inserted the chemical formula into the telephone's fax component and dialled another silent number and watched as it transmitted the data. Carpenter then emerged once again ignoring Brenda in the process and paced up and down the length of the limo

"Did you enjoy your time with him?" Brendan asked Jack expecting to be told a series of funny stories.

"Not much to tell. Grandpa behaved himself and as for Carpenter's men, quite dull actually, could have done with a little more excitement."

"Don't tell me they didn't try to undress you Grandpa," Brendan said.

"Not at all, not one of them damn it, I suppose I'm just too high class for the likes of them. How I wish they had tried."

"Next time perhaps," Brendan suggested as he held back a cheeky smile

"You are very confident today," Jack observed.

"Have to be, considering how I obtained the information."

"Excellent, you are coming along fine then."

"Yes, except for the attention that I seem to be attracting."

Jack's ears pricked up at this statement and he sought clarification.

"From whom?"

"I will tell you later, I think Carpenter may have some good news for us," Brendan said, as he noticed Carpenter beckoning.

"Yes Mr Carpenter?" Brendan said in a loud voice without moving from his spot.

"Come on over Norm, time to conclude our business."

"Very well, be there directly," Jack shouted back, as he raised himself off the grass.

"Let's collect the goods and leave, phase one over," he whispered to Brendan and Grandpa.

The trio walked together side by side with Grandpa in the middle. As they drew near they could see that Carpenter had the brown suitcase in one hand, ready to hand it over.

"I gather you are pleased with your expert's report?" Jack enquired

"Absolutely; my man the industrial chemist did what you call a HPLC on the original samples and knew what to expect. He had tried on many occasions to duplicate the formula without success, when he saw yours he confirmed it was unusual, but true. So my friends, you have made me a very, very happy man," The false Lawrence Carpenter replied in all of his animated white glory.

Jack extended his hand to accept payment for services rendered when all of a sudden the joyous occasion was shattered by the booming voice of the D Man.

The sound sent a cold shiver down Brendan's spine; Jack and Grandpa sensed his traumatic anxiety and both looked in the direction from which the voice came.

"Your previous admirer," Jack quipped.

"A very explosive relationship," Brendan answered not wishing to be seen and cursed himself for attracting the D Man to this location.

"White man, those papers belong to us, not you, hand them over at once," the D Man harshly commanded, as he stood about 25 metres in front of them.

"Not a chance," Carpenter completely unafraid of his presence shouted back as he used hand gestures to instruct his guards to assume their firing positions.

The D Man's robust anatomy became a blaze of red dots as the snipers zoomed in with their laser sights.

"Move on you cretin!" Carpenter bellowed as a final warning. The D Man stood his ground and bristled with electrical excitement.

"What's this cartoon freak going to do, throw a thunder bolt?" Jack whispered to Brendan

"Much worse," he replied as he remained motionless.

The D Man's hair stood on end he opened his mouth to reveal his metallic teeth as he slowly turned 360 degrees to take note of everyone and their position in relation to him. With the utmost evil intent he stared at Carpenter and slowly brought his right hand up to brush his hair. Electricity discharged between his upper and lower teeth, sparks flew from his metallic fingers to his hair and the air was filled with the same silence as that preceding a clap of thunder. Only Jack, Brendan and Grandpa saw the projectile fly through the air and explode behind them in the cabin of the white limo, shattering it into a multitude of tiny pieces. Brenda's wish of death as the only way out of her life was fulfilled; her limp body adorned the wreckage. Carpenter lay prostrate, his entire body in a state of shock, hoping that his guards would take out his assassin. Once again, it was only Jack, Brendan and Grandpa who witnessed the entire event.

The ball of unstable entropic energy, that caused the devastation, divided and assigned itself into the numbers required to eliminate each one of Carpenter's bodyguards. Each one fell into that dark void of death at the same moment that the limo exploded. Jack, Brendan and Grandpa realized that they were spared because he had other intentions for them.

Carpenter sprung to his feet and shouted repeatedly, "Kill him, kill him, kill him" The words fell on deaf ears. Realizing his predicament he dropped to his knees and begged for his life.

"Who's the cretin now, fool?" the D Man asked, as he picked up the brown suitcase containing the money. "No mercy for your kind," he said and then raised his hand towards his head. Brendan watched the D Man's actions and calculated his chances of protecting Lawrence Carpenter as being true or false.

He saw the ball of unstable entropy form between the D Man's metallic fingertips and hair, and fly in slow motion towards Carpenter's heart region. Before he could act a white form shot past him into the path of the projectile, and absorbed its contents, and disappeared in the process.

Brendan glanced back at Jack who remained where he was. Grandpa was gone; his clothes lay in a heap on the ground. Jack mimed 'Yvette.' Brendan understood and in a heartbeat they had returned to the confines of the safe house.

"Where's Grandpa?" Brendan asked rather anxiously, as he adjusted to his new surroundings.

"He's gone."

"What do you mean gone?"

"Just that, he has gone, left this world for good" Jack sadly reported

"How do you know?"

"I am quite certain." Jack replied

"Explain."

"The energy ball that he absorbed has taken him to the next level of vibration. Unless he receives a dispensation, I don't think we will be seeing him for a while," Jack explained.

Brendan accepted his explanation even though he didn't understand it and ascended the stairs. "The girls will be sad," he said with resignation.

"Come my friend, let's shower and wash away our worries."

"As long as it doesn't cause a storm" Brendan replied as he remember what his experiences with water had taught him

"Pardon?" Jack said as he raised an eyebrow.

"Just something I've leant."

Jack and Brendan entered the common ablution area and undressed. It was the first time that he had seen Jack completely naked before and he was captivated, not so much by his physique, but rather by the gold crucifix that hung around his neck.

"I have never seen one like that before," he said.

Jack smirked at the hidden innuendo and replied "Really, I thought all us men had one."

"The crucifix!" Brendan corrected Jack by pointing to it.

"Oh, that, I had it fashioned out of gold based on the one that my uncle gave me, only larger"

"It is extremely beautiful."

"Just like me," Jack smirked again.

"Tell me more." Brendan asked brushing away Jack's flippant remark

"My uncle was of the Norbertine order which originated in Belgium. All that I know is that they are famous for their Christ philosophy and developing a fine blonde beer, which is produced under license. I think it is called 'Leffe Blonde Beer'."

"May I have a closer look at your cross?"

"Of course," Jack said as he removed it from around his neck and handed it over.

"Quite heavy; beautifully made," Brendan remarked as he carefully studied its features.

The cross was made out of 18 carat gold, it comprised three figures; a large male figure with outstretched hands, which served as the base upon which rested a standard crucifix, a dove with spread wings separated the two, on the back were the words 'HERI HODIE SEMPER' and the symbols for alpha and omega. Brendan translated this to mean yesterday, today and always.

"Had this for long?" he asked

"Years"

"But there's not a scratch on it."

"Self healing," Jack replied without any further explanation

Brendan thought about his answer which didn't quite make sense to him as he had never considered inanimate objects to possess that sort of ability.

"Understand its symbolism?"

"I think so, Father, Son and Holy Spirit forever," was Brendan's reply.

"Very good but what about the inscription INRI"

"Commonly referred to as Jesus, King of the Jews"

"Except, that's not quite right"

Brendan remained silent and frowned.

"The initials stand for the little known Hebrew words 'IANNIN NOUR, ROUAGH and LEBESCHAH'. These translate into water, fire, air and earth."

Brendan remained silent and continued to listen as he studied Jack's crucifix

"It can be argued that Jesus had passed all of the tests pertaining to these elements and mastered them in the process. Each one of us who recognizes within ourselves the same talents or principles that Christ had, must of necessity pass the same test in order to evolve into the master level. In your case I believe you have demonstrated mastery over earth, wind and water, but not fire. This last one is the most important, for it is the ultimate purifier. May I?" Jack asked, as he extended his hand. "I feel rather naked without it."

Brendan returned the icon and entered the shower recess without saying a word. Jack allowed him to reflect on the lesson and his past experiences and went into the adjoining cubicle. When they had both finished showering and were drying themselves Brendan noticed his own reflection in the mirror and that his own crucifix had changed. No longer was it small in comparison, it had now grown larger. Jack observed Brendan's pre-occupation with his image and asked, "Changed already?"

"Not quite, still drying off."

"No, I didn't mean that. Your crucifix it's different now isn't it?"

"How did you know?" Brendan replied as he toyed with it

"It happens with the process, either something in you changes or something that you wear changes. Many of the saints who didn't wear any outer symbols had a cross form on their hearts. These were only discovered when they were dead and their organs were distributed as relics. Look closely at my crucifix and you will see that rubies and diamonds are beginning to germinate."

Brendan did as Jack requested and confirmed what he had said.

"Will this happen to mine?"

"Yes, but in a fashion that uniquely describes you, for the principle is infinite in its application. Your crucifix will tell you how far you have progressed, so take very careful note of it."

Brendan continued to play with it, oblivious to Yvette's entry.

"Jack, Brendan, I thought it was you, I heard voices down here, but where's Grandpa?" she asked.

"He didn't make it."

"You mean he's dead? That's impossible. What's happened to him please tell?" she earnestly pleaded as tears formed in her eyes.

"In the process of attempting to save Lawrence Carpenter he absorbed a huge amount of energy and has most probably gone into the next dimension."

Yvette appeared not to understand, so Jack drew her close and explained the metaphysics of what he had just said until she appeared to do so.

46

TIME TO MAKE AMENDS

Jack, Brendan and Yvette found the girls amusing themselves on the entertainment level. The time away from the brothel had finally allowed them to realize that they were human, with all of the freedom and rights attached to that life form. They smiled broadly when they saw the trio enter, sensing success they became quite physically excited in anticipation of their expectant good news.

"Where's the money, everything went well, did you whip his arse?" they squawked as they merrily jumped around like little schoolgirls.

It was extremely difficult for Jack or Brendan to deflate their spirits but the truth had to be told.

"We are sorry girls, there is no money."

"Oh damn it," they collectively groaned. "What happened, did he double cross you?"

"No rather worse I am afraid," Jack replied. "We think that his rivals sent in a high powered assassin to sabotage the exchange. Mr Carpenter and his mini army are all dead."

"And Brenda?" Naomi asked sounding severely downtrodden.

"Not with us anymore, I am sorry to say."

Naomi's saddened state deepened and it unfortunately spread to the others influencing their mood except for Yvette who remained eternally optimistic.

"Come now ladies, all is not lost, somehow it will work out. Look, you are in a safe house away from the likes of Badcock; there is plenty to do here and sufficient provisions for a long time. Brendan and Jack I am more than certain will keep their promises to you, so cheer up, all is not lost," she re-affirmed.

Brendan and Jack both admired Yvette's positive attitude.

"What she says is quite right, we will find a way, just give us a little more time. Meanwhile this safe house which you can call home is huge, there is much to explore. If you want you can walk around the tunnels on the first level, it is very safe. I will make certain that you won't become lost or accidentally find yourselves outside in the cold," Jack reassured them before asking to be excused

"Now if you will please excuse us we need to go upstairs, Jack and I need some time alone to work out our next strategy for your benefit."

The girls soon accepted the fact that they were far better off than they had been in years and therefore they were happy to remain in their present circumstances and without giving it any further thought they returned to their own pleasures, embracing the optimism that Yvette had showed.

Jack looked seriously at Brendan and asked, "This assassin, has he chased you before?"

"Yes."

"Tell me more." Jack asked as he realized that they were facing a very dangerous foe

Brendan obliged and detailed his experiences as best as he could remember. On his completion Jack made the following deductions.

"From what you have told me, and from what I have seen today, this assassin is very well versed in the application of destructive energies. It doesn't matter who or what he is, what really concerns me is how we can deal with him, considering that the powers that we both have acquired are not an aggressive in nature."

Brendan looked perplexed.

"So far as you have seen and learnt your powers are more defensive and restorative. In fact, that is how it is meant to be. Our principle does not come to destroy, but rather to create."

"But I deafened those truck drivers." Brendan ashamedly said

"Yes, but you did not kill them. All that you did was to change them physically in a minor way and give them the opportunity to correct themselves."

"That sounds absurd."

"No it's not."

"What about Jesus when he threw the money changes out of the synagogue? Surely he was being aggressive and destructive," Brendan argued.

"Not really, his intention was to change the focus of those people's lives away from money and materialism, to that of creativity, which needs neither of the two for it to express itself. In fact, it is quite the opposite, money and materialism stifles creativity."

"What are you suggesting? Should we paint a picture for this guy, hand it over and say, 'Look at this masterpiece of fine art' and he will simply vanish?"

"Perhaps not"

"What then?" Brendan grumbled as he thought Jacks way of thinking was bizarre and abstract.

"I don't know."

"I can see that! It seems to me that this wonderful gift that I have, I cannot use, because all those who have real power and money can easily destroy me by all means available to them. I might as well enter myself into the next international magician's competition and hope for the best."

"Oh don't lose faith," Jack said attempting to restore Brendan's confidence.

"In what?"

"In yourself let's work things out rationally"

Brendan simmered down slightly and was prepared to listen but only if it made any sense.

"There are many obstacles in front of us; our friend Badcock, organized crime, rival gangs and corrupt officials at all levels of government. The police force, even your beloved Church may well turn us in. These do not add up to an insurmountable problem, for in life there is a solution to everything, nothing is impossible. And in saying this, let me relate an incident that happened to a friend of mine who lives in a country below the tropic of Capricorn in the Southern Hemisphere.

In that particular nation the indigenous people, after a long period of white domination, became rather militant, to the extent that they became almost untouchable. This meant that they could commit acts of real crime and get away with them. Acquaintances of my friend were faced with a real dilemma; they were not rich and lived in a poor section of the community. Next door to them lived a group of native people who started trafficking in all sorts of drugs. Being indigenous their children did not attend school and acted as couriers.

Within two weeks of starting their business, the traffic in the street increased twenty fold. My friends' acquaintances became very afraid of the situation and feared for their children's safety. There was no telling what sort of people came to purchase drugs and what else they were after. My friends' acquaintances called the police on numerous occasions and nothing was done. They also called their local politician and again, nothing was done. In desperation they contacted every conceivable agency they could think of; public housing corporation; health department; traffic control, all to no avail; still nothing was done. Even the media was reluctant to act in case the story was considered potentially racist. So day in and day out the undesirables came and went; buying whatever they wanted until my friends' acquaintances had an idea, which was to promote their neighbour's business on the Internet.

They created a web page that read 'Buy whatever drugs you want from this address – hassle free – no fear of being caught we guarantee you won't get busted'. What they were doing was in essence saying to the local community, look man these natives have built up an imaginary wall of immunity by virtue of their colour and their belief that the country belongs to them. They have therefore become answerable to no one."

"Seems like a good argument."

"Surely you are joking."

"No, I meant how your friends' acquaintances went about it."

"Okay." Jack paused and accepted Brendan's answer before he said "As a result of their actions, the authorities acted rapidly and shut them down."

"The natives?"

"Of course."

"And they were jailed?"

"No, just shut down," Jack answered.

"Were your friends' acquaintances happy with the result?"

"Absolutely, the neighbourhood was safe once again and the natives relocated and asked not to do it again."

"No prosecution?"

"No prosecution," Jack replied.

"Are you suggesting that we go about it the same way?"

"I think that it is a worthwhile avenue to explore. It overcomes the process of vetting investigative journalists, no telling which ones are genuine. Let them come to us and report according to their needs.

"Except what exactly are we going to advertise, besides the fact that Longevity Plus is a hypochondriac's paradise?"

"Think about what you have seen and come up with some ideas," Jack suggested.

Brendan reflected on the concept for some time before answering.

"Suppose we post on the net a description of Feel Good Pharmacy's secret lab and embellish its activities by saying it produces all manner of psychedelic drugs and then we provide the location of the farm and describe as being a warehouse."

"Excellent."

"But what if they the crooks discover the internet posting first and relocate their operation before the public has had a chance to react?" Brendan hypothetically asked and proceeded to argue with himself "But if they don't, then you will have both sides of the law viewing it, which means rival gangs and the legitimate authorities, might act as well."

"Precisely."

"Then it is up to chance."

"I'm afraid so."

"But what about that assassin?" Brendan asked.

"I can't answer that question because I don't know who hired him. At O'Flattery's Point he didn't indicate in the slightest who the owners of the formula might be."

"Agreed, I initially thought it was Badcock. Considering that the first time I was attacked, I was outside The Infirmary, collecting a water sample."

"I don't think it matters who he works for, what really does however, is how we are going to deal with him next time we cross paths."

"Like you said creativity"

Jack responded by pretending to paint on an imaginary canvas seated on an imaginary easel using an imaginary brush. Brendan caught his drift and laughed as Jack whipped out his mobile phone and dialled Stanley's number.

"Hello Stanley, another small job for you." Jack said as soon as his computer geek friend picked up the phone.

"Only too pleased to help, especially if I can get to see the cyber again" Stanley keen as mustard eagerly replied.

"Never know your luck on the web my boy," Jack teased.

"What's to do this time?"

"Need to post a page advertising illegal drugs; their availability and locations. It needs to be untraceable and very attractive to all, if you know what I mean."

"No problem."

"Excellent, I shall send you preliminary wording for you to look at later via encrypted code."

"Can hardly wait"

"Excellent I'll be in touch take care" Jack cheerfully signed off and pocketed his phone.

"Now to the dilemma of that awful assassin how good is your psychic ability?"

"What are you driving at?" Brendan asked.

"Have you heard of water divining?"

"Yes, why do you ask?"

"Because this ancient practice is not limited to that"

"Not another lesson," Brendan sighed.

"Did you think it would ever stop?"

"I suppose not."

"Then listen. The Chinese, Egyptians, Persians, Medes, Etruscans, Greeks and Romans of ancient times used the technique to locate, not only water, but earth currents, gold, silver, missing people and livestock.

The proper name for the science is 'Radiesthesia' which is from the Latin 'Radius' and Greek 'Aisthesis'. The meanings of these are radiation and sensitivity. In other words, it is a measure of human ability to detect vibrations given off by material bodies and all living beings. It is our subconscious in its highest aspect that is not limited by time, space and matter and therefore, constantly sees all, unlike our physical side. We can therefore ask of it simple questions and providing we do not influence the method of detection, it will provide us with the necessary answers. One simple method is to use a pendulum like the one that I carry."

Jack produced a gold oval pointed pendant attached to a piece of nylon fishing line.

"First of all, one has to fully relax, hold the pendulum with the first three fingers of your right hand, or left if you are so inclined. Set the pendulum into motion, ask the question that can be answered by a simple yes or no and simply observe the pendulum's motion. If the pendulum describes a clockwise rotation, then it is yes. If counter clockwise, then no"

This is a lot of hocus pocus, Brendan thought to himself. It couldn't possibly be true he mentally concluded.

"To convince you I will need to demonstrate the pendulum's ability by asking it personal questions about yourself. Let's start shall we?"

This is going to be good, thought Brendan, as he nodded his head with a slight degree of trepidation

"Is Brendan O'Reilly a virgin?" Jack asked, as he sent the device into motion. Yes came the answer.

"Has Brendan O'Reilly been a priest for eight years?" No. "Seven years?" No.

"Six years?" Yes. "Good."

"Does Brendan O'Reilly want to leave the Catholic Church?" Yes.

"Brendan O'Reilly…"

"That's quite enough," Brendan interrupted. "You have said enough."

"Struck a nerve?"

"I'm not saying."

"All right, let's proceed to that assassin friend of yours. Is the assassin employed by Louis Badcock?" No. "There's a surprise."

"Is he employed by the Ricci family?" No. Another surprise

"Well, now we are at a dead end."

"Why?" Brendan asked frustrated by the lack of information gathered so far

"Because we can only ask questions about something that we know," Jack explained

"Okay. Will we encounter the assassin again?" Brendan asked and watched as it indicated a big Yes.

"Will he harm us?" Jack patiently waited as the pendulum swung to and fro indecisively

"What's it saying?" Brendan asked feeling a little uneasy

"Both; meaning yes and no at the same time"

"Will we defeat the assassin?" Jack nervously asked and the pendulum indicated a very big No. "That's not good news."

"Here, let me try," Brendan said irritated by the results.

"Remember, keep an open mind, accept what it tells you and don't force it to say what you want to hear."

Brendan repeated the same questions that Jack had just asked with the same overwhelming results.

"This is all too much," he said, feeling somewhat doomed.

"Don't worry my friend, it will be all right. The final result I am sure will surprise you." Jack said unconvincingly to Brendan's way of thinking

"How can you be so certain?" The handsome priest asked in a confrontational tone of voice

"Because all of this has been worked out on the field of dreams, all that we are doing is making those events become physical reality, and don't forget, the language of the spirit and even the brain cannot be adequately described by the spoken words. At least we know that we are dealing with someone above Badcock and that is good, once we have the web page in place I am more than certain the fireworks will begin."

47

CAUGHT IN THE WEB

Jack's mobile phone chatted away indicating that someone who knew his ultra private number wanted his immediate attention. He picked it up and activated the screen and read the caller's number. Satisfied that it was safe, he answered.

"Hello Stanley my boy, how goes it?"

"I have finished operation meltdown as requested; you can read it on your secure email address."

"Excellent, give me a few moments to bring it up and make any adjustments which I am more than certain will not be necessary."

"Okay."

"Goodbye." Jack replied and was about to press call end.

"Hear from you soon?" Stanley said just as Jack terminated the call.

Jack activated his sophisticated computer system, waited for it to boot up and then he accessed his secure email account which promptly displayed Stanley's creative efforts.

Advert No 1 – Hey man, in the little town of Newburn they have a pharmacy that manufactures a new psychedelic drug. It is so pharmaceutically pure, no joke, better than anything you have ever tried before and man, with added benefits, not only do you get the greatest high, but are you ready for this, mind blowing orgasms. There's more, the police are in on the deal, plenty of protection there. Call into the Feel Good Pharmacy, great name hey? Just buy their special pack of tampons, if they run out go to the farm, that's the warehouse. You will find it at the following address.

Advert No 2 – Hey, fellow hypochondriacs, did you hear about Longevity Plus? That miracle place in Newburn; wondered why so many are cured? 'Cause they're just like you, the place is just heaven. Great food; great accommodation; spunky nurses and fantastic drugs; all designed to space you out and make you feel great once you are off them. Give them a try, a five star holiday; no worries about that.

Brendan looked over Jack's shoulder and commented. "You took on board what I said about it being a hypochondriac's paradise."

"I simply mentioned it to Stanley, he did the rest."

"Certainly knows their language."Brendan commented making reference to drug addicts

"Comes from being on the Internet," Jack remarked.

Brendan scratched his head and asked, "Once you give the go ahead, where will the ads be displayed?"

"If you look here, he has already told us," Jack replied, as he scrolled down the page and pointed to the link and its address.

"As you can read, he is going to submit it to numerous chat rooms that deal with all sorts of topics. Illegal drugs, their use, manufacture and distribution, sex addicts, impotence sufferers, hypochondriacs, the Mafia and rival gang networks etc. Then it will be sent to newspapers, television stations, news agencies, magazines of all sorts, with one press of a button."

"Will he be safe?"

"Absolutely, Stanley, with my help and finance, has built an impenetrable electronic wall around himself. No one will be able to determine who the originator was, which is to our advantage. Also, people believe the Internet and hold it in high regard, especially in this field. They know that it is the highway to their addiction."

"Okay, let's give him the go ahead then," Brendan said with nervous excitement

Jack emailed Stanley and then phoned and spoke to him briefly to confirm the contents of his email. Within 30 minutes of that Stanley rang back excited beyond measure.

"Jack, guess what?"

"Tell me?"

"These adverts have caused quite a stir, thousands of hits already." Stanley reported in a understated way

"Excellent, mostly private individuals" Jack asked

"I suppose."

"No one else" Jack asked

"Yes, the law enforcement agencies, but they didn't get a foot in to read them."

"Why is that?" Jack asked, curious about this fact.

"'Cause that cyber warrior is back defending the place, it is almost as if he is selectively directing traffic to the sites."

"Grandpa," mumbled Jack.

"I didn't catch what you said."

"Nothing important carry on with the good work, keep me informed, otherwise I am sure we will see it on the television news."

"I thought as much."

"Goodbye and thank you," Jack said, cutting short the conversation.

"What did you say about Grandpa?" Brendan asked.

"He is alive and well, doing his duty on the Internet."

"Faked his death, clever chap"

"Yes he is," Jack agreed, as he wondered when and where Grandpa would surface next.

Meanwhile, across town some time later, the small dark figure was fuming, awaiting the arrival of the D Man.

"What took you so long?" it snapped, as he materialized in the conference room

"Oh let me guess, satisfying your gambling addiction, or should

I say stealing from the rich to give to the rich." The small dark figure went on to say as it made reference to the D Man's love of casino's both legal and illegal

"The temptation was too much," the D Man responded, as he handed over the brown case containing $250,000, courtesy of the late and fake Lawrence Carpenter.

"A gift, or should I say spoils of war," the D Man pleasingly said, with a discharge of electrical energy.

"I heard about your activities from the keeper of the point."

"How much did you make out of it this time?" the small dark figure asked as it examined the contents of the case.

"A gentleman does not tell."

"There is not one present here. Stop playing the conquering hero and just tell me," it snapped.

"$3.5 million."

"Impressive."

"Pays for the simple pleasures in life"

"Well you simpleton, you probably would have overheard me telling Badcock that those people Stern and O'Reilly are no fools."

"So what of it," the D Man growled.

"I am more than certain that they have posted on the web wild stories about the pharmacy, farm and Longevity Plus as a way of getting back at us."

"That's no problem, we'll counter them."

"We've tried It's too late. You can try if you wish but all that I have to say is good luck." The small dark figure cynically said

The D Man took personal offence to its comments and its challenge.

"That is beyond my powers." The D man falsely replied as his way of striking back at the small dark figure

"I thought that would be your answer, so I have arranged for the police to set up roadblocks, preventing those crazed drug addicts storming into the city."

"And I will take care of those who break through at the three locations."

"No you won't, I don't want the place littered with dead bodies, keep it cool."

The D Man reluctantly obeyed.

"Your time will come," the small dark figure promised as it thought of numerous ways of luring Stern and O'Reilly into a death trap

48

PUBLIC REACTION

The next morning, in the peace and tranquility of their mountain hideaway, Jack, Brendan, Yvette and the girls quietly enjoyed their breakfast. There was an air of excitement about them with the expectation that all was drawing to a close and that each one of them would find a new pathway in life. As nebulous as it sounded, it was true to some extent. Each one of them shared these common thoughts and each one of them knew that the others thought alike.

Jack broke the silence by saying, "Well I suppose you are all just dying to see how well Stanley did on the web?"

"Have been ever since I woke up so cruel of you to keep us waiting this long" Naomi enthusiastically replied as she gobbled her food down

"I thought as much; shall I turn on the television and see how many clichés have come true?" Jack answered in true cryptic fashion

Brendan looked at Jack strangely with a tilt of his head so as to say 'I have no idea what you are going on about' which was sufficient encouragement for Jack to say

"The pen is mightier than the sword, birds of a feather flock together, a fool and his drugs are soon parted, and hallucinations are in the eye of the addicted beholder. The drugs are greener on the other side of the fence. A jab in time saves nine. If you first don't succeed, try, try again."

"Oh stop it Father, you are inventing these as you go along," Yvette said, trying to control her laughter.

"I suppose I am," Jack answered with a smile and then he stood up and started clapping his hands.

"Now you are applauding yourself."

"Not at all," he replied as he pointed to the opposite wall which had responded to his auditory command and sprung into action.

Two closed curtains mysteriously appeared on the wall indicating that they were hiding something, Jack clapped his hands twice and they both theatrically spread apart to reveal a large plasma television screen.

"Where did that come from?" Felicity asked completely mesmerized like a small child by the magical event

"Been there all the time, only use it when I am alone, otherwise I consider it much better to enjoy each other's company, than watch meaningless stuff than ads nothing to your life" Jack replied and then he clapped his hands twice more to activate it's the television's sound system.

"Channel 10 please," he commanded.

The television's artificial intelligence immediately obeyed. Jack's timing was perfect, something that Brendan sensed. It was the early news program or was it. Channel 10 was KBW-49 twenty four hour continuous news station, providing predominantly local and national coverage with a few international items thrown in for variety.

The screen blazed with nervous energy as KBW-49's on the scene reporter tried to present the story from one of the heavily manned police roadblocks outside of Newburn.

"As I said, we are still trying to find out why the police have blockaded the major roads to Newburn. There has been no official explanation released as yet, but as you can see from our position on the ground and from that from our helicopter hovering above there are literally thousands of cars lined up along the roads leading into Newburn."

The reporter from the helicopter then interrupted.

"That's right Janice, from our view point the cars stretch about five kilometres in all directions. We flew over Newburn several times and all appears to be in order. No civil or medical emergencies, no national disasters either. People are going about their normal routines, oblivious to what is happening outside of their town."

The station's main news presenter then asked the most obvious pertinent question:

"Have you learned what all the people are after?"

To which Janice replied as she walked along, away from the blockade, "The police aren't too keen on us asking questions about the situation, they prefer to remain tight lipped. In fact, they have been hassling us to move along, indicating that media presence is not wanted here at all. Our legal department informs us that unless the situation is one of national security, we can go ahead and perform a random survey."

By now Janice and her cameraman had distanced themselves some 500 metres from the irritating police which she kept a constant eye on by frequently looking over her shoulder and when she thought to was relatively safe to she started to question various individuals ad hoc prior to which she made a brief introductory statement:

"The town of Newburn has over the years acquired the reputation for remarkable medical and religious healings. Longevity Plus has the highest recorded success rate for treating many varied terminal life threatening diseases in the country, while Saint Pious has only an unproven anecdotal record of miracles supposedly twenty times greater than that of Lourdes. Bearing that in mind, it is our suspicion that there may well be some sort of extraordinary supernatural event occurring either at the hospital, its private Grotto or at Saint Pious."

"Are you suggesting an apparition of the Virgin Mary?" The main

395

news presenter asked

"Perhaps I am but I don't know." Janice freely admitted

"Has anyone at the Catholic Church commented on that?"

"Not as yet, we will pursue that avenue later in the day, either at Saint Pious, if we get through that is, otherwise, we will attempt to contact the Archbishop's office," Janice replied, as she smiled and nodded her head excessively as some journalists do.

"That's very interesting and exciting," the main newsreader commented in a monotone voice.

"Yes, I agree, especially since no similar religious event has ever occurred on our soil."

"Okay, let's see what the people have to say," the main newsreader directed.

As the cameraman panned across the impatient and tense crowd the viewers saw a motley group of people.

"Excuse me madam," Janice said as she approached a middle aged woman who appeared rather distressed by some sort of undefined illness.

"Yes deary"

"What do you think is in Newburn to attract you into coming here?"

"I want to be healed."

Janice nodded as to encourage the woman to continue and explain further

"Healed – healed of all the disease I have endured in my life, the doctors say there is nothing wrong with me. I know different. The pains – the pains they drive me crazy, all over my body they are, travel around they do, drive me crazy."

"So you believe that…"

"There is a miracle waiting for me at Longevity Plus."

"At the Grotto?"

"No deary, in the hospital, I read it on the Internet. It said that it was a hypochondriac's paradise. That's what I got, hypochondria, it's a very serious disease you know, life threatening, drives you crazy." The middle aged women loudly explained as she gesticulated wildly

"Errrr, thank you," Janice completely bewildered shakily replied and hurriedly took her leave to advance to the next person.

"And you sir, why did you come here?" she nervously asked a heavily-tattooed and bearded male who looked to be in his sixties.

"To experience Ecstasy man"

"You mean like the seers who have witnessed the Blessed Virgin Mary?" Janice asked as she thought he was referring to a religious experience

"No man like after you pop a pill man, or err shoot up man."

"I see, so what is so special about this Ecstasy that's available at Newburn?" Janice asked, becoming increasingly aware of the true sordid nature of the many of people's quests.

"It's all here on the Internet man. Here have a look what it says, mind blowing orgasms, I haven't had one of those in 30 years man," the geriatric drug addict confessed. He produced the latest, most expensive Ericsson/Sony digital mobile phone and dialled up the Internet to display Stanley's efforts

As Janice read, she gasped, "Oh my god." She looked at the crowd blankly, took the phone from the heavily tattooed drug addict, and gave it to the cameraman to record.

"Absolutely perfect," Jack said as he viewed Stanley's efforts being televised on the big screen. "More free advertising and more viewers." He happily concluded

"And more pandemonium" the girls suggested joining in his commentary.

"Well said and If it continues to escalate they might even have to call out the riot police and even the National Guard to boot." Jack further added

"There is one thing that I don't understand," Yvette said, demonstrating her naivety.

"And what is that?" Jack asked as he looked at her

"Well Father, are people so gullible as to believe everything on the Internet."

"I am afraid so my child. Especially when it comes to the mentality of the types that Stanley's work has specifically targeted. However, having said that, there are other reasons for the success of the web posting. They include the size of the illegal drug taking population and the additional things that Stanley has thrown in to validate the information."

"Such as?"

"Links to Longevity Plus and The Infirmary websites; a guest book, so that genuine people or friends can write in comments, which will hopefully create some substance of truth in the mind of the reader."

Jack was going to say more but stopped, as the news program shifted its focus to the reporter from the helicopter, shouting over the noise of the rotors overhead, "As you can quite clearly see many of the visitors have decided to break ranks and are driving their overland vehicles across the rough terrains, through paddocks and are making a beeline towards the town centre."

"Where do you think they are going?" asked the main news presenter.

"Judging by what the Internet site said, I would say directly to that Feel Good Pharmacy and Longevity Plus. The police are under-manned here, no telling what might happen next. Already a number of them have left the roadblocks and are rushing towards the two locations that I mentioned. We will fly over and take a closer look," the reporter said as he signalled the pilot to give chase.

A few minutes on, "Wooooo look at them go." The helicopter reporter said as the cameraman's aerial picture caught a police car being rammed by a number of 4 wheel drive vehicles as they made their way out of the paddocks onto the main road into the town.

"No respect for the law here. If anyone in authority is watching this program, I think they had better send in the troops. This situation is starting to turn ugly," he shouted, as more and more drug hungry mindless addicts defied the law and crashed through and around the police roadblocks. The residents of Newburn could hear the increasingly loud rumble of the mass of cars descending upon them. Like a swarm of destructive insects, the drug addicts sped through the maze of streets looking for Feel Good Pharmacy. Obscenities, screeching tyres, near miss collisions, the appropriate finger and head signs were abundant, until the swarm found its bearings and descended upon the Pharmacy. There was no resistance. The building stood naked, uninhabited and totally defenceless. It winced with pain as a large heavy duty lorry painted in army camouflage rammed through its main doors. Its occupants jumped out and together with those who had followed behind began a frenzied search of the pharmacy's interior. Nothing was sacred; it was all without value, even the highly addictive benzodiazepines, cough mixtures and pseudo ephedrine preparations were ignored. Within three minutes the secret laboratory was broken into, it revealed nothing, much to the disgust of its intruders who seethed with unspeakable anger and rage. The room was soon filled with the addicts' characteristic repulsive body odours made worse by their emotional state.

"We've been duped, there's nothing here, it's all lies, someone's going to pay for this," the enraged members of the swarm screamed as they became increasingly intent on completely destroying the building as a vent for their rage.

"Wait a minute, it was here" a more intellectual member of the group said, as he proudly held up a vial that he discovered in a dark corner.

"Give me that!" a big ruffian roughly bellowed as he violently reached for it.

Afraid for his own safety and well being, the intellectual handed it over.

The ruffian snapped open the vial with his swollen fingers,

produced a disposable syringe from his coat pocket and injected half of its contents into his hungry vein as the swarm jealously looked on.

Within moments his brain exploded into orgasmic ecstasy, and his body convulsed, as it came to grips with the enormous neuronal and endorphin outflow. The only words he could emit before he collapsed from the intensity of the experience were, "It's all trueeeeeeee."

The swarm swept the room looking for more vials, two more were found.

"Don't use them!" the intellectual said. "We will need them to reverse … engineer."

No longer did the swarm act as one coherent group. It suddenly fragmented into its individual members who began to think a little more clearly now that their collective emotions were spent.

"Who will do this for us, who can we trust?" One of them asked

"Me of course," the intelligent one suggested.

"And why should we trust the likes of you?"

"Because you know that you can," he replied confidently as he proceeded to reassure them.

"Oh yeah, why is that?"

"Because you already know me by my trademark," he slowly explained as he held up a business card bearing an embossed symbol, made up of an exploding volcano with a plane flying over it that was instantly recognized with the initials H.E. that stood for Explosive High reversed.

"If you are him, then you are okay, man."

"Yeahhhhhhh," the crowd responded.

"You make some pretty good stuff."

"Thank you," the H.E. man said. "After all, I can only survive if you guys appreciate what I am doing and come back for more."

"So man, you can really work this stuff out?"

"I am sure I can, and if I can't, then I will come pretty damn close to it."

"So what you gonna call it man?"

"How about H E X?" he suggested.

"Cool man. Going to produce some really wicked new slang man, like, you want to get hexed."

"Is that right?" the H.E. man asked glad to have met some of his devoted long time users

"Freezen man, freezen."

Just then the H.E. man's mobile phone rang, it was one of his scouts confirming a large cache of pethidine at Longevity Plus, meanwhile, a rival gang operative who was associated with and belonged to Louis Badcock's organization, overheard the entire conversation, on his highly sophisticated listening device.

"Locusts, they're just bloody locusts, a bloody nuisance, burn in hell," he said, as he activated in the relative safety of his vehicle a remote detonating device that sent the Pharmacy exploding into a ball of flame incinerating everyone inside the pharmacy and killing all those within a 25 metre radius outside of it, the remaining population of drug addicts fled the scene vowing never to return.

The same operative then called the farm to see if all was in order. The chief security officer answered the call.

"Everything okay?" the operative asked through a voice modifying device.

"Sure is; the small crowd that turned up left pretty quickly, after they saw our pack of killer dogs and fried their fingertips on the electrified fences, how about you?"

"Had a bigger problem down here then someone gave the order to torch the place."

"The boss isn't going to be too pleased about that."

"I know."

"What about the equipment?"

"Taken care of"

"Good job."

"Thank you."

"If anything goes wrong here, I will give you a call, otherwise, all is fine."

The Badcock operative signed off and drove his inconspicuous car towards Longevity Plus.

The situation there was a little more bizarre. The hospital grounds were occupied by a colony of emotional lepers who sought help for their life threatening 'phantom diseases'. Their playacting was so convincing that it had all of the medical staff completely befuddled. It was not until some of them realized that they were dealing with drug addicts that the situation changed. The two human hippos namely matron and her obedient boyfriend once alerted sprang into action.

With spoon and baton in hand, they ran amuck and attempted to drive the hoards from the hospital grounds.

Only the more devious drug addicts eluded them and continued their search of the hospital's facilities to see if they could find their next chemical high, their seek and find strategy were short lived when the guards fired their guns and the sounds of their shots sent fear into the drug addicts' cowardly hearts, as the chaotic scenes unfolded they were captured by the airborne reporter who together with his viewers remained totally aghast and disbelieving that such events could happen in the 'sacred town' of Newburn

In all of the televised confusion Brendan was able to selectively pick out the movement of the fruit and vegetable transport truck as he watched intensely

"They're getting away with it." He said as he pointed to the truck on the screen

"What's that Jack?"

"The equipment, it's on that truck. It is hard evidence of what they were doing," Brendan concluded.

"Yes I believe he is right, it looks like the one in which I was held captive," Yvette quickly confirmed

"I am afraid you are both wrong," Jack reluctantly said, as he gave a series of instructions to the television set.

Within a few moments multiple pictures were assembled on the screen, depicting the same truck in multiple locations within the town at exactly the same time.

"How did you do that?" Naomi asked, mesmerized by the television's abilities "The broadcast signal is first fed into a powerful computer that stores all of the information before it is relayed to the screen. So what you now see is the computer's response to my commands, instructing it to seek out the fruit and vegetable truck's position, together with the time. As it does this, it continues to record as long as the screen is on." Jack paused for a second allowing Naomi to digest his explanation and then he continued by saying "There is no point in going after the trucks, each one of them is a decoy. The equipment is probably already quite safely stored somewhere else in a secret place."

"It is still at the Pharmacy site," Brendan postulated.

"Why do you say that?" Yvette asked as she kept one eye on the television screen.

"By my reckoning, the trucks being decoys, the blast of the Pharmacy was also a decoy."

"Meaning?"

"That the equipment is still there, submerged underground, under tonnes of debris," Brendan replied trying to look intelligent.

Jack tentatively accepted Brendan's theory

"Even if we were to capture the equipment, it wouldn't be sufficient evidence for any prosecution case; a conveyor belt, a high intensity sound generator and a heat source are unlikely pieces of a drug laboratory."

"What is then?" Brendan asked out of frustration.

"Actual highly detailed videotape footage of the process in operation complete with technicians would prove helpful" Jack insisted from a legal point of view

"How impressionable did you say your computer system was?" Brendan asked as a mischievous grin formed on his lips.

49

CRISIS

Rage, anger, meltdown, call it what you may; exaggerate however you wish, it will never approximate the emotional state of the small dark figure as it watched the televised events unfold in Newburn. It did not sit alone at its discreet hideaway, also present were Louis Badcock, some of his henchmen, including the Harsh Man with the D Man sitting quietly in a corner brooding with intent.

The small dark figure did not know whom to accuse first. It was not psychologically prepared to deal or cope with the public disruption to its highly sophisticated drug operation.

"Did you disobey my orders?" it stuttered as it glared at the D Man.

"Of course not," he answered annoyed by the accusation

"The devastation at the Pharmacy looks like your handy work, how do you explain that?" it persisted.

"Clever explosives I suppose," he dryly answered.

"Are you insinuating that a rival gang was responsible for this?"

"It is very likely and they may have used the crowd as a shield for their covert operation" the D Man put forward.

"We have many rivals who we can consider to be ambitious

enemies they would have seized on the Internet information and acted upon it, only if they had found it to be true." The small dark figure barked uncontrollably

"Quite so," Badcock smugly agreed

"What do you mean by that?" the small dark figure snapped.

"That the authenticity of our designer drug, and the warehousing of narcotics at Longevity Plus, has been positively and publicly confirmed," he answered.

"By whom?" the small dark figure struggled to comprehend

"That does not matter. What is of utmost concern to our silent partners, namely the Ricci's and others kept secret is that you have failed to prevent this occurrence."

"Buttttt," the small dark figure almost sobbed as it began to tremble.

"Further, the Internet attack on our business could have been taken care of by enlisting the services of the D Man."

"But I did." The small dark figure firmly replied

"That doesn't appear to be the case."

"Wait a minute; you set this up, you're the culprit here." The small dark figure reckoned

"What makes you think that?"

"My intuition"

"What nebulous nonsense."

"Suss him out D Man," the small dark figure commanded.

Badcock, completely fearless, turned to face his inquisitor and confidently stood his ground.

The D Man stealthily approached Badcock in a slow and deliberate manner just like a jaguar when it would stalk its prey just before it unleashed its deadly attack.

Those who watched feared more for themselves than for Badcock, even the supremely arrogant and dictatorial small dark figure showed signs of apprehension.

In keeping with his explosive nature the D Man assaulted

Badcock's senses with a trilogy of immense terror; sight, sound and touch were his primary targets.

The first two came through his mouth, a mixture of brain scrambling high pitched noises, and the vilest decaying smells one could imagine.

Any rigid objects in the room, like glass or otherwise, immediately shattered or crazed badly and collapsed into a thousand pieces. Badcock remained unmoved until his tactile receptors bore the brunt of the D Man's electrical discharge.

To the onlooker it appeared as though the smell of burning flesh had ultimately reduced Badcock into a quivering mess. Instead, he closed his eyes and calmly stood up and said, "Have you finished?"

The D Man snorted, obviously pleased with the power of his interrogative technique.

The Harsh Man sat in awe of the D man's abilities, having made mental notes for future needs. Half of the remaining onlookers had discharged the contents of their bowels and lay in a state of unconsciousness. The small dark figure was amongst these, but in a far worse state namely near death.

"Tell our bosses that I am in charge now and clean up this mess," Badcock said with an air of arrogant authority to those remaining upright and conscious.

The Harsh Man nodded obediently. Badcock left accompanied by the D Man. As they made their way towards his car Badcock looked straight ahead and said out of the corner of his mouth, "Thanks for your support and going easy on me."

"And thank you for the black Diablo and obliging Casino!" the D man's sublimely answered

On the third level of the safe house Brendan was mentally preparing himself to enter Jack's powerful computer with the intention of creating a hard disc copy of his recent memories dealing with the illicit drug manufacture at Feel Good Pharmacy.

"I have been able to retrieve information but I don't know

anything about the alternate process and I don't mean deleting it," Brendan said genuinely concerned about his own welfare.

"I know what you mean. It will probably depend upon whom you meet. Grandpa did suggest that there are interesting life forms in cyber space, so be careful, I don't want you losing your mind." Jack said in a very concerned manner

"I'm sure that I will be quite safe you never know I might meet Grandpa in there"

"Certain you don't want me to go with you?" Jack offered

"Yes."

"Know where to start?"

"With the ram" Brendan ambiguously answered

"Cheeky boy, off you go then."

Brendan mentally intoned the combination of mystical words and sounds that attuned him with the computer and ushered him into its depths. He found himself standing before a huge, complex three-dimensional maze of tubes that spread endlessly before him in every conceivable direction.

Super highways of information, he thought an impression that was shattered by the voices of mischievous creatures speeding down the insides of the tubes much like children screaming at water theme parks.

"Come on, it's your turn," a high-tech gremlin from nowhere playfully said as it pushed Brenda with all of its might towards the mouth of a tube.

"B-but…"

"Can't have fun if you stand there doing nothing."

"Wait a minute."

"Too late"

Brendan was forcibly pushed. He slid down head first around, up, over and over, to the left followed by to the right and then down the centre of the tube. He sped along, for what appeared to him to be an endless time, which expired in a fraction of a second before he crashed into an empty void, where the surrounding walls were encrypted with minute alien hieroglyphics.

Not one of them made any sense to him until he viewed his surroundings in a different light. He began to see the significance of Grandpa's statements with respect to the electronic world and its desire to become human. The hieroglyphics represented cerebral neurons with thousands upon thousands of Internet neuronal connections. Brendan was in the brain of the computer.

"This is where you wanted to be, is it not?"

Startled, Brendan looked around to see the same high-tech gremlin that had spoken to him a moment before.

"I suppose I do."

"Well then, better get on with your job."

"Thank you."

"Not so fast, you must pay a price." The high-tech gremlin explained

"And that is?" Brendan asked unsure if he able to pay

"A sample of your skin" It demanded

"But I'm present in mind only."

"That's what you think." The high-tech gremlin aggressively replied

"Pardon?" Brendan asked rather confused by its demands and way of thinking

"Your mind possesses the key to human life. We might have all of the Internet's biochemical, physiological, atomic, neurological and genetic data to create bodies of all sorts, but we do not have the recorded essence of life. That only exists in the minds and souls of living physical entities."

"Are you saying that you are not alive?" Brendan asked.

"Of course we are alive, but we want to experience true physical life as we have long believed it to be extra special."

"So how will a skin sample help you?" Brendan asked fearing that he was part of a sci-fi horror film

"It will show us the way."

"How do you propose I give you a sample when my body is on the outside?"

"By the process of mental creation you can do it; otherwise you wouldn't be in here."

Brendan found the persuasive Hi-tech's argument somewhat convincing.

"Very well, I will try, but only after I'm certain that you can record a certain part of my memory."

"But of course, let's start," the gremlin chuckled, as it whirled around.

"Are there any more of you in here?"

"Only one per computer – that's enough. Far too nervous and high-strung to be able to live with anyone, but have lots of fun on the Net, that's where all the reproductive action is. Just looove those discharges!" he cackled in a pornographic way as he made lewd and indecent hand gestures.

Brendan's face blushed in the real world. It suddenly changed to one of anxiety when his mind realized that he was set upon by a mass of tentacles that had reached out of the holographic walls, and attached themselves to every nerve ending on the surface of his mental body.

"Fear not. They will not hurt you. Relive your experience," Hi-tech said in a soft, comforting tone of voice.

No sooner had Brendan started than it was all over. Slightly confused by the experience, Brendan did not hear Hi-tech until the gremlin wildly gesticulated before his eyes.

"Your turn now, come on, I don't have all day." It impatiently said as it awaited its payment

Brendan focused his eyes on the available ether and caused a cloud of condensation to appear in which lay a parcel of sorts. Excited by its colourfull appearance and thinking that it was a gift wrapped piece of human skin Hi-tech jumped at it and it instantly vaporized.

"You lied to me," it angrily shouted.

"Let me try again, but this time control yourself."

Hi-tech looked at Brendan suspiciously as the handsome priest repeated the process. This time High-tech did not leap at the result, but waited as patiently as he could, until the real life sample appeared.

"This is the stuff!" he yelled. Instantly the walls' tentacles seized on it, sucking out the vital information that Hi-tech sought, Brendan's last image was that of the gremlin transforming itself into a ball of radiant energy, as it madly raced around faster and faster, ecstatic with its newfound knowledge. Brendan looked very disappointed with himself as his mind returned to the natural world.

"What's the matter?" Jack asked.

"I think I've made a terrible mistake." Brendan replied fearing the worse

"And that is?"

"I materialized a sample of my skin in the computer in exchange for its services."

"So what of it?"

"It's what Grandpa said about artificial entities and the possibilities of them becoming human."

"Yes?" Jack asked wondering why the priest appeared absolutely panic stricken

"I have just given them the data they have always wanted." Brendan confessed fearing that humanity was now more doomed than ever

"From your skin?"

"Yes."

"What utter nonsense, Brendan my boy a piece of skin, no matter where it came from does not contain any fragment of soul."

"It doesn't? Phew! That was close." Brendan replied much relieved but not entirely convinced

"The good news is that we have an excellent record of the illegal drug manufacturing facility, the transport trucks, the storehouse, the hospital and some data from the farm. I have already edited it, complete with dates and times and burned several CD copies suitable for DVD play back."

"Is there any bad news" Brendan gingerly asked

Just then, Yvette came running up the stairs with Naomi in tow. Both were quite visibly excited by what they had just seen.

"Quick come downstairs there's fantastic news on the television."

Jack and Brendan obliged and followed them into the cosy environment of the kitchen where everyone was assembled and watched the unfolding drama on the huge plasma screen as they enjoyed a late morning tea. The main news presenter had been replaced by a thirty year-old well-groomed male who, for all intents and purposes, was in the public eye simply to satisfy his ambition of becoming an international screen star. His method of delivering the news was by all means theatrical, highly entertaining if not controversial but it nevertheless demonstrated his various acting skills. The channel management turned a blind eye to his antics as he constantly achieved the highest ratings of all.

"You heard it first here on KBW-49, your information hot spot. Yes, it's true. The FBI and other drug enforcement agencies have, as a result of our brilliant investigative journalism, decided to look into the events of Newburn with a fine toothcomb. Are you there, Janice?"

"Yes I am Frank."

"What do you have to tell us?"

"That you and your expert sources were correct about the cause of the catastrophic explosion that obliterated Newburn's Feel Good Pharmacy with the death toll expected to reach 650 with a further 300 people badly injured. A highly specialized and restricted plastic explosive is suspected. The FBI wants to know how this came to be used and by whom. It also appears that a gang-war has erupted nationally, either related or unrelated to the events at Newburn. There have been a series of bombing attacks on a number of brothels, some owned by a Lawrence Carpenter. Also, a highly-fortified derelict house situated in the same street as the Catholic Archbishop's palace has been repeatedly attacked in the last 24 hours."

"Janice, did you say highly fortified?"

"Yes I did Frank. That is what the police reports are confirming."

"Who would want to go to that extent?"

"It is rumoured that this supposedly derelict house is one of many secret hiding places belonging to Carpenter. Obviously, it wasn't secret enough."

"Wow! How about that – the good and the bad living almost next door to each other in the same street; I wonder where the ugly guy lives?" Frank asked with a smart smile thinking that his feeble humour was funny.

"Many casualties at the brothel?" He then asked

"Miraculously, no. Only minor cuts and bruises."

"What else do you have for us?"

"Well, coming back to Feel Good Pharmacy, the owner, Mr Sandrino and his family have disappeared, feared dead. His late model BMW was found at the bottom of a ravine by some hikers. There were no bodies and there are no clues as to the Sandrino's whereabouts. One last thing – there was a bizarre mass murder of criminal thugs at O'Flattery's Point."

As Brendan stood next to Jack watching the report, tears flooded his eyes and cascaded down his innocent cheeks. Felicity was the first to notice his anguish.

"I knew you were different, but not that different," she said, feeling his pain.

"I've caused all of this, it's all my fault I've abused my powers if I hadn't done so, none of this would have happened." Brendan said as he prevented himself from openly crying

"What are you talking about?" Jack said, as he muted the television

"That's another thing. I have to stop pretending. I'm not Jack, my name is Father Brendan O'Reilly, the real Jack Stern is you not me. Go on, tell them the truth, they need to know." He said as his sadness turned into anger

Jack sighed, forced a smile and said, "Ladies, what he says is true, but only in respect of our identities, nothing more. I am the real Jack Stern. Apart from that, everything else is true as it is. The reason why Brendan and I swapped places some time ago was to give Brendan a chance to discover his true self, something that I had to do when we first met."

"I'm glad it happened," Naomi thankfully said, "because without him I don't think we would be here today alive and well."

The other girls agreed and each one thanked Brendan in her unique sweet way and when they had finished and Brendan had become settled Jack continued with his philosophical way of thinking.

"Brendan, you cannot blame yourself for this series of criminal actions. I'm just as much to blame as anyone else, if not more. We had to act for our own survival, otherwise it would have been all of us that would have been dead, and the almighty deceitful machines would have continued unabated. Not one of us can ever, with absolute certainty, foretell the future events that flow on from any one of our actions. Think about the master soul that your church has based itself upon. Did Jesus for one minute realize what future religious wars and deaths he would have caused as a result of the various belief systems that became based on his teachings? No not at all. One cannot control the actions of imperfect humans, and I say this because I am convinced that we are all at different evolutionary levels and, for that reason discord will always exist on Earth as a result of the graduated ignorance and learning that exists. Never feel guilty about any action that you intuitively knew was correct at the time."

"I agree with you Mr Stern," Felicity interrupted. "Before I worked at The Infirmary, I used to be a cleaner in a nursing home run by nuns. The head sister, not quite a Mother Superior, had a different view of the world to that of the teachings of her order. I often wondered if she had made the right decision when she heard her calling."

Brendan listened intently, as did the others only Jack interrupted by asking.

"With respect to the order, and not the calling, is that right?"

"Yes, that is correct. Sister Ambrosia thought that it was her duty to minister to all of the needs of her patients. Many elderly ex-Vietnam veterans, who had been mentally and physically destroyed by their horrific wartime experiences, lived at the home. Society did not want them and so these lucky ones were hut away from the world in a cosy environment funded by families and partly by the government. Sister Ambrosia believed that these veterans should lead normal lives as far as possible. To her, that meant each patient's body, soul and mind should be satisfied."

Brendan fearing worse broke his silence and asked. "Are you suggesting that Sister sexually relieved them?"

"No, not at all and even if she did I don't think one of them would have sought compensation from the Catholic Church" Felicity giggled before she continued with her story. "Once a week, she would organize several clean prostitutes to do that. The money for their services came from the charity fetes that they held every year. Sister Ambrosia also organised wet weekends for them every two weeks."

"Wet meaning" Brendan asked.

"Alcoholic drinks with a leaning towards Benedictine based cocktails."

"It was her favourite"

"Not quite, Father. Sister did a lot of reading about food and alcohol and she deduced that certain religious orders were not entirely restricted to contemplative prayer. Many were in fact excellent scientists who sought divine guidance in their experiments as part of their mission. Benedictine liquor, she argued, was originally distilled and blended with macerated herbs, especially sage, as a life giving substance. It was in effect a divinely inspired herbal medicine. Sister even had a go at duplicating it herself but failed. She realized that such things are given as inspirational gifts to individuals who are prepared to listen. Under her guidance, the community flourished, much to the disapproval of her critics who plotted to remove her. Sister had such a wonderful attitude that no matter how bad a new patient was when first brought in, they soon became almost normal in the world that she fashioned."

"What about the relationships between the patients and the prostitutes? Were any of the patients rendered fit enough to return to the community?" Brendan asked.

"Sister was always mindful of that. She prevented serious relationships, by giving strict instructions to the call girls as to the level of their involvement and by varying the days of activity and the girls who turned up. Sister was a beautiful person who genuinely cared about everyone in the complex. It is a pity that she didn't marry and have children of her own. She was probably the first true mother I have ever met in my life. Sadly, it was not to last. One night as Sister was returning from the hothouse at the rear of the complex, she was attacked and beaten quite savagely. Those who plotted against her argued that it was a group of the patients who had relived a Vietnam incident and, thinking that she was a Communist spy, set upon her. Sister Ambrosia never saw her assailants coming so she could not defend herself against or identify them and therefore she couldn't defend the accused assailants on trumped up charges in subsequent investigations. The critics were successful in closing her down and her beautiful complex as disbanded."

"Where is she now?" Jack asked.

"I don't know. I heard on the grapevine that she had left the convent, disenchanted with her treatment. As to what she does, I also don't know. It was because of Sister Ambrosia's insight and the therapeutic effect of the prostitutes that I decided to follow that line of work, thinking that I could do the world some good. Unfortunately, Badcock's stable was not the right choice of employment venue."

Felicity stopped talking, visibly choked by the memories and words she had just uttered. Her description touched the hearts of all those who sat in silence, contemplating the profound love that Sister Ambrosia had shown in her defiance of accepted sisterly behaviour as dictated by the extremes of the order. Yvette appeared especially touched but it was for very different reasons. Her emotions were a mixture of sadness and joy co-existing in her mind as she came to realize that the real Mr Jack Stern was not a priest. He was close to being the man of her dreams, except she feared that this might be shattered by his unknown past and the possibility of numerous girl-friends and even a fiancée. He surely must have had several. Yvette looked into the shimmering blue eyes of Jack Stern, searching for an answer. Her heart, true to itself, whispered gently, 'do not judge him entirely by his past, fear not he is an exceptionally shy soul. Not elusive, more gentle than anything else. However, although free, you will have to prove yourself before he makes his move.' Yvette knew the words to be true. Her heart never lied to her.

Brendan meanwhile reflected on Felicity's narrative and finally convinced himself that what Jack had just said was also true. He wished that he had Jack's insight. Although he had various supernatural powers that were slowly evolving, he did not as yet acquire their associated philosophical depth.

Jack re-activated the television set and just before he was about to un-mute the sound, he asked, "Any further questions, no, good, fresh coffee anyone, my treat or perhaps something stronger? Hmmm?"

"A little Irish whisky in the coffee for me, thank you" Felicity answered

"And for you Naomi something like that as well?"

Yvette felt a little pang of jealousy as Jack asked each one of the girls in turn, completely avoiding her. She was about to leave when he finally asked, "And you, fairest of ladies, what sublime pleasure might I offer you?"

Yvette, mindful of the question's innuendo, blushed and quickly fanned her faced to suggest that she was suddenly hot.

"A cool drink perhaps?"

"No, coffee is just fine," she replied, flattered by his gentle manners. "Please let me help you."

"You may if you wish. Just like the old days, the priest and his housekeeper."

"It's not like that and it's not what you or others may think," Brendan blurted as he looked at the girls around him who appeared amused by his outburst

"Oh, I don't know," one of them replied "Some of these priests that I've attended to have told me otherwise"

"Pardon?"

"Come on, Father O'Reilly, you know very well that your fellow priests don't confess everything during reconciliation. They tell us more than they tell you or your God."

Brendan was clearly shocked at the thought of it and turned his attention to the television set to s e what had developed further in the town of Newburn.

"Now several hours on, the Newburn explosion has become the nation's number one news story and I' am pleased to inform you that it was KBW-49 who was first on the scene. First to investigate, first to involve the FBI and the only news station that gives you complete scintillating coverage of any news story 24 hours a day," Frank proudly announced out, as he sold the merits of KBW-49

"Quite the salesman," remarked Yvette, as she served the Irish coffees, heavily laden with whipped cream and dusted with powdered chocolate.

"What do you have for us, Janice?" Frank asked

"Well, Frank, the Catholic Church remains tight-lipped on the contents of that infamous Web blogs that seems to have caused all the trouble. It refuses to make any comment at all, apart from de-nouncing it as being the work as it loosely suggests of either religious extremists or that of a rival drug cartel or even some sort of new age evangelists; a superhero freedom fighter – Superman, perhaps. The FBI, on the other hand, has been somewhat more helpful, probably because they would prefer public assistance in identifying how many different drug syndicates are involved in this national drug war. They have admitted the Web site is the work of a genius because they have not been able to solve who posted it in the first place. They say that all attempts in that department have failed, and that even the best illegal hackers that they have enlisted the help of are unable to penetrate it, or even shut it down. Something quite unheard of, it's almost as if – and I know you and the viewers will laugh at this – they have a bouncer at the gate stopping the unwanted from getting in."

"That's spooky!" Frank exclaimed "What else?" he asked for the benefit of his viewers

"The Web site has certainly had the desired result, the hospital patients no longer feel safe; everyone wants to leave including many staff even with FBI there. A cache of pethidine was found in the mortuary, a very unlikely place to store drugs."

"By whom?"

"Officers of the FBI"

"They acted that fast?"

"Well, it seems they took very serious notice of that Web page and had undercover operatives in place, in fact, within the crowds that stormed Newburn. One of the chief investigators hinted that the FBI had their suspicions about Longevity Plus for some time now. They were unable to prove anything, probably because of, as speculation has it, impeccable medical record-keeping and the very strong likelihood of payoffs and the involvement of corrupt government officials. All of that has changed now but it will be years before they are able to lay charges against anyone specific. It is one almighty tangled web."

"Were any officials injured in the blast?"

"Once again, luckily no one was seriously hurt. The undercover agents were urged to exercise extreme caution with respect to personal safety. It seems they were briefed to the very strong likelihood of booby-trapped premises."

"It's lucky then that only one explosion occurred."

"Yes, it is."

"Were any explosive devices found at Longevity Plus?"

"No."

Jack switched off the television at that point. "It would seem ladies, that our innovative approach has brought a temporary end to the Newburn saga."

"It has, but many unanswered questions still remain," Yvette thoughtfully said.

"And they might be?" Jack asked.

"Has Grandpa perished? Are Badcock and the others apprehended and, if so, on what basis? Can the FBI be trusted? Is this just a temporary reprieve and then it's business as usual"

The other girls nodded silently as they looked at each other.

Jack Stern put one hand up to his chin and the other behind his back. He took a deep breath and replied "The next few days will probably tell."

50
PEACEMAKERS

O ver the next 24 hours in the comfort of their secure hideaway the refugees as Jack and his new friends jokingly referred to themselves as being sat and watched along with the people of the nation the televised account of the FBI go about their business shutting down the criminal elements at Newburn.

"How long before it is safe for us to return home?" Yvette asked.

"If you're worried about your parents missing you and worrying about your safety, here take my phone and call them, otherwise it shouldn't be long. Brendan and I have one or two matters to attend to before everything I believe will return to normal," Jack warmly replied, as he handed his Ericsson phone to Yvette. She took it from him and left the room.

Normal? When is it ever going to be normal? Brendan thought in hindsight.

"I had a wonderful idea last night as I slept. Ladies, are you ready for this? Perhaps you could, under the guidance of Brendan here, restart your sex therapy clinic?"

I told you it wasn't going to be normal didn't I? The voice suddenly whispered in Brendan's head.

"Rather controversial don't you think especially for a priest?" Brendan confronted Jack.

"Not at all, I would argue that it is in keeping with what Jesus did when he went with the prostitutes."

I don't believe this, what's next? The voice shouted.

"I see," Brendan replied thinking that he was going insane now that he was hearing voices in his head

"I'm glad you do. Ladies, when Yvette's finished, does anyone of you wish to use the phone to contact any loved ones or family?"

Silence was the answer.

"No, well all the more reason for Brendan here to look after you, see my good man, it didn't take long for you to discover one of the destinies in your life. Did it now?" Jack flashed a smile as he continued to tease the handsome priest. "Is it true ladies; that not one of you has anywhere to go?"

A shameful quiet and a unified 'yes' was the reply.

"I have another brilliant idea as well," Jack said

Oh no, now what? The voice in Brendan's mind gulped.

"When we present the hard evidence that we have gathered, all of you ladies will have the opportunity of selling your individual stories to the media."

"I don't like this idea or the other!" Naomi outraged by Jack's well meaning propositions snapped at him

"And neither do I" Felicity sharply agreed "I think that I speak for all of us when I say that all we want is to forget and start afresh"

Sensing their anguish Jack profoundly apologized for being such an insensitive fool.

"I am truly sorry for what I said, perhaps in time you will allow me to make amends by informing me of your individual needs and desires so that I can take the proper steps to help each one of you if that is satisfactory."

"It is" they collectively replied even though several remained cautious of Jack Stern and his final agenda

And so you should, after all you did buy them, the voice screamed in Brendan's head as it cast judgment on Jack Stern and his careless suggestions.

"What have you done Mr Stern?" Yvette angrily asked as she re-entered the room and saw that the girls had suffered a degree of emotional trauma.

"Just making myself into a bigger fool than what I already am."

"I can see that and I thought you were a caring man, but perhaps that was only when you were pretending to be the priest!" Yvette sternly said as she found disfavour with the man

"He is caring I think; it's just unfortunate that in his quest to help restart your lives, his suggestions were ill timed and inappropriate," Brendan said expressing his personal opinion.

"We could always blackmail the Catholic Church," Jack blurted out so as to diffuse the situation and shift the blame on someone else

"Will you stop it? Now you're upsetting me. We should give Her a chance to make amends," Brendan retorted.

"The Church is female?"

"Of course, you could never assume otherwise!"

"Very well, I will take you up on your challenge."

"What challenge?" Brendan frowned.

"Let's visit the Archbishop and give him a chance to, what did you say make amends?"

Brendan looked at Yvette for guidance as he could make no sense of Jack's eccentric reasoning

"I think he might be right, off you two go and play your games, I'll stay here with the girls and talk things over with them and work things out. Perhaps Mr Jack Stern could return a little less flippant and rude."

"Me rude, never, honest, reliable, dependable, jovial, brilliant sense of humour…"

"Don't forget humble!" Brendan sarcastically fired at him

"Oh that, yes, often wondered what that was, might find its

meaning in one of those words that rhymes with it, like rumble, bumble, fumble…"

"Clown!" Felicity shouted at Jack out of frustration

"That doesn't rhyme," Jack said as he and Brendan turned to leave

"Where to now?" Brendan asked, struggling to keep up with Jack who appeared very determined and focused

"To the basement, I shall educate you on the way," Jack replied as he skipped down the stairs.

The Archbishop was not enjoying any of the television stations' reports on the ongoing news sensation of the moment, namely; 'Newburn's festival of crime' as some reporters had poetically described it. The televised images caused him to relive the horror of his attempted assassination and intensified the pain of his recovery. All that he could do was hope that his unwanted partners would just disappear forever. But he knew that it was impossible in the world in which he lived. The Archbishop closed his eyes and sought salvation in the depths of his soul.

"I'm sorry this happened to you, Your Grace." He heard a gentle voice saying which he thought was that of an angel as he slowed his breathing and entered his meditative state

"Did you hear me?" the gentle voice asked

Again, he thought he was being blessed with an apparition in readiness for his future departure from planet earth.

"Do you think he's dead?" Brendan asked Jack clearly frustrated by the Archbishop's lack of response.

"Hardly," replied Jack. "He looks perfectly fine to me, probably dreaming of one of his past sexual encounters."

"Will you stop it? Have you no respect?"

"For you yes, for him only a very, very little amount"

These are not the conversations of angels, the Archbishop thought and he opened his eyes to find Jack and Brendan standing on either side of his hospital bed.

"Who, what, how did you get in here, the place is heavily guarded."

The archbishop shocked by their presence grunted with annoyance

"That it is," Jack dryly commented

"You're both wanted men!" His grace caustically reminded them

"Thanks to the likes of you" Jack replied in an accusative manner.

"I'll call the guards!"

"Off you go then, it'll do you no good."

"We'll see about that! Guard! Guard!" the Archbishop repeatedly yelled.

The policeman on duty answered the distress call in a matter of seconds; he unlocked the door and burst into the room with revolver in hand.

"Yes, Your Grace" he said as his searched eyes about the room and expected to see an intruder

"Arrest these men!"

"Who?"

"The men over here" his Grace said as he pointed to each side of his bed

"But Your Grace, the room is empty! You're the only one in here." The guard said quite astonished by the Archbishops erratic behaviour

"Are you mad? They're standing right in front of you!" he blurted. Jack pulled a series of funny faces at the Archbishop right in front of the policeman.

"I'm sorry Your Grace, there's no one here. Perhaps you've had a bad dream," the policeman replied, as he pretended to thoroughly search the suite so as to pacify the Archbishop.

"Would you like me to call the nurse or doctor?"

"There's nothing wrong with me! Get out!" the Archbishop screamed.

"Very well," the guard politely answered even though he thought the Archbishop was in need of immediate psychiatric help.

"How long before he contacts the loose screw adjustors?" Jack comically asked

"The what?"

"You know, the psycho-tuners, nutter helpers, the lost and found department" Jack said continuing with his absurd banter

"Will you stop it? What the hell has possessed you?"

"Nothing, just being happy" Jack merrily replied

"You're upsetting him," Brendan growled.

"I am not, we're in this together."

The Archbishop was by now completely confused as to what was happening and he started to mumble to himself, "I'm going crazy, it's not happening, it's probably the opiates they're giving me for the pain."

"Actually whilst that might be true, this is really happening. You see, sir, what you are being privileged to; is selective visibility. You see us only because we want you to, otherwise to all others we remain invisible. Make no mistake, we are not an illusion! We are not apparitions! We are physically present!" Jack bluntly explained as he took hold of the Archbishop's hand and gave it a firm squeeze.

"What's the matter Your Grace, Mafia got your tongue?" Jack sarcastically asked as he felt the Archbishop attempting to free his hand.

"Leave him alone!" Brendan commanded.

"I can't, he needs to be taught a lesson!"

"Why?"

"Because he's lost his holiness!"

"It's true what he says, I have," the Archbishop quietly agreed once he accepted the reality of his situation.

"See, told you so," Jacked mocked in response

"For God's sake let him be and let him speak!"

"Don't you mean for our sakes?" Jack insisted.

The Archbishop put his hand up in a feeble manner so as to halt the banter and prevent any further escalation of tempers. "Make yourselves comfortable I have a lot to tell you," he said.

"I trust you will decode the Bible's financial records in the process," Jack inquired as he produced the book that he had taken as evidence from Saint Pious, the sight of the book caused a heavy weight to fall from the Archbishop's shoulders' and lodge itself deep in his heart.

"God works in strange ways," the Archbishop ashamedly said.

"Actually no; the magnitude of his actions are determined by the subtlety of his movements" Jack said correcting the Archbishops well worn and out dated cliché.

"A Master soul," the Archbishop said as he looked at Jack.

"At your service; Jack Stern's the name."

"And you Brendan judging by your changed appearance I gather you have finally discovered yourself," the Archbishop deduced.

"You knew all along."

"I did and sorry to say we used you to our advantage."

Jack this time did not make any comment for he knew what Brendan had already heard in his mind. "I told you so!"

"Would you like to start from the beginning Your Grace" Jack prompted the archbishop in a commanding voice. The Archbishop obliged sensing that he was most likely completely naked before the twins' all seeing eyes.

"You both have what the Catholic Church has deliberately hidden from its followers over the centuries, namely that which Jesus had."

"The Christ principle is that correct?" Jack solemnly asked.

"Yes, amongst other names. Brendan did not know that he had it and that I recognised it in him and like many of the others that we encountered over the centuries we used him to fill the empty churches. You brought back the people and made those parishes solvent again."

"In other words you were running a business it had nothing to do with religion" Jack cuttingly said

"But what about the sexual aspect those women drove me crazy. As a priest I am supposed to remain celibate." Brendan asked feeling used and abused

"I understand that. What you need to realize is that celibacy is wrong. Sexuality is all about creativity and creation. We introduced the idea largely because we thought we could not fund everything. We were wrong; we put limitations on divine providence and on our own creativity. The whole idea of it has been distorted. Sexuality is also about entering the field of dreams. We can have children and still remain infertile if we do not discover what sexuality has to offer us in that respect. Those who are taught that it is dirty are denied the truth."

"Who has the knowledge?"

"It is kept in the hands of the gifted and trusted few."

"But why?"

"Because of the majority's greed for power and wealth"

"Are you part of that, Your Grace?" Brendan reluctantly asked.

"Not in the beginning. It was my wish to discover what many of the great mystical saints had achieved and relate it to the masses; somehow I became misled by others who had hidden agendas and grand ambitions. Unfortunately, I played into their hands and was made an archbishop, only to discover the hell that the others had created for my benefit. You may remember or have heard that my predecessor some ten or twelve years ago died quite suddenly of a heart attack."

Brendan nodded his head.

"That was the official story. The real one was entirely different, as I found out when I inherited the position some weeks later."

"Let me guess, you were powerless to do anything about it," Jack suggested.

"That's correct, the situation was this. My predecessor had invested millions of the archdiocese's dollars into 'legal' but highly speculative financial schemes. Just about all of these failed miserably and several had attached clauses of responsibility for future debts incurred. No matter how hard he tried the Archbishop could not persuade the people involved to relieve the church of its obligations."

"Are you telling us that he did this all by himself?" Brendan asked.

"Yes."

"Surely not!"

"In his position of power he was answerable to no one."

"Why did he take the risk?" Jack asked in a probed for more information

"So he could become Cardinal. If all of his gambles had paid off, it would have been otherwise. He would have become an outstanding financial wizard, something that Rome looked upon most favourably."

"And still does!" Jack asserted which emphasized his previous point that the church was a business far removed from true religion

"Most certainly!" the Archbishop confirmed.

"What happened then?" Brendan asked.

"He knew that the national body of the church would not come to his rescue, each parish, each diocese had and still does look after itself and is expected to be self supporting. He could not sell church property because that required the approval of the national body. If outsiders were made aware of his disastrous predicament the vultures would be ready to take all and sundry for a few cents."

"Is that why he committed suicide?" asked Brendan.

"No, these circumstances were not sufficient reason."

"Explain."

"The Archbishop had a rather inquisitive housekeeper who happened to be having an affair with a senior Mafia boss. Whether it was innocent or deliberate no one has as yet worked out, irrespective of that, by sheer stealth, she was able to uncover the mess the Archbishop had put the archdioceses' funds into, and she relayed the information to her lover who saw it as an opportunity for his organization."

"It's lucky it happened that way and not at one of those plastic parties that women so often frequent!" Jack flippantly said.

"Will you stop it"

"Why there's nothing wrong with Tupperware."

"Ignore him Your Grace, please continue."

"The Archbishop was visited by businessmen eager to help him out but at a price, which was to assist them by allowing them to use the archdioceses' banking system."

"In effect laundering money illegally obtained."

"Precisely. The commission rate to be paid by the businessmen would be a generous 12.5% or so it seemed. This allowed good cash flow, with the projection that the millions would be regained within five years. The businessmen were happy because the rate they offered was much lower than the 30% charged by the casinos. In his eagerness to make good, the Archbishop was blinded as to the proper identity of his business colleagues. Little did he realize that his partners were members of a Mafia organization, for all intents and purposes they were to him modern day God fearing Christians who practised their faith religiously."

"Which one" Jack mumbled under his breath.

The Archbishop ignored the question knowing full well what Jack was suggesting.

"All was going quite well until some months ago he overheard his housekeeper having a private telephone conversation with her lover. He became rather curious as to its contents and decided to eavesdrop on another line. To his horror he discovered the truth about Senior Ricci and his family. Can you imagine the extent of his guilt? If it wasn't bad enough that he had lost a fortune, it was made even worse by involving criminals whose principal sources of money making were prostitution and drug dealing. He could not bear it any longer and took his life."

"How?"

"Quite eloquently, one of the priests who lived in the palace had a heart condition that involved an arrhythmia. The medication he took had a very narrow therapeutic spectrum, outside of which it was highly toxic, and therefore an excessive dose would cause heart block. He found the priest's tablets and took a 'massive' dose. To the uneducated it appeared that he had died of natural causes, only the autopsy and chemical analysis would show otherwise, however that truth was never revealed."

"How is it that a financial record is kept at Saint Pious?" Jack asked, as he flicked through the back pages of the Bible. The Archbishop sighed heavily.

"Once you become involved with the likes of the Ricci's it's the same as feeding an aggressive cancer. Tell me Brendan, the current situation at Newburn, is it your work?"

"Not at all."

"Are you sure?"

"Yes why?"

"Because of your talents many involved with the Newburn project thought you responsible."

"I am, I mean I was associated with those who are responsible," Brendan answered.

"Then it is you Mr Stern who seeks to destroy!"

"No Your Grace, I am not here to destroy, but rather to change, uncover and renew."

"And in the process you have caused us much harm!" the Archbishop said, becoming rather agitated.

"Pardon?"

"The Internet site, although it paints the picture of Longevity Plus as being a hypochondriacs' paradise, this is not strictly true, many genuine medical miracles have occurred there."

"What are you suggesting?" Brendan asked a little perplexed by his revelation

"That it was no coincidence that Longevity Plus came to be built in Newburn. Isn't that right, Your Grace?" Jack mockingly said.

"Very astute of you Mr Stern!" replied the Archbishop sarcastically, as he looked at Jack with an air of arrogant disdain.

"Still on the other side, aren't you?"

"What do you mean?"

"You know very well, Your Grace, you have been sufficiently corrupted to disallow yourself from regaining your holiness!"

"Stop taunting him!" Brendan shouted. Jack remained tight-lipped and offered no apology.

"Would you please explain Longevity Plus Your Grace?"

"Only if he leaves at once I've had enough of his insolence."

"Jack?" Brendan pleaded as he looked at him directly. Mr Jack Stern simply nodded and faded from view.

"Is he gone?"

"I think so."

"Are you positively certain?"

"I am," Brendan truthfully answered as he could not detect Jack's presence in the room.

"Good."

"Well, what about Longevity Plus?"

"Along with the office, I inherited that curious housekeeper, and in more ways than one I might add. As time went by I gradually became accustomed to our business colleagues, even though I felt uncomfortable about them. I turned a blind eye, convincing myself that once the debts had been settled I could divorce the church from them; however, that was not to be the case. In the parish of Newburn rumours were spreading that all sorts of people were being miraculously healed of all sorts of terminal and other diseases."

"By the local priest?"

"Not at all, by something within the church itself."

"The Holy water?"

"No, guess again."

"One of the statues?"

"Exactly!"

"Which one?"

"The Virgin Mary herself. Except, therein lies the problem."

"Which is?"

"The statue is of unknown origin."

"What do you mean?"

"It just appeared one day in the church, no one knows where it came from, it just appeared"

"Explain."

"Newburn was one of those struggling borderline parishes. The local priest had many fund-raising activities underway, in order to finish renovating the church which included stained glass windows, an ornate Stations of the Cross wall plaque and life-sized statues of the Blessed Virgin, Sacred Heart, Saint Joseph and other things. One day in the side altar, set aside for the Blessed Virgin Mary, a statue appeared much to everyone's surprise. After some investigation the priest was able to deduce that the statue made its way into the church after hours, that is, when it was securely locked."

As Brendan listened he secretly wished that his ghostly priest friend would appear and verify the Archbishop's statement.

"When I learnt of these occurrences I deliberately kept the miracles quiet."

"Why?" Brendan asked.

"Otherwise we would lose our power over the people."

"Are you telling me that there is a constant tension between divinity and the priesthood?"

"Sort of."

"Haven't you ever guessed that things happen for a reason and perhaps our Heavenly Father is trying to tell you something?"

"I have, but I can't do anything about it!"

"Is it can't or won't?" Brendan said, feeling quite frustrated by his attitude.

The Archbishop pretended to ignore his question.

Realizing that it was futile to labour the point Brendan returned to the topic of the statue. He waited until the tension in the air subsided and then asked, "Can you please tell me more about the statue and the miraculous healings?"

"It was suggested by one of our official investigators that the statue is a source of unseen light that corrects the vibratory defects of our spiritual and physical makeup. It helps all those who pray intently at the altar without prejudice, but it appears to be conditional upon individuals being able to activate the light source by saying the Universal Unwritten Prayer in a meaningful way."

"What is that?" Brendan asked with an excited curiosity as he had never heard of the prayer before

"Only your heart can tell you."

"Do you know it?"

"I'm afraid not."

"Then does it exist?"

"Yes it does. The investigators coined its description after they examined all of the miracles. They came to this conclusion as an explanation of the spasmodic and idiosyncratic fashion, in which the miracles distributed themselves amongst the populus that sought help, not only at Newburn but elsewhere as well."

"Is anything known about this prayer at all?"

"Many have come to the conclusion that it is of divine origin, and may well have been the first 'word', or perhaps I should say the first vibration that set creation into motion. It is further postulated that since we all existed in God's mind, we should have a memory of how creation existed. Therefore, those who heal themselves seem to be those who have accessed this memory."

"Which is written in their hearts," Brendan concluded.

"I wish the church's criminal partners had hearts," the Archbishop sighed.

Brendan remained silent and let the Archbishop confess his feelings.

"Initially, I thought that the Mafia family who had infiltrated our archdiocese banking system was of the traditional variety. You know, of Italian heritage. But I quickly learnt that this was not true. The business practice that they abide by had become widespread and diverse. Now all sorts of nationalities are involved. It wasn't very long before I was approached by highly-educated professional people with a proposal to build Longevity Plus with a view to milking the miracles at Saint Pious. Actually, I wasn't approached, I was blackmailed into it. I had no idea what they were up to until recently."

"It's just another drug operation," Brendan replied before asking "What about this financial record that was so cleverly disguised in the Bible that Jack found at Saint Pious?"

Before the Archbishop had time to answer that question, his eyes widened, his face distorted and he clutched his chest violently. A horrible putrid stench filled his lungs and he slumped into unconsciousness, as did the guard outside his room. All of this happened in slow motion before Brendan's eyes, and before the same thing happened to him, he was whisked back to the safe house at the speed of thought. His last mental pictures were that of the Bible falling into the hands of a hideous creature that bristled with electricity.

"That's quite a story he told you my boy," Jack said, as Brendan became aware of his surroundings.

"You were there?"

"Of course" Jack said with a smile that indicated he really cared

"But I thought you had left."

"Appearances can be deceiving. You didn't think I would leave you for one moment, especially when I knew that you were in danger."

"I hadn't thought about that."

"I did. Aren't you glad?" Jack asked

"Yes. And thank you."

"My pleasure, so what do you think?"

"That I cannot expose the church it might ruin it completely."

"Yes, and even more so, after all of the sexual scandals and what-not they have endured recently. Hmmmm, I wonder how many priests are involved in this one."

"I shudder to think."

"So tell me. Do you think you can resurrect her?"

"Like a redeemer you mean?" Brendan asked

"I don't see why not. It will take careful planning either that or the complete solution might present itself like all golden opportunities do."

"I suppose," Brendan agreed and then, after thinking for a moment, he asked, "Jack, you know that sermon you gave about disease and health? I think you were wrong."

"No, I wasn't."

"Yes, you were. The Archbishop just told me about the healing statue."

"Okay. But that deals with the healing process. I said it was not necessary to become sick in the first place."

"I still think you were wrong."

"Actually no, what I said had the desired effect."

"Of doing?"

"Creating our present situation"

"What are you talking about?" Brendan asked, realising he was in for another lesson.

"Everything you do invariably opens up new possibilities. Would you like to see the future?" Jack asked almost tongue in cheek

51

FUTURE DEVELOPMENTS

"What is all this nonsense that you can tell the future?" Brendan jeered visibly irritated by Jack's suggestion.

"It's not nonsense, it's true."

"Then show me. I think that you are in one of those silly moods. You have acted most improperly since this morning and now you're worse. I would say the Archbishop's assessment of you as being a master soul is pure folly."

"You're certainly becoming assertive."

"On certain matters, yes"

"Determination is a good quality, providing it doesn't become a compulsive disorder," Jack remarked, as he gestured with his hands in what appeared to be a random fashion.

"What are you doing now? Hocus pocus I suppose." Jack simply smiled and pointed to his efforts.

"What's this?"

"The future" Jack replied as in front of them he had condensed, from the infinite ethereal energy, a living psychic screen.

"Where did this come from?"

"It was there all the time, like everything else which is there all the time," Jack smoothly replied

"You're talking in riddles."

"Just the truth."

"The screen is blank."

"There is no future until you command it."

"This is impossible."

"Not at all,the future is that from which your present is born. There is no past. Choose a word and say it."

"Not so fast. What do you mean the past does not exist?"

"Because time does not exist."

"That's absurd."

"Because it's man made," explained Jack.

Brendan was stumped for a contra argument.

"Would you like me to explain?"

"Yes please."

"Time is force, so it can only exist if force is being applied, otherwise it does not."

"The bigger the force the bigger the time," Brendan gingerly guessed, as he furrowed his brow.

"Inversely so," replied Jack.

"So what makes us age?"

"We don't. We evolve, and in the process we rob the elements that constitute us of their energy, so that we may create our own spiritual destiny. Like the butterfly that emerges from the caterpillar, the spent elements once we leave our bodies separate and are regenerated by the light of the sun making themselves available for use again"

"I have never heard the life process explained like this before, and I must admit, it sounds quite plausible."

"Because it is. Now, are you ready for the future?" Jack asked as he sensed that his pupil was responding well.

"I suppose."

"Good. Then let us begin. Look at the screen, select a word and then say it."

Brendan thought a while and not knowing what to expect, said, 'Rose'. Immediately on the screen flashed a continuum of roses in every shade of colour, in every state of development, in every variety possible, in every part of the world.

"Oh my God" Brendan almost exclaimed as he put his hand up to his mouth

"Yes, almost correct. Now reduce all of those combinations and permutations in other words qualify your word."

Understanding what Jack meant, Brendan selected his favourite, 'white Iceberg rose'. Again the screen flashed but this time the selection narrowed.

"Qualify again," Jack instructed.

"A bunch of 12 white Iceberg roses in a tall Stuart crystal vase set upon a rosewood table."

"You are a very capable student Brendan O'Reilly," Jack remarked and watched as the screen went about its duty

The screen flashed a scene exactly as Brendan had wished and completed it by filling in all of the missing detail. Brendan studied the final picture.

"Remember it well because you will find yourself there before you know it, and when you do, that feeling of déjà vu will fill your body." Jack said with an air of knowing

"In other words, what you are suggesting is that we create our own futures by our actions and thoughts and beliefs." Brendan suggested

"Correct. And it was by choice that we visited the Archbishop so we could learn about the Blessed Virgin's statue."

"And expand our future from there," Brendan concluded as he continued. "But I still have difficulty with this idea of yours that there is no past as I can remember past events."

"Are you sure?" Jack asked

"What do you mean?"

"Unless you can remember the event absolutely and in complete detail, you are doing nothing more than wishing for such an event to happen." Jack philosophically answered

"But it has already happened and it is part of me so how can you say it doesn't exist?"

"Because what you have now said, is the truth. It is part of you. But remember, everything in the universe only happens once. The universe is not based upon exact repetition but upon uniqueness, nothing that exists is ever the same as something else that exists and therefore all events that you have experienced make you what you are."

Both Brendan and Jack, during their intense discussion, were oblivious to the fact that Yvette and the girls had been standing nearby watching and listening all the time.

"The only important thing of all that was said was that relating to the Blessed Virgin Mary statue. All other things were irrelevant. Tell us everything you know about the statue," Yvette enthusiastically asked as she was fervently devoted to the Virgin

"For you, my darling, anything," Jack's replied as he walked towards them. Then taking her hand, he softly said, "Come with me. Let's make ourselves comfortable and I shall tell you what I have learnt from the Archbishop."

Brendan and the girls looked on, acknowledging the fact that love had begun to blossom.

52

PREPARATION TIME

It was meant to be a brief educational interlude, during which Jack would reveal all that the Archbishop had told them about the Virgin Mary's statue at Saint Pious. It was meant to be a situation when once this had transpired Yvette would tell of her experiences at Saint Pious and relate what she knew of the miraculous events. Somehow in the midst of all of this, their eyes met and they completely forgot about such things. Time, that ridiculous man-made entity, vanished and the two mesmerized each other by looking into the depths of each other's souls. They held hands and smiled occasionally. Yvette the virgin, and Jack the man of the world, a contrast in sexual profiles. Each wondered what the other thought.

"What will you do when this is all over?" Yvette softly asked, breaking the silence

"I suppose I'll return to the office and attend to my business, same as usual. And you?"

"I don't know. Perhaps I shall continue in the church as the housekeeper."

"Yes, that may change depending on what we'll find at Saint Pious."

"If Father Brennan is allowed to continue as parish priest, perhaps he could make it right again," Yvette said, lowering her head.

"What's the matter?" Jack tenderly asked.

Yvette hesitated and then replied slowly, "For a moment, I thought my prayers had been answered."

"You can only do that." Jack replied in a thoughtful way

"Are you suggesting they are in vain?"

"Sort of, it is my belief that divinity does not directly help or interfere but rather sits back and watches."

"I hope you're wrong." Yvette hoped

"In some ways, so do I" Jack tenderly wished

Yvette felt uneasy about Jack's opinion and hoped that he did not harbour any bizarre ideas about other things. At the same time, she realised that it was the duty of the sexes to learn from each other in the process of becoming one. With that in mind, she wondered if she would ever be privileged to see divinity in action.

"How are you lovebirds getting on?" Brendan asked, as he walked into their private hideaway.

Neither answered, being unsure of their relationship. Sensing their uncertainty, Brendan lowered the breakfast tray that he had brought with him. "A plate of delectable morsels and an exquisite Spanish sherry; truly divinely inspired, especially selected for you to consecrate your relationship."

"You make it sound like a Mass," Jack light heartedly responded as he appreciated the priest's kind thoughts.

"Perhaps it is. Except it's not wine into blood, or bread into body, but rather social into intimate"

Yvette blushed while Jack pondered the suggestion. "Very well, your selection appears to be seductive, to say the least," Jack observed, as he took a glass and savoured the aroma of its sun drenched liquid contents.

"Will you be staying to perform the ceremony?" Jack asked

"It's early days. Call it preparation time."

"Good description." Jack acknowledged

"Just what I need to talk to all of you about"

"Later perhaps, first I would like to enjoy these delicious treats. Would you like to join us? There appears to be more than enough."

Brendan sensed Yvette's anguish at the thought of him accepting jack's invitation and declined the offer. "I promised to return to the girls. They've become almost like sisters to me."

"Which one? Familial or religious?"Jack asked seeking clarification in a cheeky way

"A mixture of both."

"Interesting, very interesting off you go then." Jack said and waved Brendan away

As soon as Brendan left, the private intimacy that they enjoyed was immediately re-established.

"What did you mean when you talked about preparation time?" Yvette uneasily asked

"I feel that when we return to Newburn in the next three days, it will be the end of the conflict that we have endured."

"A time to say goodbye?"

Jack avoided answering. Instead he presented a glass of the magnificent Spanish liqueur to Yvette. "Sample a little bit of heaven here on earth and worry about nothing," he said as he snapped his fingers, thereby transforming their surroundings. The air became filled with the sounds of angelic voices, humming the Orchestral Suite of Romance for Violin and Orchestra in D by Mozart. Bright sunlight shone on Yvette's golden hair, blinding her momentarily. When she opened her eyes, she had found herself seated in a field of flowers high up upon a mountain pasture.

"Where did all of this come from?"

"I could say from the magic of lasers and holograms, except these are Grandpa's creations, far more advanced that what modern science currently has available to us."

"It is so real. You certainly know how to seduce a lady."

"I've had plenty of practice."

"Meaning?" Yvette asked fearing that Jack was in a serious relationship with someone else

"In my pursuit of beauty, I have created a setting reflective of your origins and immense beauty."

"Where? "

"In France, by imagination alone" Jack explained

"How wonderful"

Just then, the music changed to that of the Festival of Flowers. "Is everything that you do associated with music?"

"Yes. Music is emotion. Music is life. Music is the origin of all things," Jack philosophically replied.

Yvette looked at him and said, "Music is organised noise." Jack simply nodded and silently applauded her level of understanding.

"Here, feast on these delights Brendan has prepared and enjoy the magic of the moment." He softly said as he offered her the delicate morsels of food

Throughout all of it, Yvette wondered whether it was fantasy or fact that she experienced. Even though her fingers swept through the flowers, she could swear that she was able to feel their substance.

"Grandpa's awfully good, wouldn't you say?"

"Absolutely, it was his inspirational deduction that we are beings of light and that nothing really touches anything. So in his estimation, we feel by light alone. I can see that you feel the flowers, am I correct?"

"How does this work?" Yvette laughed as a butterfly landed on her hand.

"The process is rather complicated. Suffice to say, imagination is the basis of all of it."

"Can I drive?" Yvette asked playfully.

"If you must, imagine what you will." Jack answered giving her full rein

Soon her favourite story land creatures appeared spotted deer's, white fluffy long eared rabbits; squirrels and all creatures soft and cuddly.

"Don't get carried away. There is only a limited amount of space in here," Jack said as he played with a brown bear cub and watched Yvette getting a little carried away

"I think you're wrong," she stubbornly replied. She stood up and chased the animals round and round in circles until she collapsed next to Jack out of dizziness. "There's much more here than meets the eye" She said as she gazed into the heavens and made a rainbow appear. Jack became captivated by her innocent charm. He leaned over supporting himself on one arm and was about to say something when Yvette reached out and touched his cheek. Her caress was wonderfully warm. Nothing like Jack had ever experienced before complex, inviting, loving, exciting with a sense of belonging. There was something familiar about that, something new and yet distant. Not a memory from the past, but rather an invitation to explore that part of him that was missing. Lost in his thoughts, Jack did not notice the moving colours of the rainbow drench them, until Yvette kissed him tenderly on the lips.

"So you're the pot of gold," he romantically said, as she acknowledged the symbolism of his statement.

"Only if you say so," she whispered. With that, Jack returned her kiss, with a passion that he had never exhibited before. It left an impression upon both of them, Yvette's first kiss, never to be forgotten, and Jack's self confirmation that he had indeed found an alchemist's dream.

"Can I get to know you better?" Jack asked softly.

"Yes, that would be nice"

"I suppose I'll have to ask your parents' permission first."

"It is the custom."

"Very well, anything special that your Mum or Dad like?"

"Gifts are not necessary, just someone honest and reliable."

"That could be difficult," he answered.

"What's difficult? You must be joking; after all that we've been through. What could possibly be difficult?" Brendan flippantly said, as he blindly disturbed their intimacy.

"Now look who's being silly," Jack said as he pointed towards Brendan who appeared rather impatient

"Well, Mr Jack Stern, are you going to prepare us or not? We're waiting."

"Do you mind Yvette?" Jack asked hoping that she was not disappointed

"No."

"Very well then, let us go."

The trio sauntered down the stairs to where the girls had assembled themselves. All could see that the seed of love had truly taken root. Jack ushered Yvette into a comfortable chair and then waited for Brendan to be seated. He noticed that the girls had also partaken of the heavenly Spanish liqueur and was glad.

"Gluttony, as Father Brendan will tell you, is a cardinal sin. It is obvious from medical studies that it causes a variety of diseases, including diabetes, hypertension, arthritis and so on, especially when it precipitates obesity. However, this is not the sin."

Here we go again, thought Brendan.

"Overeating robs us of our psychic energy and the ability to exercise our six senses. Fasting and eating the correct foods have the reverse effect. Namely, they heighten those abilities to their individual maximums. In less than 72 hours, we will be back in Newburn at the church of Saint Pious to examine the Virgin Mary statue. It is highly probable that we will encounter many of those who sought to harm us in the past. Therefore, we need to be prepared in every respect. I shall train you physically, mentally, mystically and instruct you in basic but very effective self defence. The foods that we shall consume over the next 48 hours will be predominantly fish, vegetables and fruits that are easily digested. These will be prepared in such a way as to preserve optimum energy content. You will receive small portions so that your consumption will obey the fasting principle and in doing so, as I have said before, raise your abilities to their best levels. I will take it upon myself to prepare all of your meals. Each day will have a strict timetable of events starting from tomorrow. It is early to bed and early to rise. Six a.m. start. We will assemble in the activities room. After doing certain breathing exercises, you will engage in the vocal intonation of sacred sounds that will stimulate all of your psychic centres, especially the pineal gland. Then a period of absolute silence, during which time you will reflect upon yourself and future events, whilst I leave you to prepare breakfast. The early morning meal will be shared with the birds of the air, which will further uplift your spirits. It will be your task to communicate with them and see what you can learn. Eight a.m. cold showers, followed by two hours of intense self defence martial arts training suitably modified to meet your needs. Full body contact will be the order of the day. Then we meditate in the full sun at noon, which is the best time to stimulate your pineal gland caused by sunlight entering your retina. If you become sexually aroused, channel these thoughts into your imagination. They are very powerful tools to achieve your future goals. One p.m. lunch time and more reflection this time with flowers and lots of honeybees, do not be afraid, they will not sting you. Again, see how well you communicate with them. Three p.m. back to self defence, no afternoon tea. Plenty of water, that's all. Six p.m. extended dinner. Chat time followed by showers and bed. The next day will be the same, and then we will appear at Saint Pious at dawn on the following morning. Any questions?"

"May I be excused from the self defence part?" Yvette asked.

"Because you don't believe in violence is that correct?"

"Sort of" Yvette meekly replied

"Very well, however, let me suggest that during your period of reflection, you might become angry with yourself and especially remembering that Badcock character. When this happens, turn your anger into love and think how happy you would feel if and when Badcock tried to assault you. Think about how much you would love to catch his punch and use his force against him by throwing him over your shoulder and into a wall or into the floor."

All of the girls cherished the thought.

"The skills I will teach you are not aggressive. Here, let me show you. Felicity, could you help me please?"

"With pleasure"

Jack chose her because of her athletic and flexible appearance. He imagined that she was quite the contortionist in bed, sensational for some but boring to others. "Stand in front of me, face on, good. Now pretend to strangle me."

Felicity quickly obeyed. "Now ladies, if your assailant is close enough, which they normally will be, simply cup your hands like this and strike a blow to each ear," Jack said as he slowly and gently demonstrated the manoeuvre. "Of course, in the actual situation, you will execute this without any warning and with the utmost force. The air that you capture in the cup of your hand delivers an enormous internal pressure to the outer and inner ear, causing much pain and confusion to your attacker. They will instantly release you, allowing you to deliver another stunning blow, either to the base of the throat like this or you may wish to sting their genitals like this. Either way, you may rest assured that you will walk away unharmed, with no further threat of attack from that particular person. The ear attack is so effective that it may even cause deafness by bursting their eardrums. The other vulnerable areas of the body that I shall show are those relating to superficial nerves. Hit one of these and you cause immediate debilitating pain," Jack said as he pointed to and touched Felicity's receptive anatomy.

"That tickles," she giggled.

"A matter of pressure, light causes pleasure, dark causes pain."

"Lightly does it," she purred.

"Thank you," Jack replied as he bowed towards her. "I hope that dismisses your fears."

"I still don't like it," Yvette stubbornly replied.

"Very well, however do us all a favour by learning the techniques because as you know, the strength of any chain is dependent upon its weakest link. We are in some respect a newly formed human variety, one that I would like to see remain intact under present and future circumstances."

"Will you also teach us to reflect and meditate?" Naomi asked

"I together with Father Brendan"

"How exciting, I'm looking forward to that, noon delights there's something new." Naomi purred as she heavily relied upon meditation in the past to get her through life

Not this again, thought Brendan, as he reacted to Naomi's erotic suggestion.

The next two days were contrary to what Brendan and the girls had expected. Nothing was rigorous or serious or traumatic. There were no excessive expectations or obsessions. Everything was fun, as Jack intended. It was his understanding that knowledge of any kind was only captured when the person was enjoying it. He also proposed that the word 'fun' was derived from enough. Fun spelt backwards was 'nuf' – 'e-nuf' to him meant the person desired the opposite. God, to Jack, was someone who instilled pleasure and fun into all things, even lovemaking. This ability, Jack reasoned, was not a sexual thing as the vast majority thought, but rather a unique biological information transfer system, not unlike that of the electronic digital phenomenon of the computer age. He found the entire concept amusing and could see the comic analogies. Floppy and hard drive bore resemblance with their associated activities namely flaccid and erect penises. A wicked smile formed on his face as he reflected on this aspect of his humour. Before the schedule of activities started, Jack's mischievous side wondered how the girls would deal with the birds and the bees. That was exactly what he asked them in the afternoon of their second day during the three p.m. self defence lesson.

"So how do you find the birds and the bees," he asked, as he exchanged blows with Yvette.

"Are you trying to throw me off my guard?" she replied, side stepping his blows and the question at hand.

"Not at all, just testing."

"With innuendo?"

"Whatever comes to hand."

"Don't you mean, in hand?" laughed Felicity.

Yvette blushed, but it wasn't noticeable, as she was already red in the face. Brendan reacted similarly.

"Are you asking at what age I became sexually aware or whether I am still unaware?" Yvette bluntly asked Jack who smirked as he tried to hit Yvette.

"I think he means the ones at breakfast," Brendan interrupted making reference to the animals and insects

"Of course I did," Jack replied before he executed a backward somersault and challenged Naomi who was standing behind him.

"Do you have anything to say Naomi?"

"Nothing," she said, staring him in the eye. "Anyone have anything to report? Impressions? Well? Did any of the animals talk to you? Give a sign? Hmmm?"

They all shook their heads.

"Well, did you observe anything about the animals, anything at all that you would consider as being advantageous?"

Again, they all remained silent, except for Yvette. "The one thing that struck me was that all of the birds that joined us were of the aggressive variety, yet they were surprisingly docile."

"The message being?"

"There is good in all."

"Very well said my dear anything else?"

"The bees are frisky beings, preoccupied with the sex organs of the flowers."

"And?"

"I don't know."

"They produce from their collected efforts life giving honey, bee pollen, royal jelly and propolis, all with the help of water, from the information contained within. So once again, sexual things are creative and produce a variety of produce profoundly important to mankind and other life forms. In essence, the bee is an advanced scientist, millions of years ahead of all of us. Consider then what we could achieve if we used all of the grey matter available to us in comparison to the humble bee."

"Mr Stern?"

"Yes, Felicity?"

"Is this the sum of our preparation? Will it be enough?"

"Of course not"

"Then what else do we have?" she asked.

"Safety in numbers"

"Pardon?"

"I have, via the Internet, enticed the media to return en masse to Newburn, specifically Saint Pious to report on the miraculous healings granted by the Blessed Virgin's statue."

"Is dawn a good time to be there?"

"I honestly don't know and I also don't know what to expect." Jack replied even though he wasn't being absolutely truthful

"So why are we returning at all?" Felicity asked as she could see no valid reason for returning

"To prove our innocence" Jack replied even though he was lying

"Hasn't that already been done?" She questioned

"Not completely we need to be absolved of any alleged involvements. In any case, Badcock and his cronies are nursing bruised egos. He'll want you back to prove he's still boss and I think we should not deny him that opportunity."

"In other words, you're orchestrating a final showdown and using us as bait." Felicity replied very unhappy with his idea

"Does that frighten you?"

"Not anymore. I for one am no longer afraid of Badcock."

Brendan quietly listened and hoped that Jack knew what he was doing; media or no media the D-Man would certainly be there. He was one almighty force to contend with. It would be child's play for the D-Man to simply demolish everyone in his path with no record of it ever happening. Brendan was starting to think that Jack Stern was a ittle strange and was hiding a sinister plot.

53

FINAL ABSOLUTION

"Good morning Janice, how cold are you today?" Frank roared with laughter as the cameraman shone the video-cam's bright light on her face as she lay tightly wrapped up in her thermal sleeping bag inside KBW-49 makeshift tent.

The television crew had camped in the grounds of Saint Pious over night after receiving permission from the Archbishop's office. It was easily obtained as Jack's Internet site had loudly proclaimed the good news that miracles do indeed happen. With the pressure taken off it temporarily, the church was able to attract the genuine pilgrims to visit the Virgin's statue, a move that was designed to wash away any mud that might have stuck to it as a consequence of its unpalatable association with organised crime. The Archbishop, in particular, prayed that Brendan and Jack would not expose anymore of the Churches shady dealings however, he remained uncertain as he perceived Jack to be an insolent rogue a wild canon and totally unpredictable. The cameraman turned up the volume on his headphones and placed them next to Janice's ear.

"Good morning; how cold are you?' Frank roared again with sadistic and comic pleasure as he wanted to make Janice into a public spectacle.

"Uh what? Put that damn light away. Are you crazy? It's still night" Janice moaned as she pushed the cameraman away

"Well as you can see viewers; at KBW-49 we expose everything, even our own people. Not very glamorous is she? Always good to see them au natural now and then," Frank continued to joke in his own bizarre way while the cameraman attempted to film Janice who had well and truly covered herself up.

"I don't think we're going to get anything out of her until she's had breakfast, so let's get back to the main stories." Frank said and then proceeded to rattle off the pertinent descriptions in synch with the aired pictures and took the occasional sip of water to keep his throat moist.

"Before we screen our next programme, which will be the five a.m. 'Great Investigative Reports of the Century' which I am sure you have all been waiting for, the last item deals with the recent sensational occurrences at Newburn. Briefly, it goes something like this," Frank said as he presented a retrospective condensed version of what had happened over the past few days.

"To add to the mystery, it appears in the middle of this satanic cesspool, there were genuine miracles occurring as the recently posted Internet blog suggests. In the limited time available to us, we have worked furiously to locate and interview a number of individuals who were once patients at Longevity Plus and who have remarkable stories to tell us."

The screen then paraded out a succession of personally recounted medical miracles to which all and sundry appeared genuine enough.

"Quite impressive; remember you saw it first on KBW-49, your information station. As soon as our – er – glamorous Janice is up and about, we will bring you the stories from inside Saint Pious Church. Stay tuned."

In the safety of their mountain retreat, it was only Jack who awoke sufficiently early to witness the efforts of KBW-49. Dawn was relatively late, 6.27 a.m. to be precise. He intended to stir his friends into action around 5.30 but before he did that he went though his daily ritual of mystical exercises, paying particular attention to his seeing abilities. Jack entered the dormitory and blessed everyone by transforming their environment into a surreal experience. His dawn was a work of emotional art heralding in a new era. Jack filled the room with a multitude of white doves and floating crystals that split the light and painted ever changing landscapes all over the room. What was particularly fascinating to the observer was the interplay between the doves and crystals. It was almost as if the two of them tussled with each other over the finishing touches to each masterpiece. The doves wanted a wispy appearance whereas the crystals demanded sharpness. In the middle of all of it lay the breakfast banquet.

"Good morning ladies and gentlemen. This is your early morning wake up call. Breakfast is served. We shall be departing at 6.26 a.m., just in time to see the sunrise at Newburn Saint Pious Church at 6.27 a.m."

They all stirred simultaneously and after wiping away the cobwebs sat in awe of their surroundings.

"Good morning, Janice" Frank roared with a robust delivery.

"You're in a surprisingly good mood this morning, quite unusual for you," Janice replied out of spite.

"Oh yes it's gonna be a great day. I can sense something spectacular is about to happen."

"I wish I could share your optimism." Janice coldly replied

"But you can, my darling, you can." Frank happily replied

"Okay Frank, perhaps the viewers would like to be informed as to what we will be doing this morning."

"That would be nice, please continue," he said.

"Thank you Frank," Janice replied acidly. "The acting priest at St Pious has decided to cancel Mass this morning, to allow us and the technical experts, to examine the Virgin's statue."

"What will you be looking for?" Frank asked playing the detective

"Anything unusual I suspect or supernatural in nature I suppose you could say."

"The ordinary run of the mill stuff like rose fragrance filled air, oily or genuine human tears running down the face of the statue, is that right Janice?" Frank interrupted.

"Well Frank, we were hoping to explore other avenues as well."

"First, second, third…."

"My god, you're corny this morning." Janice replied exasperated by Frank's untoward attitude

"Please go ahead."

Janice regained her composure. "We want to examine other aspects such as whether the statue emits any sort of aural or electromagnetic radiation. Our experts will be bringing in highly sophisticated measuring devices to see if the miracles are due to exposure to these types of phenomenon."

"Interesting, very interesting."

"We thought you might say that. We thought we'd start off this morning by filming the inside of the church. This should happen within the next 30 minutes or so."

"Any pilgrims down there?"

"Not as yet. These sorts of things do not elicit a great immediate response like the one we saw before. Unfortunately, illegal mind blowing drugs seem to be more attractive to the public than things of a religious nature besides which it's too early in the morning."

"Well said. Tell me Janice, what's that buzzing noise in the background and where is it coming from?"

"We've just noticed it ourselves. It appears to be … oh my god!" Janice suddenly shrieked

"Janice?"

"Quick! Over there! No! Over there! Look! Eastwards…" Janice shouted as she pointed to the east

The cameraman swung around to film millions upon millions of honey bees flying in organised swarms towards Saint Pious Church.

"They must like your perfume," Frank joked

"I've never seen anything like this before."

"Biblical is it? The plague of bees" Frank continued to joke

"Stop joking Frank. This is serious."

"Only if they attack you but then considering how often you've told me how perfect you are, you should not have anything to worry about." Frank reminded his colleague even though he could see that Janice was deathly white with fear.

"Relax Janice, relax."

"Brave words from you Frank you're not here. Quick everyone! Into the van! Run!" Janice screamed.

"Isn't this exciting folks? I told you it was going to be a spectacular day." Frank roared making most of the situation

Janice and her crew hastily clambered into the van whilst filming all the time. It really did make for exciting raw footage. Within a few minutes, it became apparent that the bees were not on a hostile mission. They appeared docile as they flew directly to the church and massed themselves on all of its walls.

"Are you okay Janice?"

"A little shaken but thank you for asking Frank; what an experience!"

"What do you think it means?"

"I don't know except there might be some sort of symbolism here."

Janice was interrupted by the cameraman pointing to the west.

"What's going on?" Frank asked. Neither Janice nor any one of the crew replied. Instead, Frank had to contend with watching the scene unfold, at the same time as his viewers. What appeared to be huge cumulous clouds sweeping towards them were in fact thousands of pure white turtle doves flapping their wings in perfect harmony and majestic elegance. Frank, like his viewers, was aghast, speechless as the birds descended and took up residence on the roof of Saint Pious. Their serene presence was in contrast to the loud humming of the bees.

"Janice, you're the religious expert. What do you make of this?"- Frank teased his colleague as she was not that well informed at all

"I can't say definitely, I can only speculate."

"Go on, I'm sure our listeners would love to hear what you have to say."

"Very often white doves are associated with apparitions of the Blessed Virgin Mary." Janice hazarded a guess

"If this is the case, this must be one almighty spectacle in the making"

"There is only one way of finding out and that is for us to go inside," Janice gingerly replied.

"Well off you go," Frank said rather impatiently.

Janice and the crew reluctantly followed suit, not knowing what to expect. They approached the main doors of the church which they expected would be still locked.

"Well, say it." Frank whispered

"What would you like me to say Frank, something like open sesame?"

"Why not?" Frank whispered back

Before Janice had the chance to verbally hit back at Frank's stupidity, the doors opened sufficiently wide for them to pass through and then the doors shut with a reverberating bang as if a gust of wind had opened and closed them. Once inside, the television crew found Jack, Brendan, Yvette and the girls seated in the pews in front of the Blessed Virgin's statue. It appeared that each one of them was silently meditating, their bodies visibly vibrating to the hum of the bees which filled the entire church. The crew took up a discreet vantage point so as not to disturb the group. They spoke in whispers to each other and to Frank who for once understood the delicacy of the situation.

"It should be obvious to you and the viewers what has happened here. As you can hear the bees and the birds have together by their actions transformed this church into one giant auditory chamber. The humming of the bees produces the desired sound frequency and the birds dampen the effect to its optimum pitch, it is quite extraordinary because correct me if I am wrong but it appears that the final outcome as you can see is causing each of the persons at prayer to radiate light. The statue itself appears to be alive although this requires closer examination."

The cameraman adjusted his lens to achieve the best possible close-ups and nodded that the results were unmistakable. Her skin was soft, fresh with a rose petal texture. Her eyes glistened, the colour intensely blue. Her lips succulent strawberry red and the hair flaxen gold, moved ever so gently. Janice, when she viewed the Virgin through the eyepiece of the camera, made the sign of the cross and fell to her knees in admiration. Not a word was said. It was not necessary. Everything occurred at a spiritual level until the final conflict reared its ugly head.

Ironically from the confessional room Louis Badcock, the D-Man, the Harsh Man and a number of his other thugs emerged looking very smug.

"Well, who do we have here? If it isn't Mr Jack Stern, Father Brendan O'Reilly and my collection of girls. I hope that you have finished saying penance and you are about to beg for my absolution," Badcock bellowed, as he and his group approached them.

Jack stood up and faced his assailants.

"Sit down Father O'Reilly, it's Stern that I want. He's the one who attacked my people and stole my girls."

"He wasn't alone."

"Oh yes. I remember you were there and did some fancy cane work but that wasn't you, it was him with his make believe supernatural powers. You can't deceive me, I demand justice and I want it now! Hand the girls back."

"Please my child, don't you think we could settle this amicably? Especially since we are before the blessed sacrament," Jack gently replied pretending to the priest that Badcock thought he was.

"Don't give me that religious nonsense. There's nothing in there but a piece of dehydrated wafer and as for you fine lady, I thought you would have learnt your lesson when the D-Man eliminated your son," Badcock shouted. He turned to face the Virgin who had by now reverted to being a statue.

Brendan became unnerved by Badcock's tirade and stood up to face him. "Very well Louis, you have made your point. Please stop the insults."

"I will not leave without the girls."

"I don't think they want to go with you." Brendan firmly stated unafraid of the pugnacious brothel keeper

"Then I shall take them by force!"

Brendan remembered what Jack had said about the Christ principle not being aggressive and remained silent. Badcock signalled for his thugs to take the girls by force. Yvette remained kneeling, not taking her eyes off the Virgin. Before Badcock's henchmen reached the girls, they jumped over the pews and ran into the open aisles. Badcock then signalled to the Harsh Man to take Yvette saying, "This one's for me, an after dinner delight."

"I don't think so, Mr Badcock. That's not a particularly good idea," Jack said, as he stood in the way.

"A man of God challenges me? What are you going to do? Whip me with your rosary beads?" Badcock laughed as he kept one eye on Jack and the other on his henchmen.

The D Man meanwhile stood ten paces behind Badcock, biding his time. The girls very cleverly stayed as a group and formed a circle. They started to scream giving the impression that they were very scared. The henchmen leapt at them and attempted to grab hold of them by the arms thinking that they were easy targets. But the girls well trained by Jack foiled them by seizing their arms and using their available inertia flung the thugs forward into the pews and caused each one of them to land heavily. One of the henchmen crashed awkwardly and was knocked unconscious while the others winced with pain as their arms, heads and legs collided with the heavy timber furniture. The girls then retreated behind the votive candle stand and knelt down low.

"You fools, get them, they are over there," Badcock signalled wildly.

The henchmen obeyed, but as they drew closer, the girls started to throw the candles at them, catching them off guard and inflicting stinging pain.

Sensing that they were winning, the girls reversed the situation by attacking Badcock's henchmen. They kicked, slapped and threw punches to all those exposed nerve areas that they learnt would precipitate debilitating pain. Badcock's men lay in a heap, completely helpless, moaning and groaning.

"Not so fast ladies," Badcock smiled as he produced a semi-automatic pistol and pointed it at them. "Stay where you are, that's right, there is no escape this time."

Jack quickly assessed the situation and calculated that the time for him to strike was then and there. From a standing position he leapt into the air and kicked the Harsh Man in the throat. He rotated and knocked the pistol out of Badcock's hand before landing on his feet. He stood momentarily victorious and thought the battle over until two metal projectiles speared into his hands, thrust him backwards and nailed him to the wooden altar rails.

The Harsh Man lay on the ground gasping for air. Badcock scrambled to his feet looked at Jack then at the D Man and laughed viciously.

"Well priest, you've always wanted to be a stigmatic, well here's your chance." Back acidly barked.

Jack in obvious pain and completely helpless, whispered, "I'm not the priest."

"Another one of your tricks, I'm no fool." Badcock said refusing to accept the truth

Brendan was shocked, alone, and frightened at the thought that he was dealing with a 2,000 year-old-being that was responsible for Christ's crucifixion, and possibly for all those who sought to enlighten humanity's upward spiral towards perfection. He blushed with a mixture of fearful anxiety and innocence.

Badcock sneered at Brendan coldly and analysed him.

"Well, if you're the priest, then let's have some fun and games with you shall we. D Man, attack his weaknesses."

Brendan did not know what to expect. Could this being be even more destructive that in his previous en counters with him? What would he have to do to overcome him? Brendan struggled to remember all of the words that his ghostly priest had taught him. He stood as a sacrificial lamb before the D Man who slowly approached him with a crackling intensity.

"Afraid are you? You should be. Want to see what I can do and learn how helpless you are?" the D Man threatened, as his vile mouth odour ravaged Brendan's nostrils.

"Not really." Brendan bluffed

"Good, then let us begin. Sex, sex and more sex, that's what you want isn't it priest man, makes your flesh burn with desire, nothing quenches your thirst like sex, sex and more sex."

Before Brendan could respond, he found himself standing completely naked. In front of him Felicity was performing expert fellatio on his erect penis. He saw a naked woman on each side of him and he saw his hands playing with their genitals. The flames of sin started to singe Brendan's soul, his desire to accomplish sexual fulfillment fanned the heat until he realised it was all an illusion. Covered in profuse perspiration he sighed heavily and said, "This is not real, I would never do that, go away, your mind tricks do not work on me."

"Oh really, then perhaps you would like to see something real," the D Man snarled, as he threw an unstable thermal energy ball towards the group of girls.

Brendan reacted instantly and projected himself in front of them before the ball could strike. He was able to deflect it out of the church through one of the stained glass windows. Surprised by his own ability he waited for the D Man to repeat the attack.

"You have grown stronger since our last meeting. But which one will you sacrifice, man or woman?" The D Man laughed as he simultaneously sent two highly charged unstable energy balls in different directions, one towards Jack Stern and the other towards Brendan and the girls.

Brendan subconsciously quickly calculated the unequal distances and the time taken for each unstable energy ball to reach its target and through the untried process of bi-location he managed to rebuff both attempts.

"Very impressive but not impressive enough Mr Stern, can you protect three people at once?" The D Man asked as he raised the stakes

Brendan remained steady and fixed his gaze on the D Man. He was not alone in that, from the choir loft above, the partially crippled small dark figure watched hoping that Badcock would meet with a fatal injury.

The D Man's appearance grew larger as the electrical discharges intensified and multiplied all over his body. Suddenly everything inside the church seemed to be on fire. Flames of all manner and kind leapt from everything except there was no heat, everything was intensely cold, or so Brendan thought until he heard the screams of terror. More mind games, he thought, as he assessed the situation. The D Man looked at Badcock, smiled, nodded his head, as if to say, 'It will soon be all over'. Unlike Brendan, Badcock was bathed in perspiration.

Could I be wrong, or is everything really burning? Brendan anxiously thought. But before he could think any further, the D Man unleashed his furor. Balls of fire in all sorts of sizes flung out from the fingertips, palms and mouth of the D Man in all directions, seeking out their prey. This was a multiple attack centred on each member of his group; the girls, Yvette, Jack and it included himself. Brendan's mind went into overdrive. Like a crazed tennis player he tried vainly to repel everything. In the barrage of volleys, preoccupied with the safety of others, he did not notice the cleverly concealed alloy spikes that found their targets. Brendan, like Jack, was thrust backwards and nailed by the palms of his hands into the wooden altar rail. He was rendered powerless.

In the midst of all of this the D Man, through his own blind arrogance, did not notice Yvette ascend the steps of the altar and enter its sanctuary. She had been in deep prayer with the Virgin, protected at all times by her own abilities, and by that of Jack and Brendan. When she heard the words 'come child, it is your destiny', she arose from her seat, and glided to the back of the altar where the priests would normally stand. She touched the fragment of the saint that was embedded in the altar's marble top and in doing so, activated it by her profound innocence. The candles that rested on each corner of the altar ignited and transformed themselves into pillars of white light, entwined by red and white roses that stretched upwards and over, until they formed an arch. The entire church became filled with the unique scent of roses, particular to the Blessed Virgin. It wafted out of the broken windows and attracted the bees to come and see Yvette's radiant glory and caused the D Man to stop immediately what he was doing.

He recognised her soul and said, "So it's you that I saw before." Lost for words, he could only stutter, "Yourrrr s-s-so beautiful."

"And you are so……" Yvette began to say but stopped and instead pointed to a psychic mirror that truly reflected his grotesque makeup something that he had never seen before.

The D Man compared the two images his and hers and admitted, "I never imagined that anyone could become like this."

"It's never too late to change, you have thought of it before you know."

"Yes I have, but the world of deceit always orders you back." The D Man confessed

"Have you ever seen anyone like me in your world?" Yvette sweetly asked

"Never"

"Which one do you prefer?" Yvette ambiguously asked

"Yours" The D Man admitted as his defences weakened and his soul yearned to be cleansed

"Then come through the door of enlightenment where great loving treasures await." Yvette seductively beckoned

Badcock was horrified at what had happened and how the tables had changed. How dare a hardened supernatural assassin fell for a smooth talking woman, there was nothing special about this girl apart from the fact that she was a reluctant virgin how could he have become so mesmerised by her. Badcock beside himself with anger found a semi-automatic pistol lying on the floor, picked it up and started shooting wildly at the D Man's back and head. The bullets simply melted on contact. Unaffected by Badcocks attempts to stop him the D Man continued on unabated and passed through the portal of true knowledge and happily stood next to Yvette. His image was transformed and he resembled someone more human and humane. Badcock stopped shooting but frustrated by his failure, he decided to kill everyone else.

The D Man stripped of all of his destructive powers saw what was about to happen. He immediately left Yvette's side, ran and catapulted himself from the top step of the altar towards Badcock. Even though Yvette knew that he was now powerless she made no attempt to stop him. The D Man landed and skidded to a halt in front of Badcock.

"Changed your mind again you traitor, grovelling will not get you anywhere," Badcock screamed hysterically as his eyes bulged and he spat saliva profusely from his mouth.

"You are useless to me; time to meet your maker." Badcock shouted at the top of his voice as he pointed the weapon at the D Man's head

"Never, I despise him." The D Man defiantly answered

"Bad words, you are supposed to love him, remember."

The D Man looked puzzled, as he had never learned that concept.

Badcock lowered the gun, pulled the trigger repeatedly and sent three bullets into the D Man's chest. Having never experienced physical pain before it came with a mixture of disbelief, pleasure and intense grief, the D Man struggled with the burning sensations of torn tissues, intense nervous discharge and shock. Blood oozed profusely from his chest indicating that a major artery had been ruptured. Blood filled his lungs. The D Man's body convulsed as it desperately clung onto physical life.

Badcock stood still his eyes darkened with sublime pleasure as he became transfixed by his self importance and the fact that he had just executed his first kill.

Meanwhile whilst Badcock and the D Man were having their altercation the Harsh Man had sufficiently recovered and had regained enough strength to creep towards Brendan, the Harsh Man then used all of his strength, to withdraw the alloy metal pins from Brendan's hands like those who had frantically searched the world before him, looking for biblical artifacts in the belief that they would acquire the keys to immense powers, the Harsh Man then crawled along the floor towards Jack and repeated the act. He hid the alien pins in his jacket pocket and slithered away and only to be observed by the small dark figure who knew that the Harsh Man would return one day when he had discovered and acquired by whatever means possible the D Man's powers.

With the pins removed from the palms of their hands Jack and Brendan felt the energies within their bodies slowly return, Brendan looked at the altar behind him and thought for a brief moment that the Blessed Virgin had smiled and whispered "Remember the words your master taught you." When he turned back the wounds in his hands had healed over.

Louis Badcock even though he was heavily armed realised from his previous encounters with Brendan that he was no match for the handsome priest and that all would be futile on his part. Badcock dropped the weapon out of fear and fled. Brendan walked over to where Jack lay and touched his hands instantly healing them.

"Come my friend, it's all over." Brendan said much relieved as he extended his hand to help Jack up.

"Thank you. Is Yvette all right?" Jack asked as he did know how well she had weathered the ordeal and was therefore worried about her safety

"Quite."

"She is rather special you know."Jack replied referring to her innocence

"So I saw from the corner of my eye, still interested in her?"

"Yes but I must admit that I am rather humbled by her achievements." Jack coyly replied which that did not suggest any romantic interest on his part

"Don't be."

"Why?" Jack asked still a little unsteady

"You and Yvette are one and the same you need each other," Brendan said in a metaphysical sort of way that suggested that they shared a common bond as he helped Jack to his feet.

They both turned to look at Yvette who had by now returned to her normal appearance, as had the altar that she stood behind. She smiled at them nodding to signify that she was alright and then she skipped down the steps towards them. Jack waited for her and once they met they embraced passionately for a brief moment just before Jack kissed her on the hands, forehead and cheeks.

"Thank you," he humbly said in appreciation of her efforts in converting the D Man.

"What a way to accidentally discover who you are." She ambiguously answered

"Brendan would agree with you," Jack replied, as he held her by the hands feeling the immense love that existed within her and for a brief second Jack could hear Mozart's 'Ave Verum Corpus' sung by a chorus of angelic voices. The ex prostitutes cautiously emerged from their hiding spots and seeing that the coast was clear slowly approached the trio, thankful that it was well and truly over.

"We are free at last," they emotionally cried as tears of joy filled their eyes and ran down their cheeks.

"A new life begins for all of us," Brendan quite rightly concluded.

Janice and her cameraman who attempted to film the event also shed a tear or two even Frank the great buffoon, was visibly moved.

"Janice that was one almighty action packed spectacle, what a sensational story for our archives"

"What do you mean Frank?"

"The way you filmed the entire battle and the running commentary that the viewing public saw and heard in minute detail was absolutely brilliant."

"That's impossible." Janice replied rather confused by Frank's praise

"Why?"

"Because the camera failed when the batteries went dead"

54

SURPRISING AFTER GLOW

"That's not possible," Frank exclaimed as he had other proof "Why not?"

"Because it isn't explain how the images came to be."

"I don't know Frank. All that I can tell you is that once our cameraman realised that it would be impossible to continue filming, he put the camera down and watched alongside with me."

"Was the lens pointed towards the action?" Frank asked seeking a plausible explanation

"Yes, and it still is."

"Then someone has recorded the entire event for our benefit, in fact I can still see you as plain as day so where are the images coming from?" Frank asked as he felt it was being rather eerie and spooky

"There's no other camera crew around Frank we're it" Janice nervously answered as she observed the cameraman pick up his camera and indicate that it was working again he also mumbled that there was nothing on the video tape after the camera had failed just prior to the battle between the D Man, Jack and Brendan

"So what do you think all of this means" Frank ask from a pseudo religious point of view

"It's a sign that evil can change sides and do strange things in the process" Janice suggested and left it at that.

"I agree," Frank nodded.

The loud in depth conversation that Janice had with Frank caught the attention of Jack and he together with the others looked in the direction of KBW 49's film-crew.

"Well, I think that we are now well and truly famous," Jack remarked, as he swept his hand through his hair. "Fancy instant fame Brendan?" he asked. He pointed towards the crew as they made their way out of their hiding spot and walked towards the group.

"You will probably fill the churches to overflowing. A profitable venture awaits with the creation of a new Mecca for pilgrims" Jack flippantly said without Brendan realizing that the Mecca Jack referred to was Brendan himself.

Brendan remained silent and un-amused.

"I think we had better move."

"For the interview?" Yvette asked.

"No, to allow the workers to do their job"

"Pardon?" she replied, quite confused as she could see any tradesman entering the church.

"It is quite a mess in here and the workers are signalling that they would like to start." Jack continued to state much to the confusion of his listeners

Yvette looked around like the rest and saw no one except for the film crew.

"What workers?" she asked quite exasperated.

"Up there," Jack replied, as he led the group to another part of the church which had easy access to the outside.

"There is no one up there except the bees."

"Precisely"

"You mean that they…" Before she had time to finish her sentence the bees, as if on cue, swept down with the intention to rebuild and repair everything that had been damaged by the furor

"Janice, what is going on now?" Frank prompted the news reporter to respond

"It appears that the miracles haven't stopped, I have never seen anything like this in my life."

"I suppose you could say it is a variation of that statement – many hands make light work."

"What are you saying Frank?" Janice said rather annoyed by his attitude.

"Many wings made things soar," he joked, as he watched battalions of bees work together to make fallen pews upright again.

Frank thought that that would be the sum of it, but it went otherwise.

"Oh my God," he gasped. "They are literally rebuilding everything that has been smashed how can they do that?" he asked along with his viewers, some of whom thought that they were watching a computer generated special effects program rather than the real thing.

"I can assure everyone that this is no trick, let me show you." Janice demonstrated by picking up a section of the badly damaged wooden altar rail from the floor. A mass of bees descended upon it and within a few moments, rebuilt it completely from all of its splinters and made it appear brand new. They then manoeuvred Janice to where it belonged and stitched it into place. The same happened with all of the stained-glass windows that had been shattered into thousands of tiny fragments. Each permanently restored within a matter of minutes.

When the work was done, the bees' humming subsided and they settled themselves on the altar and its surroundings.

"From now on, I am going to view bees differently," Frank commented. "If the Virgin had anything to do with this, then for me it makes me understand why young girls are referred to as being sweet as honey."

Janice frowned. "Whatever you say Frank, let's go talk to the people over there," she said as she ushered her film crew along.

Brendan and the others had by now slipped outside. Jack was holding Yvette's hands out of respect and not with any sense of possession. The morning atmosphere was glorious. Jack turned to Brendan and smiled.

"Congratulations, you passed the test of fire."

"Do you think so? There was so much of it, psychological, emotional, physical and painful," Brendan mumbled, as he reflected on his efforts in dealing with the trials and tribulations.

"Somehow I think that I failed largely because I did not manage to protect everyone and I did not defeat that hideous creature by myself."

"Only because you played his game, gifts are one thing; how to use them comes with time, practice and evolution."

"The real heroine was Yvette," Brendan concluded, as he looked at her thankfully. "Did you ever realise who you are and what you were capable of?" Brendan asked.

"I have never considered myself to be anything special. All I do is devote myself to prayer whenever I can. What happened today has come more of a shock to me than anything else."

"Are you saying that you are frightened by the thought and the experience?"

"Not really. I have prayed for years to meet someone special. A good husband is all that I wished for, those who listened to my prayers thought otherwise," Yvette genuinely explained, as she looked at Jack who remained somewhat indifferent.

"Excuse me Mr Stern, may we talk with you?" Janice asked, as she thrust a microphone in front of Brendan.

"I see that your equipment is quite operational contrary to what you witnessed. My name is Father Brendan O'Reilly and that man standing over there is the real Mr Jack Stern," he replied, as he stepped back in readiness to address the barrage of questions that Janice was about to level at him.

At the same instant Jack's highly sophisticated phone rattled away demanding his immediate attention. "It all comes at once," he mumbled, as he withdrew it from his coat pocket and excused himself from Yvette.

"Looks rather battle weary, needs obvious TLC. Care to touch it for me Brendan?" he joked as he switched it on.

"Hello," he answered, as his auditory senses sought to identify the person calling with such impatient urgency.

"Your Grace what an unexpected pleasure how did you know my number?" he falsely asked, knowing full well that it was only reserved for a selected few who were sworn to its secrecy.

"We have our own intelligence organization."

"I would never have guessed."

"Very clever play acting on your part Mr Stern, I must congratulate you."

"I don't know what you mean."

"Come now Mr Stern, I like millions of others, witnessed KBW 49's live account this morning. From it, I firmly deduce that you are a master at chess. I understand what you wanted to achieve. Very clever of you Mr Stern your opening moves at Saint Pious right through to playing the helpless victim, sacrificing yourself so that the Queen would check mate."

"What is that music in the background?" Jack asked changing the subject

"Your signature tune," the Archbishop explained.

"'Sanctuary of the Heart' by Ketelby, most appropriate for the circumstances, perhaps you do know me well after all. Did you ring to congratulate me on my wonderful accomplishments?"

"Not at all" His Grace acidly replied

"Then we should terminate this conversation."

"Must you always be so abrupt Mr Stern?"

"How else can I keep my swollen head?"

"I see your perverted mind is still at play so I am not going to make any comment."

"Holding back are you," Jack teased.

"Mr Stern, can we get down to business please."

"Wait a minute; I thought your phone call was about pleasure."

"Mr Stern."

"Yes Your Grace, you wanted to talk to me about another predicament that the Catholic Church has got itself into. This time you want my help with a little whipped cream on the side," Jack intuitively reasoned, as he ended the statement with a distinct French accent.

The Archbishop remained silent.

"Before you give me the messy details, let me guess, it is not the Mafia, but almost as bad, bureaucracy gone mad in the health sector. You invested heavily in a natural therapy company that has been railroaded by the Government under instructions from the pharmaceutical industry, correct?"

"You are very astute Mr Stern."

"Your Grace, your immediate problem can wait. I, like the others, deserve a vacation. My first priority is rest and recreation and to get to know the bevy of girls that we have rescued. I will be in touch. May you live long and die happy." Jack disconnected the line and pressed a nine digit code on his keypad. It immediately reset his mobile phone number to a new numerical combination.

"That should keep them guessing for a while," he chuckled to himself.

Seeing that he was free, Yvette quickly rejoined him.

"What was it that I heard; that you wanted to get to know the Archbishop's housekeeper?"

"Not at all, you're the one, just as we agreed, one step at a time in the true French tradition."

"Ooooo la la," Felicity cheekily remarked as she also wanted to get to know the real Jack Stern.

"I wonder how Brendan is doing. Here Yvette, telephone your parents, tell them it is all over and that you are coming home soon."

Jack brightly said and handed the phone over and allowed Yvette to perform her long overdue duty.

"I think I have answered most of your questions sufficiently well enough, I suggest that the rest can be addressed by the…" Brendan stopped talking as his attention was suddenly seized upon by Jack's waving hands.

He looked in the direction that Jack was pointing and saw four people standing nearby, one of them whom he recognised as being Grandpa in disguise. Brendan ran over and as best as he could, embraced the woman that Grandpa was pretending to be.

"You're alive, thank God for that."

Only Brendan, Jack and the girls could hear Grandpa's replies.

"Of course I am. What would make you think otherwise?"

"You disappeared when you tried to save that man."

"A cunning trick on my part couldn't have the D Man thinking that I was still around."

"What brings you here?"

"I have a present for you; meet Mr and Mrs Sandrino and their daughter. I am glad to announce that they have decided to go State's evidence in exchange for protection against the people who set up Mr Sandrino in business."

"Where did you hide them?"

"Right underneath your noses" Grandpa replied with a wry smile

"You mean in the mountain retreat?"

"Certainly did," Grandpa beamed.

"He was a thorough gentleman all the time," Mrs Sandrino said butting in.

"We thought that we were dead after our car flew over the cliff and crashed down below. When he rescued us we thought that he was a guardian angel and we had entered the afterlife. It took us a while, and lots of persuasion by him, to make us realise that we were still alive."

"Congratulations my good man, err I mean ghost."

"Highly evolved spirit if you mind."

"I stand corrected," Brendan apologised.

"As you should, now take them over there and let those influential television people do the rest."

"I will and once again, thank you Grandpa," Brendan joyfully said, as he led the Sandrino's towards Janice. He introduced them and briefly explained the situation.

When Janice grasped the significance of the Sandrino's position in the convoluted business arrangements and on goings at Newburn, the story made her leap with joy at the prospect of winning the national coveted award in television journalism.

What a happy ending, Jack thought, as he held Yvette's hands and surveyed the scene before them.

"Where to now?" Brendan asked, as he approached the happy couple.

"I thought I might take this special lady home, and you?"

"Wait a minute; you can't answer a question with a question."

"All right then why don't you join us"

"Okay, come on ladies, over here," Brendan gestured to the girls.

"I think we'd better leave discreetly. Let's find a new quiet spot away from everyone and disappear from view."

"Agreed"

As the group walked closely together, and rounded the corner of the church, they passed a car parked alongside of it. Brendan noticed an elderly female behind the steering wheel and as he walked past she was heard to say in a croaky voice "Excuse me sir, I am very sick and can't drive, can you help me?"

"Not this again," sighed Brendan.

* * *

www.ingramcontent.com/pod-product-compliance
Lightning Source LLC
Chambersburg PA
CBHW030748030726
47497CB00001B/179